The Girl with Stars in Her Eyes

Eleanor O'Kelly-Lynch

978-1-915502-56-8
All rights reserved
Copyright © Eleanor O'Kelly-Lynch 2023
Cover design:2funkidesign.com
Cover image: Seisyun bot

Eleanor O'Kelly-Lynch has asserted her moral right to be identified as the author of this work. The material in this publication is protected by copyright law. Except as may be permitted by law, no part of the material may be reproduced (including by storage in a retrieval system) or transmitted in any form or by any means, adapted, rented or lent without the written permission of the copyright owner. Published in Ireland by Orla Kelly Publishing.

Orla Kelly Publishing
27 Kilbrody
Mount Oval
Rochestown
Cork
Ireland

Derek, this one's for you

Invocation

Dolphin plunge, fountain play.
Fetch me far and far away.
Fetch me far my nursery toys,
Fetch me far my mother's hand,
Fetch me far my painted joys.

And when the painted cock shall crow
Fetch me far my waking day
That I may dance before I go.

Fetch me far the breeze in the heat,
Fetch me far the curl of the wave,
Fetch me far the face in the street.
And when the other faces throng
Fetch me far a place in the mind
Where only truthful things belong.

Fetch me far a moon in a tree,
Fetch me far a phrase of the wind,
Fetch me far the verb To Be.

And when the last horn burns the hills
Fetch me far one draught of grace
To quench my thirst before it kills.
Dolphin plunge, fountain play.
Fetch me far and far away.

Louis MacNeice (1907-1963)

The Girl with Stars in Her Eyes

Preface

I must confess, I never expected to write a second book. When I eventually finished 'The Girl with Special Knees,' during lockdown, I thought I'd feel relieved. The years of writing and rewriting were over, I could relax. But almost immediately, I began to miss the Redmond family, these characters I'd spent countless hours with: Sally, Dan and their girls, Andi and Doll. I wondered what would happen to them now. Would there be more tears, or would they live happily ever after? Eleven-year-old Doll – the girl of the book title – had sailed off on a magical journey to a new world, but she'd had to return to her bleak and limited life in Bluebell Grove. *Was that it for Doll?* One brief, remarkable adventure where she could be her best self? It didn't feel right. My own daughter has a rare condition that makes her life a tough battle. Writing about Doll's wonderful journey really resonated with me: I loved the idea that, maybe in another dimension, in some parallel universe, she too, could be a different version of herself. That would indeed, be magic.

And so, in the middle of lockdown I took up my pen and started to write again. This time it didn't take as long: the worlds of Glengarvan and Almazova were already drawn. I enjoyed stitching together new stories and challenges and seeing how the characters reacted.

And I found a new character. One Sunday, in Lismore, I came across a monument that mentioned a Lord Carbery. It reminded me of the stories we'd heard of our long dead grandfather, Tim O'Herlihy, who worked as a baker in Thompsons. He was, by all accounts, an amazing and hilarious character who wore a top hat and swung a cane, and who was fondly known as Lord

Carbery. I knew I had to write him into the story. His character came very easily to me, and I like to think that he was there, in his top hat, peering over my shoulder as I wrote, nodding in approval.

The book you are about to read is about an ordinary family – the Redmonds – and at the heart of that family, a child who has had enough. On another level, it's about the invisible and unknowable magic that surrounds us . . . and a reminder that all kinds of wild adventures are possible if we can just believe and follow our hearts.

Eleanor O'Kelly-Lynch
November 2023

CHAPTER 1

DOLL

Last night I cut my face till it bled. I swear to God, I hadn't done it for ages, but now that I've started, I'm not going to lie – it's hard to stop. I can feel the crusty sore on my cheek, and I'm itching to make it bleed again. Just one more time. There's an envelope in my head marked SHAME. I mean, come on, today of all days? Saturday, the third of May, my First Holy Communion day. I'd want to get a grip. Today I should be smiling, my soul spotless, making my parents proud, instead of crawling back to that shapeless, Play-Doh place where nothing matters.

I look up at my lovely dress, white satin with lace sleeves, hanging on the back of my bedroom door. The lemon sun pooling in my window lights up the cellophane wrapping. The girl in the shop where I tried it on said, 'Oh, you look like an angel.' It's what they say when they don't know what to say. My mother was standing there, cupping the back of her neck, saying, 'Hmm, I suppose we could take up the hem, and maybe shorten the cuffs, and . . . and . . . yes, we'll take it, it's perfect, and what about a cardigan? It's often cold in May, isn't it?' And the shop-girl says, 'Yeah, remember last year was a washout . . . and will we try size four/five for her? She's very, em . . . and have you her shoes bought yet?' And she draws my mother towards a rack of babyish white shoes with bows and gold buckles. The shop-girl kneels and fits the right shoe for size, then nods as she presses the top of my toe. My mother smiles. 'Perfect fit. We'll take them too.'

'All set,' the girl says, smiling at me, as my mother threads the bags through the handle of my buggy. Yes, buggy! I'm nearly twelve, but I can't walk too far and it's handy, my mom says, that I can still fit in a buggy.

I try to smile as if to say, *Yes, all set for my Big White Day*, but I'm really wishing I could throw the dress, the veil, the pearly handbag, the shoes with their silly bows . . . I wish I could throw them all into a suitcase marked DONE AND DUSTED and shove it in the back of the wardrobe. I mean, Holy Communion? Someone tell me please, *what* is all that about?

My mother isn't happy when she comes in to get me up. 'Oh, Doll, you're at your face again.'

She grimaces, rubbing her thumb along my cheek. She doesn't say anything. She sighs, though. I think sighing says a lot. Sighing says, *What's the point?* or *Here we go again* or *No, please, Jesus, give us a break*. My granny used to say you don't have to talk to say things – and she was right about that.

'You've been so good these past months, Doll.' She bites her lip and scoops me out of bed. 'It's your special day, lovey. Come on, I want you to enjoy it. Please, don't do this.'

Downstairs, it's just her and me. The birds are singing outside. She should be singing too, but I've changed her tune.

'Why now? What's brought this on?' She rubs her palms up and down her face slowly.

I close my eyes. She knows I'm trying, but the sliver of sparkle is gone, sucked clean off me. She brushes my hair into plaits, fixing little pearls and white ribbons at the ends. When she's done, she sits me at the table and pours warm milk onto my Weetabix. I watch as she shakes the sugar on top.

I want to say, *Help me, Mom.* But it comes out as a howl.

She stops, spoon in midair. She closes her eyes. Squeezes them shut. The sugar spills on the table, like snow falling. I feel her shrinking, deflating like a balloon. And it's my fault. It's all my fault. I sit at the table like a ragdoll. I'm coming undone. All the stuffing, the bits of me, is falling out across the tiles, like little tufts of tumble-wool. I can't lose any more or there'll be nothing left inside me.

The bowl of Weetabix sits in front of me, just a watery blur. I can see my face in the spoon's reflection. I'm upside-down. *Even the spoon knows.* My mother rubs the back of my head. She knows too.

'Is she all right, Mom?' Andi, my sister, teeters into the kitchen on pink platform shoes. Mom takes in her short pink dress and matching eye-lining. 'Andi, you're not wearing that to the church? Wait till your father—'

My sister rolls her eyes. 'Give it a rest, Mom. I'm sixteen.' She hunkers down next to me, and I can smell her perfume, like summer flowers. 'Doll, dry your eyes, love.' She tears off some kitchen paper from the roll on the table and dabs my lashes, soaking up the wet. 'Come on, girl, you can do this.' She looks at Mom. 'I'll get her ready, if you like,' and my mother nods and mouths a thank-you.

Later, in the church, the St Mary's girls are gathered up ahead in the first three rows, fairy brides with handbags, sparkly tiaras holding their ringlets in place. Eyes cast down in prayer. Butter wouldn't melt, as my granny would say. Angels with dirty faces. She was funny, my granny.

I gaze up at the coloured windows, where stained-glass men huddle together and pray. The children's choir is singing 'Walk, walk in the light', and the sweet notes float down like feathers on my shoulders. They're singing about Jesus healing the sick and raising the dead. Imagine. You're a goner, and he can flutter you back to life. I believe it. Miracles are real, and I must keep remembering that. The magic is out there – you just have to stretch out and grab it.

There're only three of us from St Teresa's unit, and we stay sitting with our parents for the Mass. We don't have to eat the bread or drink the wine like the St Mary's girls. Thank God for that. It's because we're already perfect, my dad says, so it's just a quick trip up the aisle so the priest can bless us.

When it's my turn, my mother holds my hand. A quick trip up the aisle is right. I nearly fall over twice. *Je*s*us*. Everyone stares. I'm mortified, feel like a right plonker. What must I look like – silly bows, lace socks on stick legs, clunking along behind the delicate girl-angels up ahead? I mean, I'm nearly twelve, and . . . and the altar is blurring and all I really want to do is press my thumb into my cheek till it hurts.

Afterwards, outside the church, Father Joe says to my dad, 'She's a great girl, a child of Jesus. God's own. Aren't you, Doll?' He taps my shoulder kindly with a blue-veined hand, but who does he think he's kidding?

One good thing about today, though, was what Father Joe said from the top of the ladder during Mass. He said prayer can blow away your troubles – all that stuff that tangles round you till you don't know which end of you is up. 'Believe,' he said, thumping his fist against his chest, 'and your prayers will be answered.'

The man is right. You must walk, walk in the light.

Last year when I prayed, a miracle happened to me. Didn't I burst out of my life in Misery Street? I'm not making it up. I soared across the universe with Nan-Nan, a doll that arrived in the post for my birthday. She brought me to Almazova, a world behind the moon. I was reborn. The things I did, the people I met, the adventures I had . . . I swear on my white soul, cross my heart and hope to fly.

The only bad thing was, I was back home after a couple of weeks. And I promised myself I would be a better girl, a fighter, that I wouldn't be feeling sorry for myself anymore just because I couldn't talk or think straight or even feed myself. I was told before I left Almazova that I needed to cut through the skin of despair and not curl up inside my own dark head. And that worked for a while. But lately, the little packets of joy I carried have begun to leak. Hopeless, my old friend, is muscling in, cosying up to me, insisting I listen to her side of my story. And she's a bitch, telling me I'm a loser, that there's nothing for me up ahead in this valley of tears. The thing is, she's no fool, and I know she's got a point.

But today that priest reminded me – look, maybe I can walk in the light again. I can escape back to Almazova. If it happened once, it can happen again. The trick is believing it.

Back at the Plaza Hotel for lunch, as I sit under the clatter of plates and happy voices all round me, I feel a sudden spark, an invisible whoosh of something flowing towards me. It lasts only for a tingling moment, but it's telling me not to give up yet. My rosemary beads are on the table next to my dad's pint. I reach out and say three Hey Marys in my apple crumble head, a jumble of words, but God knows what I'm saying, and that's what counts. He knows he needs to get me out of here again, sooner the better. He knows I need to walk, walk in the light.

I smile up at my mom, and she smiles back.

CHAPTER 2

SALLY

'Good morning, Sally. Nice to see you again.' I glance around the thankfully empty reception area. It's not that I'm embarrassed to be seen in Glengarvan Counselling Centre. I mean, there's no stigma anymore around therapy, not like years ago.

She taps the keyboard. 'Dr Winters, isn't it? Half two?'

I nod, smoothing my hair. 'That's right. I'm a few minutes early.'

She gestures to her left. 'No problem, I wish everyone was this punctual. Room two, on the right. Go on in. She'll be with you in a couple of minutes.'

'Thanks, Tina.'

The room is much as I remembered it – brown floral carpet, cheerless walls with framed certs. *Dr Mary Winters, Irish Association for Counselling & Therapy.* The smell of beeswax polish.

I slide into the scuffed leather chair, remembering back to my first visit here last year. I don't even hear the door opening.

'Hello, Sally. How are you doing?'

Mary Winters closes the door quietly behind her. She is wearing a cream skirt and a blue silk blouse, the bow tied neatly at the throat. Her hair is swept into a chignon. The first time I met her, I thought she was too fashionable, too perfect, to be a therapist. I was wrong, though.

'Good, thanks, Mary.'

She shakes my hand, smiles, takes the seat opposite mine.

'How is Doll? And all the family?' She leans back and crosses her legs. 'It's been a while, Sally.'

'Yes, it's about six months. Hard to believe, isn't it? I remember the very first day I walked in here.'

She smiles. 'Me too. You weren't very happy to be here. I don't think you were too keen on the whole counselling idea.'

She was right. I was raised to keep shtum. Feelings were for weak people. And crying, telling people your troubles? Well, that was for the birds. At the time, though, I was beginning to realise those ideas weren't working for me and I needed help.

'Yes, I was very reluctant, wasn't I?'

She cups her hand under her chin. 'Doll was just out of hospital after pneumonia, am I right?

'Spot on. That was the funny thing, Mary – once she'd recovered, I started to fall apart.'

'That often happens.'

I nod, remembering back to last November. 'The panic attacks forced me to face the demons, I suppose.'

It was true. After Doll recovered from a serious bout of pneumonia, instead of feeling relieved, thankful that she'd survived against the odds, I slammed into a wall – and Mary helped put the pieces of me back together again. Dan even came to a few sessions with me, and then Andi did. Who'd have thought it? That family therapy works? I know that now. We all changed – in a good way. But deep down, and I hate admitting it, there's still a hollowness inside me that I can't fill, a sense that I'm simply not enough. And never will be. And I don't like to think about that.

'You're right, Sally. Panic attacks are often a signpost pointing up what needs attention.' She pours two glasses of water from the jug on the small table next to her and hands me one. 'They can be a reminder that we need to let go, to face up to something. We're all human; sometimes we need a helping hand to guide us through the maze.'

I loosen my scarf and take a sip of water. 'It's true.'

'But you got there. You worked through it. You embraced it, eventually.'

We both laugh. 'Eventually, yes, I saw the light,' I say.

She nods. 'How are you now?' She's not asking just to be polite. It's not the usual how-are-you. She waits, a manicured finger resting on her chin.

'I'm good, I mean . . .' Truth is, I'm not sure where to begin.

'Go on, Sally. Take your time.'

I take a breath. 'Doll's started to injure her face again. Last week. I don't know if I can go back there. Watching her deteriorate. I can feel myself sinking into the quicksand again, Mary.'

She takes a sip of water, wets her lips.

'It's a tough one. I can hear it in your voice.'

'She's been good since she came out of the pneumonia – not exactly happy, but somewhat contented. More interested in what's going on around her, you know. But now that she's started to self-injure again and seeing her dip . . . well, it breaks my heart.'

She nods. 'It's very hard to watch someone suffer, Sally. Especially when it's your child.'

'She's struggling again, Mary. And when she's in pain, she can't tell us where it hurts. It's like she wants to escape her life . . . like a death wish. I can feel it, can feel her starting to fall apart again. Does she know what she's missing, that's she's different? Maybe she just doesn't want to keep going? That tortures me.'

The words hang there like cobwebs. *Death wish. Escape. Missing.* I can hear the screech of an ambulance siren in the distance. The phone rings in reception. But the room is as hushed as a graveyard.

'Sally?'

'Yes.'

'Why are you really here?'

The question startles me.

'Sorry?'

She folds her arms. 'You made the appointment a number of weeks ago. Doll's distress seems to be more recent, am I right?'

'You are.'

She waits.

'Y-yes, there is something else. You'll think I'm crazy.'

'Try me, Sally.' Her voice is soft, pulling me in.

I give a little laugh. 'It's probably all in my head.'

'All the more reason to get it out there.' She folds her arms. 'In your own time, Sally.'

I can hear the clock on the wall above us. Seems like it's suddenly got louder, trying to drown out what I'm going to say.

'I think Dan is having an affair.'

There. I've said it. Aloud, to another person. My heart is hammering. Saying it out – *I think my husband is having an affair* – makes it more real. But maybe I'm being paranoid. I can't trust myself to think straight. I haven't slept, I can't eat. I'm driving myself insane thinking about it. Turning it over and over in my mind.

'Are you sure? Do you know this for a fact?'

'Not for a fact, but the evidence is there.' Last year, there was that thing with Shirley Lovett at the bank. It was a brief kiss. I believed him at the time. But now I'm not so sure what to believe.

My mouth is dry, and I sip some more water.

'Go on, Sally.'

'It started with a call about six weeks ago.'

She nods, tuned in to every word.

'We were just finished dinner, and Dan's mobile went off on the table. He was stacking the dishwasher, so I answered it.'

I swallow. 'It was a woman's voice. An English accent, saying, "Hello, Dan." When I asked who was speaking, the caller clicked off.'

'Could have been a misdial. It happens all the time.'

'I know, but it was Dan's reaction. He grabbed the phone and turned it off. "Just a client," he said, "I'll ring her back tomorrow." A couple of nights later when his phone rang again, he took the call upstairs.'

Mary says, 'That's hardly evidence, Sally.'

'A few weeks back – I shouldn't have – I checked his phone. I just wanted to be sure, to put these suspicions out of my head for once and for all.'

'And?'

'There was one text from the previous Wednesday evening. It went like Dublin perfect. A drink or dinner? With a pink heart. I felt sick, Mary. I couldn't look any further. That was enough.'

'Sally, have you asked him about the text? There may be a simple explanation. You need to know for sure.'

My tongue keeps clinging to the roof of my mouth. I take a gulp of water.

'No, I haven't said anything. He's gone to a meeting in Dublin this morning, though. The bank's annual review, he said. He might do an overnight, just in case things ran over, he said.'

Hmm. Just in case you get lucky, you mean, I thought to myself when he told me earlier this morning. He was in the hall searching for his keys. 'You don't usually overnight.' I said it lightly. 'Is there a dinner afterwards?' He didn't answer me directly, just turned away to check himself in the hall mirror and run his fingers through his hair. 'Not sure, we'll see.' He was wearing his grey suit and the new pink shirt I'd bought him the week before.

Looking good, I thought to myself. My husband is a dead ringer for Kevin Bacon. Last year at Cheltenham, two women approached him for a selfie. They wouldn't believe him when he said, 'Sorry to disappoint you, ladies,' and that wasn't the first time. We've often laughed about it. But I can't deny it: women find my husband attractive.

'You're avoiding the conversation you know you need to have, Sally. What's stopping you asking him? What's your plan?' Mary says, and to be honest I don't have a plan, unless being a rabbit in headlights is a plan.

'What if he denies it?' I say.

'Do you trust him, Sally?'

'I do.' I bite my lip. Well, I thought I could, but can you ever trust any man? I won't lie; after Doll was born, we drifted. Didn't see things the same way. It was hard. The world of disability opens up in front of you like a lion's jaw. It's a jungle, you don't see it coming. You lose your way, and you start pulling in different directions. And your suit of armour – the one you keep in the wardrobe for battle – well, you soon realise it's made of tinfoil. It's a shocker.

'Well, I think I do.'

Last year I was heartbroken when he told me about the beautiful Shirley, his colleague at the bank, and how, thankfully, it came to nothing because he stopped it. And after the counselling sessions last year, I really felt we were back on track. After twenty-two years, we could see we had something worth hanging on to.

But do we?

'It doesn't *sound* like you trust him. Sally. Where is that distrust coming from? Do you agree that you both need to sit down and talk frankly?'

I know she's right. I'm driving myself crazy, but now, with Doll sliding down again, I'm not sure I can handle a confrontation. Life is messy. Well, that seems to be the way it works for me. It wants you on your knees. In the valley of tears. Life is a bitch. An absolute bitch. Is it the same for other people and they're just not admitting it? I often wonder about that.

'Why are you avoiding this conversation with him, Sally?'
'It's not a good time. I need to get my head around it.'
'It's been six weeks.'
'I'm not avoiding it, Mary, it's just that . . .'
'It strikes me that you are, Sally, and my question is, why?'

There's a silence in the room. The seconds fold into each other like baby mice. She's waiting for me to answer but there's a stone in my throat and the words can't squeeze past it. It takes an age.

'I'm afraid. If there was another woman, I couldn't bear it. Losing him.' The words come out as a whisper. 'I don't think I even want to know. If I did . . . my life would shatter.' My hands are shaking, and I tuck them out of sight.

'You're not angry? If he was having an affair, I mean. Would you feel any anger?'

It's a reasonable question. If my husband was playing away, I should be raging. I should be confronting him with my hands on my hips, demanding answers, taking charge, fighting back. Being strong, like other women. But anger takes energy and I have none.

Afterwards, on the drive home, I make a decision. Well, two decisions. First, I'm going to bring Doll to that new neurologist in Cork University Hospital. I read about him last week in one of the Sunday papers. He's a Canadian specialising in behaviour and mood disorders. There must be something we can do, and as Mary said, action is a good antidote to anxiety. And two, I'm going to confront Dan this weekend. Get those scorpion suspicions out on the table and face the possibility he's meeting another woman. Jesus, I have to say, I didn't see that coming.

Having a plan diffuses some of my stress. I switch on the car radio and sing along to Blondie's 'Heart of Glass' at the top of my voice. I'm not the only one – even the gorgeous

Debbie Harry is singing about her broken heart and losing her mind over a man she couldn't trust. It cheers me up to remind myself I'm not alone.

I turn onto the Mill Road, swing right into Bluebell Avenue, and park up in front of the yellow door of number six Bluebell Grove. My mobile buzzes. Staying over, Sal. Mting running late. C you tmrw.

My heart swerves to the right. How much evidence do I need? I switch off the engine and stay in the car for a few minutes, taking slow, deep breaths.

On impulse, I ring the bank and ask for Claire, Dan's right-hand woman. I make sure my voice is cheerful when she comes on the line. 'Hi, Sally, is everything all right?'

'Hi, Claire, just a quick call – I can't get my hands on Dan right now. What time is the review over, do you know? It might drag on after six, and I was wondering . . .'

'No, not a hope, Sally. Don't worry, they'll have it wrapped up by four p.m. at the latest. And that suits everyone – they all want to get out of Dublin before peak traffic, you know yourself.'

I laugh lightly. 'No drinks reception, so, or late dinner?'

Claire laughs too. 'Those days are gone, Sally. It's all family-friendly hours now, and no harm either.'

I ring off and stay sitting in my driveway. I can't trust my legs to carry me to the front door. I knew it. The bastard. Now I know for sure. Now I need to be strong. Now I need to plan exactly what I'm going to say. And it's not going to be pretty. I mean it.

CHAPTER 3

DOLL

Today it's Thursday, or so I hear. It's just after eight a.m., and we're stuck in the traffic outside Andi's school. Andi's my sister, sweet sixteen and pretty as a peach. Her boyfriend, Steve, is from the wrong side of the track, even though we don't even have a train in Glengarvan. Steve is a mechanic and he loves Andi. I wish I was Andi. We're stuck at the school crossing outside Murphy's shop and my dad is drumming his fingers on the steering wheel and cursing under his breath. He's going to a meeting in Dublin and keeps looking at his watch and shaking his head.

I see all the girls going into St Mary's Academy, red blazers, loose ties, white smiles. Some of them gather outside Murphy's, standing around in little circles – high ponies, hairbands, gossiping and giggling. I wish I were them, not me. Strapped into a car seat like I'm three. I slither down as far as I can so they don't see me.

I spot Ruth Meehan from number nine, just down the road from our house. She's fourteen, a real clever-clogs, Andi says. Her hair is plaited, blonde wisps falling across her forehead. She's linking her friend Amy. If your thoughts were coloured and seeped through your skin, mine'd be nettle green. I bet they're talking about weekend plans and girl guides and football games. And I'm mad. Mad jealous.

Ruth's mother jogs past the car, sees my dad, stops, and reverses. She's wearing a purple-and-green leggings and vest and looks like that annoying dinosaur, Barley, on the telly.

'Hi, Dan.' She leans her chest on the open car window, pushing her hair off her face and curling it behind her ear. 'All this running has me worn out.' She winks and slaps her bum. 'I'm training for the 5K, you know. Hope it'll be all worth it in the end.'

She smiles at my dad, blinking a lot and touching his arm every chance she gets. She nods at me. 'You've your hands full, Dan.'

'I won't delay you, Lucy. You're a busy woman.' My dad looks at his watch again.

'You never get a minute, do you? I'm always saying to Sally you're a wonderful father. I don't know how you do it.' Her eyes open and close quickly. She's flirting with him. I've heard Andi say flirting is when you want a boy to notice you. Granny said flirting means you're a hussy, but she never said what a hussy was. I miss my granny.

I can see my father's face in the mirror, lines of annoyance on his forehead. The traffic begins to edge ahead. 'I'm heading to a meeting in Dublin, Lucy. Good luck with the running.'

She gives him a little wave and puffs off like a steam train. He buzzes up the window. 'Can't stand that stupid woman.' I smile to myself, 'cos I'm thinking the same.

We stop at Texaco. Dad puts the card in the slot, and the car wash sprays foam all over the car, like snow. It's like me and my dad are in an igloo, quiet and white. Walk, walk in the light. I can't get that hymn out of my head. The brushes whiz across the windows like spiked monsters. This white world is a magic place, like the world at the back of the wardrobe in that film I saw on the telly. You're in a dark wardrobe with coats and furs; next thing you're in a snow-world. It reminds me of Almazova, the otherworld I travelled to last year. Everyone thought I was lying in a hospital bed with pneumonia, but that was only the shell of me. I was gone. I was on the other side of here. I rode a horse and nearly drowned. And I helped kill Ramish, a man who was liquid evil, the darkest kind of bad. And then I had to come back. The Council of Grandmothers *sent* me back. As my granny used to say, eaten bread is soon forgotten. They got what they wanted, and then they spat me out.

So here I am, back in Misery Street, still mute and miserable in my fuzzy world. It's not fair.

The car is getting a blow-dry now, rinsed clean, shiny and new. I know how that feels. In Almazova I was shiny and new. And people there said I was a powerful girl. A proper hero. Nell, the head honcho from the Council of Grandmothers, said I was unconkerable. Invincible. Well, it's better than invisible. Better than being a goner or not right upstairs.

Nell told me, before I left Almazova, 'Doll, when you go back, you must break through the skin of despair.' But it's hard. Much easier to break through the skin on my cheek, feel the blood trickle down. The sharp pinpricks of pain make me feel so alive.

I look out on the pine trees whizzing past now.

When you think about it, it was easy for Nell to talk about 'the skin of despair'. Like it was custard, something you could slice through with your spoon. But despair is a lot thicker than custard. And it's not yellow. It's black, with wings, beating around your head when you close your eyes. And it's not sweet. No, despair is gooseberry-sour. What'd Nell know about despair? She didn't live my life. Talk is cheap, as Granny used to say. *She* didn't have to come back into a stale hospital room, back into to my bony shell. Huh! Wasn't my choice to return, but that's typical. When do I get a say in anything?

We pull up outside my school. Dad switches off the ignition. He helps me out of the car and into my buggy. Marianne, my assistant, comes out to wheel me in, and my dad waves goodbye before driving off.

Behind Marianne, there's a figure approaching. She's wearing a black top hat, a navy suit and – my heart stumbles –

red-laced shoes. The lunch box on my lap clatters to the ground. I open and close my mouth, forgetting for a moment that I can't talk.

'What's wrong, Doll?' Marianne says, reaching down to pick up the lunch box. My mouth's gone dry. She straightens up and turns towards the woman in the tall hat.

'Come over and meet Doll Redmond, Nan-Nan.' Marianne smiles down at me. 'Doll, meet Nan-Nan; she's our visiting teacher, and she's looking forward to meeting all our kids over the next few days.'

Nan-Nan smooths her skirt and lifts off her hat before replacing it. 'Hello, Doll, pleased to meet you.' She winks at me. I can only stare.

She leans in, takes my hand in hers, and squeezes it. The smooth black skin feels warm and worn, and I can feel a bolt of electricity fire through my body.

I reach out and wrap my arms around her skirt. I need to know it's not a dream, some cruel trick of my mind.

'I think you've made a friend there,' Marianne says, laughing. 'Consider yourself lucky. Doll pushes most people away.'

Nan-Nan laughs, a familiar tinkling sound, and I almost forget to breathe. She takes the handles of the buggy. 'I'll take Doll for a little walk around the gardens, Marianne. See you in ten minutes.'

We take the gravel path towards the rose garden, and she leans down and whispers, 'Let's find a quiet place to talk, Doll.' I stare straight ahead. Nan-Nan is back. Has she come to rescue me? Or kidnap me? I grip my lunch box as we disappear behind the line of oak trees skirting the school grounds. She stops the buggy when we're out of sight and hunkers down in front of me. Her red curls peep out from under her hat. Her voice is stern as she brings her face close to mine. 'It's time to fly again, Doll.'

Her words are a necklace, a string of diamonds falling from her mouth. There's a tip-tapping in my feet as an invisible dance begins, glitter-stepping up my legs, pulsing up through me, a secret stream of lightness. My future, fluttering to life, pulling me to a world beyond my skin of despair. A pied-piper world where everything is possible.

CHAPTER 4

DAN

'Good trip?' It's the way she says it, pursing her lips and looking away quickly. It's like she knows.

'The usual.' I nod, unzipping my bag, folding a sweater, hanging my suit in the closet. Avoiding her gaze, I snap the suitcase shut and shove it under the bed. 'Traffic was murder, though.'

She nods. 'Yeah, that's Dublin for you.'

I pull a T-shirt over my head. There's an awkward silence. She folds her arms, looks out the window.

'I'm going for a run,' I say, lacing up my trainers. 'I won't be long.'

She shrugs. 'It's starting to drizzle. Bring a rainproof.'

'Is there something wrong, Sally?' I can't stand the tension, but I'm not ready yet to tell her what I need to tell her.

'No. Why are you asking me that?'

'Well, you're very quiet. It's not like you.'

She rubs her palms over her face, sighing. 'I'm worried about Doll.'

In one way, I'm relieved she's not asking awkward questions, but I feel a frustration – a sense of *here we go again*. 'What is it now?'

She looks up sharply, reading my impatience. Her voice rises. 'What is it now? Are you blind? Don't you see the change in her?' She stops. Straightens the blue throw on the bed, smoothing out imaginary wrinkles.

'Doll is self-injuring again. She's shutting herself off.' She looks up, folds her arms. 'Or are you too busy at work to notice what's going on under your nose?'

She switches her hands to her hips – it's what she does when she's looking for an argument. When she's ready to erupt and looking for someone to blame. And I'm not in the bloody mood.

'You know what, Sally?' I zip up my windcheater. 'Maybe you need to get out for a run yourself. Get rid of some of that stress. And then we'll talk. When you're calmer.'

She brushes past me. Her eyes flash. 'I'm not even going to answer that.'

The door slams behind her. She opens it a fraction. 'By the way, I'd love to go for a run, but someone has to mind Doll. Enjoy yourself, though.' She disappears down the stairs, and I can hear saucepans banging loudly in the kitchen.

Do I need this? This bloody interrogation? As if I haven't noticed Doll's form. Her face, scratched and torn. Her wails in the early hours of the morning. As if I can't see the way she stares out the window, the light switched off inside her head, the invisible sign saying there's no one home. For Chrissake, I'm not blind.

I bang the front door shut and jog down the avenue. I take a right onto the link road and then the first left onto the river path. The rain is hammering down now, but it's good to get out into the early-summer evening and let the hassles of the day behind you. But they're hard to shake off, clinging like suckers, and I quicken my pace, seeing if I can outrun the bastards. I decide to take the longer route; who'd want to go home to that?

I sprint across the school grounds, exit onto Monastery Road, and take the path that skirts the Lainey River and cuts through Durrow wood, a good hour's run. The rain is warm against my face, and I can feel the layers of mental grime peel away as I fall into a steady rhythm.

Sally knows something. The way she wouldn't meet my eye. And not just this evening; she's been in odd form for the last few weeks. She's concerned about Doll – I don't blame her for that – but there's something else. Something she's *not* saying.

I hop over the gate onto the path that crisscrosses the wood. The rain is a soft drizzle now, and there's a rainbow arching through the beech trees. I stop for a second to admire the hazy blues and pinks and yellows filtering through the dripping leaves. For some strange reason, I feel like crying; how dumb is that? I must be getting soft in the head.

I push on, but I can't escape the guilt, winding itself around me, squeezing tight like a too-small shirt. Guilt? Shame? Is there a difference? No doubt someone could tell me, but would it matter? They're only labels anyway – at the end of the day, names for feelings that fill you with regret. And confusion. But there's love too; last night I felt it. Love and guilt. Mary Winters at the Counselling Centre said feelings need to be expressed, not suppressed. There's something in that. Still, certain stories are best left untold.

Deeper in the woods now, I can smell honeysuckle, wild jasmine, nettle, the deep earthy smells released by the drenched grass underfoot. The world being washed clean. Wish I could be washed clean of the lies and secrets. I've seen secrets destroy families. You hear a lot of secrets in my job at the bank, stories unfolding in the back offices. Confessions. Confidential conversations whispered across the desk over cups of coffee.

Like Ger Mac – one of our clients in with me last week. Local boy made good. His mother died when he was six, and his father starting drinking. Ger ended up in a care home, left school at fifteen, disappeared for a while to the UK. He came back to work in a local waste disposal company on Finbarr Street. Today he owns the business; he's got thirty employees and has tripled his turnover in the last five years. 'There's money in shite.' He always said that. And he'd laugh then. He's not even forty, and he could retire now and still be able to look after his three kids, set them up for life.

Truth is, he's a gambler, he told me. An addict. Late starter, he said. A few bets here and there on the horses. Then online. I could see the withdrawals in his account over the past while.

When I asked him what was going on, he said it was the buzz. Beginner's luck had gotten him hooked. In the last year he'd thrown away close on sixty grand like 'twas Monopoly money. The wife didn't know. Yet. He was convinced he could win it all back.

I know Eileen, great girl. She'd have his back, but he can't tell her. It's the shame, he said, the self-disgust and betrayal. She wouldn't understand, he said. But she probably would.

I spot a deer behind the trees to my left, her red-brown coat glistening in the rain. She's standing still, watching me. I stop, panting hard, trying not to disturb her. I can see her eyes, brown and languid. She bolts as I move towards her, disappearing into the undergrowth.

I walk for a while, get my breath back. What would Sally say if she knew? Would she understand too? Or would she walk away? Would she say, *It's the last straw, Dan?*

I break into a run again. I need to talk to Sally. And what would I actually say, how would I frame it? *Sal, there's something you should know, and let me explain?* And then what? How to proceed from there?

'Dan! Wait up.' The sound is like a bullet. I turn around and groan silently. It's Lucy bloody Meehan, a vision of purple and green emerging from the woods. I wait as she catches up, huffing and panting. 'Slow down a second.' She leans forward, hands on her knees, breathing heavily. 'Just. Spotted. You. There.'

'Hi, Lucy.'

She straightens up, looks at the sky. 'Isn't it lovely, running in the summer rain?' She smiles, nodding towards the trees behind her. 'And that rainbow in the mist? Very romantic.'

She waits for me to say something, and I nod. Christ, I hate small talk.

'Are you heading home?' She gestures to the path on the right.

'Yes, em . . .'

'Great, let's do it.' She giggles. 'Take it handy, though. I'm not as fast as you, Dan.' Inexplicably then, she winks. What is that woman *on*? It's all I need, but it's only a ten-minutes run back to Bluebell Grove and, knowing Lucy, she'll talk for the two of us.

And she does.

'You're back.'

I know by Sally's face she's in a better mood.

'I met the dreaded Lucy on my travels.'

'So I see. Did she tell you that she's lost 9k in Slimming World and that she feels so toned, so energetic?'

'Oh, she did. I got it all.' I puff out my chest and slap my thigh. 'Soooo energised now, transformed, I'm a new woman.'

We both laugh. The ice is broken.

I take the stairs two at a time. I don't want to kill the mood. Tomorrow there'll be more opportunity to open up the conversation. Over dinner, maybe. A bottle of wine.

I turn the water to hot and step into the steaming shower. Maybe a cup of coffee when we're out for a walk on Sunday afternoon. I'll say, *Sally, there's something you should know.*

That's it. Once I get started, well, it will roll from there. I close my eyes, let the hot water run over my face.

As I get into a tracksuit, I feel a bit better. I've a plan.

A shout from downstairs. 'Dan, there's a fish pie in the oven, ready in five.'

'Coming.'

Sally's in the kitchen setting plates and cutlery on the table. She unscrews a half-empty bottle of sauvignon, refills her glass, and takes a large gulp.

'We need to get Doll to a neurologist, Dan. There's a new guy, Dr Bartley, from Canada, in the Cork University Hospital. He's meant to be a top man in his field. Might be worth a try. A different angle.'

I pour myself some wine.

'Good idea. We have to keep trying.' Safe ground here; we'll have the real conversation on Sunday.

We clink our glasses, both of us with a plan. A plan to make things better.

'Cheers,' Sally says, smiling, taking a sip.

The guilt is like a tumour in my throat. 'Cheers,' I say, raising my glass. But a voice inside is telling me that there's going to be a train-wreck and that there's no going back.

CHAPTER 5

DOLL

It's Saturday. The Bee Gees are on the radio, singing about going back to Mass in Chusetts. Maybe it was Father Joe's idea. Something's telling them they must go home. And something's telling me *I* must go home too. Home to Almazova – the place where I can be me. The best me. Where people think I'm the berries; a world where I can walk like a proper girl, where I can talk and crunch my food and I don't have to take medicine and I don't get sick and smell of vomit. In Almazova I can climb a mountain, ride a horse, read a map, talk to important people who take me serious and tell me I'm a topper, a Child of Summer, a special person – not just someone with special knees.

Like Father Joe said, when you believe, magic happens. Last year my brother Will, who's studying in Ethiopia, sent me a doll called Nan-Nan for my birthday; I didn't know *she was real*. That she had come from Almazova, that she was a scientist with the Space Agency there. That Almazova was a world among many worlds up behind the moon. She said they needed me to complete a mission. I thought it was a joke. But I took a chance and flew off with her and escaped my lemon-life here. And now Nan-Nan is back! Pretending to be a teacher – visiting my school for a few days and telling me that Almazova needs me again. I have another mission to complete, she said, and will I come back?

Does a swim duck?

'Doll, well done,' my mother says, sitting on the couch next to me. 'You haven't touched your face, and you've almost finished your tea too.' She smiles and goes off to get my Weetabix. *Bring it on, Mom*, I think. *I will finish that too. I will do anything you want me to.* Because soon, I'm off. Across the skies to Almazova. Back to freedom and adventure, and this time, this time, I might try and stay a bit longer. But Nan-Nan doesn't know that. It's my little secret.

My sister Andi is just back from her school trip to Paris. She drops her rucksack on the wooden floor with a thud and plants a kiss on my face. She smells minty. 'How're you, Doll?' She rubs my head and marches into the kitchen.

I can hear her telling Mom about the trip, about how three girls were caught drinking and someone called Triona got lost for an entire afternoon. Panic search. In the end, they found her asleep in her bed, back at the hostel. My mom laughs. The Champs-Élysées is beautiful, Andi is saying, and she's talking about the markets and the cool French guys. I hear more laughter, shared jokes, and I envy Andi that. The sharing, the fun. I wish I could join in.

Still, I hug myself inside. Soon, I'll have that. I'll be talking and laughing with Tiger, my best friend in Almazova. I'll be having fun too. It's enough to make me whoop with joy.

My mom comes rushing in, followed by Andi. They look worried. 'Are you all right, Doll?' She smiles when she sees me drinking my tea. 'You gave us a fright.' She looks at Andi. 'Put on the kettle, love.'

She takes my hand. 'Come on, Doll, we'll all have breakfast together and get more juicy stories of the St Mary's history trip.'

While they're talking, I'm thinking about *my* trip tonight. Nan-Nan didn't say exactly when we might be leaving, but I'm all set. 'Think about it carefully,' she said in the rose garden on Thursday. 'It's up to you. It's your decision. To accept the invitation. Or not.' It had to be my own free will, she said. 'Don't forget, it's hard coming back to reality, Doll. Remember the last time, how tough it was having to return. Having to get used to a more confined life again.'

Confined life? Huh! That was one way of putting it. In Almazova I was a real eleven. When I came back, I had to get used to being like a baby again. Pureed food, beakers, not being able to talk or read or run or figure out problems. Back to pain and getting sick. Back to a girl-cage. Would I go? Hello! I didn't have to think about it too long – about three seconds, I'd say.

'Did you miss Steve, Andi?' my mom is saying, pretending the answer doesn't matter. 'You haven't seen him for five whole days; that must be a record.'

Steve, Andi's boyfriend, is from Brandon Terrace. Brandon Terrace is up the town. Up the town is not a good place to be from, according to my dad. I dunno why. I've often heard him say that a lot of pups live up the town. I'd love a dog myself, but obviously my dad isn't into dogs. Especially ones that live up the town, around Brandon Terrace. My mom sort of agrees with him, and they do argue about Steve when Andi isn't around. And I don't think she knows that.

'You can't stop her seeing him,' Mom tells him. 'That will only make her more determined. You know how stubborn she is.'

He tut-tuts then, shakes his head. 'She's sixteen, Sal, young enough to do what she's told. We're her parents. We need to look out for her.'

I think my mom thought it would fizzle out, but actually Andi is proper in love, and she was only fifteen when she met him. I think my dad blames my mom for letting it go on.

'He is not the type of boy for our daughter,' he said just last week when Steve called to bring Andi to the cinema. 'No education, no prospects, a dreadful tattoo, and a family history.' He rolled his eyes.

'Jesus, they're only kids,' my mother said then. 'They all have tattoos these days. Anyway, it won't last. It's a crush, Dan; we have to choose our battles.'

Andi is always smiling when she's with Steve. She was so grumpy before she met him, and now she's always humming to herself. Like me now. Fizzing up at the thought of my trip.

Sometimes when Mom and Dad aren't here, Andi sits on Steve's lap at the kitchen table and she kisses him. For ages. They drink Coke and hold hands, and he strokes her hair and tells her he loves her. Before her, he says, he didn't have a clue where he was going, and then, he says, she changed his world. Oh God, they're so boring. Loads of girls fancy him, Andi says, but far as I can see, he only has eyes for our Andi. I love Andi. And I think Steve is cool. He looks like Justin Bieber. My dad says she has everything going for her, and Steve, he says, has nothing going for him. So how is all that going to end? Everything and nothing – it's like they're going in opposite directions.

'I can't wait to see him,' Andi is saying. 'I missed him so much, Mom. We talked every day, but it's not the same, is it?' She checks her Fitbit. 'Oh, look at the time; I'm going to be late.' She gets her rucksack and hoists it onto the kitchen table. 'Look, I got him a present.' She pulls out a red bag.

'Lovely,' Mom says when she sees the grey Calvin Klein T-shirt. 'He's going to love that.'

Andi digs out another T-shirt for me, a pink one with a heart, and a green scarf for Mom. She hugs us both. 'Good to be back,' she says, getting up. 'I better get ready. See you later.'

She takes the stairs two at a time. Mom purses her lips. I think she's disappointed. Maybe she hoped the trip away would have helped Andi see Steve in another light. No chance. We can hear her singing a Taylor Swift song in the shower about how no one gets her like Steve does.

Mom rolls her eyes and looks at me. 'Teenagers,' she says, shaking her head as she fills the dishwasher and clears the table.

I go back to my couch, pull my tartan rug around me. I'm excited for tonight. Nan-Nan must never guess my plan, though – that this time I mightn't be coming back. They made me come back the last time. Protocols, they said. They were sorry, but no, the Council of Grandmothers was not for turning. I had to go back to my half-life, no matter how much I pleaded or sobbed. And I expect it will be the same this time.

But this time, I'll be ready. This time I might find a way to disappear when my mission is completed. This time maybe I can stay in Almazova and be all the things I can be – the girl who isn't afraid, the girl who's a hero, the girl who will grow up like Andi and bring colours into a boy's life. The girl who is invincible, not invisible. The real Doll, stepping out.

Yes, I'll miss my mom and dad, I'll miss my family and Marianne my teacher, but it's not enough. It's just not enough. Already, thinking about Almazova, I can feel the misery dropping off me. Life, it's a crazy thing. I love it. Bring it on.

CHAPTER 6

ANDI

I see him scrolling through his phone in the booth at the back of Pizza Pizza. He looks up, sees me through a sea of diners, and waves me over.

'Girl, you look stunning. Love the dress.' He leans forward and kisses my cheek. He places his palm across his heart. 'Missed you, babe.'

It's a bit awkward for a few seconds, with us not seeing each other for nearly a week. It's almost like our first date all over again. He smiles then. 'Don't let on to the lads, though – my reputation will be shagged.'

I know he has – sorry, *had* – a reputation. He was a player. His best friend Rizla told me he was a love-'em-and-leave-'em kind of guy. Until he met me. And then, Rizla said, he was all in.

But I was too. All in, that is. Steve gets me, he adores me. We have something special, that's what I'm trying to say. People say he's trouble, but that's just first impressions. Deep down he's sweet and kind. I'm his princess. His words, not mine.

The girls in school don't think I should be dating a boy from Brandon Terrace. Pure St Mary's snobs. Just because of where he's from, just because his mother's a junkie who walked out on him at seven, just because he's a trainee mechanic, they say he won't do at all. But they don't know Steve. How he makes me feel. I think they're jealous, though. Girls are like that. They want what you have. Or they call it something else.

'He sounds possessive,' Ciara Lane said one day as we walked home from basketball.

'How do you mean?' I said, surprised and annoyed and thinking to myself that Ciara Lane had never had a proper boyfriend and what would she know?

'Oh, you know. He seems to want you all to himself. Just him and you. It's a bit over-the-top.'

'And what's wrong with that, Ciara? He loves me; it's the real thing. You've no idea how it feels, do you?'

She shook her head then, switched her sports bag from one shoulder to the other. 'You're right. I don't. But look, you're only sixteen; don't get sucked in, Andi. That's all I'm saying. And,' she said, making a slicing motion across her throat, 'I'd say it's only a matter of time before your father puts his foot down.'

Like I said, jealous.

'Missed you too, Steve,' I say, sitting opposite him, letting him wrap his fingers around mine, feeling the familiar thrill zipping down my spine.

We order a pepperoni pizza to share, and we catch up. He laughs when I tell him about Triona going missing in Paris and the drinking and the mad stuff that goes on during school trips away, including the bits you'd never tell your mother. I pull out the red paper bag. 'Something for you,' I say.

He holds up the T-shirt, grinning, and pulls it over his head. 'Perfect fit,' he says, puffing his chest out, all muscle, like a catwalk model. We both laugh.

'How's your gran?' I say. 'You said she had to go into hospital on Wednesday. Poor Joanie. Was it the emphysema?'

Steve lives with his gran, Joanie, and he's so close to her. She's his real mam, he says. His mother comes back from London once in a while, but he doesn't have any relationship with her. She told them recently that she was clean now, getting her life together, but he's not holding out for anything new there.

'Yep, Gran's home tomorrow. And she's promised to give up the fags.' He rolls his eyes like he's heard it all before. 'She's in better shape, though, after being on the drip and getting some TLC. It'll be good to have her home again, though she says she's missing Molly more than me.' He laughs. 'She argued with the doctors about the hospital's no-dogs policy, but they wouldn't listen.'

After lunch, we walk along the prom and scramble down onto the beach. We stop at the bend where the sand gives way to gigantic granite rocks. It's cool for May, and there's a light breeze blowing my hair across my face. He stops and curtains it behind my ear, and we lean in against a rock and kiss, his tongue exploring my mouth, insisting on my attention. *Don't worry, Steve, I'm all yours*, I'm thinking as I massage the warm skin under his two T-shirts. I'm afraid someone will spot us, mid-afternoon, snogging in the sunshine, but it's private down here. Well, usually. A group of boys roar across at us from the prom, 'Get a room!' and we laugh and I blush.

'That reminds me,' he says, nodding towards the boys. 'I have something to ask you.'

He cups his palm around the back of my neck, our foreheads touching.

'You being away, Andi, it made me think how much you mean to me. I don't deserve you.' He frowns. 'Girl, if anything happened between us . . .'

'It won't,' I say, slamming my mouth onto his.

After a long time, he pulls away. 'Listen, Andi?'

I plant kisses on his eyelids. 'I'm listening.'

'Will you stay over tonight in mine?'

'You know I can't, Steve. If my father found out . . .'

'He wouldn't need to know, babe, would he?'

I sway against him, feeling his hand slip through an opening between the buttons at the back of my dress and stroke my spine.

'I suppose he wouldn't. But your gran wouldn't approve, Steve, going behind her back like that.'

His mouth grazes my cheek. I love when he does that. 'She loves you. I don't think she'd mind if it was you, Andi. She thinks you're a good influence.' He rolls his eyes, shaking his head and grinning. 'If only she knew the real you!' He waits.

'I dunno,' I say, but inside I'm on fire. On fire.

'It's your call, babe, but a whole night together . . . ?' He sighs, his breath ragged. It says it all for me.

'Okay,' I say, my heart pounding. 'I'll tell them I'm staying at Stacey's.' Stacey is the one real friend I have at St Mary's. And my mom and dad like Stacey.

He closes his eyes as he kisses my forehead. 'Thank you.'

'But Steve.'

'Yeah?'

'We're not doing it, okay? I'm not ready.'

'Sure, Andi, I respect you, babe. No pressure.'

We've talked about this so many times. Our 'first time'. We both want to wait, for it to be special. But now, with his gran away till tomorrow, we have a free house for the first time ever. It's too good a chance to miss. And we don't have to go all the way. But can I trust myself? I know I can trust Steve, but can I stop myself? Even thinking about it makes me shiver. But hey, I'm sixteen, not a child. Still, I don't want to walk into something I just can't control.

'You're gone very quiet,' Steve says. 'Are you sure you're okay with this?'

'Absolutely. Let's head back, and I'll set it up.'

*****

Stacey's up for it. Mom's okay, all sorted. Back in my bedroom, I pack a bag. Toothbrush, makeup, hairbrush, jeans and top for tomorrow. I slip the half-empty naggin of vodka into my handbag. I bought it for a rare girls' night out at the Rugby Club a few weeks ago. I shower, take out my new yellow halter-neck dress and sneakers. Do my face, straighten my hair. Good to go. My fingers are shaking as I button up my dress and slip on my leather jacket.

Mom pops her head around the door. She looks surprised. 'You're looking very glam for a night in,' she says.

'We might go out for a pizza,' I lie, 'but we have to be back to mind Conor at nine o'clock while her parents are at the fundraiser.' I finish putting on my lippy.

'I'll drop you off if you like, in a half an hour, if you can wait?'

My heart drops. 'Ah, no, Mom, thanks anyway – I need the exercise. See you tomorrow. I'll be home before lunchtime.'

'Okay, suit yourself, and say hi to Stacey and her parents for us.'

She swallows the story. I feel bad lying like that. But if I told her the truth? I smile inside at the very idea. *Hey, Mom, can you drop me off at Brandon Terrace? Steve's gran is away and we have the place to ourselves, so I'm staying over, okay? Sex? Well, we'll see what happens. I can't wait!*

Steve is at the door when I arrive. He takes my bag upstairs and I wander round the sitting room, too nervous to stay still. It's chilly outside, and he's lit a small fire. The room smells of turf and cigarettes.

Steve gets me a glass of Coke, and I take the vodka from my handbag. 'Just one, Steve, to celebrate our first proper night together.'

He grins and raises his can of Coke. 'Cheers, babe.'

He pulls me down on the couch next to him, and I turn on the telly, scrolling through Netflix.

'I've ordered a takeaway. You can choose the movie,' he says, swinging my legs across his lap.

We watch *What Men Want*, but it's hard to concentrate. I'm thinking about what might happen later, upstairs in his bed. What might he want? What's he expecting to happen?

I can't face the Asian street food when it arrives, and instead I slip a generous splash of vodka into my Coke.

No Dutch courage needed for Steve. He seems totally chilled out. It's probably not the first time he's brought a girl back to his, and the thought of this punctures me.

I take his hand in mine. 'Come on,' I say, switching off the telly before the movie even finishes. 'Let's go to bed.'

He leads me upstairs and into his bedroom. The walls are covered with posters of motorbikes and heavy-metal bands I don't recognise. No trace of clothing, magazines, cups, glasses. The room has been cleaned and has a fresh citrus scent.

'All this, for me,' I say, looking around and smiling. He pulls down the window blind and comes close, kissing me slowly. He turns off the bedside lamp so it's only the landing light casting a dim glow through the open bedroom door. There's an awkwardness between us.

'Come here, babe.'

My head spins as he opens my dress and it slips off my shoulders. He pulls me towards the bed and he's whispering in my ear and my limbs are liquid and I forget any resolve I had earlier. It's like I've been waiting, without even knowing it, waiting for this moment for the last seven and a half months, waiting to *not* hold back, waiting to say *don't stop* instead of *don't*, to lose all resistance and collapse into him. I have to catch my breath, and what was I thinking? How did I think I could resist his fingers running from my shoulder down the length of my body?

Nothing else matters right now. It's too late to turn back. Too late to plan ahead. The vodka is saying, *Lean in and go with the flow, girl*, and I yield to my dissolving body and my spinning heart.

Afterwards, in the early hours, I watch him as he sleeps. His smooth chest falling and rising, his fringe damp across his forehead. I coil myself next to him, like an eel.

He stirs, murmuring something I can't catch. *Princess*, I think he said. I ease his head against my shoulder and I know I have never, ever been this happy.

The phone won't stop ringing. It takes me a second or two to realise where I am. I run down the stairs still naked and grab my mobile from the table in the hall. It's Mom. What the fuck. It's not even nine o'clock.

'Hi, Mom. What's up? Stacey and me are still in bed. It's only—'

'Andi, are you in Steve's house? Don't answer that! I know you are, because I'm here in Stacey's house and she's spilled the beans.'

'I can explain, Mom.'

Her voice is flat. 'Just get home now. It's Doll. She's had an accident.'

'Wha-a-at?'

The line is dead, she's rung off. I race up the stairs two at a time.

Steve is pulling a T-shirt over his head. 'What's up?'

'I dunno, Steve. Doll's had an accident. Mom's in Stacey's. Holy fuck.'

I pull on my jeans and top, grab my bag, and I'm out the door, down across Hettyville, racing along St Joseph's Avenue and out onto the Mill Road, my breath ragged by the time I get to number six Bluebell Grove. I hear sobbing from the kitchen, and guilt wraps itself around my neck like a rope.

CHAPTER 7

DOLL

I yawn six times before they notice. I wish I could talk. I'd say, *Come on, come on, bring me to bed, for heaven's sake. Hurry up, please.*

The news is just starting on the telly.

'She's tired,' Dad says.

'I'll bring her up,' Mom says, taking my hand. 'Sounds like you're ready for the sack, Doll.'

I can't wait to get up the stairs and into my bed. Nan-Nan will be waiting for me. She'll be getting ready for our trip. The thought makes me stumble, and I nearly fall down the stairs.

'Steady on, Doll. Take it easy,' my mother says.

Little does she know – my stomach flips when I think about it – I may not be back again. Am I crazy? I stop for a moment. Peer at the photos on the stairs wall. There's one of me with my granny leaning down to kiss me. But she's gone this while now. Disappeared out of our lives and left a hole in my heart as big as Galway Bay. But I know my granny will turn up in Almazova like she did the last time. My granny isn't dead. There's no such thing as dead. She lives in another corner of the universe, working her way to heaven. I'll see her soon. I know this. I push on up the stairs again, my mom behind me, her hand on my shoulder.

I grab her sleeve as she helps me into bed. She looks surprised.

'Is there something wrong, Doll?' She waits for a moment, and then as I turn away, she leans over and kisses me. And she says what she's said every night, as long as I can remember.

'Sleep tight, love.'

She closes the door softly behind her.

I half sit and keep my eye on the strip of sky between the half-pulled curtains. Clouds hurry along as the sun slips behind the roof of number eight. The top window is ajar and I fix my eyes on it, waiting for Nan-Nan to appear.

After a long time, my lids grow heavy. It's dark now, and I hear my mom and dad climbing the stairs to bed. Andi is in Stacey's. The bathroom tap runs. A door bangs, a light switch is flicked off. Silence falls over the house. I force my eyes to stay open.

Maybe she's not coming. Maybe someone is playing a trick on me. Maybe there is no Nan-Nan and it's all in my head.

A long time passes. Out of the darkness, a strawberry glow appears on the horizon. I have to face it: she's not coming after all.

Tonight I thought I was going to be born again – into a new life, a new world where I'd walk, walk in the light. But that's not gonna happen now. My eyes freeze closed.

I dream that Nan-Nan is here. The doll version of her, not the visiting-teacher version.

She places her hand on my forehead. 'Sleep, child,' she says. 'Not long now, not long at all.'

She settles herself, hands laced across her middle, and her breathing is slow and even. She looks tired, small lines fanning out across her temples. Her red curls peep from under her tall hat.

I open my eyes. The main window is open, and Nan-Nan is shaking me awake. It's not a dream. I stare.

'It's not a dream, Doll.' She's on her feet now, smoothing her skirt. The curtain is pulled back. I can see the moon hurrying along, making way for the day.

Nan-Nan stretches her arms wide. Her lips move, and she's whisper-chanting words I can't make out. It's like she's in a trance, somewhere else entirely. I know there's a rigmarole to go through before we sail out of here. She looks at me. Puts her finger to her lips.

'Ready, Doll?' she says in a hushed voice.

I nod, keep nodding. She pulls her hat down over her curls, undoes her belt, which is embroidered with pink shells, and tethers herself to me, wrist to wrist.

'Close your eyes. Do *not* make a sound.' Just like last time, I feel myself being sucked off the bed, hovering briefly in midair, and then we're moving toward the window. I can feel the sharp breeze on my face. An owl hoots, and in the far distance, a dog barks.

Now we're sailing out the window. Quantum levitation, Nan-Nan said.

I open my eyes. One last look before I float off. It's like the world has slowed down for a moment. The breeze dies. There's a stillness, silent as snow.

And then, Jesus, Mary, and Holy St Joseph, instead of sailing away over the rooftops, I'm falling. Tumbling towards the toolshed and the decking in our back garden. In a flash, I can see the flowerpots and the mossy roof of the shed coming up to greet me. I hear a splintering crack, like when a bird is shot down. A thud, and then, a whimper.

I can see lights – on, off, on, off, on. There's a trickle gently dripping inside my forehead. The lights are switched off. Thank you so much; they were blinding. Darkness is soothing. *Hello, darkness.* The orchestra is playing a song, and the conductor is singing about darkness being his friend and he's distracting all the musicians with his singing.

I hear Nan-Nan gasp. I feel a tug, a separating, like a butterfly shaking off his old caterpillar coat. I see my old body-casing crumpled beneath me on the deck, and then I'm lifted by helium hands up, up into the starlit night. I can see the waves crashing onto the prom and the strings of yellow lights zigzagging through the streets of Glengarvan. The Lainey River is glistening in the moonshine. Car lights flash and wink along the motorway, and way in the distance, I can hear the scream of an ambulance siren. Someone in trouble. I say a prayer for them, breathe it out into the chill air.

I'm still tethered to Nan-Nan. I look up and see her above me, her brow furrowed, her face chalk white in the moonlight. We're speeding through the silence of the night. My pyjamas flaps and clings around my legs, and my head hurts. The fizz is gone out of me. I feel dizzy, cold, and oh-so-tired.

I sail through a sea of ink. A rib-freezing wind carries us along in her arms, begging us to hurry, hurry, hurry. It cools my scalding head. Thank you, wind. The moon shines down like a giant pearl. In the distance I hear a palace of music, an orchestra and a chorus of silvery voices. They sweep up the bits of my heart that were scattered across the darkness. The voices echo across the heavens, filling the world with song, promising wonders to come. Are those mermaids singing to me? Oh lord, I hear my granny's voice. And she's singing, 'Walk, walk in the light.'

I hum the tune, curl into myself; let the notes fling us across the night, away toward the red glow in the far, far distance.

CHAPTER 8

SALLY

The ambulance screeches off, turning onto the Mill Road and racing towards the motorway. The siren blasts through the night air.

Dan fumbles with the ignition. 'Christ, what's wrong with the damn key?' The engine roars to life and we speed off. His hands shake as he grips the steering wheel. Crashing three red lights, we're on the motorway in under two minutes.

'How the fuck could it have happened, Sal? It's not possible, is it? Doll fell out her bedroom window? There is no way!'

He's right. He's right. I don't understand it myself. That window was definitely closed.

I stare at the road ahead, hands shaking.

'It's like a nightmare; I can't believe this is happening. How, when that window was closed, did Doll fall? It just doesn't make any sense.'

'Was the window closed? Are you sure? Think, Sal.'

'Of course I'm sure. That window is never open. The top window was ajar, that's it.'

'You're absolutely sure?'

'Stop asking me if I'm sure! I told you: that window was closed, and it is quite stiff to open. You know that, Dan.'

'So, Doll opened the catch, pushed the window wide open, and, what? She leaned out and lost her balance?'

I can't argue with him. It sounds ludicrous.

'Leaned out,' I say, 'or jumped.'

'Ah, Sal, get a grip. Jumped? Stop it, she wouldn't do that. She wouldn't be able – physically, even.'

Silence crackles in the air between us.

'But why would she even lean out?' I say. 'Why would she bother, even if she could? It's cold and dark; there's no reason for her to do that. It's impossible.'

Dan veers off the motorway, takes the slip road, and we arrive at Cork University Hospital as they're wheeling Doll towards the emergency service doors.

There's pandemonium inside. Nurses and doctors in green scrubs push the gurney through double doors and down a corridor towards theatre four. We follow. Doll's face is milk white, her eyes closed. There's blood matted in her hair. Her forehead is swollen. I stifle a scream. 'Will she be all right? Will she be all right?'

One of the doctors turns to wave us aside. 'Mum and Dad?'

Dan nods.

'Please take a seat. Leave this to us. We'll keep you updated.' He places his hand in front of Dan's chest. 'Please, sir, leave us do our job.'

The doors swing shut behind him. A nurse hurries towards us. She's carrying a file and stops when she sees us. 'Mr and Mrs Redmond?' She beckons us towards a tiny room. 'Please wait here, and someone will be along to talk to you soon.' She nods towards the double doors. 'They're doing everything they can in there. Don't worry; your child is in expert hands.'

Don't worry. Is the woman serious? I feel like screaming at her. She smiles and bustles off down the corridor. I sit in the cramped space while Dan paces over and back, four steps forward, four steps back, four steps forward.

'Would you stop pacing? It's driving me crazy.' I lean forward and take some deep breaths. I feel like I'm going to pass out. 'Get some water, Dan. I think I'm going to faint.' I can't stop my leg shaking.

Dan comes back with two paper cups. A woman follows him in. He passes me the water and I sip slowly, feeling the violent storm in my chest abating. Slow breaths. *In*. Count to four. *Out*.

'Mr and Mrs Redmond?'

We nod.

She looks at me. 'You've had a shock,' the woman says. 'Take it easy. It will pass.'

I straighten up. 'Thank you. I'm . . . I'm okay now.'

She sits down opposite me and Dan, folding her brown pleated skirt carefully under her. She smiles. 'My name is Emily. Emily Murray. I'm a social worker. I need to ask you a few questions. Is that okay?' She opens a file with a single sheet of paper inside. 'It's routine, nothing at all to be alarmed about.'

'Why should we be alarmed?' Dan says, scowling at her. 'And what exactly do you need to know that the emergency services haven't told you already?'

I try to give Dan a look, but he's choosing not to see it.

'Of course,' I say. 'We understand. Ask away.'

'Just need to fill in some details,' she says, snapping her pen into writing mode. 'Now, your daughter's name is Doll. Doll, short for Dolores. Aged eleven.' She looks up for confirmation. 'Number six Bluebell Grove, Glengarvan. Special needs. Third child in the family. Correct?'

'Yes. Yes.'

From my plastic chair, I can see the doors of theatre four, willing them to open, willing the doctor to emerge with a smile. *The child is going to be fine* – that's what he's saying. *The child will be fine. A nasty fall, but no real damage done.* That's what he'll say. He must tell us this. Then my heart can return. It went off about its business an hour ago, and now – I can feel this – it's lying in a filthy drain somewhere. Pounding away in foul-smelling water.

Come back to me, heart. All will be well. No real damage done. And I'll cry then, in relief, in gratitude, and I'll visit Father Joe on my way home, and I'll slip into the beautiful gloom of the church to say a prayer. I'll light candles, thank Jesus for miracling away the nightmare. I will never ask for anything again. I'll tell Him that. In gratitude. And I'll—

'Mrs Redmond, are you okay?'

I start. Take a sip of water. 'Yes, of course, carry on.' Annoying Emily is still asking questions, ticking a list of boxes about Doll's medical history. She's making notes now of the timeline of events, biting her lower lip as she writes. A bad habit, someone should tell her – lip biting is a sign of nervousness, that you're not comfortable in a situation. Either that or she's flirting with Dan, and somehow I don't think she's the type.

Emily is saying, 'So when you heard the sound out on the patio, you looked out your window and immediately rushed outside?'

'Yes,' Dan says, 'we were in bed. It was four twenty a.m. We heard a noise outside. I looked out, and I could make out a figure lying on the deck. We ran downstairs, through the sliding door, and we found Doll.'

I flinch, thinking about it.

'Was she conscious?'

'No, her eyes were closed. She was lying on her side.'

'Was she bleeding?'

'Yes. From a head wound, as far as we could see,' Dan says.

'What a dreadful shock. You called an ambulance, you didn't move her?'

'Yes, obviously. They talked us through what to do. Keep her warm, not to move her.'

'How do you think it happened?' She bites her lip again. *Emily, stop doing that.* 'She was sleeping in the back bedroom upstairs. Was her window left open?'

'No.' I say it firmly. 'The window was definitely closed.'

'Was the clasp loose?'

'No. On the contrary, it was quite stiff to open. She couldn't have opened it herself.'

Emily looks from me to Dan. 'Was there anyone else in the house at the time?'

'No,' Dan says, 'our other daughter is staying at her friend's house tonight.'

'So? How do you think it happened?' Emily sucks on her pen, looks at us both.

'We don't know,' I say, 'it doesn't make any sense. We are as baffled as you are.'

'I see,' she says, biting her lower lip again. 'I hope you won't be waiting too long.' She jerks her thumb towards theatre four. 'I'll have to file a report, and I may need to talk to you again.'

I nod, glad to see the back of Emily bloody Murray. 'We understand.'

'I'm not sure what else you need to know,' Dan says, his blue eyes flashing. 'You're making it sound like we're negligent parents.'

She smooths her skirt as she stands up. 'Not at all, Mr Redmond, but we need to know exactly what happened. This was a serious incident. And very upsetting for you.'

Dan stands up, digging his hands in his pockets. He does this when he's angry.

'Do what you must,' he says, rolling his eyes. He turns his back on her and looks at me. 'Want a coffee, Sal?'

I shake my head, and he's off out the door.

Emily smiles weakly. 'We're just doing our job.'

'Of course.' *Just go, Emily.*

As she moves towards the door, she turns to me. 'Just one last thing: has Doll suffered any unexplained falls or injuries in the past?'

'No. What are you suggesting?' I want to shake her till her teeth fall out.

'Nothing, Mrs Redmond. Just routine questions. Thank you.'

I stare at the theatre doors. *The child is going to be fine*, the doctor is saying. *A nasty accident, but no real damage done. All will be well.* I want to put a notice on the door: STAY AWAY. DO NOT DISTURB. I'm staying here in my secret capsule of consolation, where nothing bad happens and where life hums and sparkles and there's always a happy ending. I like it in here. *A nasty accident, but no real damage done.* Alleluia to that. My heart flutters home. *No real damage done.* That's the business. A happy ending.

A boy walks towards me. He's wearing scrubs, black-rimmed glasses. Oh, he's not a boy; his voice is too deep. But he's still young – thirties, maybe. Behind the glasses his eyes are ice green.

The first word he utters is a spear. Its sharp point skewers my heart like a barbecue steak. I don't hear what comes after that first word. I feel dizzy; I need to lean forward on fizzle-stick legs. I'm sinking towards the tiles. The cool, cool tiles. I want to tell the boy, the young man with the black-rimmed glasses, I want to tell him not to be bothering me, upsetting me with his stories . . . can't he see, for Chrissake, can't he see I'm busy? Would he show some respect? But the words get lost inside my chest and I can't get them into formation, they keep flying off like bats, refusing to line up.

Through the din inside my head, I hear Dan's voice. Oh, Dan. He's sitting me forward on the chair; he's rubbing my hair, bringing warmth to my fingers. His touch is light and firm. I hear him say to the boy, I mean, the young man, the young man in the black-rimmed glasses hiding his green eyes, I hear him say, 'Start again. Please, Doctor, start again,' and I cover my ears with my palms and I can still hear the word, the word I don't want him to say – *Someone stop him, please!* – but he says it anyway.

'Unfortunately,' the doctor says, 'unfortunately . . .'

CHAPTER 9

DOLL

I'm tumbling through the air towards a grassy bank. Nearby, my granny is kneeling in prayer, and somewhere – I can't see him – Father Joe is saying the Lord is his shepherd; there is nothing he shall want. Granny is singing that there's nothing she shall want either, and a chorus of voices are singing about fresh and green pasta and the Lord who is, who was, and who will be, forever and ever. Up above me, red balloons drift up into the sky, floating along like souls, like they know there's something beyond, some magic wind to lift them, carry them like a melody, up and out of the ordinary everyday.

There's a hand on my shoulder. A breeze feathers my cheek. Then it comes to me with a surge of joy: I'm back in Nan-Nan's house with the pale-blue shutters – in the same bed I woke up in last time. Outside, I can see the gardens and the hills in the distance.

Footsteps on the stairs, along a corridor, and a head of red curls appears around the open door. Nan-Nan – yes, hurray! A full-sized Nan-Nan comes and sits on the bed. She's wearing a red skirt and white shirt, and I can smell her perfume as she leans towards me.

'You're awake, Doll.'

I manage a smile. 'We're home, Nan-Nan. Are we home?' The sound of my own voice thrills me.

She nods and touches my forehead. 'How are you feeling, sweetheart?'

She doesn't wait for an answer but takes a glass from the bedside table. 'Here, Doll, drink this. Your head might still hurt a little.' She holds the glass to my lips, and I drink the sharp liquid. 'Good, you're much cooler. You've been poorly for a few days. You had a nasty fall, but no real damage done.'

I stretch out, feeling the warmth of the bed beneath me. I move my fingers, making fists and releasing them. I wiggle my toes. I start to laugh. I can't believe I'm back.

Nan-Nan laughs too, and busies herself around the room while I trampoline on the bed. 'This is even better than last time,' I say.

'Less of that, honey,' Nan-Nan says, frowning. 'Take it easy, now.' But I know inside she's happy – relieved, even – to see me well and recovered.

'We have a visitor arriving' – she checks her watch – 'at nine bells.'

I stop jumping and sit on the edge of the bed, panting. 'Who is it, Nan-Nan?' My voice is music, a gift, opening me up. Word-miracles rising up, turning thoughts into sounds.

'You'll see. Hurry along now. Take a shower and get dressed while I make breakfast.' She lays out a purple skirt and white shirt, white shoes, and a purple hairband on the wicker chair next to the bed. 'These arrived for you, Doll.' She gives me a hug. 'Today is an important day, child. Don't delay. Look smart.'

Her red shoes click-clack down the stairs, and in the distance I can hear crockery, the whirr of a juicer, the hiss of food grilling, and I realise I'm starving.

In the shower, my first life falls off me like scales. I holler and whoop, curling my tongue around the sounds. I pretend-play the piano with my fingers. There's a scent of coconut as I wash my hair.

I thought, I really did, that the second time couldn't be as magical as the first. That maybe somehow I had exaggerated the wonder of my first visit here. Things can appear rosier looking back, my granny often said. Or what if I'd imagined the whole thing, like a fake memory? Those were the dark thoughts I had after Nan-Nan spoke to me in the rose garden.

Actually, this time is even better – because this time I know the drill. Almazova isn't a new scary place. I've been here before, completed my mission, saved the day, survived. I was a hero, I was invincible. I was known as the Child of Summer. I can do it again. I can be somebody again.

I rinse off my hair and wrap a towel around me. I look at myself in the mirror when I'm dressed, then fix the purple hairband in place. I'm a new person, shiny and clean. Ready for anything.

'I'm ready for anything,' I say to the mirror, and the girl in the mirror smiles back.

Downstairs, Nan-Nan is sitting on the patio pouring orange juice into two glasses.

She turns around. 'Oh my, you look lovely,' she says. 'Come here and sit down.' She pats the seat next to hers and raises her glass. 'Here's to new adventures.'

'To new adventures,' I say, raising mine.

We sit in the sunshine under a pink parasol, sharing breakfast like two old friends. I want this moment to go on forever: the birds singing, the buttercup-scattered lawn, the hum of bees and the warmth across my shoulders. And Nan-Nan, my friend, dressed to the nines, her red shoes tapping to the beat of the music coming from the kitchen.

'Well, Doll?'

'Sorry, Nan-Nan, I wasn't listening.'

'You'd better listen when our visitor arrives, Doll. Now, have you any questions you'd like to ask? And don't,' she says, raising her palm to me, 'don't ask me about your mission, because I'm not privy to that information.'

'Will they let you come with me, Nan-Nan?'

'Certainly not, Doll. My job was to get you here. Tomorrow I must return to my work with the Space Agency. Your fate will be out of my hands.' She frowns for a moment, then smiles. 'I'm sure you will be well briefed, and your safety will be paramount.'

'My safety?'

Nan-Nan runs her tongue over her teeth. 'Your mission will carry some jeopardy. As on your first visit, Doll, there may be challenges, danger, risks you have to take.' She furrows her brows. 'It's not a holiday; you are aware of this. There's work to be done.'

'I know.'

'You chose to come here, Doll.'

'I know. I'm not sorry. I'm ready for anything.'

She comes over and wraps her arms around me. Kisses my forehead. She smells of maple syrup.

'That's the style. Ready for anything. That's exactly what you need to be, child, ready for anything.'

'How long will it take, Nan-Nan?'

She taps her chin, looks off into the distance. 'As long as it takes, sweetheart.'

'And my family?'

She avoids my eyes. 'Your family are at your beside. You are unresponsive.' She sees my face then and takes my hand. 'It's the way it works, Doll. It's the best we can do, given your dual existence.' She squeezes my hand. 'It's complicated, honey. Trust us.'

'Can I die, back there in my first life? What if I die here?'

Nan-Nan begins to gather up the dishes, placing the cutlery into a little pile on the stack of plates. 'That's enough for now, Doll. You need to go up and brush your teeth and come back downstairs. It's almost nine bells.'

In the far distance, a giant golf ball purrs across the sky. We both shade our eyes and look up.

'Our visitor is approaching. Quickly, we need to be ready.'

I stare. 'What is it, up there?' The ball is circling downwards.

'That's a hovercar, Doll. A simple enough technology. Go now quickly, child.'

I watch the hovercar/golf ball from my bedroom window. It swoops down and comes to a smooth stop on the lawn. Nothing happens for a minute, then curved doors snap open and a man in uniform steps out onto the grass. The medals across his chest catch the sun like tiny mirrors. He fixes his cap on his head – it's white with navy-and-gold braiding. He looks like a diet Santa, and I recognise him: it's Jasper, president of the Space Agency and Nan-Nan's boss. He stands to attention as a small wiry woman steps onto the grass. She's dressed in black, her grey hair coiled neatly at her neck, her metal claw hand by her side.

I gasp. It's Nell, Chief Grandmother, Matriarch of Almazova. Nell, who wouldn't let me stay last time. She slips on dark glasses and strides across the lawn towards Nan-Nan's house. I lean forward to get a better look. The front door is wide open and Nan-Nan is standing there, extending her arms in welcome. Jasper follows, hands clasped firmly behind his back.

I hear my name being called. 'Child of Summer, come quickly to the library.'

I tiptoe down the stairs, take a deep breath, hold my chin high – like a princess would – and follow the voices to the room at the end of the hallway.

CHAPTER 10

DAN

Dr Valera is saying, 'So, because of the subdural haematoma, we've put her in an induced coma. As I said earlier, it will give the brain a chance to heal. She took a nasty fall. She's lucky to be alive.'

He's standing at the end of Doll's bed. The ICU is hushed and smells of antiseptic.

'For how long?'

He shifts his weight from one foot to the other. 'It depends. Right now, it's too early to say. We'll have to give it a few days.' He turns his palms up. 'If the swelling recedes, we may be able to lighten the drugs. All going well, she has a reasonably good chance of recovery. But too early for guarantees.'

It's something, though – *a reasonably good chance of recovery.*

'So, this induced coma, is it safe? She's very small; can her body take it?'

He nods, folding his arms. He looks like a schoolboy, his thick dark hair falling across his forehead. But he's heading the team, and you just have to trust that these guys know what they're doing and that they'll do everything they can to save your daughter's life.

'Very safe,' he's saying. 'The coma is completely reversible, and by effectively shutting down brain function, we can help reduce the inflammation.' He pauses for a moment, looking at Doll's ashen face. 'It's not something we do lightly.'

'She doesn't feel any pain?'

'No pain. You can be certain of that, Mr Redmond.'

I can't think of anything else. The main thing is that she has a good chance of recovery. That's what we must hold on to. That's all that matters.

Dr Valera's bleeper goes off. He glances at it, a look of impatience sweeping across his face.

'Excuse me, I have to go. If you have any further questions?'

'No, thank you, thank you so much.'

He hurries off – another patient, another emergency, another trauma or tragedy. How do they do it?

I check the time; it's after eleven a.m. Sally may have gotten a few hours' sleep at this stage. I'm just about to text her the latest update when Andi puts her head around the door.

She hugs me, wrapping her arms tight around me.

'Mom told me what happened. Dad, you look exhausted.' She rubs my forehead. 'Will she be okay?'

'We don't know for sure, Andi. She has a good chance of recovery, but we'll have to wait and see what happens over the next few days.'

'She'll pull through. Doll's got nine lives.'

I nod. It's true. Doll's been through a lot. She's a survivor.

'How's your mom? Did she sleep much?'

'She's gone to bed for a couple of hours. You should do the same, Dad. I'll stay here for a bit.'

'Maybe,' I say, but I'm not sure if I could sleep. I'm still trying to process what happened last night. Doll could have been killed. How did it happen? And then Thursday night in Dublin – was it really only three days ago? I'm still trying to work out how I'll break it to Sally, but it won't be anytime soon now. With Doll on life support.

I look at the machines attached like telephone wires to her body, see the tube in her mouth, hear the whirring of the respirator breathing for her, inflating her lungs. Monitors check her vitals, blood pressure, heartbeat, all finely tuned like a violin. Technology keeping everything working away at a steady pace to ensure maximum chance of recovery.

Life is a fragile thing; hospitals remind you of that. We're all Lego people when it comes down to it, toy-creatures who can fall over or be pushed this way and that by some remote deity who pulls the strings and decides your fate. Life is a lottery, when all is said and done. A bloody lottery.

'Dad?'

'Sorry, Andi, yes, I'll go home for a few hours.'

'I'll call you if there's any change.'

I grab my jacket, fish out my car keys.

'Dad?'

'Yes, love?'

'I didn't stay in Stacey's last night.' She holds her palms up. 'You might as well know. Mom's going to tell you anyway.'

'Tell me what, love?'

She hesitates. 'The thing is, don't freak out, Dad.'

'Jesus, don't say it, Andi; you stayed over in Steve's house?'

She stares at me, says nothing.

'Are you serious, Andi?' But actually, I'm not that surprised. I've said it to Sally so many times. This guy has always spelt trouble. And I can't understand what Andi even sees in him.

She nods her head, close to tears. 'I wasn't to know this would happen. If I'd known—'

'You lied, you deceived us. Where was his grandmother? Christ, you're only sixteen.'

She's not even listening. 'If I was home last night, I might have prevented this.' She sweeps her arm across the bedside, tears running down her face. 'I might have heard her; I might have been able to stop her.'

'But you *weren't* home.' It comes out harsh, judgemental.

'My room is next to hers – I could have . . .' She's sobbing and I want to comfort her, but I can't get past the fact that she lied to her mother and went off to sleep with that waster Steve Thompson.

'Was his grandmother there?'

She looks away, avoiding my eyes. 'No, she's in hospital.'

'So you took advantage? I hope you're proud of yourself.'

She looks at me then, her eyes flashing. 'It's not like that. We didn't plan it. Why are you making such a big deal about it? I love Steve, and he loves me.'

'You love him? Are you for real, Andi? Steve Thompson isn't fit to polish your shoes.'

She rolls her eyes. 'I'm sorry for lying, but I'm not sorry for sleeping with him. We love each other, and it feels right.'

I snort. 'So that makes it okay, it *feels* right? I'm going to have words with his grandmother about this.'

The irony isn't lost on me. Here I am, grilling her, accusing her of deceit, but what about my deceit? My lies? What a fucking mess. There are more tears. I feel bad now.

'Don't cry; it's not worth fighting about, Andi. We've more important things to worry about now.' I pluck a tissue from the box on the bedside locker and hand it to her. 'And stop blaming yourself; you couldn't have prevented this accident, so stop thinking like that.'

She sniffles. 'Dad?'

I ruffle her hair.

'Please, Dad. Don't say anything to Steve or his gran about this. Leave her out of it. Promise me.'

'Well talk about this tomorrow, Andi. Dry your eyes.'

She blinks, blows her nose. 'Thanks, Dad.'

I tune in to the Brendan O'Connor show on the way home. The panel is discussing insurance scandals, women's football, house prices, the ordinary blessed distractions of life, tearing us away from our own messy problems. The debate, laughter, and disagreement all capture my attention, and I'm grateful for the respite, the opportunity to get caught up in the affairs of the nation.

As I kill the engine, the nightmare returns: my baby girl is comatose on life support, *no guarantees*. Andi has just spent the night with a guy from Brandon Terrace – I shudder to think where that went. Christ, what if she's pregnant? And now I have to tell Sally about something I've been hiding, something I thought would stay in the past. But the past has a way of sneaking up on you when you least expect it with a gun in its hand. And a bullet with your name on it.

I twist the key in the front door. The house is warm and welcoming with the scents of fabric conditioner and fresh coffee and the spicy aroma of yesterday's lamb tagine. It's like nothing has changed. And the clock in the hall is a comforting and familiar heartbeat. Tears prick my eyelids, and I blink them away.

I put the kettle on, toss a tea bag in a mug. Suddenly, I feel tired. More than tired. Weary. Deflated, like a balloon near the floor long after the party's over. All the puff gone out of it. I pour the boiling water into a mug, add the milk, and stir. You think life is manageable – good, even. You're doing okay, and all of a sudden, everything starts to collapse around you. And it doesn't matter how clever you are, how well off, how positive, how lucky you are or well connected; at the end of the day you have no control over things. We're all just flotsam and jetsam, tossed this way and that, across the oceans, before being spat onto the shoreline.

I hear footsteps on the stairs.

'Sal! You're supposed to be asleep.'

'I couldn't relax. How are things? Any further news?'

She pours herself a coffee from the pot on the Aga.

She knows. The conversation feels awkward between us.

'I just met Dr Valera again before I left. He explained about the induced coma; they can't say for how long. It depends on how quickly the swelling goes down.'

She sits down, takes a sip of her coffee, wrinkles her nose. 'They think she's going to be okay, don't they, Dan? They're hopeful, yeah?' She closes her eyes and sighs, afraid to hear the answer.

I squeeze her hand. 'A good chance of coming through this. That's what he said, Sally. No guarantees, but a good chance.'

She opens her eyes, smiles. Tears leak out. 'I'm so relieved. It's something positive to go on. Thank God. I mean—' She stops. 'They wouldn't say that unless they were pretty certain, would they?'

'Of course they wouldn't. Andi's with her now, so why don't you get some rest?'

'I rang Will and spoke to him. He's so far from home and I don't want to worry him, but he is her brother.'

'Good. He needs to know. He'd have heard about it anyway before long.'

It's like we're skirting around the unsaid.

'I know about Andi staying over in Steve's; she told me.'

Sally rolls her eyes. 'I'm so angry with her, all the lies. I told her we'd be going straight to the pharmacy first thing tomorrow morning, but she said nothing happened.' She purses her lips. 'Still, it's only a matter of time. We'll have to put a stop to it, Dan. It's gone too far.'

I'm glad the focus has shifted to Steve. 'I agree, he's not a good influence, I've always said that. I hope, you know . . . she's telling the truth, when she said that nothing happened.'

Sally massages her temples. 'Jesus, don't even go there. I'll have to have a chat with her.' She takes my hand in hers. 'You look exhausted. I'll go up to the hospital to Andi.' She puts her coffee cup in the sink and stretches. 'You get some sleep.'

She pulls on her red jacket, zips it up, and runs her fingers through her spiky blonde hair. Her face is pale, and she looks fragile. I want to pull her into my arms, but I stay sitting at the table. 'Mind yourself,' I say. 'Take it easy driving.'

She takes her car keys from the hook inside the kitchen door and turns to me as she leaves. 'Later, Dan, we need to talk.'

I look up at her, rub my eyes. 'Talk? About what?'

Her shoulders slump. 'I think you know,' she says as she disappears into the hall.

I don't answer. The front door slams shut.

Silence.

I close my eyes and see the storm clouds gathering, and I realise I've only myself to blame.

CHAPTER 11

DOLL

The library is hushed and dim, only a trickle of light filtering through the coloured-glass windows. It feels like a church, with books instead of statues, books and books stacked to the ceiling with a ladder to reach the highest shelves. Nan-Nan is lighting a candle, placing it at the centre of a polished table. Four green velvet chairs are arranged around the table, and Nell is already sitting down.

I step into the gloom and Jasper approaches, arm outstretched. 'Welcome back, Doll.' He pumps my hand. 'An honour to have you amongst us again.'

He leads me to the table and pulls out a chair for me.

Nell reaches over and puts a slim hand on my shoulder. 'My dear, dear Child of Summer, how wonderful to see you. You are most welcome.' Her voice is strong, but her words seem to shimmer, light as feathers. There's an airy magic about her.

'Thank you, Your Majesty, I mean, ma'am. Thank you, ma'am.'

She sits back. 'You are rested, child? You are ready to begin?'

'Yes, ma'am, I'm ready for anything.'

She cups her hand around her ear. 'Speak up, child.'

Jasper says helpfully, 'She says she's ready for anything.'

Nell smiles and keeps nodding. 'Very good, very satisfactory. A remarkable girl, to be sure.'

Nell's hair is as white as a rabbit's, and her skin is like buttermilk. She's the visionary, Nan-Nan said. The leader of the Council of Grandmothers. A wise old bird.

'Thank you,' she says, bowing slightly. 'Thank you for your services to Almazova. We are proud of you and indebted to you for completing your first mission so spectacularly well.'

I blush. If only my family could hear this, about me being remarkable and stuff. If you just get the chance, really, you can do anything. Almazova gave me that. So why in the name of Diamond Jesus would I choose to go back to my first life? Who could blame me for deciding to stay here? Who'd choose a life of acid reflux and fuzzy thinking? A life of silence, being different, being sad and mad? Mad jealous of Andi, and Will in Addis Ababa University, and Ruth Meehan with her blonde plaits and cool friends? They're all living the life. Except me.

The four of us sit around the table, waiting for Nell to speak.

'Now,' Nell is saying, 'it's time. This story I am about to recount is about mystery and death, about innocence and darkness.'

I straighten up. I like a story.

Her watery blue eyes are fixed on the books behind me. 'I'd like you to listen, Doll,' she says, and I whisper that yes, of course I will, ma'am, and I lean forward, all ears, afraid to miss anything.

Nell leans back and begins. 'Let's start with a boy, Matthew. A very bright child – curious, creative, a wonderful artist. He's twelve years old.'

'I'll be twelve next birthday.'

She doesn't seem to hear me. 'He attends Almazova's finest Academy for High-Performing Children.'

'Like a school for tall children?'

'No, child.' She smiles. 'High-performing as in clever, creative, children who excel. Those with multiple intelligences, talented, capable.'

She takes a sip of water from the glass in front of her, runs her tongue across her lips. Her left hand is a metal claw, and it rests on the table. I try not to stare at it.

'A school, Doll,' she says, 'run by an order of druidesses, wonderful women within whom flows a river of learning and sacred inspiration.'

What is the woman talking about? I stare ahead, nod like I understand.

Nell sweeps her good arm in a circle. 'These incredible sisters can raise the seas and winds with their incantations, they can call up spirits, and even' – she makes an O shape with her finger and thumb – 'decipher someone's secrets from their clothing. Imagine! All in all, their matrix powers can open horizons that no man can hope to.'

I glance at Jasper.

'Even me.' He nods, mock-serious.

Nell smiles. 'You may be the exception, Jasper.' She takes a sip of water and continues. 'They are the intellectual elite and can access portals to other worlds in ways even we scientists' – she looks from Jasper to Nan-Nan – 'cannot understand.'

'Jasper here attended the Academy,' Nan-Nan says. 'Many moons ago. Didn't you, Jasper?'

He nods. 'That is correct, Nan-Nan. It was a very adventurous education, I remember. And those sisters have vast knowledge and wisdom.' He strokes his beard. 'They study for twenty long years, you know. It's a gruelling path. But they inculcated in us a love of learning. That's what they taught me above all else – a love of learning. It's a gift.'

'That is indeed a gift,' Nell says.

'They are a powerful community of women, I have heard that,' Nan-nan says. 'But is it true that when they die, their lower jaw is removed so they cannot speak of what they've learnt, what they've seen and heard?'

I shudder at the thought of someone dragging the jaw out of you. That's demented. I know you'd be dead, you wouldn't feel it, but still, a kid shouldn't be listening to all this.

I look at Nell. 'Can we go back to the boy, ma'am?' I whisper, just to keep her on track. We've gone away from the story completely.

She clears her throat. 'Ahem, yes, Matthew. The boy. One moonlit night not too long ago, he leaves his dorm. Takes a small craft out on the lake near the Academy. After dark, the lake is strictly out of bounds. Nevertheless, this wonderful, talented child rows across the lake, stands up, and throws himself backwards into the water. He doesn't surface. He drowns.'

'He falls in, you mean? Can he not swim? Maybe he hit his head.' I feel sorry for the poor boy. Maybe he had enough. That's another story, but who knows?

'The boy is a strong swimmer. He doesn't fall. He allows himself to topple back into the dark water. Now, why would he do that?'

'Were there witnesses, reliable witnesses?' Jasper asks, scratching his beard.

'Yes, a caretaker gave a good account of what happened. He had seen the boy take the boat out, and he had come to the shoreline to investigate. Also, one of the druidesses was meditating on her balcony and saw it happen. She heard a cry first, saw the boy topple back, and heard the splash. The two accounts tally.'

'Does anyone know why he did it?' Nan-Nan is shaking her head.

I can't understand why Nell is telling us this. So much for the clever druid-dresses. They didn't see it coming. How wise can they really be, in fairness?

'It's a mystery. The boy was a happy child. Popular, gifted, well balanced. His family shed fierce tears.' She puts her finger to her lips. 'Wait, I have more to tell.'

Nan-Nan fills her glass with water and takes a sip.

Nell continues. 'There are two young girls in the Academy. Two firm friends, thirteen years old. These children excel at maths and science, and I'm told that when they sing, the very hills weep, such is the sweetness of their voices.'

'What are their names?'

'I was coming to that. Kristin and Ava. One afternoon almost three weeks ago, they decide to climb up to the bell tower in the grounds of the Academy. We don't know why. The afternoon is sultry, the birds resting, heavy rain is imminent. The parapet on top of the bell tower is low. The girls appear to struggle, and Ava falls to her death. Or is pushed. It's impossible to say for sure.'

'And Kristin?' Nan-Nan asks, a look of horror on her face.

'She is in a catatonic state; she can't or won't speak. She's in trauma. Her parents are caring for her, and she's attending psychiatric services. Tragic.'

I've never come across such things. Andi's friend Stacey fell in school last year and broke her ankle, but she just slipped on spilt Coke. But this carry-on – well, it wouldn't happen at St Mary's. If it did, my parents would be taking Andi out pronto.

'I hadn't heard about this,' Nan-Nan says, shaking her head. 'These are shocking incidents.'

'Shocking, Nan-Nan, and puzzling. There is something not right here.'

'You're right, Nell. It's sound like it's more than coincidence. These children are the future of Almazova, and we are failing them,' Jasper says. 'It's ironic, isn't it? The Academy is a powerful incubator of the principles of living in harmony with nature, and yet, these unspeakable and unnatural events . . .'

'The Academy, the druidesses, the children, the parents are all shattered,' Nell says. 'But there's something we're not seeing.' She taps the table with her claw hand. The sound is like a drum.

No one speaks. The only sound is the *tap, tap, tap* on the table.

'There is a black energy in the Academy. The sisters know it. I know it. I can feel it deep inside.' Nell places her right palm across her chest.

'Last week, another boy, Thomas, leaves his dorm around midnight. He's heard stumbling back at dawn. The next day the boy cannot speak, cannot communicate in any fashion. This boy has now left the Academy; his parents are very distressed, looking for answers among puzzled doctors.'

'It's like a virus,' Nan-Nan says. 'Some dark, lamentable force field burning through the school community. What's to be done? What do the sisters say?'

'Bodica, mother of the order, a dear, dear woman, admitted that she is distraught. The sanctity of the space has been defiled – vile deeds visited on the innocents. *On her watch*. The sisters are bereft. The community are sure of only one thing: someone has been dreaming evil.'

'But who and why, that's the question,' Jasper says.

The candle flame stretches towards me as if straining to leave its waxy body behind and leap into my arms. In this world, candle flame follows me.

Jasper notices and raises his eyebrows. Nell looks at me and smiles. 'Nature knows everything. Nature understands everything.' She nods towards the candle. 'I am not surprised. Nature recognises you as the Child of Summer.'

'Indeed, and now, I assume, you are calling on the Child of Summer to solve this mystery. What happens now? Have you a plan?' Nan-Nan asks.

Nell looks at the others, and then her blue eyes catch mine. Her voice is a whisper, slow and deliberate. 'Child of Summer, your mission is to discover what is happening at the Academy and who and what are behind these tragic deaths and strange happenings.'

Jesus, I knew it. I saw it coming.

'I'm not sure, ma'am. I'm not clever. An Academy for High-Performing Children? I can't see how I might fit in.'

Nell smiles. 'We have consulted the Ancient Manuscripts, and they spoke to us of your return. The Manuscripts do not lie.' She leans forward. 'You are resourceful, you are courageous, you are charming and disarming. You have many unique gifts.' She stops for a moment. 'Your multiple intelligences will emerge. Trust yourself. Trust us. Trust Almazova.'

I shudder inside. She is joking. That all-too-familiar doubt clings like ivy around my heart. I think back to the first time I met Nell and the Council of Grandmothers in the Cathedral of Light. I thought I must be dreaming. I didn't believe in myself. I only knew that I was helpless, hopeless, useless. A goner. I didn't believe in the magic of life. In the possibility of being shiny and new in another world. But still, fair dues to me – it has to be said – I jumped, and instead of crashing to the ground, I rose like a bird through the skies. I didn't look back, I didn't give in or give up. I wanted so badly to win . . . and I won.

I can do this. I can surely try again. I remember from earlier that girl in the mirror who said, *I'm ready for anything*.

I sit up straight. 'Ma'am, the truth is, like I said, I'm ready for anything.'

'You understand what is required of you?'

'I do.'

'You understand you must tell no one of your real identity?'

'I understand.'

'You understand there may be danger?'

'Yes, I understand, ma'am.'

Nell breathes out a long, slow breath.

'The clothes you are wearing are the Academy uniform. A travel bag has been packed with everything you will need: books, clothing, information, a new identity. You can retain your name, but your backstory will be much simpler.'

'Is the Academy far from here, ma'am?'

'You will travel with Nan-Nan by hovercar; the journey will take about an hour.' Nell looks at Nan-Nan. 'All students at the Academy must wear a small purple tattoo behind the right ear. A badge of honour, much sought after in life. You can apply a transfer instead of a genuine tattoo, Nan-Nan.'

'That's correct,' Jasper says, showing us a tiny purple flower tattoo behind his ear. 'A constant reminder of the joy of learning and how lucky I was to attend the Academy.'

Nell says, 'For Doll, we can use a temporary dye which doesn't pierce the epidermis. This way' – she looks at me – 'we're not sending you back altered in any decipherable way. It will dissolve in time.'

Huh, if only she knew. I'm planning to stay around this time.

She pushes a large envelope towards Nan-Nan. 'All the instructions you need are here. Read carefully and discuss before you set off.'

'We will study it well, be assured,' Nan-Nan says.

Nell rises and comes around the table to put her arms around me. 'May the Gods protect you and guide you,' she says. 'I wish you success in your mission, Child of Summer.'

And then she turns and sweeps out of the library, beckoning Jasper to follow her. 'We must be away,' she says, 'Jasper will send a hovercar to collect you within the hour. Bodica and the sisters await your arrival at the Academy. A new term starts tomorrow. Good luck.'

Jasper shakes our hands and waves goodbye as he strides across the lawn after Nell. The engine purrs and they are up, twirling into the sky and away over the purple hills.

Back in the living room, we curl up on the couch and drink hot chocolate. Nan-Nan's affixed my tattoo behind my ear, and it looks just like Jasper's. 'Very authentic,' Nan-Nan said when it was done. 'No one will guess it's not the real thing.'

We've gone through my instructions three times, and I'm still worried I'll forget something.

'The thing is to remain below the radar,' Nan-Nan says. 'Use these' – she points to my ears – 'rather than this.' She places a finger on my lips. 'Mother Bodica thinks you are a distant relative of Nell. Your parents have passed; your guardian is a woman called Nan-Nan. That's me.' She points to herself, smiling. She consults the sheets of paper in front of her. 'Report in to me each night. You have a journal-screen. Make your entries without fail. What you dictate, I will read simultaneously.'

'Wow, that's cool.'

'I have a bit of good news too.'

'Tell me.'

'There is someone attending the Academy whom you know.'

I nearly spill my hot chocolate. 'Tiger?'

Nan-Nan nods. 'She's not aware you're coming, but she will be a powerful ally, as she will be familiar with what's been happening and may have important insights.'

Whatever fear I had inside me starts dissolving. Oh, the excitement of meeting Tiger! The girl who saved my life. We climbed mountains together; we cried when her father lay shot in her heartbroken arms. I would trust Tiger with my life. I thought I'd never see her again.

'Oh, Nan-Nan.'

She comes close and hugs me. We stay like that, saying nothing, locked together, and it feels good.

Later, when the hot chocolate is well cold, Nan-Nan says, 'Come on, Doll, it's time to go.'

The travel bags are at the front door. When I put on my new purple school blazer with the Academy crest, I feel a thrill of pride. In the distance we can see the hovercar coming over the hills. 'Ready?' Nan-Nan says, squeezing my hand.

I smile up at her and nod.

I think about Mom and Dad and the hospital where I am unresponsible. A snake of guilt slithers around my throat, but I cast it off. *Leave me alone.* I must follow my own dream, and someday, you know, I will go back. Of course I will.

We step up into the hovercar. The door closes, and we strap ourselves in. A woman in a white uniform turns to salute, and she smiles and says, 'Welcome aboard,' and then she switches the dials with a white-gloved hand, and we are whirling up and off, across the skies.

In the distance, a clothesline of flowery tablecloths swoops towards us. I gasp. It's the Headscarves. When I saw them first, Nan-Nan explained how they were a chorus of old souls in haggard bodies, earning their way to heaven. Their coloured headscarves hide their crabby old faces, she said, as they sing of things to come, foretelling danger and betrayal. They are a spirit-force for good, and in amongst them, last time I was here, I found my granny.

I shade my eyes to see if I can catch a glimpse of her now, but they've flown off ahead of us, into the horizon.

Nan-Nan squeezes my hand. 'The Headscarves have come to welcome you, Doll.'

I nod. I'm so excited to see my granny again. I know she's one of them now, and I'll surely see her soon. It takes a while to make your way to heaven, so she'll be a Headscarf for a few years yet. And with her here to mind me, how could I put a foot wrong?

Nan-Nan looks at me. 'There is one thing you need to know, Doll. The Headscarves cannot come to your rescue this time.

Because they are a spirit-force, they are not permitted in the vicinity of schools, playgrounds, and childcare establishments.'

'So I won't be meeting my granny again?' My heart sinks to my boots.

'I'm afraid not, Doll. These are the protocols. The Academy would be strictly out of bounds for the Headscarves.'

I'm gutted. I can't believe what she's telling me. I won't be meeting my lovely granny after all. I turn away and look out the window so Nan-Nan can't see my tears falling.

CHAPTER 12

ANDI

'It's been three days, Stacey. Three whole days and . . . nothing.'

'I know, Andi. That's the tenth time today you've told me this.' Stacey swings in the door of Pizza Pizza and slides into a booth by the window. She grabs the menu and looks at me. 'It does seem a bit weird, but remember that time his mother came home from London? Remember he disappeared off the radar for a few days? And then he contacted you and everything was fine. He just needed to sort things out with her.'

I nod. 'But this is different. We're together seven and a half months, and we talk every single day. There's something going on, Stace.'

'Did you text him again?' She points to my phone. 'Text him now. One last time. Go on.'

She runs her finger down the menu. I don't know why she bothers, because she always orders the same thing. 'How about a Hawaiian to share with fries? And a Coke, yeah?'

I nod. 'Fine. Whatever.'

She shrugs off her jacket and folds it next to her. 'Look, you need to tell him to ring you ASAP. Tell him it's urgent. If he doesn't get back, well, maybe you have to face it – he's dumping you. But I doubt it, Andi.'

I stare out the window onto Glengarvan town square, hoping Steve will materialise, maybe even walk in and join us. I'm distraught. I check the time. He'd be working till five at least, so that's not going to happen.

'Look, Andi, maybe his gran has taken ill again?'

'But why would that stop him calling me? Doesn't make sense. He's definitely ghosted me.'

'I know you're upset—' Stacey stops as the waitress approaches and takes our order. 'But you're in bits for the last few days, and it's got to stop.' She snaps her fingers. 'Girl, you need to take action. You need to find out what's going on.' She takes a napkin, knife, and fork from the box on the table and puts them in front of me.

'Action? What action? I've rung him, I've texted him over and over, I even called round on Sunday night. No response. A big fat nothing. I have to face it. He's dumped me.'

Stacey plucks another napkin from the holder on the table and hands it to me. 'Dry your eyes, girl, your mascara's running.' She smiles. 'Come on, don't be so dramatic. I'm sure there's a perfectly good explanation.'

'Oh yeah? Like what?'

The waitress arrives with our order. I take a gulp of Coke, keep my head down. I feel like bawling my eyes out, but this is not the time or the place.

'Maybe,' I say, 'maybe he thinks I'm a pushover.'

Stacey knows about me sleeping with Steve. I didn't mean to tell her, but I felt I owed it to her, considering I put her in the firing line so I could stay at his on Saturday night. And anyway, it was good to confide in a friend. Stacey might be a bit of a swot, but we really click. And the more time I spend with her, the more I like her. I can tell her about Steve and she's not judging me. Or judging him. That counts for a lot.

She bursts out laughing. 'Oh for God's sake, Andi, don't be an ass.'

'Well, I did sleep with him. I haven't heard from him since. Hello? Is there a connection?' I blow my nose. God, if he could see me now. 'It's probably why he hung around so long. Probably all he ever wanted and now that he's got it . . . well, he can tell his mates. Another notch in his belt.'

'Rubbish.' She loosens a triangle of pizza and takes a bite. The juice runs down her chin, and she rolls her eyes. 'This is to die for.'

'I feel such an idiot,' I say, 'letting him use me like that. I really did think he loved me, but once a player, always a player.'

'That's nonsense,' Stacey says, taking another bite and popping stray pieces of pineapple into her mouth. 'Steve Thomson *was* a player, but he is totally in love with you. And that is clear to anyone who has a pair of eyes.'

'But what if he was, you know, disappointed? Maybe he was expecting, I don't know . . . more?'

'You said it was amazing.'

'*I* thought it was, but he's had, you know, way more partners.' I dab my eyelids with the napkin. I know my face is a mess. 'Don't say a word to anyone about this, Stace; I don't want it getting around.'

She finishes another slice of pizza and taps the side of her nose. 'Mum's the word.' She hands me another napkin. 'It's nobody's business but yours anyway, but look, it's tough. I feel for you. Boy trouble ain't easy.'

I push the plate towards her. 'Have mine; I'm not hungry.' I take another sip of Coke. 'I hope he's okay, that he's not sick or had an accident.'

She starts on the fries, dipping each one in ketchup. 'Unlikely, I'd say. I saw him going into the Carlton last night with Rizla and Jacko.'

'You never said. Did you talk to him, did he say anything?'

'No, I just saw him from my dad's car.' She finishes off another slice and wipes her mouth with the back of her hand.

'You're a savage!'

'I needed that.' She grins and takes a long drink. 'I have to ask, Andi. How's Doll doing? Any change since last night?'

'No. No change. She's stable. And that's another thing. He knows Doll's in hospital, and he hasn't even asked about her.'

'That's good, though, that she's stable. Every day now, she'll get stronger.' She finishes the fries and checks the time. 'Have to dash, hon. I've a physics grind at five o'clock.' She makes a face and pulls on her jacket. Stacey wants to do med in college, so she's getting extra science tuition before the senior cycle starts in September.

'Is my face a mess?'

She smiles. 'You'll get away with it. Just keep the head down.' We leave the money on the table and head out into the drizzly afternoon. She slings her rucksack over her shoulder and gives my arm a squeeze. 'Give me a call later if you need to talk.'

'Thanks, Stace. Will do. See ya.'

I take the long way round to Bluebell Grove, hoping I'll bump into Steve, maybe catch him heading home from work. I pass Brandon Terrace, but the blinds are drawn and it's hard to see if Joanie is home. There's no way I'm calling again.

Heading through Hettyville, I spot Rizla up ahead, smoking outside O'Driscolls Pub. He half waves when he sees me. I decide to ditch all self-respect and cross the road to talk to him.

He grins, takes a drag. 'How's amazing Andi?'

I hate when he calls me that. I think he's being sarky. I never know what his problem is, and I usually ignore his smartass comments.

'How's it going, Rizla?'

'Grand, girl.' Rizla looks me up and down, holding his rollie to his mouth with his thumb and forefinger. I always get the feeling he doesn't like me, though Steve said Rizla thought I was hot.

'How's Steve?' I say. 'Haven't seen him for a while.' I'm trying to sound chilled.

'Steve is just fine,' he says, then hesitates for a moment, as if he's debating whether to say something else. 'And, if you ask me' – he drops his cigarette and crushes it with his foot – 'he's better off without you.'

Before I can even think of a reply, he's heading back into O'Driscolls. At the door, he turns around. 'A bit of advice, Andi?' He doesn't wait for me to answer. 'Stay away from Steve. You and him . . . it's going nowhere, girl. It never was. Trust me.' He disappears inside the pub.

I'm stunned. My legs feel wobbly. My heart is hammering. Has Steve told Rizla about sleeping with me? What's he been saying? *It's going nowhere?* How can you love someone and then three days later not love them? Steve Thompson was a player, everyone knew that. Every girl in town fancied him, even if they didn't admit it. But when he met me, well, everything changed. I brought colour into his life – that's what he told me, that's what I believed. What an absolute idiot I've been. I fell for it all.

I walk along the Mill Road. The drizzle has turned into heavy rain hopping off the pavement. At least it hides my tears. My world is shattered. Nothing matters now.

Since I met Steve, my heart has been humming, note perfect. Now the music's stopped. I just didn't see it coming. The thought of a Steve-less life is a fist pressed to my throat as I trudge home.

I let myself in the front door and go straight to my room. My phone pings as I'm peeling off my sopping clothes. OMG. It's Steve.

Everything's going to be all right; I knew he'd contact me. I feel myself uncoil, and I punch the air.

I stop for a second. Hang on, I may have overreacted, but I'm still annoyed, upset that he left me hanging there for three days. But, look, he's going to tell me why. And if something dreadful has happened, I'll be there for him. Whatever it is, I'll make it right. For my Steve. My beautiful boy.

The message blurs before my eyes. I read it again. There must be a secret code I'm not getting. Is it a joke?

He *is* dumping me. I've lost him. I read the message again, but it couldn't be clearer. How idiotic am I?

It's not me, it's him. We need to give each other space now, he says. I'm not to contact him again. Sorry.

Sorry? Is he for real? Sorry? He's dumping me by text. The ultimate humiliation. I can hear the girls in school sniggering in the corridors. The chorus of *We told you so; Steve's a player.* And my mom saying, *There's plenty of fish in the sea. You're only sixteen; you'll get over him.*

I sit on the bed, let the phone clatter to the floor. It's over. We're done. I can't even cry. I stare out at the rain, my heart exploding like a shell in a silent war movie. And there's only one thought going round and round my head: my life will never, never be the same again as long as I live.

CHAPTER 13

DOLL

'There's the Academy. Can you see it, Doll?' Nan-Nan points to the valley below. Through the hovercar's curved glass doors, I can make out a large circle of domes like ice-cream scoops.

The biggest ice-cream scoop has a fountain outside it, and beyond the fountain, a long white table has been set with juice and fruit.

'Do you see the biggest pod, behind the fountain?' Nan-Nan says. 'That is the druidesses' temple – their living and sleeping quarters.' She studies the map in the Academy brochure on her knee. 'All the other domes – they're called pods here – are interconnected by glass corridors.' She peers closer, reading out loud. 'Each pod is a centre for, let me see . . .' She reaches in her bag for her glasses. 'There's one for meditation, one for science, library, sports . . . there's a whole list here.'

I'm trying not to think sad Granny-thoughts. I know that if there's any way my granny can find me, she will.

Nan-Nan hands me the brochure. The words are clear; reading and understanding them is easy. 'The arts, homemaking, history, the humanities. What's that, Nan-Nan?'

'It's the study of human culture and self-expression. Oh, you'll soon learn, Doll. This is wonderful.' She taps the page in front of me. 'This Academy has a reputation for greatness. Did you hear what Jasper said? How they imbue their students with a love of learning? What a gift. You're a lucky girl.'

Lucky? Well, I've never been told that before! And has she forgotten about the two dodgy deaths?

Just behind the druidesses' temple, I can see a lake and a thick forest spreading out into the hills.

'That's a sacred oak wood,' Nan-Nan says, following my eyes. 'Druidesses are very close to nature, and they believe spirits dwell in an oak forest.'

I shiver. The hovercar is circling now, and a sea of green is rising up to meet us. I can see the clock tower and the arched entrance gates with gold lettering: ACADEMY FOR HIGH PERFORMING CHILDREN. And underneath, in smaller letters, THE FUTURE BELONGS TO US.

'The future belongs to us,' Nan-Nan says, stroking her chin. 'What a glorious message for youth. An acknowledgement that the future is yours, that an adventure awaits you.'

She's right. It's saying that even if you're only a child, you can shape your life, shape the world, shape the future. You can write the pages. Before, I could never write my pages. I could never hope to make anything happen. The future to me was as flat as the past and as flat as the present. Nothing had changed for me in my eleven years. But *The future belongs to us* – these are words of a different colour. They whiz and fizz, they punch the air, they make you realise all the things you can do, the difference your life can make. The future is cupped in your hands. Imagine!

Jealousy zigzags through my chest. I can taste it coming up my throat, the acid of resentment. The future belongs to all these smart children with their beautiful hair and clear skin and perfect teeth. Clever, happy children who know, deep down, deeper and down, that the world is for them. That the future belongs to them. But not to me. I'm different. I have special knees. I don't have a future where I come from.

Any minute now we will be landing. I need to pull myself together. But the thought gnaws at me: imagine if they knew where I came from. My history. Making my face bleed on purpose? Hello! Who does that? Only a loser. If they knew

I couldn't even talk, couldn't eat proper food . . . What would they say, those perfect children? I know. They'd pity me. Pity is like someone spitting on you. It hurts that much.

We're circling towards a set-down area just outside the Academy grounds.

I want to become invisible – like a dancer inside a jewellery box, disappearing as the lid closes over her. I could hide away in a velvet drawer, out of sight. I just hate what I am. I'm a fraud. Who am I kidding? I'll be found out.

Nan-Nan unhooks her belt. 'What's the matter, honey?' she says, pushing my hair behind my ear. 'What ails you, child?'

'I'm not like them.' I try my best to trap the tears in my throat.

She hands me a hankie.

'You are the Child of Summer, remember that. The candle flame follows you – and what does that tell you, sweetheart? Remember, too, that you have saved Almazova. Our world has a future because of you. These children can only dream of your experiences and adventures.' She puts her finger under my chin. 'Now, chin up, walk tall, child.'

She's all talk, I think to myself, but I don't say that to Nan-Nan.

'But the future doesn't belong to me, does it?' I finally say.

Nan-Nan doesn't answer for a moment. 'The future belongs to all the children,' she says after a while.

'Do you honestly believe that, Nan-Nan?'

'Quick, look.' She points to a line of druidesses walking in pairs out of the forest, around the temple, and towards the fountain at the front of the building. Even though the sun is shining, the hoods of their sky-blue cloaks are pulled up so their faces are mostly in shadow. Their palms are crisscrossed over their chests. 'They're probably coming out to welcome the children back.'

The hovercar has come to a smooth stop, and Nan-Nan is buttoning up her jacket. She gives me a kiss on the cheek as she runs a tissue across my face. 'Come on, miss, your time has come.' The doors swing back, and I step onto the grass. At least, I think, the present belongs to me. I'm here, now.

The first thing I notice is the scent of lavender and just-cut grass. A flutter of pink butterflies sails past and disappears up into the blue.

I take a deep breath, feel something in the air. A lightness. Lifting my heart, dusting it off, setting it right way up inside me. *The present belongs to me.*

Nan-Nan carries my bags, and we walk through the gates, into the Academy grounds, making our way towards the pod marked RECEPTION.

Inside, children and parents bustle around, chattering, hugging goodbyes, screaming hellos. Kids reuniting, excited, noisy. I feel like an alien.

A bright-blue cloak floats towards us. It's only as it gets closer that I realise there's a woman inside it. Her eyes are the colour of her cloak, the brightest blue, and her skin is like bark, lined and grooved and lived in. No lipstick would feel at home here. She reaches for my hand and smiles at Nan-Nan. 'Welcome, welcome. We are expecting you. Nan-Nan, the guardian, isn't it? Yes, yes. Welcome, dear Doll.'

Nan-Nan smiles and nods. I nod. We're all nodding.

'I'm Mother Bodica, and on behalf of all my wonderful tutors' – she sweeps a crabbed hand towards the line of druidesses dispersing outside the fountain – 'may I welcome you to the Academy.' She still has my hand caught in a tight grip. 'Inspiration through education,' she whispers, 'is what we are about here. Transforming children. Unlocking gifts.'

'Very pleased to meet you, Mother Bodica.' Nan-Nan looks down at me. 'Doll is very much looking forward to the experience. Aren't you, Doll?'

Mother Bodica hunkers down so she's at my level. She must be at least one hundred, but she can bend like a dancer. She looks into my eyes and up at Nan-Nan. 'I sense a special child.' She cups her hands around mine and closes her eyes, breathing in deeply. 'Nell's great-grandniece, am I correct?'

'That is correct,' Nan-Nan says. 'She's missed the first term, unfortunately, but I'm sure she'll settle in.'

Mother Bodica looks into my eyes. 'I can see you've come a long, long way, child. An arduous journey of stars and stones and skeletons.' She sighs, releases my hands, and straightens up. She places her hand on the top on my head and looks at Nan-Nan. 'Of course she'll settle in. Please.' She gestures us outside towards the long table set out with bowls of peaches and jugs of pink lemonade. She calls one of the children, who is standing nearby, eating a peach. 'Lia, come here, please.'

A brown-eyed girl with a yellow hairband drops her peach on the table and hurries towards us.

'Yes, Mother.' She straightens her hair, adjusts the hairband.

'Meet Doll, our new student, Lia dear. She'll be sharing your dorm, so please escort her to the dining hall for lunch. Afterwards, you can bring her to her sleeping quarters to unpack.' She takes a large silver watch from her pocket and turns to Nan-Nan. 'Come with me, Nan-Nan, and we will complete the paperwork and registration.'

Lia flashes me a smile. 'Come on, Doll, I'll show you around.' A boy in a white tunic whisks away my bags, and Lia takes my elbow, leading me towards the table of drinks. She pours us lemonade and clinks my glass. 'Welcome to the Academy, new girl,' she says. 'I think you're going to like it here, despite the . . . you know.' She lowers her voice. 'Despite what's been happening. Have you heard?'

I remember Nan-Nan's advice: *Use your ears, not your mouth.* Easier said than done, I'm thinking, when you haven't spoken for eleven years.

'Yes, I heard a bit.'

'It didn't put your parents off?'

'I don't have parents. They, em, they died.' I feel so guilty even saying it, thinking of Mom and Dad in the hospital in Cork waiting for me to wake up. Worrying, while I'm here, living the life.

'Oh, I am sorry,' Lia says, putting her hand over her mouth. 'How did they die?'

Me and Nan-Nan prepared for this.

'My father,' I say, 'died in a riding accident.'

She looks at me with puppy eyes. 'That is terrible. And your mother?'

Oh Jesus, I feel terrible. I cross my fingers behind my back. 'She was ill and died.'

'Oh, tragic,' Lia says, biting her lip.

I'm sweating. I take a sip of cooling lemonade. Lia sets down her glass and puts her palms over her eyes as if she can't bear to picture the scene.

'Poor you.'

'I don't really want to talk about it,' I say, my lips disappearing into my mouth.

She squeezes my hand. 'I understand, Doll. I shouldn't have asked – it's none of my business – but thank you for sharing with me.' She drains her glass. 'Come on, I'll bring you over to lunch.'

We walk back past the bustling reception and across to the library pod – a huge white space with books stacked on shelves, on platforms, on balconies, and even on the steps of the spiral staircases reaching up into the roof. Pink, green, and purple beanbags are strewn everywhere, and large posters on the walls say *Inspiration through Education*.

'Come on, Doll, you've seen a library before,' Lia says as she pulls me towards a doorway and through a glass tunnel into the adjoining pod. She swings through double doors. 'Here we are, the great dining hall. Ta-da!'

Two long wooden tables run the length of the room. One lies empty, but the other is set for lunch, plates heaped with salads and rice, baskets of breads and fruits. Seated along the table, a gaggle of children fill the room with a buzzing din.

'It's so noisy the first day back,' Lia says, covering her ears. 'They're all excited.' She waves to a group of girls halfway along the table, and they beckon us over, scrambling to make space on the bench for us.

Lia blows kisses to the three girls, who are tapping the bench, saying, 'Lia, sit here, good to see you. Who's that?'

'Doll's the new girl,' she says, pushing up to make space for me. 'Doll, this is Mollie, Sophia, and Lou.'

The girls smile. 'Hello, Doll.'

'Welcome, Doll.'

'Nice to meet you, Doll.'

Lia says, 'Don't ask Doll about her parents. It's off-limits, okay?'

They all nod. 'Sure, okay.'

Phew. Glad I don't have to tell that story again.

'Anyone seen Amber?' Mollie asks, putting a chubby finger to her lips. 'Is she coming back? I haven't seen her anywhere.'

Lia turns to me. 'You'll love Amber,' she says. 'Won't she, girls?'

Sophia tightens her ponytail and nods, laughing. 'She's crazy, but in a good way. She's always in trouble, but she doesn't care, does she, Lia? She's such a rebel.'

'Remember the time she took a blue cloak from the temple and paraded up and down the dorm with it, taking off Mother Bodica? And Hopely walked in and caught her?' Lou says. The girls all burst out laughing.

'Yes, at least it was only Hopely. She's on our side. She didn't report it, to be fair.'

'Who's Hopely?' I say.

'Dr Hopely Ashe. She's our medical officer, and she teaches some science modules. She's lovely,' Mollie says, 'not like some of the Cloaks.'

'You shouldn't call them Cloaks, Mollie,' Lia says crossly. 'It's disrespectful to the druidesses.'

'Oh, get a life, Lia,' Mollie says, 'you're such a Goody Two-Shoes.'

'There she is,' Sophia says, pointing to the doorway, where a girl with green eyes is rocking back and forth, like she's deciding something important. Her blonde curls bounce as she moves. Her smile shows a gap between her two front teeth.

'Where's she going?' Lia says, as Amber starts to skip towards the long empty table across from ours. The girl with the curls then leaps onto the table, light as a deer. She looks around her, smiles, and begins to dance along the tabletop, clapping her hands as she goes. Kids stop talking and nudge each other. The girl jumps, half turns, skips, points her toes, and twirls, then tap-dances on the spot. Everyone stares. The only sound in the room is her shoes clacking on the wood. Then she cartwheels and starts the routine again.

Everyone starts to clap and whoop and stomp their feet. There's a man in a white tunic stacking plates, and he turns and watches the girl. His mouth drops open. All eyes are fixed on Amber, and she knows it.

'Step down from that table.' The man marches towards the twirling girl, his finger wagging in the air. 'Step down, this instant.'

Amber grins at him, raises her arms like a ballerina, and then somersaults right over his head, landing on steady feet three steps behind him, arms outstretched.

He turns, looks confused. There is laughter and applause all round, and shouts of 'Whoop-whoop, Amber!' She's the coolest girl in the school. A show-off. I feel a stab of pure jealousy.

The clapping stops abruptly. Mother Bodica is hovering in the doorway, her frame casting a long shadow across the tiles.

'Amber!'

Amber swivels towards the voice. Her smile vanishes. *Good enough for her*, I think.

'Please leave the dining hall!' Mother Bodica's voice is the loudest whisper.

Amber has to walk past Bodica. 'Sorry, Mother.' But she says it defiantly.

Bodica moves about the dining hall like a bird, half gliding – I swear to God she's not quite touching the ground. The children talk in whispers till the druidess is well out of earshot.

'Amber is some girl for one girl.' Lou giggles. 'You just never know what she's going to do next.'

'She's sharing our dorm this term,' Lia says. 'Mother Bodica asked me to keep an eye on her.'

'Teacher's pet,' Mollie says, but she's smiling at Lia and giving her the thumbs-up. 'You're the right girl to keep an eye on her for sure. A safe pair of hands. The Cloaks know that.'

*****

After lunch, Lia shows me to our dorm. There are four beds in a row, with four wooden chests for all our stuff. A long window overlooks the lake, and a smaller one to the left looks out over the forest. We pack away our things and make our way back to the reception pod, where Nan-Nan is waiting to say goodbye.

'Keep your journal-screen safe. Don't trust anyone. Keep your ears open. Bless you.'

She hunkers down, and I wrap my arms around her, feeling salty tears in my mouth. 'Goodbye, Nan-Nan,' I whisper into her red curls, and then she's gone. Out through the gates, across the green. I watch her till she's out of sight.

I can't see Lia anywhere, so I go back to the dorm. There's a girl sitting on the bed next to mine. Her dark hair is tied up with a purple ribbon. Some stray bits have come loose, and she tucks them behind her ear. Her arms are tanned, the skin smooth, and she's writing in a notebook.

Is it . . . ? My heart is hammering. 'Hi, Tiger.'

She looks up then, her blue-green eyes widening.

She hollers. 'Doll? Is it you, Doll? Blow me down, what are *you* doing here?'

She jumps up and throws herself at me, and we hug each other tightly.

'I can't believe you're back.' She holds me at arm's length. 'Hang on a sec – I know why you're here,' she says. 'All the weird stuff going on. Am I right, Doll?' She closes the dorm door, putting her finger to her lips. 'You need to be careful, Doll.' She lowers her voice to a whisper. 'We all do.'

'What's going on, Tiger?'

She chews her lip. 'I wish I knew. But one thing I do know is I'm scared, and you should be too.'

CHAPTER 14

SALLY

'It's not looking good, Sally. You're right.' Terri wraps her hands around her mug of coffee and blows on it.

'Keep you voice down, Terri,' I say. 'The walls have ears in here.'

In here is the *Cork Observer* staff canteen, a square florescent-lit space with lousy acoustics. Terri manages sales and I'm editorial, but we've been best friends since we started here ten years ago. We're sitting at a Formica table near the door, and there's a loud lunchtime buzz.

She glances around her, lowers her voice. 'First things first, Sally – how's Doll doing?'

'Okay, so four days in and she's still in the induced coma. But the good news is they're saying no deterioration. The swelling is actually reducing. And they think she has a good chance of recovery.'

Terri takes a sip of coffee. 'That sounds positive, Sal. I asked my brother-in-law about it last night when he was over – he's a doctor – and he said that shutting down her vitals can cool the brain, allow it to heal itself.'

'Yeah, that's the idea, I think. I have a good feeling, I don't know why; I think she's going to be fine. It's just tough this week, the waiting and the hospital visits . . .'

She nods, places her palm on her chest. 'It's a mother's intuition, Sal. Don't underestimate it. Deep down, a mother always knows.' She unwraps her cutlery and points the knife at me. 'Y'know, you shouldn't even be here. You must be wrecked.' She takes a forkful of chicken. 'You need to head home straight after lunch. Rest up. Get a break from this mad place.' She rolls her eyes behind blue tortoiseshell glasses. 'I'll cover for you. It's quiet today for a change.'

Terri wouldn't admit it, but she loves the stress and the pressure of the job. And I do too. We don't always agree, we've had our moments, but whether it's work or life, Terri always has my back.

'Look, I had to turn up for the features editorial meeting this morning,' I say. 'There's a lot going on. If you can cover for me this afternoon, though, that'd be fab.'

'Hello? Consider it done, girl.' Terri sips her coffee, takes another forkful of chicken-and-rice salad. 'Okay, now go back to Dan and the texts. What is going on with you two?'

'Well, you said it yourself, Terri. *It's not looking good.*' I shove my phone towards her. 'I took a pic of these messages sent to his mobile last Thursday.'

'The day he was in Dublin?' She loads up her fork. 'And stayed over?' She points a blue-painted nail to the top of the screen. She peers closer, her mouth full.

I take a sip of coffee. I pick at my ham salad. Food lately is starting to taste like cardboard.

She swallows. 'Would that be unusual, Sal? Him staying over?'

'Yes, it's unusual, unless there's a dinner or a big networking event, but there was no after-hours last Thursday. I checked.'

'I mean, come on.' She flicks to the next screenshot. 'Who calls themselves Lavinia? Sounds like a makey-uppy name.'

'Sounds exotic,' I say, 'though it's not that unusual. There are about a hundred and fifty Lavinias on LinkedIn.'

Terri points her fork at the screen. 'Her flight was in at six thirty p.m. on Thursday. She's looking forward to meeting him.'

'Please, Terri, don't remind me.' I have the texts memorised anyway. Lavinia had arranged to see Dan at the Gibson Hotel at seven thirty p.m. Can't wait to meet you. Smiley face. A missed call. I've arrived, where are you?

At the bar, he said.

That's all I've found. It was all very quick and furtive; I felt like a spy or some pathetic wife trawling though her husband's texts, looking for evidence to hurl at him. What did it say about me? That I didn't trust him? That I couldn't just ask him straight out because . . . because I couldn't handle the truth? Was I better off not knowing?

'Maybe I'm better off not knowing, Terri.'

'Well, you *do* know, Sal. Have you said anything?'

'Jesus, no – well, not yet.'

'Why not?'

'He'll know I've been sneaking through his texts. That's appalling.'

'So what?'

'He's probably going to lie anyway, isn't he? He might say, oh, that was an old friend, no big deal. And what then?'

Terri doesn't say anything; she's still flicking though the texts.

'Her flight was in at six thirty p.m. I wonder where she was flying from. You could check that, Sal.'

'I already did.'

She laughs. 'And what did you find, Sherlock?'

'There was a flight from Heathrow at six thirty p.m. on the nail. Another was coming in from Malta and one from Berlin at six thirty-five p.m., but my money is on London.'

She finishes her salad and pushes the plate away. Dabs crimson lips. 'You know, Sal, it's not like Dan. Not the Dan I know.' She looks undecided. 'Maybe it is just a friend and you're just putting two and two together and getting five.'

'So why the big secret?'

'Well, one way or another, you're going to have to ask him straight. It's the only way.'

'I said to him on Sunday, I said, "We need to talk, Dan."'

'What did he say?'

'He said, "Talk about what?" But it was his reaction, like that rabbit-in-headlights look. I'm not a fool, Terri.'

They say body language never lies. He couldn't look me in the eye. He was uncomfortable, like he had something to hide. You just know when someone isn't being truthful. It's what they don't say as much as what they say. It's the way they might avoid the conversation, cut it short, avert their eyes, make a joke or an excuse to change the subject.

'The timing is horrendous, Sal. All the grief and stress with Doll – it never rains and all that.' Terri takes my hands in hers. 'Whatever it is, whatever happens, you'll get through this. You've come through a lot worse, girl.'

I feel the panic – invisible to all – surge up my throat. Twenty-two years with someone and you end up like this, suspicious, afraid, vulnerable, crushed. Betrayal is a bitter pill. You hear stories, but you never think it's going to happen to you.

I finish my coffee, push away my plate. The salad looks just like I feel – curling at the edges, limp, withered. Defeated. It doesn't have the energy to sit up on the plate and be noticed. It can't be bothered.

'I better get back,' Terri says, reapplying her lippy and running her fingers through her hair. She squeezes my shoulder. 'Hang in there, girl. Choose your moment, and I'll be here for you if you want to rant, bawl, or share a bottle of red.'

We head towards reception, and there's a queue for the lift.

'I'll walk to the car with you, Sal. I'm not trudging up to floor four in these,' she says, pointing to her blue velvet heels. We head out into a sunny afternoon and start towards the car park round the back. 'How's Andi doing?'

I've been so caught up with Doll and tracking down Lavinia that I've forgotten to tell her about poor Andi.

'Devastated.' I blink in the bright sunshine and put on my shades.

'About Doll's accident?'

'No, it's Steve. He's finished it. I don't know the details yet, but she told me last night.'

'Ah, Jesus, what next? She was cracked about him, wasn't she?'

'Head over heels in love, but look, maybe it's for the best. You know he's from Brandon Terrace, a bit of a rough diamond. Dan didn't approve.'

'And you?'

'I thought he was a good guy, but Dan has a point – he might not be what you'd want for your daughter. Does that make me sound like a snob?'

'Poor Andi, she'll get over it. No, I get it, I'd feel the same. Still . . .' She fans her face and smiles. 'First love can be intense. You'll always remember it.'

I zap my car open, and we hug. 'Mind yourself,' Terri says, and I smile as she totters round the corner. Those shoes are killing her, but she'll never admit it.

I switch on the engine, take a left out of the car park, and make my way up the motorway to the hospital.

On the way, I rehearse what I'm going to say to Dan. When the time is right. Maybe when we know Doll is out of the woods. I'll ask him then. Straight out. *Who's Lavinia*, I'll ask? Just like that. And then I'll wait. I won't interrupt. I won't react, no matter what. I'll stay calm. I won't cry or shout or rant. I won't throw a plate at him. Or hurl abuse. I want it straight. The truth. I'll say, kindly, *Look, I just want to know, Dan. No, really, love, I'd prefer if you're honest*. I'll pretend I understand, that I'm strong and capable, and I'll assure him there'll be no tears or threats.

I'll be resilient, so I will. I must be resilient. It'll be a challenge. Like Doll, I'll make it through. Don't marriages break up every day? Anyway, it's better to know.

My phone is ringing as I pull into the hospital grounds. I park up. A missed call. It's all I need – Emily bloody Murray, the social worker with the sensible skirt. The phone beeps a voicemail message. Emily wants to meet us again, please return her call.

You can fuck off, I think to myself. I switch the phone to silent and sling it into my bag. In the rearview mirror I smear on some pink gloss and pat the shine from my face. I march towards reception then, smiling, walking tall, capable, determined, strong. Fake it till you make it, as the book says.

CHAPTER 15

DOLL

From my bed I can see a skyful of stars, silver, white, and gold. They wink and shimmy, and every now and then one shoots out of nowhere, like an arrow falling. Where is it going? Could someone back home spot it flashing by too?

Back home. Somewhere out there, behind the pearl moon, far beyond the stars, is home. Where people laugh and celebrate and worry and struggle and cry their salty tears all over the earth. My granny said life was a vale of tears. Well, it was for me, anyway.

Was. Past tense. My heart tilts with happiness. The future belongs to me now. And I'm not going back to the past.

There goes another shooting star, falling away into the blue-black. And out there, behind the blue-black, *is* my past. If I stare hard at the silvery sky and focus, I can see a window forming, a square of yellow light, and behind it there's a girl in a bed, wired up like a robot, surrounded by whirring and beeping, and my mother is there, reading, watching over me, turning her ring around her finger again and again like a prayer. There I am on the antiseptic bed. Another me. A frail me. A lemon me. A silent me. Two of us, her and me, living our separate lives in different corners of the universe.

I prop myself up against the pillows and lace my hands behind my head. I don't want to be that girl anymore. *Mom, if only you could see me now!* Could she understand? I think she could. She'd be happy. She wouldn't cry over me anymore, 'cos she'd realise I'm on the inside now, looking out, not the other way round. I'm in the sweetshop, not out on the frozen street, pressing my nose to the glass.

Here I am in my purple-and-white uniform with a box full of sparkly slides, schoolbooks I can read, and cool trainers. Tomorrow I'll be sitting cross-legged, meditating, studying in the library, eating peaches with my friends. I'm living the life.

Today, after Nan-Nan left, we all assembled in the meditation pod. We lay on our purple mats, listening to slow piano notes as Sister Fidelma counted back from twenty. 'Breathe deep and slow,' she said. Her voice was like a lullaby, and we drifted into TRM – total relaxation mode.

'Close your eyes. Imagine a peaceful place, a forest, the seashore, a garden . . .' There were a few giggles at the start, then silence.

'Imagine your best self,' she said then. 'Visualise the best you. Remember your greatness. See it, feel it, touch it.'

I wasn't sure what I was supposed to be thinking. I sneaked open one eye. Everyone was in the zone. So I settled into it. I saw myself living the life, having Amber and Tiger by my side. I saw it all like a video, me sitting around a campfire sharing drumsticks and jokes and singing and climbing rocks and learning hard stuff and Amber coming up and saying, *Please can I be your friend?*

'How does it feel?' Sister Fidelma was saying, her long dark hair like a silk rug over her shoulders.

I felt I was floating off the mat – holding on to the string of a balloon drifting up towards the ceiling. How did it feel? For me, it felt like a fluttering, a beating of tiny wings, something being born inside my soul. A shifting of the furniture in my heart-home.

'Remember, your spirit is invincible. Be grateful for your gifts.'

When I opened my eyes, I realised I'd been crying. They weren't sad tears, though. Was I crying over something I'd lost and found? Over something inside me that had broken open or realising that I might have a best self? That dreams might be possible and – who knew – maybe the future did belong to people like me?

It was joy. I'd had a visit from joy, and it felt good.

Afterwards, we all gathered for garden time. Which, to be honest, is just another name for backbreaking work: picking peas and strawberries, weeding, planting seeds. But it was fun too.

Amber came up to me as we were tidying up in the greenhouse. The light was fading. Quiet moths were out, and I could smell the sweetness of nettles.

'Hi, Doll. Lia told me about you. We haven't met yet. We're in the same dorm. I'm Amber, your roomie.' Her curls bounced when she talked.

I smiled at her, envying her all her gifts. 'I know who you are, Amber. I saw you earlier in the dining hall. You're an amazing dancer.'

'I know I am.' She giggled. 'The trouble is, I can't stop dancing. My feet have to keep moving, moving, moving.' She tapped her feet and did a little shuffle, and we both laughed.

'It's inside you, it wants to come out, it *has* to come out,' I said.

She burst out laughing at that, gave me a gentle dig. 'That's exactly it, Doll. Dancing is like breathing for me.' She made a face then. 'Meditation is a real struggle, but Sister Fidelma told me to harness my energy and pour it into visualisation. And that works some of the time.'

'That's a good idea,' I said. 'You can still dance in your head.'

'I'm going to be a prima ballerina when I grow up.' Now she was rubbing the dirt off her hands and washing them under the greenhouse tap. 'It's written in the stars. It's my destiny.' She grinned, then, in the half-light. 'What's yours?'

'How do you mean?'

She dried her hands on her apron. 'What's your destiny? You have to have one.'

'I'm working on it,' I said, scrubbing my hands, grateful when Tiger came up behind us and put her arms around our shoulders.

'Come on, you two, hot chocolate time. Hurry up – it's a quick shower and lights out at nine bells.'

By nine bells I thought I could sleep on a clothesline, but now here I am, still wide awake, staring out at the diamond sky. I sent Nan-Nan a message on my journal-screen, but I didn't have much to tell her.

The others are out cold, Tiger on my left, Amber on my right, and Lia near the door. Amber groans in her sleep, pushes the cover off. Then she gives a little cry and sits up. Her eyes open wide. She looks at me for a few moments.

'I had a bad dream,' she whispers, rubbing her eyes with her fists. 'Hope I didn't wake you.' She sighs and reaches for the glass of water on her bedside table.

'I was awake,' I say. 'I can't sleep.'

She keeps looking at me like she's still a bit dazed.

'Are you lonely, Doll? Lia told me about your parents. Tragic.' She shakes her head. 'Don't know what I'd do if it was me.'

I take a deep breath. I feel so guilty for my lies. 'Not lonely,' I say, looking across at her. 'A bit scared, really, to be honest, you know, over what happened to the others.'

She nods. 'You mean Matthew and Ava.'

'Imagine, even the druidesses with all their powers and learning can't figure it out.'

She nods again. 'I know. It is scary, what's been going on.'

I wait. *Use your ears*, Nan-Nan said, so I say nothing, leaving Amber fill the silence between us.

'I knew him,' she says then. 'Matthew, the boy who drowned in the lake. We were close.' She doesn't speak for a while, just stares out at the stars. 'He told me things.'

'Like what?'

'I don't like to talk about Matthew.' She puts her hands over her eyes. 'It hurts to remember him.'

'You must miss him so much.'

More silence, only the even breaths of the other girls sleeping, unmoving.

'I do,' she whispers, and a tear snakes down her face. 'Matthew was an adventurer,' she says quietly. 'He had no fear – water rats, cave bats, black eels coiling around our legs in the water – nothing scared him. We were partners for all the class expeditions. He was my buddy; he had my back.' She smiles, remembering. 'He was like a brother.'

'Sound like he was invincible.'

'Yes, but he wasn't in the end, was he?' She starts to cry quietly, so I go and sit on her bed and rub her tears away with my sleeve.

'Don't cry, Amber.'

She squeezes my hand. 'I saw his body, dripping, when they took him from the lake. It was like he was just asleep.'

I say nothing, just hold her hand tight.

'He told me he heard voices, you know. Especially at nighttime. He was worried.'

'What kind of voices?' She was putting my heart crossways.

'He said 'twas hard to explain. They'd come into his head. He'd have to move about – he'd feel restless, not himself. He was afraid.' She twists the sheet around her finger.

'Did he tell someone? A grown-up, I mean?'

'For sure, he went to Dr Ashe. She gave him some herbs, then some meds to relax him. Sister Fidelma did some yoga and meditation with him too.'

'Did it work?'

'No, but he told them he felt better. He didn't want to be sent home. His parents would worry. And he was proper scared.'

'Scared of what? The voices?'

'Scared of losing his mind, Doll. He didn't want his father to know. His father is Almazova's greatest explorer. Have you heard of JB Morley?'

I shake my head.

'Matthew wasn't close to his dad, but he was so proud of him, and he so wanted his father to be proud of *him*.'

'I'm sure his father was proud of him. But why didn't he want his dad to know what was going on?'

'That's the thing. JB's own father had some sort of mental illness, and he died young. Matthew's gran told him it was suicide, though his parents never spoke of that.' Amber takes another drink of water. 'Poor Matthew thought he must have the same illness. He was convinced for a while.'

'He should've told his parents. They would've helped him.'

'I know. I told him a hundred times.' Amber stops, her eyes filling up again. 'But then he was gone, the brightest star in the Academy.' She stares out the window. 'Gone in a heartbeat.'

'There's nothing you could have done, Amber.'

She keeps looking out at the night sky and whispers, 'I know. But still.'

Something clicks. 'You said he was convinced he was ill for a while. Did he change his mind?'

'Definitely. We were hiking across the Long Valley the morning before he drowned, and he told me he didn't think he had his grandfather's illness. He was in a good mood, I remember that.'

'Had the voices gone away?'

She shakes her head. 'No. But another boy, Thomas, told him he was hearing voices, feeling confused and restless.'

'So it wasn't just him?'

'Exactly. And not just that.'

'Kristin and Ava too?'

She shakes her head. 'I don't know about them, but Matthew said he thought he knew what was wrong with him but no one would believe him. And I wasn't to tell a soul.' She rubs her palms over her face. 'I said, "What's to tell?" But he said he had to do some checking first before he told me anything.'

'What happened after that, Amber?'

'The very next morning he was gone. Rowed out to his death.'

'Did you talk to anyone afterwards? Tell them what he'd said?'

She bites her lip. 'I did say it to Dr Ashe, about him thinking he knew what was wrong with him. But she just said, "Poor boy, we'll never know now, will we?"' Amber rubs her eyes and sighs. 'I did ask Thomas how he was feeling, though, if he had any problems with sleeping, or voices.'

'What did he say?'

'He laughed at me. Said no way, was I joking?'

'So that was that.'

'Yes and no. A week later, Thomas got sent home with an unnamed illness, and he's not coming back, Lia said.' Amber puts her head in her hands. 'I should have said something. Maybe if I did, I could have saved Matthew.'

Poor Amber. Behind the white smile and the curls and the dancing and the mischief, there's a lonely, grieving girl. I put my arms around her. I know what lonely feels like – it's a puddle around your heart.

'We'll have to find out what's going on,' I say. 'Things are not right at this Academy.'

'Don't say a word,' Amber says, putting her finger to her lips and closing her eyes.

I slide off her bed. Away on the horizon, a shoulder of crimson and orange is bursting its way through the dark.

I close my eyes, and soon I'm in dream city. I see a boy rowing in the moonlight. A silvery fish leaps onto the boat, and the boy jumps. The fish turns into a grinning mermaid with long golden hair. And far above the water, I'm attached to a red balloon and I'm floating across the night sky in search of my best self, my best self, my best self . . .

*****

'Doll, rise and shine, it's seven bells. Time for prayers. You can't be late on your first day!' Lia says.

I roll out of bed, brush my teeth, fix my hair, scramble into my uniform. In the mirror, my scarred cheeks are healing well, just a little puckered skin around the sealed-up wounds. A reminder of my worst self. My old self. My ex-self. *Forget about her, Doll!*

We troop down to the dining hall, us four girls, me linking Tiger and remembering my gifts and my new best self. Bring on the day. It belongs to me. Despite the dreadful mystery, inside I whoop. *Look at me now – I'm drinking summer, I'm living the life!*

CHAPTER 16

DAN

I was never much good at juggling stuff. Not in the way women are – multitasking, managing the bills, the holiday plans, the kids, the house, the groceries. And the job. Firing all the balls into the air and catching them as they cascade back down. Hats off to them. It's not my thing. I drop the ball, or don't see it coming, or swear as one falls and rolls away.

I fire up the engine and swing left out of the hospital car park. It's only seven p.m. on Wednesday, but I feel burnt out already. Rain drizzles down the windscreen. I switch on the wipers and turn off the radio, grateful for the silence driving brings. Everyone out there separated from you, cut off by a glass-and-metal shell. Quiet time to think, put things right in my head.

And when you're trying to think things out, you try to compartmentalise, keep the problems separate in their own boxes, minimise the confusion. But you end up with a headache that won't go away, no matter how many painkillers you take.

I inch out of the hospital grounds onto gridlock. It'll be bumper-to-bumper all the way to the motorway. For once, it suits me. I'm in no hurry to get home. And this is about me, not Sal.

The phone purrs a message. It's Sally. Telepathy. It often happens with us. I'll be thinking about her, and she rings me at that very moment. Or I ring her at precisely the same time as she's WhatsApping me.

Though lately there's a distance between us. Women definitely have a sixth sense, like an emotional radar system built into their brain. Which means that no matter what you're hiding, they sense it, and what's more, they'll unmask it. It's unnerving.

The traffic lights are out of action up ahead, and the traffic is flowing through, makes you wonder. I'm nearly at the slip road to the motorway already.

Sal knows me better than anyone. And I admit I'm dragging my heels on things, but dammit, I'm wrecked – from work, the hospital vigils, the sleepless nights, and Jesus, Andi's meltdown over Steve Thompson.

I mean, that kind of dependence is dangerous. It's not love, it's bloody addiction. Which is what I told her. And that went down like a lead balloon when I looked in on her last night. 'You're a jerk. Get out,' she said. How can't she see him for what he is? Love really is blind.

I switch on the aircon, glad of the cool jet of air on my forehead.

Thank God it's over with Steve. He's out of the picture. She'll get over it. From September she'll be studying for the Leaving Cert. Time enough for boyfriends in college. A good degree, a master's, a career doing something she loves. She's bright. She'll go far if she can focus on the prize.

The traffic has thinned out a good bit. I swing left, up the slip road to the motorway. From here, it's looking like it should be a clear run home.

There was a time when me and Andi were inseparable. She was my little star. *Was*. Then she turned into a stroppy teenager overnight. Tantrums. Moods. Grumpy.

'She's just a teenager,' Sally would say, as if that explained it. When I was her age, I wouldn't have gotten away with that. This generation gets away with murder.

Of course, cool-hand Steve changed all that. After her first date, she turned into Miss Happy. A personality transplant! What did she see in him? A tiger tattoo the length of his arm – what's that about?

'Body art, Dan,' he said one day when I asked him. When I pressed him further, he grinned and said, 'Tats can be a game changer – girls love 'em.'

He might get the girls, I thought, but he'll never get a decent job with that monstrosity on his arm. And his ear pierced too. Jesus wept.

I press the accelerator, and the car roars along the motorway. I know where the speed cameras are, so I'll pull back in a couple of minutes. Been caught too many times.

Steve is a nice enough guy; he's treated Andi well, I'm not arguing with that. But he's the last one you'd want her to end up with. And it happens. Look at Kate Marron – a lovely girl from Bluebell Avenue, wanted to study medicine. Started going out with a waster from Hettyville. She got pregnant in Leaving Cert. Had the baby three months after the exams. Moved into an apartment in Finbarr Street. Jesus, can you imagine?

We knew the parents, Pat and Ang. They were gutted. What about the morning-after pill? they said to her. She could've sorted it, but no, she told them, she *wanted* to have his baby.

That was about five years back. She came into the bank last week, two little boys in tow. She's working part-time in the local deli, but God, what a waste of a life. That could have been Andi.

If I hadn't put a stop to it. At least that was one ball I could catch. One box I can tick as sorted. We can all move on now, once the tears and tantrums subside. As they will.

At the Glengarvan roundabout, the traffic is light. Murphy's Law. If I was in a hurry, it'd be tailbacks all the way. I turn into Bluebell Grove. The rain is gone, but it's still overcast. The weather in this bloody country would get to you sometimes.

There's a scent of laundry in the hall and what smells like satay chicken wafting from the kitchen. Sally is laying the table for three. She doesn't look up, just says, 'Hi. How's Doll? Any news?'

I sling my jacket over the back of a chair. 'No news. I met Dr Valera again. Says she's holding her own.' I pour myself a large glass of wine from the bottle on the table. 'They're going to reduce the sedation after the weekend and are confident she'll respond. The scans look positive.'

Her shoulders relax. 'That's good, isn't it? There's light at the end of the tunnel.' The last few words get stuck in her throat. She takes out some plates and puts them in the warmer.

'Where's Andi?' I say. 'Is she eating with us?'

'Andi is in bits.'

'Such drama. Over a boy. It's nonsense.' I take a drink of wine.

She's washing some cutlery at the sink and stops for a second, leaving the tap run.

'It's not just a boy, Dan. It's Steve. The love of her life. Remember?'

She runs a cloth across the knives and forks.

'And don't snort like that,' she says, over her shoulder. Her voice is brittle. 'She loves him. Or thinks she does. Whichever. It doesn't matter. Her heart is broken.'

'She'll get over him. You shouldn't be encouraging her. You need to be a parent. He wasn't right for her, and you need to reinforce that with her.'

Her eyes flash. 'Have you forgotten how it feels? Were you ever a teenager? I wonder sometimes if you even have a heart.' She dries the cutlery vigorously, clattering everything into an open drawer.

Did I really come home from another twelve-hour day to listen to a lecture? I bite back the words. Which isn't easy, the way I'm feeling.

Instead I say, 'It's for the best, in the long run. You're with me on that, surely?'

'I'm not disputing that, Dan. It's just the way he dumped her. By text. Just like that.' She clicks her fingers. 'No excuses, no explanations. That is tough on her.'

She folds the tea towel carefully over the Aga door.

'Did he say anything at all, Sal?'

'Nothing. He's cut off all contact. It's shocking, really. But it's too early to be saying *I told you so*. It's too raw.'

'I'm glad he saw the light,' I say. 'I admire him for that.'

She looks up from stirring the chicken. 'How do you mean?'

'Well, he saw reason.' I loosen my tie. It's hot in the kitchen.

'Reason?'

I'd better tell her. 'I spoke to him Sunday evening.'

She drops the spoon and puts her hands on her hips. 'You spoke to him on Sunday?'

'Yes. Her staying over with him was the final straw. I won't have her ending up like Kate Marron.'

'What did you say to him, Dan?'

'I told him to stay away from her.'

'And he said, *Okay, Dan, no problem*?' Her eyebrows arch.

'More or less.'

She sits down and rests her chin on her palm. 'I can't believe it. What exactly did you say?'

'We had a man-to-man.'

'Tell me. I need to hear this.'

I can't work out if she's being sarcastic, but there is scorn in her voice. Is she spoiling for a fight?

'Look, basically I told him we didn't think Andi was right for him. She has a career to think about and he shouldn't hold her back. I told him straight, Sal – if he really did love her, he'd leave her follow her path.'

'And?'

'He said he loved Andi. Wanted the best for her. I said, "If that's the case, you'll leave her alone." I may have said that Andi herself was also feeling a bit conflicted.'

Sally closes her eyes, takes a sharp in-breath. 'That is *not* true. She is *not* conflicted.'

I feel annoyed that I have to defend my position. I shouldn't have to justify what I did. After Saturday night, well, I had to do something. Someone had to parent.

'Well, it's true he's not suitable, Sal. You said it yourself. He wasn't right for Andi. I mean, for Chrissake, his mother is a heroin addict.'

'And Steve agreed to this, did he?'

'Well, I wasn't asking. I was warning him to step back. Why make it hard for Andi to choose him or us? I told him she'd have to choose. I said we'd made a decision.'

'*We?*'

'Yes, *we*. You were furious over Saturday night, her sleeping over. For all we know, she could be pregnant already. Do you actually believe her, when she said nothing happened? You need to stick with me on this one.'

She says nothing.

'I told him if necessary, I'd speak to his grandmother. I think he understood me, Sal. Andi'll see it our way in time. That we had her best interests at heart.'

'Her best interests? Is that what this is about, Dan?'

'Of course. She'll thank us in the end. Trust me.'

She stands up and folds her arms. 'I can't believe you did that. Without consulting me. You said nothing till now about what *we* had decided. You have some nerve.'

'*I can't believe you did that!*' We both turn towards the doorway. Andi is standing there, shaking.

Dan steps back. 'I didn't hear you coming in.'

'Evidently, Dad.' Her eyes flash. 'How dare you make those decisions for me! I'm sixteen. You went behind my back. You let me think it was his idea. You knew, and you said nothing.' Her voice trembles.

'It was in your best interests.'

'So you keep saying. If you ask me, Dad' – she points her finger at me, tears welling – 'you're just jealous. Jealous of what me and Steve have.'

'Keep your voice down! You're being childish, Andi,' I say. 'Get a grip. Listen to yourself.' I'm getting angry now, and there's no talking to her while she's in this state.

'You're not happy and you don't want to see me happy. That's what all this is about.' She grabs her rain jacket from the chair.

'Where are you going, love? Dinner is on the table,' Sally says, throwing me a dirty look.

'I'm going to Steve's house. Try and stop me.' She marches out the hall, and I can hear the front door being wrenched open. 'And don't expect me back. Ever.' The door slams behind her.

'Happy now?' Sally walks past me and snatches her car keys from the hook inside the kitchen door. She never has to search for them; they're always there.

More hysterics. I hate these scenes. All high emotion rocketing around the walls.

'Let's sit down and eat and talk things through.' I say it calmly, though it's the last thing I feel right now.

'I'm not hungry.' Sally fires a tea towel across the room, narrowly missing me. 'Help yourself.'

The front door bangs shut, and I hear her car engine starting.

I switch off the bubbling satay, bang a lid on top. My head is spinning. I break open two paracetamol and wash them down with the rioja.

The silence is deafening, the calm after the storm. I refill my glass, turn on the telly. I need serious escape time.

The doorbell rings. Christ, I'm not in the mood. I use the remote to turn up the sound, but whoever's outside isn't giving up. Damn. Through the side panel I can see a woman in a dark jacket, a scarf wrapped around her throat. I open the door.

'Mr Redmond?'

'Yes, yes, can I help you?' I can hear the impatience in my own voice. The woman steps back a little.

She smiles politely. 'I'm glad I caught you in. My name is Ann Brophy. A colleague, Emily Murray from the hospital, made contact with me.' She pushes her lapel badge towards me. 'I'm the public health nurse, and I wondered—'

'Yes, what did you wonder? Please tell me? I can't wait.' *Calm down, Dan*, I tell myself. I know I'm looking for a punch bag, but being rude and sarcastic is not the way to go here.

'Is your partner in, Mr Redmond?'

'My partner? Do you mean my wife? No, Mrs Redmond is not here. If you call back tomorrow—'

'I'd hoped to talk to you both, actually. It's about Doll, your daughter. She had a serious accident recently, and—'

'Oh, really? Fill me in, if you will. Please do. An accident? Tell me something I don't know.'

She steps back again, a look of alarm crossing her face. Her eyes flicker towards the glass of wine behind me on the hall table. 'This is obviously a bad time. You're busy.'

'Yes, you could say I'm busy. My wife is busy. We're all busy, as you can imagine, with our daughter on life support and juggling work and worry.'

'I can understand that.' Even through the haze of wine in my head, I can detect a note of annoyance in her voice. 'However . . .'

'However, you still incessantly ring my doorbell late in the evening, like a bailiff. What is it that cannot wait until tomorrow?'

'Mr Redmond, I have left a message on your wife's phone. She hasn't returned my calls. I called here yesterday, but there was no one home. Emily has also failed to get a response from either of you.'

Her mouth is set in a straight line. Her eyes tell me she is not impressed. She probably smells the wine on my breath. I can imagine her report. *The father is arrogant, could be controlling, at the very least a heavy drinker, one to watch.*

'Well, Nurse Bromley, perhaps you might restrict your calls to office hours in future. I will have my wife call you tomorrow.'

I don't wait for a reply and close the door firmly. I can see her hurrying to her car. She's already on her mobile, and God only knows what she's saying.

I lean against the door for a minute, take a deep drink, and finish the glass. Not a smart move, really. I know they're following up on Doll's accident. It's procedure, they're just doing their job. But it doesn't mean I have to like it.

On the coffee table, my phone rings out. I'm not answering any calls tonight. I check to make sure it's not the hospital. The name flashes up. *Lavinia.*

I need to hear a quiet, cool voice. I sit down, turn off the telly, and wait five minutes. Then I'm calmer, and I ring her back.

She answers on the first ring. "Hi, Dan, how have you been?"

If she only knew the half of it.

CHAPTER 17

DOLL

'And so,' Tiger is saying, 'I ended up getting a scholarship to the Academy.' She takes another scoop of strawberry ice-cream and waves the spoon in the air. 'Supposedly for my brilliant zoology project, but I think Nan-Nan and Jasper had something to do with it.' She puts her ice-cream tub next to her on the grass and lies back, closing her eyes.

'I'd say it *was* your project work, Tiger. You earned your place here,' I say. 'And people like you *belong* here. This is the start of your path to the Space Academy – what you always wanted. The future really does belong to you.'

'And *you*, Doll.' She sits up and squeezes my hand. 'I'm so thrilled you're here. I didn't know if I'd ever see you again.'

I scrape the last spoonful of her ice-cream and chew on a piece of strawberry. 'Me neither. But you being here, Tiger – well, it makes me feel safer.'

She laughs. '*You* being here makes *me* feel safer.' Her brows furrow and she stretches back on the grass, soaking up the midday sun.

'Did you know Matthew?' I ask.

She shakes her head. 'Not really. Amber did, though.'

'I know, she told me.' I fill her in on what Amber said last night.

'Blow me down, that's weird. What did he mean when he said if people knew, they wouldn't believe him?'

'Dunno. But the next day he drowned.'

She sits up again. 'He jumped in, Doll. He wanted to drown. No one pushed him. There were two eyewitnesses.'

'Did you know the girls, Kristin and Ava?'

'Not really. We were in the choir together, but they kept to themselves. But Doll, those two could sing. Mr Cage loved them. He adored them.'

I met Mr Cage, the music tutor, earlier in music appreciation class. He's a nice man with one blue eye and one brown one, set under a pair of bushy grey eyebrows. His topping of frizzy black hair makes him look like a kind spider.

Lia told me after class that Mr Cage is actually a genius who wants to breathe music, not air. To him, she said, music is oxygen. I think she's right. I've never met a genius, but when Mr Cage played the piano this morning in class, his fingers fluttering over the keys, I felt the notes spring up and dance across the room.

'He used to call the girls his two canaries,' Tiger says. 'He'd tell them they were destined for greatness.' She smiles and rolls her eyes. 'When they sang, he'd shout, "Magical" or "Bravo, Bravo."'

'So he must've known them well?'

'Definitely. They were forever practising for some concert or recital.' Tiger fans her face. 'Wow, it's getting hot.' She stops for a minute. 'It might be worth talking to him, though. He might know something.'

'Does anyone believe Kristin pushed Ava?'

'That's the thing. It happened so fast. Poor Ava. It's how it *looked* – Kristin seemed to push her, but no one really believes it. I mean, they were best friends.'

'And Kristin left the Academy. Does anyone know how she is?'

'According to Lia, she hasn't spoken since, and doesn't even seem to know what's going on. It's so sad.'

'And how are you, Tiger? After your dad? Do you dream about him? Do you think about that night on the lake?'

I was there that night with Tiger. She'd just met her dad. An hour later, he was killed saving her from a bullet. He died in her arms. I'll never forget the blood turning pink in the rain and her screaming.

'I think of him every day, Doll. Some nights I can't sleep.'

'It's tough. I can understand that. You loved him. You found him. You lost him.'

She plucks a daisy, twirls the stem between her thumb and finger.

Then she nods. 'But I'm not the only one awake at night, Doll. Other kids come and go in the darkness here. I've seen them.'

'Come and go where? It's lights out at nine bells.'

'I'm not sure. I see figures walking along the lakeshore some nights, or coming out of the oak forest.' She shrugs. 'I didn't think too much about it at the start. But' – she breaks off a daisy petal – 'after what happened with Matthew, I wonder, is there a connection?'

She looks at her watch. 'Come on, I'm down to get my tattoo done after history class.'

We stand up and shake the grass off our tunics. I show her my transfer.

'Looking good,' she says.

I wink. 'It's not real,' I say, putting my finger to my lips, 'but I so wish it was. It's a sign you're special. An Academy girl. A mark of pride.'

'You're right, Doll. It's an honour. And Mollie said it doesn't even hurt.'

A woman in a big pink dress is beavering across the grass towards us. 'Is that you, Tiger?' She leaves her gold-rimmed glasses fall to her chest, where they sit snugly, held there by a silver chain. 'Ah, yes, it is. Good, good.' She notices me. 'You're the new girl. Doll, isn't it?' She shakes my hand vigorously. 'Welcome, darling, welcome. I shouldn't call you *darling*, but what matters, what matters.'

'This is Dr Ashe, Doll,' Tiger says. 'Our medical officer and science head.'

Dr Ashe smiles and winks at me. 'Hopely Ashe. Call me Hopely, darling. Everyone does.' She puts her glasses back on. 'Hate all these formalities, Doll. No need for them.' She produces some notes from a file under her arm. 'Tiger, please drop these off to the admissions office if you will, pet.' She checks her watch. 'I've a meeting in five, and admin needs these records straightaway.'

Tiger flashes her smile. 'Of course. We're going that way now.'

Hopely beams at her. 'You are a star. Thank you, dear.' She turns to me. 'If you need anything, any help, darling, come to my office. My door is always open.' She winks again. 'There's always a chocolate drop or a sherbet if you ever feel homesick.' Before I can say thanks, she whirls away, bustling across the lawn towards the science pod.

'What a twirlwind,' I say, laughing. 'So that is Hopely Ashe.'

'She's so different to the others,' Tiger says. 'She's one of us. Like our Academy granny.'

I couldn't think of anything further from my granny, who would never have worn a pink dress or carry a file or wear a chain with her glasses stuck on it. Still, I like Hopely. She isn't scary like some of the druidesses. And I like her idea of having me drop by for a sweet or a sherbet. She makes you feel like a grown-up, like you're important and good for a chat. I wouldn't tell her, though, who I really am. No one knows that. Only Tiger, and she would never tell.

By six bells, we're back in our dorm. Tiger and Amber compare tattoos, both tiny purple flowers covered over in a clear plaster.

'Did it hurt?' Lia asks. 'I got mine last term, and it was sore for days.'

'That's because Sister Evalina did it,' Amber says. 'She's not as good as Hopely.'

'You got yours, Doll.' Lia lifts my hair back. 'Nice and neat.' Before I can answer, she looks at her watch. 'Come on, we'd better get a move on. Tea is at five bells this evening 'cos the showcase is at six.'

Everyone is excited about the showcase event.

'What happens tonight?' I ask Tiger as she pulls a comb through sleek wet hair. The dorm smells of soap and shampoo and coconut cream. I have to pinch myself to make sure I'm not dreaming this perfect life. I fix my purple hairband, keeping the bow to the side. Amber says the bow to the side is cooler.

'The students perform for the Cloaks,' Amber says. 'There'll be stories, songs, plays, dance, and artwork. All the stuff we've been working on across the last term.' She spills some hand cream onto her palm and rubs her hands together. 'It was meant to be at the end of term, but with the accidents and . . . and Matthew drowning and Ava falling, it was postponed until tonight.'

'We didn't have the heart for it,' Lia says. 'It's a night for celebration, and we were all too upset.' She takes the hand cream from Amber and smiles. 'Caring is sharing, Amber.' She jerks her thumb towards the music pod. 'It was Mr Cage's idea. The druidesses were delighted with him – all the talent and skills on show. They love all that.'

Tiger hinges forward, mimicking Mr Cage, pointing an imaginary cane across the room and saying in a high-pitched voice, 'Bravo, bravo, wonderful talents, my dears. Absolutely wonderful. Remarkable. Stupendous.'

We all collapse about, laughing. Amber has a twinkle in her eye. She starts to dance across the room, twirling and kicking her legs in the air. 'Look at me, Mr Cage. Am I stupendous, sir?' She dances around Tiger, and they both fall onto the bed, giggling.

'A round of applause for the star of the showcase,' Lia says, handing over a vase of flowers to Amber. She mock-bows. 'Thank you, my dear, I'm honoured.'

She leaps onto her bed, spilling water from the vase as she flips it onto her bedside table. Tiger steadies it. We all clap and whoop.

'Come on!' Lia says. 'We better not be late.'

Amber somersaults off the bed, and we all troop along to the dining hall for tea.

Just after six bells, Mother Bodica opens the showcase in the great hall with a speech about new beginnings. It sounds to me, listening down in the back rows, like her heart isn't in it. She doesn't believe it. She knows there's something bad underneath, some crawling thing she can't see.

'Tonight is tinged with great sadness. We remember the terrible events of last term. But here tonight, we celebrate the creative, the magical, the wondrous gifts within all present.' She takes a deep breath. 'Life asks us to carry on. Demands that we pursue our dreams. We, who are the living, must live – must endeavour not just to live, but to live our best lives. We owe the dead that much.' She raises her arms. 'Eternal Spirit of Life, grant us protection.'

We all answer, 'Ago-ye.'

'And in that protection, security. And in that security, knowledge.'

'Ago-ye, ago-ye.'

'And in that knowledge, awareness. And in that awareness, the awareness of the rightness of things.'

'Ago-ye, ago-ye.'

We join our palms in prayer. Long white candles are lit, and sage burns in small bowls. The Academy choir sings softly, the voices rising and filling the room. They hover above us, blessing us, showering down some droplets of peace.

Someone sobs quietly near me. It's Amber. Her shoulders are shaking, and I reach over and hold her hand. She closes hers over mine and squeezes it.

The druidesses, a sea of blue silk, take up the first three rows of seating. Mr Cage introduces the various acts as the students come onstage, to loud applause.

When Amber goes up to dance, there's a hush. She slips off her cardigan and shoes and glides onto the stage. There is only the sound of a chorus of violins as she swirls and slides across the floor, turning like a bird, stretching her arms above her head like wings. I wish I was Amber. My blood runs green, and I hope no one notices. We all know we are watching a star rising. She knows she's a star too, knows it is written in her destiny.

Next up is a play, and poetry that makes us laugh. Tiger sings in the choir, and a dancing troupe tells stories through movement. The Academy orchestra raises our spirits. We all forget to be sad and get lost in the magic.

Afterwards, we sip hot chocolate as we circle the room, admiring the paintings and the stone sculptures hammered from the lakeshore rock.

'You were the star, Amber,' Tiger says as we stop by a painting of Mother Bodica, a long figure wrapped in blue. 'You danced with the grace of a swan.'

Amber stares at Tiger, then turns her head to look at the painting. Then she swivels abruptly and walks away. Her curls don't bounce tonight.

'She's probably still upset about Matthew,' I say to Tiger as we climb the stairs to the dorm. 'She was crying earlier.'

Lia nods. 'And she's exhausted, I'd say. She was working on that dance for weeks.'

*****

Nine bells chime as we brush our teeth and get ready for bed.

'Where's Amber?' Lia says. 'It's lights out.'

'Probably chatting to Mollie or Lou in the next dorm,' Tiger says. 'She might want a break from us.'

Moonlight pools into the room. The lake below is like glass. Outside, nothing stirs the silence but the *yip-yip* of a sugar glider in the distance. Tiger says they're everywhere. They sound like lonely birds calling to each other over the still waters of the lake.

'We need to find Amber,' I say. 'It's trouble for us if Hopely or Sister Fidelma drops in.'

'I'll check with the girls next door.' Lia hops off her bed and slips on her socks.

She's back three minutes later. 'That's odd. They haven't seen her since the showcase. She must have sneaked out.' She purses her lips. 'You know what she's like – a rule breaker through and through.'

'What'll we do?' I say, feeling my skin tingle with fear. Sharp little pinpricks shoot up my arms. 'What if something's happened?'

Lia says, 'We need to wake Sister Fidelma. Even if it means Amber will be in trouble. It's almost ten bells, and I'm worried.'

We scream when we hear a sharp rap at the door. The handle moves, and Sister Fidelma's head appears. She looks cross, like she just woke up and didn't want to.

'Is it true Amber is missing?'

We all whisper, 'Yes, Sister.'

'You should've come to me directly. Mollie said she didn't return with you tonight after the showcase?'

We nod. 'We thought—'

'Stay where you are,' she says, pursing her lips. 'I will raise the alarm. You girls stay here and get some sleep.'

Is the woman joking? How could we sleep? As she disappears, we pull on our tracksuits and trainers and follow her, at a distance, down the stairs and out into the moonlight.

The druidesses are roused. They hurry down towards the lakeshore, picking their way over the rocky ground. We can see shadows fanning out towards the oak forest, and through the stillness we can hear the word repeated over and over. It floats up through the trees. *Am-ber. Am-ber.* But no one answers except the sugar glider.

CHAPTER 18

ANDI

There's a light on in Steve's house. Yes! I ring the bell, and I can see a shadow through the frosted glass. *Come on, Steve.*

The door opens a fraction.

'Yes?'

'Hello, I'm looking for Steve?'

The door pulls back. A tiny woman in a long navy raincoat and pink slippers is standing there. She tilts her glasses and hunches forward.

'You're looking for Steve, love?' She smiles, running her tongue along the roof of her mouth and behind her teeth. The teeth move. 'I thought you were selling something, or one of them collectors – you know, charity people.'

'Is he here? Is Joanie here? It's all right. They know me.'

She shakes her head. The frizz of white curls doesn't move.

'No, love. No one here only myself. Joanie's just out of hospital. Gone to her sister's in Limerick for R & R, as they call it these days.' She stops. Lowers her voice to a whisper. 'She's not great at the moment, you know. But' – she smiles again – 'she'll be fine by and by. Please God.'

'Oh, I'm sorry to hear that. Are you . . . ?'

'I'm her neighbour. Teresa Chapman. Number seven, two doors down.' She nods her head to the left. 'I'm here to collect Molly's dog food and mind the place for Joanie.' She leans past me, her watery eyes darting up and down the terrace. 'Some right pups around here after dark, you know.'

'And Steve, is he with her, then?'

She peers at me. 'Who's asking?'

'I'm sorry, I'm Andi Redmond. Steve's girlfriend.'

She laughs. 'Well, Steve's girlfriend, hello. He was always one for the girls.'

'Is he with her then, Mrs Chapman?'

'Well, if you're the girlfriend, you'd know, surely?' She waits a beat. 'He's gone over to his mam's for a while. Went yesterday. Didn't he tell you?'

'To his mother's? For how long?'

'That I do not know, love. I didn't ask. Wasn't in the best of form, which isn't like him. Such a gentleman, Steve is.' She fixes her scarf around her throat. 'Did you ring him at all?'

'He's not answering.' I bite my lip, feel the tears coming. What if I never see him again? 'I need to talk to him. Urgently.'

She steps back from the door. 'That important, eh? Come in out of the cold.' She buttons up her coat. Looks up at me kindly. 'Maybe he doesn't want to see you, lovey? Is it finished? Did ye break up?'

I nod. It's hard to stop the tears. 'But it's all a misunderstanding,' I say. 'He needs to know. I need to tell him. To explain.'

Mrs Chapman nods, plucking a packet of tissues from her coat pocket.

'Here. I can see you're upset, child.' She shakes her head. 'That Steve. Always breaking some lassie's heart.'

'Do you know where his mom lives, by any chance?' A plan is forming in my head. I just need the address.

'I know Linda's in London or near London. Could be Dartford or Dagenham. Joanie and herself didn't always see eye to eye, you know, so she didn't talk about her much.'

'I know. Steve told me. Would Joanie have her address, do you think?'

'You're not thinking of going after him, are you?' She does the tongue thing against her teeth again.

'Oh no, not at all,' I lie, 'but I might write to him.'

'That's a good idea, love.' She pats my hand with soft, shiny fingers. 'A letter will help you get this off your chest. Wait there, and I'll check Joanie's address book in the cabinet.'

As she disappears into the sitting room, I look around the dim hallway. Was it really only last Saturday night we walked up those stairs to spend our first night together? Our first time. So much can change in a heartbeat.

Mrs Chapman reappears with a small black notebook.

'Here we are. Linda Thompson. Have you got a pen, child?'

I pull out my phone and take a picture. *Flat 3, 27 Morley St, Dagenham, KM9*. My heart is thumping. 'Thanks so much, Mrs Chapman. And please tell Joanie I was asking for her.'

'I will, to be sure. And mind you read over that letter before you send it. The written word is very powerful, so be sure you—'

I nod and wave my goodbyes.

I can't wait to voice-message Stacey. I need to tell someone about my plan. I make my way towards the river path, checking flights on my phone. Yep, Cork to Stansted. Tomorrow at seventeen forty. Perfect. Another hour and a half by train to Dagenham Dock via Liverpool Street. It's not a big deal. I'm sixteen. Entitled to do as I please really, legally. Still, I won't be telling my parents. Obviously. And I'll be in trouble.

It's almost dark, and I can feel a soft drizzle falling. I break into a jog to release some of the stress in my head. So tomorrow I'll be there. I'll explain. We'll make up. And then I can come back. Doll looks like she's on the mend, so I shouldn't feel guilty. But still. How selfish am I? I run faster, but it's hard to outrun my head.

I slip in the front door quietly. The telly is on; I head straight upstairs. Google Maps tells me it's a fifteen-minute walk to Morley Street from Dagenham Dock.

I check my debit card. More than enough for my flight and train. Good to go. I get my passport, download my boarding pass, shower, pack my rucksack. It's an adventure, I tell myself. A way back to Steve.

*****

The one thirty p.m. Cork City Express is nearly empty. The fewer people I meet, the better. No awkward questions about where I'm off to on a Thursday when I should be in school. I change out of my uniform in the bus station in Parnell Place. The shuttle to the airport only takes twenty-five minutes. I arrive at the airport with buckets of time to spare. I fix my face, do my eyes carefully in the airport loo mirror, and have a Coke while I'm waiting to board.

Stace thinks I'm mad. She was still trying to get me to change my mind this lunchtime in the school canteen.

'He'll be back in a week, maybe less. Why don't you wait?'

'I can't, Stace; I have to get him back. You don't understand. I have to tell him . . .'

She rolls her eyes. 'Tell him what, exactly?'

'Tell him that my dad was out of order. And that we don't have to break up. Tell him that my mom didn't even know about all this. And that I love him.'

She dives into her bag of Taytos. 'He probably knows all that already, Andi, in fairness. He just doesn't want to come between you and your parents.'

'That's the point – *he's not*. I need to make him understand that. My dad was just doing a solo run.'

She sucks the salt off her fingers. 'Can't you just say all this on the phone? Message him. Text him. It's a bit dramatic heading off to London, isn't it? And you know his mom is an addict, yeah?' She empties the last tiny crisps into her mouth and folds the bag over and over into a tiny envelope shape.

Why did I tell her that? My big mouth.

'She's clean at the moment, Stace. She's in a new relationship, and she's happy.'

Stacey sniffs.

'Stace, for all I know, he could be looking for a job over there.'

Silence.

'Stace, are you listening to me?'

'Yes. Go on, then. But, Andi, say what you have to and then come home, okay?'

'Will do. I promise.'

She wipes her mouth with her sleeve and takes a packet of Polo mints from her pocket. 'Want one?'

I shake my head.

'One more thing: don't sleep with him again without . . . you know. Saturday night was a risk. Don't be stupid, take precautions.'

'I know. I know. I'll be careful. Look, I have to catch that bus or I'll miss my flight.'

At the Ryanair gate, I sip my drink, feeling an edge of guilt top-sewing around the corners of my mind. I was careless last Saturday, wasn't I? I should have got the morning-after pill on Monday, but with Doll's accident and everything, I forgot about it. What if . . . ?

I shake it off. I mean, who gets caught their first time, right? You'd want to be dead unlucky. I won't make that mistake again.

The flight is smooth, and I read for half of it. In Stansted, I make my way down the elevator to the Liverpool Street train on platform three. I text Mom while I'm waiting. I'm meeting Steve. Back tomorrow. Ur not to worry. A x. I switch off my phone as I get on the train.

After Liverpool Street, I have to change at Tower Hill, walk to Fenchurch Street, and take the Dagenham train from platform two. I don't turn my phone on again till we arrive in Dagenham Dock.

Six missed calls and three messages from Mom. My heart flips. *Not now.* I go straight to Google Maps to plot my route for

27 Morley Street. I button up my denim jacket against the chill night air and head right past a string of busy kebab takeaways, grocery stores, and restaurants.

I check the time: a quarter to nine. I take a right at the traffic lights, turn onto Newingham Road, and ten minutes later I turn right down Morley Street, a quiet cul-de-sac of tall redbrick houses with small front gardens. Number twenty-seven has a motorbike in the garden and four bins of various colours. There's a dim light on in the hallway.

I ring the bell for flat three. No answer. I keep ringing. Nothing.

I take a step back when the front door opens. A man steps out with a dog on a lead.

'You okay, love. Looking for someone?'

'Flat three. There's no answer.' I never thought about what I'd do if there was no one home. Wait in the dark? Call back later? Check into a hotel or a hostel – but do I even have enough money? What an idiot I am.

'Ray and Linda, is it? Are they expecting you?'

'Linda Thompson, yes. And, um, no, this is a surprise visit.'

The dog is straining against the lead, eager to be off. 'You won't find them home tonight, love.' The dog is barking now. 'Easy, boy, easy.'

He sees my face fall.

'Your best bet, love, is the Rose and Crown. Take a right here' – he points back towards Newingham Road – 'and it's five minutes' walk, on your left. You can't miss it.' He tucks the lead under his arm and pulls a beanie cap from his pocket. 'There's a fundraiser for the Daggers tonight. Y'know, Dagenham Football Club? A community table quiz. Some of the players will be there.'

'Are you sure that's where they'll be?' I'm not so happy heading into a pub on my own on some random chance I'm going to see Steve there. I mean, I don't even know his mother.

And I'm underage. What was I thinking? My dad will have blue murder if he finds out where I am.

The man with the black beanie hat says, 'I'm dead sure. Wasn't Ray organising the night, trying to rope us all in?' He smiles, opens the gate. 'And they play cards there every Thursday night anyway. So, like I said, that's your best bet, love.'

Once he's out the gate, I ring the bell one last time, but still nothing, so I head for the Rose and Crown.

I read my mom's texts on the way. Angry first. Where are you? Come home straightaway! Then firm. Andi, please answer your phone. Then pleading. Please, please, just let me know where you are?

I text back. I'm fine. I'm safe. Back in Cork tomorrow. I switch my phone off again.

Across the street the shiny gold lettering of the Rose and Crown is lit from above. Like the man with the dog said, you couldn't miss it – all mahogany and stained-glass windows. I linger outside. The door opens to a surge of noise, and two girls emerge to light up. They're wearing short skirts, and one has a sparkly top and glitzy heels. And here I am with my faded denim jacket and red sweater and jeans.

I run my fingers through my hair, rub some gloss on my lips. I take a deep breath and pull on the brass door handle.

There's a gush of welcoming warmth from the plaid carpet underfoot. The polished mahogany bar is gleaming, and there's a smell of ale. Beer. Whatever. A real pub smell. The place is teeming. Plates of sandwiches and cocktail sausages are being passed round, and there's a din of laughter and conversation. I scan the room.

And then I see him in the far corner booth. He's talking to a girl with cropped blonde hair and red lips. She's laughing at something he's said. Linda is sitting opposite him. I recognise her from the photos he's shown me, though her face is more rounded.

A man in a red-and-blue striped football jersey goes to the table with a tray of drinks. He leans over, says something to Linda, and she pulls him closer and cups her hand around his ear. The girl with the red lips – who the hell is she, anyway? – sees me staring and nudges Steve.

He looks over at me. The world lurches. I steady myself. The shards of noise around me fade to mute. I see his face, his mouth slightly open, his blue-and-amber eyes staring at me. He's saying something, but he's too far away for me to catch it. The world freezes for a moment.

I feel faint, remembering I haven't eaten since breakfast. There's a grey sweatshirt approaching, a tiger's paw peeping from the rolled-up sleeve. Someone is putting their arms around me, whispering into my hair. A hand strokes my cheek. *Andi.* I fall against the sweatshirt, inhale the Pour Homme. *Babe.* It's oxygen, it revives me. I can breathe again.

'Is she okay, mate?' a voice asks from behind me.

I try to shout, but I hear my own voice only as a whisper. 'I'm fine,' I say, 'not a bother.'

And then we're outside. I feel the cool night air and a taut body pressed to mine. 'Missed you, girl.' He kisses my hair, hard. I bury my face in his chest, my hands massaging the warm skin of his back. He catches his breath as I scrape rough lines along his spine with my fingernails.

CHAPTER 19

DOLL

Amber is asleep in her bed, her eyes flickering under half-closed lids. Outside the sky is pale blue, flecked with pink. I nudge Tiger awake. 'She's back.' I point to the sleeping Amber, who's beginning to stir. She looks startled for a moment and turns to me and Tiger.

'We were worried about you,' I whisper, trying not to wake Lia.

Her brows knit, and she sits up straight. 'What?'

'Last night,' Tiger says, 'you went missing.'

'I went for a walk, down by the lake.'

'Why did you go off by yourself like that, Amber? We were all looking for you – before the Cloaks sent us back here.'

She bites her lip and, after a long silence, says, 'I don't know.' Her face crumples.

'We were afraid something happened to you,' I say.

She draws her knees up to her chin, clutching the sheet. She doesn't say anything for a while, then, 'I just felt like a walk. And it's so strange.' She closes her eyes. 'I remember my shoes getting wet. I was in the water, and it was so cold. And I was standing there for ages, the water slapping against my skin.' She shivers, hugging her arms. 'Now, why would I do that?'

She looks at us, puzzled.

'I don't know,' Tiger says. 'Why did you?'

'And I was thinking I might go in deeper but not really wanting to. But still, wanting to.'

'That doesn't make any sense, Amber,' I say.

She presses her hands to her face and looks up after a while. 'I know. I'm confused. It's like part of me wanted to keep going, y'know, but a voice inside me was telling me to go home.'

I rub her arm. 'It sounds terrible, Amber. Did you talk to Dr Ashe? She'll be able to help you.'

'No. Sister Fidelma found me on the shoreline, and the Cloaks brought me back to theirs and made me tea and gave me something to help me sleep. They were very kind. I hope they're not going to tell my folks.' She clutches my hand with both of hers. 'Do you know what stopped me wading in deeper?'

'Tell us, Amber.'

'I knew if I kept going, I'd never dance again, and I couldn't bear that.'

'You're a dancer in your heart, in your soul; it's the deepest thing. It's your destiny. You knew that.'

'I did, Doll. I knew it. So I filled my head with the music. I was humming it loudly, trying to lock out the thoughts that were shouting at me, saying, *It's a beautiful thing; keep walking in deeper, Amber, keep walking.* And after a while my head was bursting with the music and I couldn't think, only feel, and I felt like dancing, tapping, twirling, and it was hard because the water was heavy around my shoulders and my legs were getting numb. And I . . . well, I sort of half-danced my way to the shore.'

'Dancing saved you, Amber,' I whisper.

Tears hover on her eyelids, and she blinks them away. 'Dancing saved me. You are right, you understand – dancing saved my life.'

'Do you think you'd have kept going in deeper? That you'd have drowned?' Tiger asks, glancing at me and raising her eyebrows.

'I do. I was close.'

A silence follows. We are all imagining the picture: Amber wading through the freezing water, hesitating, then dancing her way back to shore, her head bursting up with music and the Cloaks with their lanterns scurrying along the lakeside and finding the dancing, shivering girl.

Lia stretches awake. 'Amber! You've come back to us!' She leaps out of her bed and comes over to hug her. 'They sent us back to bed last night. What happened?'

'She'll fill you in on the way to breakfast, Lia,' Tiger says, looking at her watch. 'We're going to be late.' We dress hurriedly, and soon we are all heading towards the dining hall.

'What do you think?' Tiger whispers as she fills her bowl with muesli and peels a banana. 'Do you feel she's telling the truth?' She pours milk and scoops a spoonful of cereal into her mouth.

'Of course she is. Why would she lie? And it sounds to me like what happened to Matthew.'

'I was thinking that too,' Tiger says. 'Except, unlike our Amber, he went ahead and jumped in.'

'Exactly. But why? And is it the same reason Kristin pushed Ava? Something or someone told her to do it and she couldn't resist?'

'It's a bit far-fetched, though, isn't it?' Tiger says, taking some raspberries from the bowl on the table. 'We all have free will. We can't say, *Oh, a thought entered my head and I was compelled to obey it*. I don't think that would hold up in court. Unless you were pleading insanity, I suppose.'

'But the incidents must be connected, though, yeah?' I say. 'At least, what happened to Amber and Matthew.'

'Yes, for sure, Doll. I think so. But that doesn't get us any closer, does it? I mean, who'd want to kill children and make it look like they did it themselves? Only a monster. It makes no sense.'

'And they knew each other – Matthew and Amber. They were best friends. That's a connection,' I say, finishing my pancake and getting up to go.

'So? It could be just a coincidence.'

'Come on, hurry up,' Lia calls to us, linking arms with Amber. 'We better not be late for class. It's double history.'

'For you two, maybe,' Tiger says, laughing. 'We've a science practical with Hopely, so that should be a bit more fun. Catch you later.'

Tiger pushes the glass doors into the science pod lab, and we take our places for today's experiment. Hopely Ashe is handing out packs of baking soda and vinegar and getting her materials ready for the class. She explains as she goes about chemical reactions and acids and bases, and today, she says, we are going to be making rockets.

It's only my third day at the Academy, and already I can feel my brain expanding at the speed of a rocket. This is my best life. I don't have to dream it; I'm already living it. I look around me at the chattering children, the glass tunnels and the greenery outside. The sour memories of my days back home are slipping away like river fog now, a wispy grey thing getting smaller and smaller every time I look behind me. My granny was right – it was a vale of tears. The present belongs to me now, though. I can soak it up, become my real self. The self I couldn't be back home.

Back home, there was no *becoming*, just a never-changing *is*. Now, all is possible, a cloth of hope with my name stitched across it in silver letters.

Dr Ashe hurries over to our workstation, her orange dress billowing out behind her, making a swishing sound as she moves. She takes a tissue from her pocket and dabs her forehead.

'Welcome, girls, welcome. How *are* my girls?' I can smell lemony perfume and fresh sweat off her. She leans closer and whispers, 'How is the talented Amber? I heard about last night. Poor darling. She seems to be losing her mind.' She shakes her head. 'A dreadful business indeed.'

'She's fine, Dr Ashe,' Tiger says. 'Just a bit shaken.'

'Did she say what happened? What possessed her to wade into the lake in the darkness?'

'Maybe you should talk to her, Dr Ashe,' Tiger says. 'She could do with some adult support, and the druidesses – well, they're a bit otherworldly, you know.'

Dr Ashe smiles, and her face crinkles up. 'I've spoken to Sister Fidelma. We agreed a chat might help. Tell her to see me after last class today, Tiger. Say, four bells at my rooms in the temple.' She rests her hand on Tiger's shoulder. 'You come with her. She'll feel more comfortable with you two nearby.' She gives us a thumbs-up and moves on, stopping to talk to students and then clapping her hands for silence as she explains how to start building our fizzing rockets.

After class, we head towards the library for free reading. In the tunnel, Mr Cage calls us over. 'Well done last night,' he says to Tiger. 'You were all pitch-perfect. I'm very proud of you. After all that's happened last term, you really stepped up and gave us a stunning performance.'

Tiger beams, a sunflower drinking rain.

'And you, miss.' He gestures with his cane to me. 'I'll want to see you at rehearsals next week too. The junior choir interschool competition is only three weeks away. I believe we can win it.'

'The seniors are competing tomorrow in Vanistra, aren't they?' Tiger says.

'Yes, another wonderful choir. Stupendous. They'll do well. We are off this evening at six bells, and we'll hopefully bring back the trophy the day after tomorrow. I'm very excited about it.'

'You'll miss Kristin and Ava's harmonies though, won't you, sir?' Tiger says.

He shakes his head. 'A huge loss, those two.' He taps his cane against the path absently. 'A mystery. A tragedy. My heart truly bleeds for them.' He looks as if he's about to cry.

'Have you any idea what happened?' Tiger asks. 'I mean, why would Kristin push Ava off the tower?'

He looks at her sharply. 'How would I know, my dear? It is a complete mystery. Most uncharacteristic.'

'And you knew them well, didn't you, sir?'

'I wouldn't say that. No better than the other tutors.'

'I'm wondering if someone made her do it. What do you think?'

His brow creases. 'I have no idea whatsoever. What evil child would do that?'

'Or evil adult?'

He smiles then. 'I don't think our little band of tutors would qualify as evil, Tiger. And the druidesses are life-enhancing and spiritual creatures.' He sighs, a cloud passing through his face. 'We'll let the psychiatrists and the detectives do their work, shall we? Eh?' He checks his pocket watch and flicks his cane. 'Dear, dear. I must be off. Lots to do before we go.'

'Good luck tomorrow, sir.' We both say it together, and he waves without looking back.

When he is out of earshot, Tiger says, 'What do you think, Doll? He wasn't giving much away, was he?'

'Well, he's our teacher. He's not going to tell us anything, is he? I thought you were a bit cheeky, actually, asking all those questions. I think he was getting uncomfortable.'

We walk towards the dining hall. 'Exactly. *Uncomfortable*. Now, why would that be?'

It's a question I don't get to answer, as Amber, Mollie, and Lou join us. 'Dr Ashe wants to see you after class today, Amber,' I say.

She makes a face. 'I'm not sure, Doll.'

'She said we could come with you,' I say. 'Have a chat with her; she's cool. We'll wait outside.'

She chews her lip and sighs. 'I'd better do it,' she says. 'Otherwise I'll have the Cloaks on my tail.'

I've never been to the temple where the druidesses live, and I'm looking forward to seeing inside.

'This is the grand atrium,' Tiger says as we arrive. The sunlight flows through the glass dome overhead like a waterfall splashing over the cornflower-blue chairs set around a table. We shade our eyes. 'Down there' – she indicates left and right – 'it's all meeting halls and workspaces here on the ground floor.' Our shoes make a clacking noise as we cross the black-and-white tiles towards the grand staircase.

'Upstairs,' Tiger says, 'are the druidesses' sleeping quarters and their dining and recreation area. On the very top is the prayer room overlooking the oak forest.'

She grins at me. 'We don't ever, ever get to climb those stairs, but we are free to visit the basement. That's where Hopely's office is. Come on down.'

We are about to step down the marble stairs when a voice calls out. We all jump, and I scream.

'Shh,' Tiger says crossly. We look for the source of the sound, but all we can see are the portraits of long-dead druidesses lit by the sunlight, which gives their faces an eerie liveliness.

We are about to take another step when the voice calls again. 'Child of Summer!'

This time I snap my head back. There, at the top of the steps on the first floor, a druidess is crooking her finger towards me. My legs wobble. Tiger nudges me. 'Answer her.'

'Y-yes.' My voice is a whisper. Amber is rooted to the spot. She's staring at me.

'Come here.'

Tiger nudges me again. 'Go on, hurry up and go.' Her face is white.

'We're not allowed up those stairs, you said.'

'You better do as she says,' Amber whispers.

My footsteps clatter on every step. I haul myself up by gripping the banister. I can see the blue cloak far above me, wrapping the druidess like a baby. The sun catches half of her withered face. Her eyes stare straight at me, and I'm beginning to think it's a statue, maybe a puppet, some prop from the drama room. But the scrawny finger moves again. I swallow hard as I reach the top of the stairs.

'Follow me,' she says in a whisper. I look down at the girls and they're standing in the same spot, staring upwards. I bring my palms up in a question, but they gesture for me to carry on.

I walk behind the druidess down a gloomy corridor past door after door, till she stops and motions for me to follow her through an archway onto another, narrower corridor. She stops at the last door on the left and takes a key from inside her cloak. She fumbles with the lock, and the door swings open.

Fingers of sunlight are creeping through the curtained windows. Stuffed birds with red feathers and savage beaks stand lifeless in glass jars along a table, their eyes as dead as raisins.

The druidess shuffles towards a faded armchair by the window and folds herself into it, drawing her cloak around her like a blanket.

'It's chilly, isn't it?'

''Tis, Sister.'

She points to a stool with a pink silk cover. 'My name is Dagda. Sit.' Her voice is thin like a bird's.

I sit, tugging my purple skirt over my knees.

'I know who you are.' She sits back, almost disappearing into the chair, her mouth making a chewing motion.

'My name is Doll,' I say.

'Shush! Stop it. I know what name you wear.' The mouth keeps moving.

I look down at my shoes. They're covered in grass, and it's messing up Dagda's wood floor. I feel her eyes on me.

'Why are you afraid? You won't achieve much by being fearful.' She shakes her head.

'I'll be in trouble if you tell,' I say. 'I'll be sent home.'

'You're in trouble already, child. I can smell it.' Her tongue slides around her mouth as if it's trying to find some annoying crumb.

'I'm ready for anything.'

'That's not how it looks to me.'

'I'll figure it out. Please don't tell. The future belongs to me here.'

'You plan to stay?' When I don't answer, she says, 'You cannot stay. Remember that, dear.' She leans forward. 'Come closer, Child of Summer, so I can see your eyes.'

I bring my stool closer to her chair. She reaches out a clawlike hand, and I rest my fingers in her curled palm. I can smell thyme off her, and when she folds her fingers over mine, I can feel a dizzying vibration run through me, bone to bone. I gasp and pull away.

She smiles then, closing her eyes. I'm thinking she may have drifted to sleep, but when I get up quietly, her eyes fly open.

'Wait, one thing,' she says, sitting up straight and touching my forehead. Her hand is cool. 'Bless you, child, and may the forest protect you. Ago-ye.' She slips something into my palm, and my fingers close over it.

I back-tiptoe out of the room. The birds' dead eyes seem to follow me, and as I close the door behind me, I can see the old woman has gone off to sleep.

Walking quickly along the dark corridor, my heart thumping, I uncurl my fist. Dagda has given me a dainty white pearl bracelet. I slip it on my wrist and step quickly down the staircase. I can see the girls are waiting for me, sitting on the bottom step of the basement stairs. As I get closer, I look at my arm, and I nearly get sick.

My white pearls have turned black.

CHAPTER 20

SALLY

It's just before nine when I hear his car in the driveway. The front door bangs shut, and I don't look up as he comes into the kitchen. He yawns, lets his keys fall on the kitchen table.

'Doll's stable, no change.'

'You took your time coming home.' I continue emptying the dishwasher.

He doesn't answer as he takes off his suit jacket and fits it carefully around the back of the chair like it's a tailor's dummy. He loosens his tie, runs his fingers through his hair.

He sighs. 'I was at the hospital. You knew that.'

His voice is flat. And in the tone I can hear the unspoken, the holding back, some angry thing he wants to keep the lid on.

'But you had time to stop off for a pint. Lucky you.' I can smell the beer.

'So what if I did? Is that not allowed?'

'You know Andi's missing. You saw her text. Are you not concerned?'

'She's not missing, strictly speaking. We know she's with him. She'll be home tomorrow. Let her off; I'm sick of this whole Steve saga.' He takes a bottle from the wine rack behind him and holds it up for my inspection. 'Want one?' He doesn't even wait for an answer, just unscrews the cap and pours himself a glass.

'No, thanks. One of us had better keep a clear head.'

He takes a sip. 'What's that supposed to mean?'

'I've been over to Steve's house. The place is deserted. She's not there. We might need to drive over there again. Well, obviously, *you* can't now with drink on board.'

'The grandmother is in hospital, isn't she? The happy pair are probably gone out for a pizza and back to Brandon Terrace then for a cosy night in. Happy days!' He smiles sarcastically and raises his glass in salute. He takes a long drink.

'You've changed your tune.' I snap the kettle on and line up a mug. 'She's staying with him tonight again and you're okay with it?'

He tops up his glass and leans back against the table like a visitor who's popped in and only plans to stay a moment. He folds his arms. 'Look, I took a stand on this . . . this . . . this *relationship* with that moron, and you didn't even back me up. So don't come running to me, Sal. You can deal with it now.'

'So this is my fault, is it?' I slosh some boiling water into the mug.

He doesn't answer. Just stands there, stroking his glass slowly.

I slam the dishwasher door closed. 'You had no right to go and talk to Steve without telling me first. Charging in with your ultimatum. What good did that do? She's chosen him. Big surprise, Dan. I could have told you that if you'd have bothered to listen.'

I know I'm pushing his buttons. I'm being a bitch. He's wrecked. Straight from work to the hospital. It's been a long day for both of us. And he comes home then to Greenland. A chill wind blowing around the kitchen.

And I know – and I hate to admit it – that this is really all about Lavinia. *The mystery woman*. The woman he sat at the bar in the Gibson Hotel with. Just last week. That's what's really crushing me. She's like a Berlin Wall stretched across the kitchen, dividing us. A shadow dimming all the light.

But I'm not telling him that. I can't face that conversation now, with Doll in hospital and Andi running off to Steve's.

'Oh, Sal, I'm pretty sure you have all the answers, as usual.' He walks out of the kitchen.

'Don't walk away, Dan!' I shout after him, but he's out of earshot. I hate when he does that, makes himself invisible. So infuriating. Upstairs, I can hear the shower buzzing on.

I really want to smack him. I want to make him pay. I want to shout, *Who is she, Dan? Who is the wonderful Lavinia? Tell me, Dan! Do you think I'm a fool? Do you think you can play away and not get caught?*

Maybe this isn't the first time. The thought dangles there in front of me like a noose, sending a cold sweat through my skin. Of course. I hadn't thought of that, but it makes sense. This isn't the *first* time.

I feel the panic searing through my chest like a firework. I sit down. Take some deep breaths. Try to gather myself. Cool my heart. Maybe Shirley Lovett wasn't just a kiss either. I only have his word for it. How do I know he didn't have an affair with her? The wife's usually the last to know – isn't that what they say?

My phone pings. I'm fine, Mom. Back in Cork tomorrow.

Back in *Cork*? So she's gone away with him for the night. I just pray she's safe and sensible. I dial her number, but her phone's switched off. That girl is so self-centred. Can't she think of someone other than herself for a change? I'm beginning to think this love affair with Steve is unhealthy. She couldn't stay away from him for five minutes. Dan had a point: is it dependence?

Dan reappears in sweatpants and a T-shirt. I tell him about the message. 'Fine,' is all he says. He switches on the TV, flicks through with the remote, and settles on CNN. We sit there emptily in a grey silence, staring at the dramas unfolding across the planet. Distant dramas, not the ones swirling around the room like a fog.

I know I won't sleep. Not a wink. 'Dan, we need to talk.'

He sighs again and switches off the TV, throwing the remote onto the coffee table. It slides and clatters to the floor.

He yawns, stretching his arms over his head. 'I think we've enough talking done for one night, Sally. At least you have.' He gets up and rubs the back of his neck. He looks shattered. Worn down. 'So if you don't mind, I'm going to bed.'

'Running away again, Dan?' I can't help it. I shout it after him, but he's gone, up the stairs, and I can hear a bedroom door slamming shut. And by the sound of it, he's in the spare room.

I turn off the lights and sit there in the quiet shadows, the street-light across the road casting strange shapes across the furniture.

You never really know someone, do you? You think you do, but you don't. It's all an illusion. You spend twenty years living with someone, sleeping with them, raising a family, sharing your dreams, and poof! It means nothing. You can't know what goes on in someone else's head, not even if you're with them for a hundred years. Scratch the surface, dig down a little, and we're all strangers to each other. And often – and I know this – we're strangers even to ourselves.

CHAPTER 21

DOLL

I walk along the corridor with the girls, my head spinning after meeting Dagda.

'What did she want?' Amber asks.

'I'd say she thought I was someone else. She seemed confused.' I say nothing about the bracelet and pull my sleeve over it. Tiger is looking at me with a silent question, but I change the subject quickly. 'Okay, so what's down here in the basement, then?'

'The tutors have their offices down here,' Amber says, pointing to a line of closed doors on the right. 'This is the laundry room. And this is the porters' storage rooms, sports equipment – all that stuff is along here.'

At the end of the corridor, we turn left towards Dr Ashe's rooms. 'Sick bay is here too,' Amber says, opening the grey double doors so I can peek inside, but my mind is elsewhere.

What if the old hag tells Mother Bodica who I really am? If she does, there'll be trouble. I'll be marched home, back to my old life, and they won't be asking me to visit Almazova again. And I really want to stay this time. I don't care if it's against the interplanetary rules – that was just Nell's excuse. Why couldn't I stay? What harm could come of it? At the Academy, I have a future.

So here's the thing: I need to find a way to disappear when all this business is over.

'Doll, you're not even listening.'

'Sorry, Amber, yes, sick bay. Hope we never end up here.' I smile at her.

Dr Hopely Ashe is waiting for us when we arrive at her rooms. She smiles an orange-lipstick smile as she ushers us into a waiting area with a row of chairs and a table with science magazines and a jug of something pink with ice. She gestures for Amber to follow her into the room marked STRICTLY PRIVATE.

'You stay here, girls – have some lemonade – and we won't be long.'

Tiger pours two glasses and hands me one as the door closes behind Amber.

'Well, come on,' Tiger says, 'what happened back there? How did she know you're the Child of Summer?'

'I don't know. She didn't say much. Warned me there was trouble coming. I was going to say, *Tell me something I don't know.*'

'That was it?'

'Yeah, that was it.' I don't even know why, but I'm not mentioning the bracelet. I glance under my sleeve, and the pearls are still black. I shiver.

We sit in silence for a while. The only sound is the quiet hum of voices inside Hopely's office. 'Hope Amber will be okay,' I say. 'She's worried about what nearly happened last night.'

'It's so weird,' Tiger says, nodding. 'It's like a fire spreading through the Academy. Who'll be next?'

After a few minutes, the door opens and Amber emerges, sobbing.

'Leave her be, girls,' Hopely says as Amber runs off down the corridor. 'She's confused and upset. It's good for her to cry.'

'Will she be okay?' I ask.

Hopely nods. 'Come in for a quick chat, both of you.' She ushers us into her office and swings a second chair in front of her desk. 'Sit down.' She smiles and spills some lemon sherbets from a jar into a bowl. 'Have a sweet.' She sits in her swivel chair, looking at me from over the top of her glasses. 'Are you settled in, Doll?'

'I am, thanks, Dr Ashe.'

Her voice is kind. 'It's tough. On you both. You are Amber's roommates. Poor child, she's very upset. I told her Mother Bodica would have to contact her parents.' She purses her lips. 'Especially when you consider what has been happening.'

'Do you think they were accidents, Dr Ashe? I mean, Hopely?' Tiger says.

'Do *you*?' Hopely picks up a pencil and twirls it back and forth between her fingers.

Tiger shakes her head. 'Ava was pushed. People saw it. But nobody believes Matthew drowned himself.'

'But he did. People saw it.'

'But why? And why did Kristin push her best friend to her death? And why did Amber walk into the water last night?'

'Why indeed? We may never know.' Hopely purses her lips. 'These are strange and unsettling times. Amber is a sensitive child; she's reacting to the trauma. Matthew was her best friend, I gather.'

'That's right. She loved him like a brother.'

'Did he confide in her at all? Was there anything he might have said?'

'No,' I say, 'just that he was worried he was losing his mind, but then he was relieved when he realised he wasn't.'

'Yes, she told me that. But we'll never know now what was going through his head.'

'Yes. He drowned soon after that.'

'It's all very worrying.' Hopely rearranges the pins in her haystack hair and pats her bun. She gets up to ensure the door behind us is firmly closed and comes back to her chair. 'There's something I've discovered. I'm loath to mention it, but . . . '

'What is it?' we both say together, glancing at each other.

She lowers her voice and leans her elbows on the desk. 'I have brought my information to the attention of the investigating officers, but they tell me that it leads nowhere.' She waves her hand crossly. 'Basically, there's no evidence to support my claim; they followed up, but nothing came of it.'

'What?' We both look at each other.

Hopely takes a deep breath. 'Mr Alastair Cage is a convicted murderer.' She reaches for a sweet, unwraps it, and pops it in her mouth. 'I know. You are shocked. But please trust me when I tell you I know this: our musical genius, Mr Cage, *is* a killer.'

Tiger gasps. 'How can you be so sure?'

Hopely sucks her sweet. 'Many years ago, as part of my doctorate, I was involved in research on how neural network models can be used to assess and predict criminal behaviour using facial imaging.' She pauses, sees the puzzled look on my face. 'Simply put, we used artificial intelligence to see if certain facial expressions, traits, and details could predict a criminal nature.'

'And where did Mr Cage come in?' I ask.

'We were given hundreds of anonymous photographs of convicted killers for our study. They were from all over the prison system, and I remember his face and especially those eyes. How could you forget someone whose eyes are a different colour?'

We nod. 'It is the first thing you notice when you meet him,' I say.

'Yes, heterochromia is very unusual; less than one percent of the population is affected.' She reaches for another sweet. 'I recognised him the moment we were first introduced last year, but I convinced myself I was mistaken once I got to know him. I found him to be a gentle and kind soul. But now . . . I'm not so sure.'

'The police didn't find anything, though?'

'No. They assured me they'd check his name and details against the system, but there is no record. They think I am mistaken.'

'So now what?' Tiger says. 'If he is a murderer, maybe we need to take a closer look at him?'

'We can only let the investigators do their work,' Hopely says, sighing. 'We'd need proof. Some evidence to prove he did time, and I don't have that.'

'We could check out his house, see if there's anything we could use.'

'Nonsense, child. You can't break into and enter someone's property. That is a crime in itself.' She pauses. 'No, I just want you to keep your eyes peeled on Mr Cage and let me know if you spot anything unusual. That is all.' She stands up and stretches. 'Darlings, look at the time. I must leave you girls go. Our chat today is confidential. Please respect that.'

'Of course, Dr Ashe, we won't breathe a word,' Tiger says.

Hopely looks at me, waiting.

'We won't tell anyone,' I say. 'Not even Amber.'

A storm cloud passes over her face. 'Especially not Amber! She's very vulnerable.'

We say our goodbyes and make our way upstairs, out of the temple and into the bright-yellow sunshine. It feels good to be outside again.

'Are you thinking what I'm thinking?' Tiger says as we head for our dorm.

'I am. Mr Cage will be away in Vanistra.'

'Tomorrow, after class?'

'Do you know where he lives?'

'It's not very far. If we follow the lake path and cut through the wood, we can reach it from there without being seen. It's one of those shepherd cottages on the hill overlooking the Long Valley.'

'He's not back till the day after tomorrow. No one needs to know,' I say.

'What are we looking for? And how will we get inside the cottage to search?'

'We'll know when we find it,' I say.

Later, in the dorm before the others arrive, I send another message to Nan-Nan. I tell her about Mr Cage and about Hopely's story and about Amber going missing and nearly drowning and what she told us about Matthew. I don't mention Dagda or the bracelet. I dunno why; maybe I just want to forget it ever happened.

As I'm washing my hands, I push my sleeve back and glance at my bracelet. The pearls have turned white again. I'm not sure whether I should be glad or spooked.

CHAPTER 22

DAN

Claire, my assistant manager, puts her head around the canteen door.

'Morning, Dan. Happy Friday. You're early.' She bustles in, chest heaving, and drops her handbag on the chair opposite mine. She consults her watch. 'It's only just after eight – how about a quiet coffee, eh?' She shrugs off her cream jacket and hangs it up in the closet behind the door. 'You'll have one, Dan?'

I nod my thanks.

She fills the kettle and switches it on and takes two mugs from the cupboard overhead. She crosses to the fridge. 'You look exhausted. Were you at the hospital again overnight?'

I put the newspaper aside. 'No, just didn't get much sleep.' I don't add *in the spare room*. Though if I did, I know Claire would make some clucking noises of sympathy and it would never be referenced again. Claire is what my mother would have called a brick. Solid. Dependable. Calm in a storm. She's a rock and she's kind, a rare combination. But work colleagues are just that – colleagues, not confidants. I envy women, the way they can share what's going on in their heads, intimate stuff, personal stuff. Men rarely do that. Far as I know, anyway.

'How's Doll doing?' Claire closes the fridge with the back of her red patent shoe and smiles. 'Sorry, Dan. I'm sure you're sick of answering that question.'

'She's good, Claire. The swelling's going down, so the doctors are optimistic. Hoping she'll be off the machines after the weekend.'

'Thank God. I'm glad. It's not easy, is it?' She pours me a coffee and milks it. 'Here you go.' She lowers herself onto the chair opposite and rummages in her handbag. 'Come on. A Friday treat.' She takes out a packet of chocolate fingers and shoves it between us. 'My favourite time of the day.' She rolls her eyes and joins her hands in mock prayer. 'A fifteen-minute window of peace – and chocolate – before the work begins!'

She takes a biscuit from the pack, snaps it in half, and wraps her palm around her mug.

'You heard about Ger Mac, I suppose?' She blows on her coffee.

'No, what about him?'

I haven't thought much about him since our meeting a couple of weeks ago. I remember afterwards thinking about his gambling and the fortune of money he'd lost and how he couldn't tell his wife and was hoping to win it back. I can never understand why gamblers think they can win back what they've lost. They somehow think they can outwit the monster in the end. Right. Who are they kidding?

'He's missing. You haven't heard?' She licks a crumb from the corner of her mouth.

'I don't understand. Missing? As in disappeared?'

Claire snaps another biscuit in half. 'I met Eileen yesterday morning – you know, the wife, small, dark hair? She was worried sick.' She takes a sip of coffee. 'He was heading to Dublin on Tuesday to collect some machinery parts for the plant, but he never turned up there. And she hasn't heard a word from him since.'

'Christ, that's three days ago.' Something slippery is uncoiling inside my stomach.

'Eileen was frantic, as you can imagine. She said the Gardaí weren't classifying him as a missing person when she called them on Wednesday, but I'd say it's a different story now. If he hasn't turned up yet, that is.'

I get the sense of a cord being pulled tight around my chest. A knot of guilt. Did the gambling get to him? Hardly. I'm getting ahead of myself. I should have said something to somebody, though. I should have followed up on it. My heart feels like a hammer on wood.

'I'm sure he'll turn up,' I say. 'Maybe he needed time out – you know, to clear his head. Still, it's odd.' The words sound like someone else is speaking them. There's a red flag waving at the edges of my mind.

'Dan, are you okay?' Claire comes around to my side of the table. I can smell her perfume, strong and sweet. I want to retch. 'Dan, you're scaring me now. Your face is grey.'

I knew. And I did nothing. I loosen my tie. 'Just a bit dizzy there, Claire. I'm okay now.'

She fills me a glass of water. 'Here, drink this.'

I'm running away with myself here. *Get a grip, Dan.* The cord loosens. 'Thanks, Claire. I'm actually fine now. Just felt a bit off there, you know.'

'You should go home, Dan. I'm going to ring Sally.' She pulls her mobile from her bag.

'No.'

She spins around.

I smile at her. 'I'm fine, really, Claire. Thank you.'

Back in my office, the numbers on the spreadsheet blur. It's mid-morning and I wheel back my chair, rest my face in my palms. What if Ger Mac was confiding in me for a reason? He didn't have to tell me. Maybe he wanted me to intervene. To do something. To save him from himself. And I did nothing. I said nothing. Too caught up in my own problems. And now, *what if?* There's a serpent inside me rising up, swaying from side to side, its jaws extended like rubber bands. I can hear it hissing at me. A forked tongue spitting a poisonous thought: *Did Ger Mac take his own life?*

I grab my jacket and buzz Claire. 'I'm off to a meeting. I'll be back after lunch.'

'I have Eileen on the other line there, Dan; she's looking to speak to you. Will I put her through?'

'Any news on Ger's whereabouts yet?'

'Nothing. God love her. The Gardaí are on it.'

'Take her number, and I'll get back to her in the afternoon, Claire.' My mouth is dry.

The sun is out, the morning as crisp as an apple. I head towards the Glengarvan Arms Hotel in Main Street, an imposing granite building with wrought-iron railings that could well use a coat of paint. Inside, the red flock wallpaper and mahogany furniture are a shrine to the seventies. The bar is gloomy and smells of fried breakfast. Two senior ladies are sharing a pot of tea and scones in the corner. There's a boy wearing a bow tie behind the counter. He's stocking the cooler with bottles of beer, but he springs up as I slide onto a barstool.

'What can I do you for, sir?' *Do me for.* What a little smart arse.

'Double Scotch and water, please.'

'Coming right up,' the boy says. 'Johnnie Walker?'

'Fine.'

I just need something chemical, some fake fix to see me right for now. So I can rationalise my thoughts. Ger Mac is not my responsibility. I slosh a drop of water into the glass and drink half the amber liquid. It hits the spot and begins to unjangle me. I can't control what a client does in his personal life, can I? Anyway, for all I know, Ger could be back home by the afternoon, and all this stress and worry for nothing. I'm crossing bridges way too soon here.

I finish off the Scotch and order a single. But still. I screwed up. Let's face it, I should have at least logged it. Should have sent the information up the line to Regional Office. A red flag. I should have done *something*. Why didn't I?

The boy refills my glass from the optic, and now he's started to roll cutlery into red paper napkins. I check my watch. Don't want to be here when it starts getting busy for lunch. In a town like Glengarvan, you don't get away with drinking Scotch in the middle of a working day. Not if you're the local bank manager. Tongues wag. People gossip.

On impulse, I text Andi. Anything is better than thinking. And we have to repair this. Are you on your way home? I add a heart.

She gets back straightaway. Hme tmw no flights 2day.

Flights, where you? I tell myself to take it easy.

London. With Steve. Talk tomorrow.

She not only defied me, she sneaked off school and left the country, and not a word to me or her mother. That girl has absolutely no respect. She's gone too far this time.

I jab her number, and I'm shocked when she answers.

'Andi.' I try to keep my voice calm and friendly. 'Where in London are you?'

She sounds cheerful. 'In Dagenham, Dad. We're staying with Steve's mom. Look, we need to sort this out.'

We need to sort this out. You bet we do, young lady. I can feel the anger crisscrossing inside me but try to keep my voice steady. 'Bloody Dagenham. I can't believe I'm hearing this. You're with his mother? She's the heroin addict, am I right?'

'Don't say that,' she hisses, and I can hear a door closing behind her. 'She isn't an addict anymore. She's clean now, and her partner, Ray—'

I drain my drink. 'Spare me the details, Andi, please! Are you in your right mind? Get yourself out of that den of iniquity and get on the next flight home. I'll cover the cost.'

'I'm not a child, Dad, so stop treating me like one. You lied to Steve. You told him I wasn't into him, that he'd better back off.'

'It was for your own good. Let's not rehash this here.' The boy behind the bar is glancing at me and starts to move away discreetly.

'You don't get it, Dad, do you? You can't break us up. I followed him to London. And now he knows I do love him, and we're stronger than ever. Thanks to you.'

That girl knows how to twist the knife. 'You haven't a clue, have you? You're a disgrace. Get yourself home today, Andi, and tell Steve you're done, or else.'

'Or else what, Dad?' She's crying now. That's all I need.

'Or else don't come home at all.' I'm realising now that I've been shouting. The two women in the corner stand up and brush the crumbs from their chests. One keeps looking my way as she puts on her coat and settles her cap over her ears. Nosy Parkers. The town is full of them.

I lower my voice, and it sounds like a hiss. 'It's him or home. Would you give up everything for Steve bloody Thompson? Make your choice, Andi; you can't have both.'

She hangs up. There's silence in the bar. The two women shuffle past me, sliding their eyes over me, smiling and nodding politely. The old biddies. Tuned in to every word, fodder for their next gossip session.

I leave a twenty on the counter and get up to leave. The phone pings. *Choice made Dad. I'll be staying in Brandon Terrace.*

She knows the very name Brandon Terrace will make me livid.

I buy a ham sandwich and a packet of extra-strong mints in Centra and make my way back to the bank. There's a yellow sticky on my desk. *Ring Eileen – Urgent.*

I take a deep breath and dial the number. She answers straightaway. 'Hi, Dan, thanks for getting back. Look, I know you're busy, and I'm sorry to hear about poor Doll. Please God she'll be fine.'

'Thanks for that, Eileen. Any news on Ger? Claire told me.'

'It's not good, Dan. The Gardaí have located his van. In Fermoy. Parked up off the main street.'

'Does he know someone? Does he have family there?'

'No.' Her voice falters.

'And no trace of him?'

'No trace.'

There's a pause.

'Dan?'

'Yes, you wanted to talk to me?'

'Was he in trouble? Financially, I mean?' She gives a little laugh. 'I don't have the passwords to the accounts. You know, he did all that stuff himself. Is the business solvent?'

'It is, Eileen. It's healthy. I can tell you that.'

'So it's not about the money.'

'What are you getting at, Eileen?'

'I found receipts. Bookies' receipts. But lots of guys have a flutter, don't they?'

'Well, I suppose so. No harm having the odd bet.'

'If he had a problem, you'd know, wouldn't you, Dan? He liked you a lot, you know. Often said that to me. That you were a sound guy.'

'You know, Eileen, let's wait and see what happens. I'm sure there's a good explanation for his disappearance. I mean, did he say anything to you before he left? Anything strange or odd? Looking back, I mean?'

'Nothing. He was just himself. Christ, Dan, if he was in trouble, he'd have told me, wouldn't he?'

'I'm sure he would, Eileen.'

She rings off, and I stare at the family photo on my desk. Disneyland, Paris, about seven years ago. Andi in a pink Minnie Mouse T-shirt, shading her eyes from the sun. Sweet and happy. Now she's in some kip in Dagenham planning to move in with loverboy Steve. At sixteen! I could strangle him. And Ger Mac is still missing. And I failed him. I didn't follow the protocols. That's bad enough. But I failed him as a friend, as a person. As a human being. Have I failed Andi too? As her father, I should be protecting her, not driving her away.

The buzz from the Scotch is wearing off. My head hurts. I swallow a couple of paracetamol and look out the window onto the busy street below. I never saw myself as inferior, but now, today, I can see the flaws, the threads of failure woven through my life to date. I'm not being honest with Sally. Andi hates my guts. Lavinia thinks I'm wonderful, but then she doesn't know me five minutes. I'm lying to Eileen. And Ger, I know I let him down.

Later, I gather up my keys and walk through the bank, past silent offices. Only the porter is left, sweeping the floor, emptying the wastebaskets. 'You're off. Have a good weekend, Dan.' He raises his hand absently as I salute.

I decide I'll head home and sleep for an hour before I take over from Sally at the hospital. My mobile rings as I'm in the car park. It's Lavinia. My heart leaps as I hit the green button.

'Hello, Dan.' The voice is breathy and soft.

'Hi, darling.' *Darling*. What am I saying? Jesus. Let's face it, I hardly know her. *Darling*. What must she be thinking?

'I just wanted to check in,' she says, 'see how you are.'

'All good. Thank God it's Friday and all that. And you?' *Keep it light, Dan.*

'I'm in Dublin next week, Dan. I got a callback. Be lovely to meet up again. Is it too soon?'

'I'd love to, Lavinia,' I say, 'there's nothing I'd look forward to more. But . . .'

'You're busy. I see. You don't have to do this, Dan.'

'It's complicated,' I say.

'Yes, I know. I understand. Of course. And it's short notice.'

So sweet and polite. She's disappointed, though.

'Lavinia?' She's still there. 'Listen, I'll work out something. Leave it with me, and I'll call you.'

'Will you? I look forward to that.'

'Me too.'

'Goodbye, then, Dan.'

'Goodbye, Lavinia.'

She lingers next to me in the car on the drive home. I can smell her perfume, feel the touch of her delicate hand on mine. I can see the gold necklace at her throat and the way she'd constantly pull at her yellow dress, smoothing it over her knees, as we sat at the bar in the Gibson. And I can see her clearly in my mind's eye as she came towards me – the wide smile and her short blonde hair, cut like a boy's.

When I saw her, I loved her instantly.

CHAPTER 23

DOLL

I wish our trip was done. It feels wrong, heading off to sneak through Mr Cage's personal things, but if he's involved in the deaths at the Academy, we need to check him out.

After tea, we slip on our rain jackets as it starts to drizzle. Insects hover in the sticky air, and there's a mist blanketing down over the lake. Alastair Cage's cottage lies at the far side of the Long Valley. Tiger said the main path was a much shorter route, but then we'd risk being spotted. Instead, we could cut through the forest. 'It'll take twice as long, but we'll have less chance of being seen,' she said. *And we can't afford to be seen.*

Now she looks up at the sky, which is now a thick quilt of grey. 'At least we'll stay dry under the trees.'

She's right. The leaves are a giant roof above us and the ground is dry, crisp twigs snapping under our shoes. In here, there's a green, perfumed hush. The whispers of the breeze through the trees, and the scent of wildflowers are like fairy prayers urging us to walk, walk in the light. Birds call out to each other, swapping stories.

'It's like an otherworld in here,' I say. 'A magical place.'

'Well, it belongs to the druidesses, and they are all about the otherworld. You know, mystical beings, communing with the afterlife and all that stuff.'

'Cool.' I remember what Nell said about them, how clever they are.

'They've been around for thousands of years, you know,' Tiger says. 'They were spiritual leaders way back in our ancestors' time.' She lowers her voice. 'They could cast spells, foretell the future. They were healers and plant experts. They even practiced human sacrifice.'

Tiger grins when she sees my face.

'They believed the sacrifice of the innocents would attract the admiration of the Gods. But don't panic' – she laughs – 'that was thousands of years ago.'

Nell didn't mention that shivery little detail. Isn't that called fake news?

'I'll show you,' Tiger says, grabbing my hand and leading me off the path towards a clearing in the wood. 'Look.'

She points to a circle of trees, where five altars stand side by side on a thick bed of shells. Tied bundles of twigs have been placed on top.

'People were sacrificed here.' Tiger points to the altars. 'A chieftain might be burnt here to please the Gods or enlist their help in battle.' She leans against a tree and folds her arms. 'Or they'd behead their enemies or cage them and set fire to the lot.' She shakes her head. 'A gruesome bunch.'

'Why are the altars made of shells?'

Tiger smiles. 'Shells? They're not shells; they're smashed bits of human bone.'

'From thousands of years ago, I hope?' I back away.

'Ha, you're scared, Doll.'

'Who puts the twigs on top?'

'Who do you think? The druidesses, of course. That's mistletoe. They still honour the ancestors.'

There is a rustle behind us. My heart freezes when I catch a blur of blue. Dagda emerges from behind an altar. She's shaking her head slowly. Tiger has started to walk ahead.

I call out to her, and she spins around. 'Doll? What?'

Underneath my feet, the moss feels like glue. Dagda stays watching me.

Tiger looks over her shoulder. 'Doll, what is wrong with you?'

'Look.'

She stops for a moment. 'There's nothing there.'

Dagda has melted into the green.

'There's nothing there. You imagined it.'

'I saw the druidess I met yesterday at the temple. Remember?'

'There is no one there. Trust me, Doll.'

'But there was, I swear it.'

'So what if she was? Look, you said yourself she was confused. She's not going to report us. If she's out here wandering around, it's nothing to do with us.'

All of a sudden, Tiger breaks into a run. 'Come on, race you to the Long Valley.'

I run, fixing my eyes on the purple rain jacket and the glossy head, trying to keep up, not wanting to lose sight of her. I keep looking behind, expecting to find Dagda following me – or flying over my head and swooping down to block my path.

Tiger has disappeared from view. 'Tiger! Wait up!' I stop to get my bearings, my breathing heavy. And then I hear it. Someone is whispering my name, over and over. To my left, I see a blue cloak half-hidden behind an oak tree. The forest is silent now, waiting, holding its breath. My legs are marshmallow. I open my mouth, but no sound comes out.

The cloak approaches, a hand outstretched. The fingers are weathered, the knuckles slightly misshapen. There's a silver ring on the middle finger, and I know the engraving inside that ring. I know, because it belongs to my granny.

She pushes back her hood, and I can see the fear in her eyes as she grasps my hand.

'I'm not meant to be anywhere near the Academy.' She sighs. 'But I had to let you know, Doll, my beautiful, brave little Doll; you need to know I'm doing my best for you.'

I reach towards her, feel her warm hand in mine.

'I won't let them . . . Dagda told me . . .' Granny stops and looks up.

There's a screeching sound from above. A brightly coloured bird is flapping its wings above the trees. As we both stare, I realise it's not a bird. It's the Headscarves. Skinny arms stretch down, lifting my granny up and carrying her away through the trees, spinning towards the western sky. She's shouting something at me, but the words get tangled in the branches and I can't hear what she's saying. But it doesn't matter. All that matters is that my granny came to me. She broke the rules to let me know she's watching over me. No harm can come to me now. I feel safe.

I race off after Tiger, buzzing with energy again, and I'm elated when I spot her waiting for me on the hillside leading to the cottage.

'You took your time, Doll,' she says, giving me a gentle dig.

'Let's avoid the forest on the way home,' I say, and Tiger nods and gives me a thumbs-up.

Three cottages stand side by side on the steep slope facing the forest. Only one is occupied, Tiger says, as most of the tutors opt to stay on the Academy grounds, but the cottages are there if tutors prefer a more peaceful environment.

We scramble up the hillside and make our way along the rough track to the middle cottage where Mr Cage lives. An ancient stone wall surrounds the property. There's a gate with a hinge missing, and we have to jiggle the latch to open it.

'I didn't expect the front door to be locked,' Tiger says, pushing her shoulder against it. 'Not up here.' We scoot round the side and find the back door unlocked.

'I feel like we're robbers,' I whisper as we tiptoe into the gloom.

'We *are* robbers,' Tiger says. 'That's why we're here. Come on.'

Inside the kitchen door, there's a small table heaped with books. In the corner near the fireplace, a violin case stands against the wall next to a guitar. Everywhere there are books of music, sheets of music, music magazines. On another table, there's a keyboard and a page with squiggles and markings. Even the mug on the table has musical notes on it. Can someone so in love with music really be a killer? Is that possible – to feel the spirit of music inside you and at the same time pull the bath plug on someone's life?

'You start in here,' Tiger says. 'I'll check the bedroom.' She waves her hand towards a door off the main room. I look around me. Now, where to begin?

There's a shaving mirror on the windowsill, and I catch sight of my face. My eyes surprise me. There's a light behind them I've never seen before. Their greenness dazzles me. I pick up the mirror for a closer look. Inside my head, I'm whirring, chiming, clicking, connecting the dots. And you can see it in my face. The mask of misery has melted away. I can figure things out now. I can read. I understand things. I'm not dull Doll anymore, I'm a new girl, fizzing to life. Or was I always there, underneath the layers? Waiting for my turn to shine?

I am the girl in the mirror.

'I am the girl in the mirror,' I say, and the girl smiles back at me. The girl with the bright eyes who's lost her scars and looks like she's ready for anything. 'The future belongs to me,' I whisper.

I put the mirror down. Almazova is weaving its magic over me. Almazova found me. She wants me to stay. She's letting me unfold, like a flower. I love it. And I'm not letting go.

'Find anything?' A shout from the bedroom.

I jump out of my daydream and start the search. 'Not yet.'

A small dresser holds only a few pots and plates and a dusty frying pan. I sift through the papers and notebooks, rummaging through drawers and a stack of boxes lying against the wall. But the books and notes have nothing to give, and the boxes are full of harmonicas, whistles, and spoons.

'Come, quick.' An excited whoop from the bedroom.

A suitcase lies open on the floor. Tiger is sifting through photos, letters, cards.

'Lots of cards,' she says, tossing a bundle towards me. 'People thanking him for his expert tuition, his masterful gifts, his patience, his ability to instil . . . blah, blah. Alistair is very popular.'

She waves her hand at the contents of the suitcase strewn around her. 'There are medals and certificates, diplomas and degrees, all proof that our Alistair Albert Cage – that's his full name, apparently – is a musical genius. But' – her eyes shine – 'look at this.'

On her lap, she has a white cloth bag and a stack of letters. She hands me a blue envelope. 'Read the address.'

We both look at each other.

'Read the address, Doll.'

'It says, *Mr B Cage. Wing 4, Sanderhow Penitentiary, Sanderhow, Kolpina Province.* This is Mr B Cage?'

'Alistair Albert Cage. Albert? Bert. Bertie.'

I close a hand over my mouth. 'I can't believe it. So Dr Ashe was right. Where's Kolpina?'

'It's very remote. And Sanderhow is a snowy city you wouldn't visit unless you had a good reason to.' Tiger pulls a sheet from an envelope in her hand. 'Listen to this.' She reads the letter aloud:

My dear Bertie,

I trust you got the parcel of books I sent you last month. What a joy it is to hear you are using your time in prison well. You are to be commended, son. Please do not be disheartened by the appeal. You must never give up. This dreadful business will be resolved and your conviction will be overturned. As if you could kill another human being. The truth will out in the end.

'Maybe he's innocent?'

Tiger rolls her eyes. 'That was his mother, Doll. Mothers will always think their sons are innocent.' She taps the letter. 'I think we have our proof here.' She shoves it into her jacket pocket and puts everything back into the case, sliding it under the bed. 'Come on, it's going to be dark by the time we get back.'

Outside, the drizzle has turned to heavy rain and the path is a mud bath. We lift the gate closed behind us, then slide down the hillside and cross the valley floor.

'Dr Ashe will be pleased when she sees this.' Tiger says, tapping her pocket.

'It could still be a coincidence,' I shout above the din of the rain. 'Even if he was a killer, he may not have anything to do with the deaths at the Academy.' The thing is, I quite like Mr Cage and can't see him as an evil person. I just don't want this to be true.

'Let the police do their investigations,' Tiger says. 'Our work is done.'

We tramp on, the water dripping down our faces and soaking through our jackets. The light is fading fast, and there's a rumble of thunder in the distance.

'Hurry on,' I say to Tiger as she trails behind me. 'You know where we're going, right?'

She doesn't answer.

'I'm lost,' she says at last. Her voice is small, fearful.

'Are you okay?' She doesn't look right. Some of her Tiger-light has dimmed, like some part of her has snapped off and she's only starting to realise it. Maybe she's feeling guilty about what we've done. I know *I* do. '*Are* we lost, Tiger?'

She hesitates for a moment, then quickens her step. 'I know where we are, sorry.' She grins at me, recovering her voice. 'Quick, the light is fading. Follow me up the hillside. We'll avoid the forest, like you said.'

We have to scramble up the muddy slope on all fours. It takes an age to get to the top, the rain bucketing down, stinging our faces. My pearl bracelet has rolled down on my wrist, and I notice it's changed colour again. What do black pearls *mean*?

'Tiger, do you know anything about black pearls?' A wind has whipped up, and I have to shout to be heard. She turns around and stands there in the driving rain, her face now just a shadow in the near darkness. 'Do you mean snake pearls? The ones found in snakes' heads, the ones that change colour?'

'Snake pearls . . . ? Yes, what does it mean when they change colour?'

She comes towards me.

'Danger,' she says. 'Black pearls mean danger.' She reaches out to help me up the last bit of the slope, and then I'm tumbling back down, down, down. The sharp shove of her palm on my chest has sent my breath from my body, and I'm rolling, speed-bumping over mud and rocks that jut out and jab my bones. It hurts. A lot. I scrabble for a handhold, but I'm moving too fast. I can taste blood in my mouth as I spin back down to the valley floor and shudder to a stop.

A flash of darkness. And when I open my mouth to call out, I can see my mother. She's calling to me, and then she sees me and she's running towards me. She folds me into her arms, and I can smell her perfume, the one in the red bottle, musky and clean. 'You're back, Doll,' she says as she cradles me. I can feel the throb of her heartbeat against my cheek. It feels so good, so wonderful to be back home.

CHAPTER 24

ANDI

'I'm not going home tonight, Steve. I can collect my things there tomorrow.'

He doesn't answer. I stare out into the dusk. The bus to Glengarvan feels like a spaceship hurtling through the night. There are only a handful of passengers farther up, and they're lost inside their phones or staring out at the green-grey landscape.

Steve squeezes my hand. 'Shh. Andi. Listen.' Declan O'Rourke is singing 'Galileo' on the bus radio. 'That's our song,' Steve says. I smile and close my eyes. Inside me, I feel a deep glow, like some magic, peach-tinted dust has settled on me. Steve is whisper-echoing the lyrics in my ear, massaging my palm with his thumb. The words are warm stones around my heart.

My thoughts take off, hover beyond the song, back to our shared nights in London. The two of us in that single bed, wound together, gazing out at the glittering lights of the city. Away from small-town Glengarvan, we could both imagine a new world and a future, together forever. It was only a little room with a small window in Dagenham, but compressed into that space was a world of love and dreams and longing. I hate coming back home, back to school uniforms, curfews, sleeping alone, back to the cold tap of reality.

I stroke his hand. 'I want to be with you tonight, Steve.'

'I know, girl. Me too.' He squeezes my hand. 'But you've got to put in an appearance. Let them know you're back. See what they've got to say.'

'Dad has already told me it's you or them, Steve. What else is there to discuss?'

'He didn't mean that, Andi. That's just him being stubborn. Your mom will have something to say about that.'

'I know. I just don't need the aggro right now.' I lean my head against his shoulder.

'I know you don't. But I'll come with you if . . .'

'No. You don't need to be in the firing line. It's not fair on you, Steve. They're the problem, not you.'

'I'm just glad we're back together, Andi. I'm not lying, girl. I'm nothing without you.' He kisses me, full on.

It's just after ten when we arrive at the Glengarvan bus depot. Along Main Street, everyone is spilling in and out of pubs and restaurants, dressed up and perfumed. Saturday night laughter lingers in the air. Short skirts and high heels skitter past.

Steve walks me back to Bluebell Grove. 'Are you sure?'

I put my finger on his lips. 'No, you go. I'll talk to you later at Brandon Terrace.' It's an ache to see him disappear down the avenue.

The Honda in the driveway tells me only Mom is home. Alleluia for that. I let myself in the front door and follow the light and the smell of garlic bread to the kitchen. Mom is sitting at the table reading a magazine. John Spillane is singing about cherry trees on the radio.

She looks up, hurries towards me as I drop my rucksack onto a chair.

'Thank God you're home, Andi.' She hugs me. 'I don't know whether to strangle you or make you a cup of tea.' She doesn't let go for a good minute.

'What were you thinking of?' she says then, stepping back. 'I mean, London? Anything could have happened.'

'I'm really sorry, Mom.' I notice little lines around her eyes I never saw before. 'I don't blame you for being mad at me. I just had to see him, put things right between us.'

She pulls out a chair for me. 'Your father is not happy, Andi. He was concerned about you. About where all this will end up. That's all. And you defied him and ran off without saying a word.' She's trying to hide her annoyance, but you can see it in her face.

'Give me a break, Mom.' I roll my eyes. I knew this would happen. The guilt trip, typical. 'He lied to Steve for starters and then bawls me out of it yesterday morning on the phone.'

She shakes her head and goes to switch on the kettle. 'Let's not go through all that again, Andi. There are faults on both sides.' She smiles weakly. 'Come on, have a cup of tea and a slice of tart.' She points to the plate on the worktop. 'Lucy Meehan dropped it over earlier. Still warm.'

She tosses the tea bags into two china mugs. 'Your dad will be back from the hospital soon. He'll be happy and relieved to see you home, trust me.'

'Will he? Seriously, Mom? Yesterday he told me not to come home unless I'd finished with Steve. And that is *not* happening.' I take off my denim jacket and roll up the sleeves of the pink top Steve bought me yesterday. 'So when did he change his mind?'

She spins around. 'How do you mean? When did he say that?'

He evidently hasn't told her the full story. I sit at the table and milk my tea. 'Yesterday morning, he rang me. Told me – and he was serious – give him up or else don't come home, he said. I think he'd been drinking, Mom, to be honest.'

'Drinking? He was working. You father would never drink during the day. That's absurd.' She takes two plates from the cupboard and cuts two slices of tart. She hands one to me.

'Is it? He's acting a bit weird lately.'

She passes me a fork, and we eat in uneasy silence.

'I'll miss this,' I say, pointing to the plate.

She smiles. 'How do you mean?'

'Mom, I can't stay here. I'm just home to collect my things. Dad meant what he said. And I don't need all this aggro. I'm going to stay with Steve for a while. Just until Dad comes round. *If* he comes round.'

She places her fork quietly on the table. 'You'll do no such thing. That is ridiculous. The very idea.'

'Tell Dad that!'

'I will tell him, Andi. You're going nowhere. Anyway' – she rubs her palms up and down her face – 'I'm sure Steve's grandmother would have something to say about you moving in with her.' She pushes her plate away.

'She's not even there, Mom. She's recuperating in her sister's house in Limerick.'

'All the more reason you can't stay in her house. Have some respect for the woman, Andi.'

'Joanie likes me. She wouldn't mind.'

'You don't know that. Did you consult her? It's her home, and you can't just shack up there with him.'

'*Him* has a name, Mom. I love Steve. Get over it.'

Her eyes flash. 'You love him? You don't know the meaning of the word. You have no idea.'

I knew this would happen. There's a lecture coming on now, and I couldn't be arsed listening to it.

'I know you're in love with him, but that's not the same thing. One day, Andi, you'll learn that, and you'll move on.'

'Mom, I'm not listening to this.' I head for my room and gather my stuff into a wheelie bag. She follows me up the stairs.

'Please, Andi, don't do this. I'll speak to your father. I'll ring him now. Please see sense.'

'If Dad says I can come back, I will. How's that, Mom? But tonight I'm staying with Steve, whether you like it or not.'

She follows me down the stairs now, agitated and cross. 'You're so self-centred. It's all about you. But what about your family? What about your sister lying in a hospital bed? Don't you care?' She's shouting now.

'You're such a drama queen, Mom. You said Doll was going to be fine, so don't bring her into this.'

'We don't know that for sure. Can't you see how horrendous it is for all of us? Your father is out of his mind with worry.'

I get my jacket from the kitchen, and she follows me.

'And you swan off to London in the middle of it all – you are so immature. Maybe it's time you took a good look at yourself in the mirror.'

I've never seen her this mad before. 'Don't put all this on me. Dad started it.'

I wind a scarf around my neck and wheel my bag to the front door.

She stands there, tapping her foot, arms folded. 'So you're going, after all I said?'

I move to hug her goodbye, but she steps back.

'Yes, I am. I'm sorry, Mom. We all need a bit of space.'

'Your father will be devastated, you know that.'

I open the front door, and the chill night air hits me. 'He'll get over it.'

She purses her lips and sighs. A cloud passes across her face. 'There's no more to say, is there?'

'No, Mom.' I half want to change my mind, to unwind the conversation and go in a different direction. But it's too late for that. The 'immature' accusation stings me, and so does knowing that underneath, they both feel the same about Steve. *He's not good enough.* That destroys me. They never gave him a chance, just pretended to. How can I ever live here as long as they feel like that?

Her phone rings as I'm buttoning up my jacket. She mouths *the hospital* to me and jabs the screen, her hand trembling.

I watch her face, stricken. She's saying, 'Doll? Oh, thank God. I got a fright when . . . oh, I see.'

Alarm sweeps across her voice. She's nodding. 'Yes. Yes, I'm his wife.' She's concentrating, making sure to catch every word.

'What, sorry? When?' She's confused. 'I don't understand. No. I mean, yes.' She looks up at me, gestures for me to wait. I shift from one foot to the other, not sure what's happening.

'Are you sure?' she's saying. 'You're sure. Jesus. Yes. Yes. I'll be there. Oh God.' She hangs up. Holds the phone to her mouth like she's afraid of what will come out. A scream? A swear word? She sways in the doorway.

'Mom, what is *wrong*?' I hold her and she feels weightless, fragile in my arms, a light wispy thing. Not my mother.

'I need my car keys, Andi.' She only whispers it. I usher her into the warmth of the kitchen, rub her white fingers between mine. 'Mom, what's happened? Say it.'

She looks at me like she's just discovered me there. I'm frightened. She begins to wail quietly as she lowers herself into a chair. 'Andi, love,' she says, gathering herself, steadying her voice. 'Andi, it's your dad. They think he may have had a stroke. A stroke, that's what they said.'

There's a thick feeling inside me, like my blood has turned to honey and is now loitering in my veins. Slow and sticky and sucking the energy out of me. When I talk, my words feel thick too, like glue in my mouth. 'A stroke?'

This happens, doesn't it, to other people? Obese people. Strangers. Old people. People in the news, people on cocaine. People who have a family history. Yeah? It doesn't happen to good dads who go to the gym and run and who are still young. Does it?

My mom is putting on her red quilted jacket. She's fixing a scarf around her neck. She's saying, 'Phone, keys, money, a bag. I'll bring some things. What else does he need?'

We pack a bag between us. 'Are you okay to drive, Mom?'

She's recovered herself. Takes a few deep breaths. 'All good to go.' Her hand shakes, though, as she puts her key into the ignition.

We speed away into the night, both of us caught in a head-spin. Both of us thinking Dan thoughts. Will he make it? Will life ever be the same again? Thinking, *Jesus Christ Almighty, don't let him die. Mind him, God. Please. Don't screw this family. Give us a chance. One chance. Please.*

The moon, like a giant host, follows us all the way to the hospital car park. Simple stars look down on us, the only ones to witness the click-lock sound of the car shutting down as we hurry away, down the steps towards the yellow hospital entrance.

I always saw my mother as strong, capable, a fixer, a solver of problems. The mom who could kiss things better, talk things better, wave her wand and make things better. The go-to when you were in trouble. Tonight the wand is gone. It's as if she's suddenly morphed into a Barbie doll. A tiny thing with a fixed plastic smile. She needs *me* now. A piece of her heart has broken off, and I need to be there to catch it. And I will.

'You okay, Andi?' She smiles thinly, squeezing my hand. 'I'm so glad you're here. Such a comfort, darling.'

I squeeze her hand back. It's better than words. But I couldn't answer anyway. There's a horrible, choking drip-drip sensation in my throat, and I know it's the lozenge of guilt and regret wedged firmly at the back of my mouth, out of reach. No matter how much I swallow, I can't shift it.

CHAPTER 25

DOLL

She's gone. My mother disappeared. One minute I was warm and safe, and then – *poof* – I was alone. A moon weaves across the sky. A damp breeze scrapes across my face, and when I turn my head, there's a stink of rotting clay. When I pull the skin of leaves off my face, an ant darts out from underneath and marches across my fingers. Places to go, things to do. Rain-light makes the leaves glitter, and in the distance, up beyond my quilt of giant ferns, I can hear the drowsy dripping oaks. I drift off to sleep.

When I open my eyes again, I try to sit up, but my bones won't allow it. I'm fastened down in my green nest. The sky above me is a roof of hissing grey, the sun just a sliver of orange on the far horizon.

My head hurts, but it's my heart that's in pieces. I thought I had a friend, but it didn't go deep. Why would I want to stay here in this cold world, where even your best friend is happy to kill you and walk away? Is she whistling now? What evil is inside her? When I close my eyes, I think I can hear voices calling – *Doll, Doll* – but they fade away into the air.

Do I matter at all? Will I be just another peculiar child who hurled herself off a hillside? Back home, in the hospital, are my switches being turned off, one by one? Are the doctors shaking their heads as they're unplugging me? Are they saying to my family, *It's for the best; she was too far gone?*

Maybe I am too far gone. Too smart, pretending I could be somebody. An Academy girl with a future. Who was I kidding, thinking I had a silk-life mapped out for myself?

Tears feel warm on my face, but I'm frozen. I try to turn my head, but it won't budge. There's dried blood on my fingers.

My first life wasn't enough for me, was it? Then I tasted Almazova, and I got greedy. I was willing to walk away – run away – from my old life; I wasn't even planning to look back. See where that got me!

I watch as the ant reappears with some friends, and each one waits his turn to take a crumb of dry blood from my hand and carry it off. One after another they march away, like soldiers. How clever they are.

I close my eyes. I shouldn't have dreamed; I should have made the best of what I had, like Nell said. But no, I wanted more, and I was happy to betray her and Nan-Nan. And somehow, for planning to break the rules, I'm going to be punished. Even my mom has deserted me. I wail.

The ants are back again, and now a worm appears, wriggling away from my fingers. So much life down here in this drowning world. The light is thickening into a melon-yellow glow. A newborn day. It makes me sad. I was part of all this, and now, soon, I'll be on my way, slipping off into the frozen dark. A huge pink emptiness stretches out inside me.

And then I hear it behind me – a hissing sound, and it's not the rain. A thin tongue appears, touches my face. I scream. A snake slithers over my chest. I can feel its body steamrolling past my shoulder, its skin warm and musky.

I close my eyes and scream a prayer in my head: *Blessed is the foot of Diamond Jesus.* Will it sting me dead? Would a snake squeeze the life out of you, or would it bite you? Or would it pick your eyes out?

After a minute, I open my eyes. The snake is still, resting its head on my pearl bracelet. Even if I could, I dare not move.

I close my eyes, and after a while I hear my mother's voice again. She's singing about red roses and blue violets and sugar being sweet. She lifts me up and wraps a blanket around me. I can smell warm bread. 'Poor child,' she says, 'poor child.' I can hear her breathing hard as she carries me away unsteadily, and she's saying, 'You're safe now, you're safe.' I try to say, *Sorry, Mom*, but nothing comes out, and I'm glad I'm not vanishing into the dark after all. I'm glad I'm going somewhere – because anywhere is better than nowhere. And I don't want to be a Headscarf, not yet anyway. I see now that any life is better than no life. And I realise that, whatever happens, I don't want to miss the melon sky and every precious thing that's happening under it.

CHAPTER 26

SALLY

'All I can tell you,' the nurse with the plump face says, 'is that he was talking to me in the corridor outside ICU at around ten past ten. And right in midsentence he just stopped all of a sudden and brought his hand to his head, like this—' She presses her temple. 'Then he turned very pale. I knew something was wrong; he wasn't making sense. I knew the signs. And then he collapsed. Right there in front of me.' She nods sombrely. 'That's what happened.'

Andi holds her hand to her mouth and clutches the sleeve of my jacket. 'Oh my God, poor Dad.'

'I'm sorry,' the kind nurse says, looking from Andi to me. 'I know how upsetting this is to hear.' She touches Andi's arm. 'Well, we got him straight down to A and E – thankfully, he was in the right place. I know they're assessing him now and doing all the tests as we speak.'

'Are there any results back yet?' I say. 'Do they know it's a stroke? I'm out of my mind with worry. Did he regain consciousness?'

'It *may* be a stroke. We don't know for sure. He's still undergoing tests, Mrs Redmond, so we'll have to wait for the final prognosis. Dr Forde and the A and E team are excellent. He's in the best of hands down there.' She looks at her watch. 'I know all the bloods are taken at this stage, and he's had an ECG. They've taken him for a CT scan now, so Dr Forde will have news for you shortly.'

'And he's able to talk? I mean, can he walk? Is he . . . ?'

'He regained consciousness very quickly, Mrs Redmond. Even before the gurney arrived. That is positive, I can tell you that.'

She points to the sign for the hospital canteen. 'That's all we know for now. Why don't you go and have a cup of coffee and come back here in a half an hour? Dr Forde will have all the results by then. And we have your number.' She smiles and touches my elbow. 'Don't worry. I know it's hard, waiting, but it's quiet tonight, so there will be no delays, I promise you that.' Her voice is soothing, compassionate. It helps. I can almost believe things might not be so bad.

'Will we drop in to Doll, Mom?' Andi asks, and we climb the stairs to the ICU and sit by her bedside. A nurse hovers like a ghost. She checks the fluids and adjusts one of the monitors, casting her eyes over the sleeping form as she passes. She smiles at us before gliding off, her soft white shoes making a squeaking noise on the polished tiles.

I hate this place, this alien moonlike place. I hate the hushed suffering, the blood bags and the tubes and the cables and the drips attached to paper-thin arms. Life, withheld. And all the while in the background, the orchestra of whirring and beeping and mechanical puffing and wheezing. It unnerves me. Sometimes I avert my eyes as I pass them by, those pale and wordless bodies. Like frail birds. And I hum to myself to block out the soft drone of pumps and ventilators. *Even as they're keeping my child alive.* I should be grateful. Robot angels are watching over her. I *am* grateful.

Sometimes, in here, when I close my eyes, I hear a sigh. It startles me. And I can't tell if it's a weary patient or some hissing instrument, exhaling.

We still in silence, me and Andi. Doll is in a state of *profound unconsciousness*. I looked it up. A *temporary hibernation. A state of rest.* It sounds so peaceful – a pleasant interlude between the fall and life-after-the-fall. I watch her tiny body, pinned down like Gulliver, the bandage around her head like a hairband. Life, interrupted. The monitors shine down on her with their waves and graphs and numbers, calculating, measuring, calibrating. Is she dreaming? I wonder. Is she singing and happy in some deep unreachable world beyond ours? Is she with mermaids now, or sitting having tea with a chorus of elves?

Andi's phone pings, and I jump. I know it's probably Steve. 'Go outside and talk to him,' I say. 'He'll want to hear from you.' I push her gently. 'Go on, love. I'm fine here for a while.'

She squeezes my arm and gets up to leave. 'I'll be back in ten,' she says. She kisses my forehead. I love that girl.

I shuffle my thoughts like a pack of cards. Hearts are trumps. I need to explore Dan territory. I need to face my terror. There are sheets of water behind my eyes, ready to bucket down. I'm afraid if I tilt, even a little, I'll spill across the floor. My eyelids are burning, *but hold fast*, I tell myself. *Hold fast. Be strong. Dan will be well. All will be well.* But it's not looking good, is it? Jumbled speech, collapsing down like a straw-man. There's a rat gnawing inside me. I can hear the squeaking. *Go away*, I say. *All will be well.* But he scurries back, his claws scratching against the walls of my heart. Disgusting creature.

A nurse passes, and I rearrange my face. She smiles at me and I smile back. All is well, all is good.

But the thoughts rise up like a sea of bile. *What if?* What if Dan dies? What if a stroke alters his life forever? What if I never see the old Dan again? No, it's not hysterical. No, it's not beyond possibility. I must face the possible. And the rats, they scurry up and over my bones. There are so many of them, I can't count.

I need to tell him . . . things. Because, you know, when someone is gone, they're gone. And all the things you think might matter, the petty things, the small hurts – well, they don't. When a person's gone, they can't hear you anymore. You can never make them understand how you're feeling, how you love them, how they light up your life, how they're actually quite funny and very, very kind. You know you need to tell the person this while they can still hear it. That they make the world a shinier place. And that if they were gone, there would be a gaping hole in your life and it would take an awful lot to fill it. Actually, stop! You couldn't fill it – there would always be angles and gaps and hollows and . . . and . . . well, the very idea, that would be unthinkable, actually.

My hands are trembling. I hope the nurse doesn't notice. She's giving me funny looks. Thinking, maybe, *This mother can't cope, poor woman.*

Mind your own business!

And anyway, I need to get back to my card thoughts. I need to follow the thread, to soothe myself.

Like, if someone were to die. Just, say, anyone. Not just Dan. Anyone who's loved. You'd want them to *know* that they were loved. That they were regarded. That they mattered. And you'd have to tell them this – that if they went, they'd be leaving something special behind, some silvery cloth that shone and caught the sun and reflected it back on the people they loved.

And we don't say these things. These precious, lovely things. We don't say them, and then, one day, we discover a breath-less body and we wail and weep and rant against the God who snatched them away before we got to tell them . . .

So we shouldn't let our chance to say these things slide by. One day, we all run out of road. Everyone needs to hear they're loved. Everyone needs their heart warmed. And, in bleak and lonely times, those words of love could be shaken out, like tinfoil, and they'd catch the light, and maybe even save them.

So I need to say it. I need to tell Dan. If I can. Because he has a right to know that he did measure up and that he was . . . *is* wonderful. I'm going to tell him: *You light our lives. You are a trooper.* And that there's a Dan-space in our hearts that could never be replaced. He needs to know that. And that I love him, no matter what.

I shift in my seat. A poison-thought rises up. *Lavinia.* Sitting in the bar of the Gibson Hotel. But the more I think of her now, the more I realise that my imagination has been running away with me. She exists, sure. But she's a friend, some casual acquaintance or someone who, God love us, might have a crush on my husband. My heart relaxes around Lavinia. I will relegate her to the dustbin and concentrate on us. And I know what I need to do now – if, please God, I have the chance. I'll tell Dan I love him. And Doll will come out of her induced coma next week. Like they said. It's not me. *They* actually said it. They were quite clear. Soon, everything will be just fine. I know it will.

Andi is back. We meet the kind nurse at the bottom of the stairs, and she steers us towards a small, dark-haired woman in her fifties. 'Dr Forde, this is Mr Redmond's wife and daughter.'

We exchange brief smiles and hellos. There are goosebumps on the back of my arms, and I arrange my face so she doesn't guess the chaos in my head. Doesn't see that, any second, I could keel over.

Dr Forde wastes no time. 'Your husband has had a TIA – that's short for transient ischemic attack, a brief interruption of blood flow to the brain.'

I swallow. I need to get this right in my head. 'I see. Is that the same as a ministroke?'

'The symptoms are stroke-like, but there is no damage to brain cells and no permanent disability. His tests are clear, no blood clots, no heart issues, reflexes are normal, but we need to find the cause. He's still a young man.'

Is it too early to punch the air? I love that word – *normal* – it sings to me. 'And have you?' I hold my breath. Her body language is cheery. A positive signal.

'Yes, we've found the culprit.' She checks the file in her hand. 'Hypertension. Your husband's blood pressure was extremely high. A common complaint, I'm afraid. It can be a silent killer if it's left untreated. This was a warning, and he may need medication to bring it under control.'

I release a long breath. 'I'm so relieved. He's going to be fine.'

'We're going to keep him in overnight, just to keep an eye on him, but, yes, his health is good overall. Does he have much stress in his life? Any kind of stress can exacerbate this condition.'

'Well, I'll make sure that's minimised,' I say, as Andi bites her lip. 'He doesn't talk much about it, to be honest.'

'That's not unusual in men. We see it all the time, and it's not good,' Dr Forde says, her brow furrowing. She shakes her head. 'Well, see that he takes it easy for the next few days. We'll recommend he uses a twenty-four-hour BP monitor to assess his blood pressure patterns, and his GP will follow up with meds if required. You can see him now.' She smiles. 'He's in room twenty-one at the end of that corridor, last door on your left.' She points over her shoulder.

Andi wraps her arms around me and cries. I hold her, stroke the back of her head like a baby, tears pooling in my eyes. Some moments are beyond happiness. Some moments are beyond the scope of words. How could words be enough? They're only letters stitched together, lines and circles, too primitive to capture the joy of this. Dan is well. Therefore, all is well. It's a mathematical principle. A new theorem.

'You go in first,' Andi says outside room twenty-one. 'Go on, I'll give you a few soppy minutes on your own.'

I see him before he sees me. He's hooked up to an IV, and a blue screen counts the beats and waves of his heart. He is staring straight ahead, his face pale, almost childlike, in the dim light. There's a smell of disinfectant.

'You'll do just about anything to get attention!' I say. He turns towards me and laughs thinly and reaches for my hand. I lean in and hold his face between my palms. 'Don't ever do that to me again, Dan.'

He smiles. 'I thought I was a goner, to be honest, Sal.' His face clouds over.

'Well, you're not. You're going to be fine.' I sit at the edge of his bed, take his hand in mine. His grip is weak and he looks shrunken, just a little too small for his skin. So what if I let the damn tears escape. Sue me. Those drops of relief won't stop anyway, and as they fall, quietly – I don't want to upset him – I feel myself retilting, steadying, soothed. And then I tell him. The words fall out, spill out onto the covers. They leap through me and find a home. And he kisses me. And he keeps holding me. Saying, 'Sally, Sally.' And we stay like that. And I sense something has shifted. Some icy shard inside me has melted, and I know, tonight, I will sleep.

'Ahem, can I come in?' Andi approaches the bed. I step back as she leans in to kiss her father.

'Dad, I'm so sorry.'

'How's Steve?' Dan asks. 'I'm sure he knows more about what happened tonight than I do.'

But he's smiling when he says it.

'We'll talk about Steve another day.' I say, not wanting to break the comfort bubble around us.

Dan says, 'We'll work it out, Andi, don't worry. We'll work it out. Everything will be worked out, you'll see.' He closes his eyes. It's twelve thirty a.m.

Me and Andi, we pull up two chairs and sit by his bedside. We hold hands, watch him drift to sleep. I feel light, like gossamer. I memorise the theorem. Dan is well. Therefore, all is well. Even the rats have gone home.

CHAPTER 27

DOLL

The stone walls seem to shrink in around me, and the glass of water next to the bed spins as I reach for it. I try to focus. A finger of light squeezes through a narrow slit of window. Am I in prison? Am I dead, in a waiting room for God? I drift off.

The door opens and a girl appears and sets a steaming bowl on the bedside table. She's not much older than Andi.

'Hello. You're awake. How're you feeling?' She lifts the glass of water and holds it to my lips. My throat is dusty and the liquid rinses it clean.

'My head hurts.'

She smiles and gently taps my forehead. 'You've had a fall. A few cuts and scrapes and bruises. You're probably still stiff and sore. You're safe now, in Mistletoe Castle. Lord Carbery found you early this morning.' She adds, 'I'm Tessa. You're from the Academy?'

'Yes. My name is Doll. They'll be looking for me.'

'No, they won't. Lord Carbery has already sent word to Mother Bodica that you're safe and well. You'll probably be okay by tomorrow. Today, you'll need to take it easy.'

'Lord Carbery?'

'He owns the castle.' She fixes the covers around me. 'We're high up, overlooking the Long Valley. Beautiful views.' She passes me the bowl and a spoon. 'Here's some chicken soup.' She fixes the pillows behind me so I can sit up. 'Take it slowly. You've had hypothermia, so you'll need warmth and rest.' She pats my head. 'Tomorrow you'll be stronger.'

She turns away towards the door. 'The bathroom's through there.' She points to a carved wooden door behind her. 'I've left a tracksuit for you; your own clothes should be dry soon.'

I smile my thanks and eat my soup. I'm so glad I'm not dead. Or in prison. I'm still here in Almazova and that feels good, as long as I can scrape Tiger off my mind. It's hard, though. Hard to forget her eyes, like glass, as she sent me tumbling down the hillside.

After a while, I push the covers back and feel dizzy for a minute before I steady myself and tiptoe through to the bathroom. Soon, the warm bathwater is soothing my aches and bruises. In the mirror, I run my finger over the cuts and scratches on my face and hands. I have bruises all over and the wound along my leg stings, but, hey, I'm alive. And I'm grateful. But how can I go back now? Who can I trust? Next time I may not be so lucky. It's not a game anymore. Now I'm really afraid.

I pull on the tracksuit, which is three sizes too big, and tie up my wet hair with a piece of string I find in the bathroom closet. There's an old pair of slippers, snug and warm. I feel I've been spinning through a washing machine, sparkling clean but battered.

Tessa comes in as I've just finished dressing.

'Oh, good. You're up. I'll bring you down to meet His Lordship if you feel up to it. He's just finished choir practice.'

'He's got a choir here at the castle?'

'Yes, a choir of birds. They join him in the great hall every afternoon. And the harmonies . . .' She places her palm on her heart and rolls her eyes. 'He's blessed with a wonderful voice, and he's taught them so many of his songs.' I'm back to being speechless again. *A choir of birds?*

The chandeliers glitter in the sunlight as I follow Tessa along a panelled corridor and down the pink-carpeted staircase.

'He's a good man and so worried about you,' Tessa is saying. 'He feels Alexander may have traumatised you.'

'Alexander?'

'Lord Carbery's python.' She laughs. 'Another of his friends. He keeps picking up new friends, but Alexander never leaves his side. They have, I don't know what it is . . . a connection. That's how it looks to me, anyway.'

'I remember the snake.' I shudder. 'I thought I was a goner, to be honest.'

She smiles as she leads me down another corridor and gestures ahead. 'This is the library, and don't worry. Alexander is harmless. Don't forget, he found you and stayed with you. You can thank him for your life, Doll.'

Tessa knocks at the library door and opens it gently. 'The child is here,' she says. Beyond her small frame, I can see a lamplit wall of books. There's a rug hanging over the fireplace with pictures of birds and tigers and snakes.

A voice from a fireside chair says, 'Come in.'

I step into the room. On a low table by the fire, a pair of green velvet gloves sit next to a top hat in the same colour. Tessa nudges me forward, and there, sitting in the glow of the fire, is the most peculiar man I've ever seen.

'Well, well, well,' he says, gesturing for me to sit opposite him. I sit and watch him quietly from under my eyelashes. A white lace frill covers his throat and his jacket is blue velvet, catching the light when he moves. Coiled around his crimson trousers and polished boots, Alexander appears to be asleep, resting his head against the old man's knee.

'I'm delighted to see you, Doll. To see you up and about – that is a wonderful thing to see.' He smoothens a bushy eyebrow. 'It *is* Doll, isn't it?'

'Yes.'

'I've sent word. They're so relieved you're safe. So relieved. They were frantic. Absolutely frantic. You're a lucky girl.'

He sits back, watching me. I'm grateful the snake doesn't move. Lord Carbery follows my eyes.

'Harmless, absolutely harmless, child. He saved your life, remember. I wouldn't have found you without Alexander. His whistling led me to you. He was attracted by your snake pearls. They glowed so brightly, and Alexander was attracted to the light.'

'Really? Why are they called snake pearls?'

He points to my bracelet. 'Snake pearls are formed inside the head of a snake. They are very rare and are said to possess supernatural properties. My father was given one when he was travelling up north by a local shaman many years ago. I was only a boy at the time, but the story captivated me.'

'Really? What else did the shaman say?'

'He told my father that snake pearls could ward off evil spirits and would warn the wearer of danger. They could even emit sounds the human ear could not hear. Those sounds were probably picked up by Alexander too. '

'So you think my bracelet saved me?'

'Without a shadow of a doubt, Doll. Without a shadow of a doubt. My father said his snake pearl saved his life many times. I do believe they are magical gems, indeed I do.'

'But without you and Alexander, I would not be here, so thank you, Lord Carbery. And thank you, Alexander,' I say.

He rings a bell, and Tessa reappears. 'Tea for the young lady, please, Tessa. And biscuits. Chocolate wafers.' He winks at me. And then, as the door closes, his face changes, his brows knitting together like tangled wool.

'The birds speak of destruction. Do you know anything about that?'

What is he talking about? Is he mad?

'No,' I say.

'No, indeed. You're only a child. Still . . .' He takes a cane from underneath his chair and leans forward. 'But children, they understand things. They are closer to the natural world and its secrets, yes?'

He doesn't wait for an answer, just shakes his head sadly. 'The birds have tears in their eyes, you know; something is gripping them of late. Have you noticed at all?' He waves a hand about as if he's looking for words, but they've scurried away from him, hiding in the shadows. A huge diamond glitters on his middle finger.

'Even the flowers, they're casting off their petals much too soon. Are they protesting, giving up? What do they know? Can't you smell something rotten in the air? Can't you, child?'

I shake my head.

When he smiles, his mouth is like a bucket.

'Don't mind me, Doll. Too much time spent in the world of nature.' He waves his hand towards the window. 'You know a bear can sniff out food from twenty miles away?' He taps his nose. 'I feel I've acquired a nose – for trouble.'

He leans towards me. 'Here's my theory. Nature has been roused, her natural rhythms interrupted.' He jerks his thumb towards the window. 'The birds, they sense the terrible things approaching. Nature is crying out, screaming out to alert us.' He shakes his head slowly. 'What is happening, child?'

Tessa comes in with a tray, and she pours us peppermint tea.

'Thank you, Tessa,' Lord Carbery says.

I take a biscuit. The chocolate melts on my tongue.

'Delicious. Thank you, Lord Carbery.' I'd better keep listening.

He sips his tea, blowing on it to cool it.

'Speak up, Doll. What have you to tell me? I'm all ears.'

I'm not sure how much to say. He knows Mother Bodica. I'll have to be careful.

He plucks a polka-dot handkerchief from his pocket and runs it along his forehead.

'Unwrap your secrets, Doll.'

There's a silence in the room.

'I'm afraid to go back.'

He looks around him and puts his finger to his lips. 'Be not afraid. Speak to me.'

There's a log in the fire, and it collapses, hissing. Alexander raises his head for a moment, then goes back to sleep. The hush returns.

'We sneaked out, my friend and me. We got lost in the dark. And then she pushed me and I fell a long way back down into the valley.'

'She pushed you? Tsk-tsk. Why would she do that?'

'I don't know, but some of the other children—'

He waves a hand about. 'Yes, yes, I know about that. Terrible accidents.'

'They're not accidents, Lord Carbery. Two nights ago my friend Amber nearly drowned herself. Only her music saved her.'

His eyes light up like stars. 'Her music? How's that?'

'The music in her head guided her home, and she danced to it. She's a dancer, heart to toe.'

I don't know why I'm telling him all this. He's like a magnet that you get drawn to, like I *have* to tell him. Maybe he even has some answers.

'And now your friend tried to kill you and left you alone in the valley in the torrential rain. You're not imagining this, are you?' He rubs his beard. 'I mean, child, you had hypothermia, and you also hit your head.'

He sees my cross face. 'Okay, I believe you. Well, well, well. What is going on? What, I do wonder, is going on? There is something not right.'

'Now I'm afraid to go back.' I try to push the tears back inside my lids.

'I can see why, yes, I can see why, right enough.'

'I actually don't want to die.'

'Of course not.' He looks horrified. 'The very thought. You're a child. You must be safe.'

He puts down his cup and gets to his feet, disturbing Alexander, who slides off his legs and settles under his chair. Lord Carbery turns to me, his hands clasped behind his back.

'Where you ended up last night, well, you would not have been found for days. You could've easily died. And you were completely invisible under those giant ferns. Another hour or two in the soaking rain, and poof' – he clicks his fingers – 'you'd be gone off with the angels.'

He leans down to stroke Alexander. 'We take our walk at first light. I love to hear the dawn chorus, and Alexander leads the way. The creative spirit is at its peak in the early morning.'

I drop off my slippers and tuck my legs under me. So, the pearl bracelet is more than just a bracelet. Did my granny talk to Dagda? Could Dagda see the future, and is that why she gave me the snake pearls?

'Wow. You know a lot,' I say.

'I know nothing. I have so much to learn.' He looks around the room. 'All those books?' He shakes his head. 'Only nature can make us wise – *if* we're prepared to stop and listen. The power we have in here . . .' He taps his chest. 'Such power and wisdom in our hearts.'

He grabs his cane, then, and taps it on the floor. 'Come, child, we must bake bread.'

I scramble to my feet, wincing at the pain in my leg. I hurry after him and follow him to the kitchen at the back of the castle. He walks smartly, swinging his cane in circles, and I have to step back in case I get a belt of it. I like Lord Carbery, and I can't believe we're now off to bake together. He is full of surprises; you never know what's coming next.

In the kitchen, I whisk eggs as His Lordship ties on an apron and fires up the oven. He gathers the ingredients and starts to sift flour and seeds and sugar together. He gets me to add the buttermilk from a brown jug, and he hums softly as he turns and flours and kneads the dough, getting me to cut it into triangles. I sprinkle seeds on top, and he swishes the trays into the oven.

'You're an expert baker,' I say as I sit on a high stool, drinking hot chocolate. He washes his hands, replacing his diamond ring carefully and rolling down the sleeves of his frilly shirt. He frowns when he spots a stain on it.

'It's only flour,' I say.

His mouth tightens as he rubs it with a cloth. 'It'll be ruined. My beautiful handmade lace.' He looks at me and shakes his head. 'This is my shame, my terrible flaw. I am so vain. Vanity is a terrible vice, Doll.' He looks upset.

'You just like clothes. You're fussy. There's nothing wrong with that.'

'Yes, but can't you see? Vanity stunts my spiritual growth, Doll. I love fine silks, tweeds, velvets, the purest weaves.' He rolls his eyes. 'It's pride – a shallow attachment to image – and it harnesses me to a lower energy frequency.' He shrugs. 'Why am I telling you? You're a child; you cannot understand vanity.'

'What's wrong with being proud of yourself and how you look?'

'We are not here to be proud, Doll. We must detach and nurture humility if we are to fit through the portal to higher awareness.' He closes his eyes. 'Clothes are image. Image is a projection, nothing more.'

An alarm buzzes. 'Oh, our bread, I'd nearly forgotten.' He lifts the baking trays from the hot oven and sets the crispy brown bread and scones out on a wire rack. He's forgotten about his clothes for now.

'Baking is meditation,' he says, inhaling the delicious aroma. 'Our guest will be pleased.'

'Guest?'

'Yes, Doll. And you shall join us. We are celebrating tonight with fine music and fine food.'

'Is it your birthday, Lord Carbery?'

He taps his cane against the stone floor and laughs. 'No, indeed, no. You didn't know, of course; how could you? The Academy senior choir won the trophy in Vanistra last night. The wonderful Alistair Cage is joining me – us – for dinner this evening.' He claps his hands in delight.

My heart sputters. 'He's coming here?'

He does a little dance with the cane and giggles. 'Yes, he's a regular visitor to the castle. He twirls his cane. 'Evening dress essential!' He places his finger on his chin, and I can see he's planning his outfit for later, lost in clothes thoughts.

'I'll ask Tessa if there's something nice you can wear, Doll. Yellow is your colour, I think.'

I stifle a giggle. Maybe he is addicted to fashion after all. *Yellow is your colour.* Lord Carbery would brighten your heart.

On the way back to my room, I think about Mr Cage. My heart shrinks. What if he knows about me and Tiger being in his house? What if he is the killer? Am I even safe here? I sit in my turret room. I know now what I have to do, and I don't have much time.

CHAPTER 28

Dan

Outside, the trees are dripping wet, their leaves glistening and restless. Sheets of rain pour down, frantic, hammering on the windows and gulleying down the driveway. The water streams out onto the tarmac in waves, tumbling on down past the Mill Road on an urgent mission, or so it seems, to join the Lainey River. Above, the skies are leaden, full of the frenzied rain. In here, in this oasis, the fire is lit, an orange-red glow. The armchair is plumped with downy cushions arranged just so, and I sink into them, grateful for the familiar. I want to cling to the familiar like a boy clings to his favourite teddy. A comfort blanket to grip in the darkness.

She brings in a tray of tea and toast and leaves it on the coffee table beside me.

'Will I turn on a lamp?' she says. 'It's so gloomy outside.' She disappears and returns with the *Sunday Times*. 'Here, I got the paper in Centra.' She tosses another log on the fire. 'How're you feeling, love?'

'Glad to be home, Sal,' I say. Which is true. Last night feels like a bad dream. It rattled me, I have to admit. That sensation of losing control, collapsing, forgetting – it shatters your confidence. It makes you ask, *What else don't I know?* I sip my tea. 'Get some rest, have a nap,' she says, fixing a grey wool rug over the arm of my chair.

'I'm not an invalid, Sal,' I say, smiling, though in truth, that's exactly how I feel. Shaken up. Unnerved. Like the ground beneath me has become, suddenly, unstable. Booby-trapped. I feel old now. More a patient than a man. It's hard to explain it. And I wouldn't admit it to anyone. It feels shameful. Ungrateful, even. I mean, when all is said and done, it was a thing of nothing, a minor blip.

I hear the door closing softly, and I breathe in the silence and the scent of wood smoke and peat. A log crackles, and I watch as it falls sideways, flames leaping on it hungrily, the wood snapping and spitting underneath. I made it, though. I've got the chance now to put things right between Andi and me. And with Sal. I've been pushing that away for too long. And what if I had died last night? There would have been such hurt left behind. Stuff unspoken. Sally does not deserve that. I'd never want to do that to her. She's got a right to know. She needs to hear it from me first, and then she can make up her own mind. It's a risk I have to take.

I open my lids slowly. My mouth feels furred, my head heavy with sleep. The fire is still glowing, red coals keeping watch. Outside, the rained has eased, just the *drip-drip* sound from the eaves. The door opens slowly. A whisper. 'Dad, are you awake?'

'Come on in,' I say, straightening up. She switches on the lamp in the corner and sits near me on a low leather stool, stretching out her legs. The light finds her face troubled, her brows knitted together.

'I just wanted to come and say hello.' She stops for a second, winding a coil of dark hair around her finger. 'And to say I'm sorry, Dad, about the whole London thing. I was out of order.'

'Well, I'm glad you're saying that, Andi. It wasn't your best idea. But maybe me talking to Steve mightn't have been my best idea either.'

She stares into the fire. 'I know you hate him and you think he's—'

'I don't hate him Andi. It's just that—'

'It's just that he's not good enough, Dad? I know what you think, but you're wrong.'

'It's not that. I've nothing against the boy, but, yes, I think you could do better than Steve Thompson. I don't think he's suitable.'

She folds her arms. 'It's the same difference, Dad.'

'Hold on a minute, let me finish, Andi. You don't have to agree with me. Just listen. I worry about you. You're my daughter.' She rests her chin on her fists and looks at the fire again.

'You're smart. And you're beautiful. I worry you'll end up staying in Glengarvan, skipping college, ending up in some dead-end job just so you can be with him. And when you realise what you'll have lost, it'll be too late.'

'That's not going to happen, Dad.'

'Maybe not. But I am concerned. I mean, there are drugs in that family, addiction, and God knows what else. You're better than that, Andi. I want you to have a career, to travel the world, to achieve your goals, have a good life.'

'I know. And that will happen, I swear. I'll study next year, I'll get my points. Steve won't stop me. Don't judge him by his mother. He wants me to go for it.'

'Really, Andi? That's what he says now.'

'You're getting way ahead of me, Dad. That's two years away, in fairness.' She rubs her palms over her face. 'I wish we could get past this.'

'We will. We are past it, okay? I'm not going to stop you seeing him. And I'm going to talk to Steve, tell him I was wrong. We're going to draw a line under this.'

She gets up and sits on the arm of my chair. Her left hand touches mine. 'Dad, you don't have to do that.'

'Andi, there'll be rules. No staying over at his, for starters. You're sixteen, under the legal age of consent.'

She leans over and gives me a hug. 'Thanks, Dad. I won't let you down.'

She gets up to go. 'You know I'm making dinner this evening. I better get cracking before Mom gets back.'

'Andi?'

'Yes, Dad?' She stops in the doorway, looks back at me.

'You look after yourself too. You know what I'm talking about.'

'Dad, please!' Her face colours.

'Look, talk to your mother. I'm just saying. I don't want you coming in here with any news, you know.'

She nods, avoiding my eye.

'What's for dinner, then?'

'Chicken casserole. Very healthy.'

I groan. 'No roast, on a Sunday? That's disgraceful.'

She laughs as Sally arrives in the front door. 'Did you hear that, Mom? He's not happy with the menu!' She winks as Sally drops her car keys on the kitchen table and comes into the room.

'Good news,' she says, shaking off her leather jacket and running her hands through her hair. She stands with her back to the fire. 'They've started to reduce Doll's medication, and tomorrow morning they'll be taking her off the ventilator.' She does a little pirouette on the rug and claps her hands. 'If all goes to plan and she responds well, she could be out of hospital by the end of the week.' She stretches out on the couch, kicking off her shoes.

'That's brilliant,' Andi says. 'Once they take away the ventilator, will she come round straightaway?'

'Not necessarily; it might take a few days,' Sally says. 'But all the vital signs are good.'

'Let's celebrate with Andi's award-winning chicken dish!' I say.

We're just sitting down to dinner when my mobile purrs.

Sally looks up from filling her plate. 'Who's ringing you at this time on a Sunday, Dan?'

Andi jumps up from the table. 'I'll get your phone, Dad.'

'Let it ring out, Andi. They can leave a message.' It wouldn't be Lavinia; I spoke to her only on Friday. God, it seems like a month ago, considering all that's happened since.

Halfway through dinner, the phone rings again. 'Are you going to get that, Dan?' Sally says, sighing, and there's an edge to her voice. I sense her eyes trained on me as I go to grab my mobile from the living room. 'It's Claire, from the office,' I say.

'What on earth does she want?' Sally says impatiently. 'You better take it. It must be important. I hope there wasn't a break-in.'

'Hello, Claire.'

'Sorry for calling you on a Sunday, Dan.'

'Is there something wrong. Has the alarm gone off?'

'No. Nothing like that. I didn't want you hearing it, just in case it's on the news tonight.'

I can feel the earth shudder beneath me. My reptilian brain is telling me there's a mine underfoot and it's about to explode.

'Hearing what, Claire?' Though I know the answer. The tadpole thought is already formed.

'It's Ger Mac,' she says.

My heart curdles. I lower myself into a chair. My legs feel like sticks of chewing gum.

'What about him?' But I know. I'm buying time. My heart is flapping its wings. *Steady on, girl.*

'They've just pulled his body from the Blackwater this afternoon. I'm sorry, Dan. I know you were close to him.'

Close to him. Yep, you could put it like that. We often had a pint together in Whelan's over the years. I really liked the guy. One of the good ones. Worked like a dog for his family. Wore his awful early years lightly. A quiet hero. Life was full of them.

'Dan?'

'Yes, thanks, Claire. You're very good to call. Poor Eileen – and the kids. That is shocking news.'

'You never know,' she says. 'You never know what's going on inside someone's head, do you? It's tragic.'

I put the phone down.

'It's Ger Mac,' I say, over my shoulder. 'His body's been found in the Blackwater today.'

'Oh, no! I know his daughter Emma. She plays basketball for the under-fourteens. That's terrible news,' Andi says. 'I saw the Facebook post on Friday about her dad going missing.'

I slide back the patio door and stand out on the deck. The weak evening sun lights up the wetness of everything. The air is crisp and clear. Sally follows me outside. I can hear the puff sound as the door closes behind her. 'You're very upset.'

'It's my fault. I knew.' My skin is a suit of armour, even my voice is metal.

'That he was suicidal?' She takes my arm, rubs my sleeve ever so gently.

'No, that he was gambling. He was in my office just three weeks ago. He told me he'd lost a lot of money, Sal. A small fortune. He thought he could win it all back.'

'Why does knowing something make it your fault?'

'I should have done something, said something to somebody. But I didn't.'

'There would have been a confidentiality issue there, Dan. You couldn't divulge that to anyone.'

'No, Sal. At the very least I should have flagged it up with the Regional Office. I don't even know why I didn't.'

'And what would they have done, Dan?' Her voice is cross now. 'I'll tell you. Nothing. It would have remained a red pencil mark in some file in Dublin until the business was seriously affected. Until loans went unpaid.'

She's right. 'Still. I knew he had a problem, and now the man is dead. Gone. Husband. Father. Never to be seen again. All avoidable.'

She slips her arms around my waist. 'It wasn't your fault, Dan. It wasn't your responsibility. What could you have done? Suggested counselling? Advised him to get help? What good would that have done? Why would he listen to you? Gambling is an addiction. It's complex.' She hesitates for a minute. 'Did Eileen know, do you think?'

'No. She rang me Friday to ask if he was financially okay. She was looking for a reason for why he might have disappeared. Poor Eileen. I didn't say anything, Sal. I couldn't. And now . . .'

She comes around and cups my face. 'Listen to me: you couldn't have known he would do this. You're not God, Dan.'

I hold her in my arms, grateful for the touch of her skin, her strength. The familiar. I need to hold on to the familiar. She's right. Sort of. But I can't shake off the feeling that I screwed up. A crime of omission. Who knew – if I'd followed it up, if I'd made contact with him, if I'd set up an appointment for him, persuaded him to tell Eileen . . . If I had done something, things might have turned out different. *If, if, if.* All the ifs of our lives, like a barbed-wire fence of regret and guilt and lost opportunities.

'You're not going to work this week, Dan. I'm going to ring them tomorrow. You need to rest and get your blood pressure sorted. You need to mind yourself, for Chrissake.'

I'm thinking I should ring Eileen. I'll need to tell her. Maybe not straightaway, but she'll need to know.

'You're the boss,' I say, kissing her cheek. And she smiles up at me. And I can't imagine living life without this woman . . . though it's a strong possibility that I'll have to.

CHAPTER 29

DOLL

My mind's made up. I have to come clean. When Tessa comes in with my bundle of clothes, I thank her and ask if I can talk to Lord Carbery again.

'I saw him in the garden gathering peas for dinner tonight.' She lays the clothes on the bed and looks out the window on her tippy-toes. 'He's still there. Why don't you go down and join him now?'

I slip on my own shoes. 'Thanks, Tessa. Will he mind?'

'My mother is cooking dinner this evening. Get a bowl from her in the kitchen and fill it with raspberries from the garden.' She winks. 'That'll be your excuse.'

He's surprised to see me. 'Ah, Doll, hello again, my friend.' I see he's swapped his white frills for an orange polo shirt. He nods to the fruit bowl in my hand. 'I see they're making you pay your way.' He laughs. 'Come on, I'll show you the raspberry beds.' I follow his gleaming blue wellies along a gravel path towards the back of the walled garden.

'I need to tell you something. It's important,' I say. He stops, pushing back his straw hat, and takes a seat on the low wall separating the vegetable garden from the fruit beds. He lays his basket of peas aside and gestures for me to sit next to him.

'I'm all ears. You have my complete and singular attention.' He folds his arms and stares down at his boots. 'Off you go, Doll, tell me everything you need to tell.'

So I do – well, almost everything. I leave out the bit about the Child of Summer and me crossing the universe, shamefully willing to leave my family behind forever. Lord Carbery would not approve at all, and in a funny way, though I hardly know him, I'd hate it if he were disappointed in me.

I tell him of Dr Ashe's suspicions about Mr Cage being a convicted murderer and the prison letters we found in his suitcase.

'I mean, two children are dead, so we had to find out, you know.'

I can see his woolly eyebrows knitting together. 'And Amber nearly drowned, and last night my friend Tiger . . . I could be another dead child, you said so yourself.'

He bends down and rubs some imaginary spot of muck off the toe of his boot. After a while he looks at me and says, 'You shouldn't have done that. Doll, Doll, what are you telling me? Breaking in and stealing? Tsk-tsk. You had no right. It was a foolish and criminal thing to do.'

My face burns with shame. 'We had to find out if it was true,' I say. 'And it is. He is a killer, and we have proof.'

He looks at me, but his face is kinder now. 'Not at all, child. Mr Cage is a good and decent man. He is not responsible for these terrible accidents – I mean, terrible deeds – at the Academy.'

'How can you be sure? Aren't you shocked to hear he was in prison?'

'I knew that. He told me all about that business. He was pardoned, Doll. Handsomely compensated by the courts. He never killed anyone.'

'Well, he would say that, wouldn't he?'

'Mother Bodica knows.'

I gasp. 'What?'

'From the very beginning. She knew. He told her. Alistair is an honourable man. He can tell you his story himself. After all, it is his to tell. We all have a story.'

'And Dr Ashe?'

'Evidently, she didn't know. But I'm curious why she confided in two students.'

'I think she told the police about her suspicions, but it went nowhere.'

Lord Carbery takes off his hat and smooths his hair.

'So, Mr Cage is definitely innocent?' I say.

I'm disappointed that all this has been a waste of time and we are no closer to finding out what's wrong at the Academy. Nan-Nan is going to be disappointed. Nell will be cross – so much time wasted, and we are still in the dark.

'Certainly. He's one of the good ones.' Lord Carbery breaks open a pod and crunches on a pea. 'I'm glad you told me the truth, Doll. You did the right thing. Now you must tell Alistair what you did and apologise.'

He pops another pea into his mouth and shakes his head. 'What is going on, Doll? What is going on?' He fixes his straw hat back on.

'Did you know the druidesses used to offer human sacrifices? I saw the altars in the oak woods. Do you think they could be involved?'

He looks sideways at me and laughs. 'That was ancient history, Doll. Are you suggesting they might be sacrificing children now?'

'I met one of them in the wood near the altar. She'd given me a present of the snake pearl bracelet the day before.'

'So?'

'Maybe she's lost her mind and thinks she's back in the old days.'

'Ah, Doll. The druidesses are spiritual and peace-loving women. Who was it that you met?'

'Her name is Dagda.'

He guffaws then, throwing his head back and steadying his hat.

'What's so funny? Do you know her?'

'Do I know her? No! She's been dead for over two hundred years, child. Dagda was a legendary horsewoman and spiritual leader of the druidesses. There's a portrait of her in the atrium at the temple. A highly revered soul.'

'Well, I met her.'

'You met someone who *said* she was Dagda. There is only one Dagda.'

'Why would she pretend?'

'Maybe the poor lady has parted from her mind. She *thinks* she's Dagda. It happens. At times I fear I'm losing mine too.' He taps his temple. 'No, I don't think the druidesses are harbouring secrets. The question we must ask is – who else is?'

He stands up and picks up his basket. 'You pick your fruit, Doll, and don't be late for dinner at eight bells.'

'I might miss it. I'm tired, and I shouldn't be up late really at my age.'

He clicks his tongue. 'Now, now. It's bad manners to refuse a dinner invitation on the basis of fatigue. Come now.'

'But . . .'

'No buts. You must apologise to Mr Cage. I'm sure he'll be magnanimous once he knows your intentions were pure. And he will. I am sure he will.'

As he marches off, he turns back. 'Face the music and dance, Doll. Face the music and dance.' And with that, he disappears into the kitchen, leaving me in the raspberry patch with my thoughts. Can I trust Lord Carbery? Is Mr Cage really innocent? How did Tiger flip from friend to freak in a moment? Are there secrets Mother Bodica and her sisters are keeping? And who is the woman who calls herself Dagda?

And the biggest question of all – will I live long enough to find out?

CHAPTER 30

ANDI

School's finished for the day. Stacey takes her wallet from her locker and turns the key. She checks the time. 'Are you free for a burger? It's only just four, and my grind isn't until five.'

'I'm up for that. How about the Yummy Café?' I say. 'Their two-for-one special is divine.'

We take a shortcut through the basketball court and join the throng of students spilling out the school gates, a sea of chattering red and grey waiting for lifts home while the older ones cycle off or dawdle, smoking, along the river path. We wind down Main Street and follow the heavenly aroma of chips and fried chicken wafting up from the new café on the corner of Bridge Street. Their chips are the best in town, thick and chunky and homemade with two dips, no extra charge. Hard to resist, now that I'm eating again. For a while there, food tasted like wallpaper, but my appetite's back and, as I said to Stacey earlier, everything's turning up roses.

'Tell me about Doll anyway,' she says, linking my arm as we weave through the crowd on Main Street.

'Like I said, she hasn't really surfaced from the coma yet, but it can take a bit of time, so I don't think anyone is too concerned yet. And she's breathing on her own since yesterday, and that's good.'

'That's a big development, being off the ventilator,' Stacey says. Those things are horrendous. I saw it in a documentary.'

We cross the street at the lights. 'I know. We're all relieved. Spent most of yesterday mooching round the hospital with

Mom and Dad. You know, my Dad had a ministroke on Saturday night. Don't say it to anyone, will you? I think he wants it kept quiet.'

'Jesus, Andi, is he okay? I thought only old people got those.'

'He's fine, just his blood pressure skyrocketing. I felt so bad, Stacey, over London and everything. After fighting with him, all the arguments – imagine if he died? But we have a truce now. He's letting me see Steve, as long as I study and toe the line at home.'

We swing in the door of Yummy Café. There's a great buzz, mostly students from St Mary's meeting up with the St Brendan's College boys. Harry Styles is singing 'Adore You' on the radio. We're lucky to find a table for two in a tight corner spot.

'Love this place,' Stacey says, sitting down and sizing up the boys at the next table. She scrolls through the menu and taps the special. 'Two for one – cheeseburger, slaw, and fries? With barbie sauce, garlic mayo, and a drink?'

I give her a thumbs-up. 'Good choice. Coke for me.'

We don't have to wait long to order.

'What can I get you lovely young ladies?' The waiter, in a long black apron, mock-bows from the waist and clicks his heels. 'At your service, girls.'

He looks like a heavyset Robbie Williams with a West Cork accent. We giggle. He winks as he sets down our cutlery and glasses on the tabletop.

'These are on the house,' he says, grinning as he fills our water glasses.

After he takes our order, Stacey rolls up the sleeves of her cardigan, like she means business. 'Anyway,' she says, 'London sounds amazing. Like a honeymoon.' She rolls her eyes and laughs. 'It all worked out. Happy ever after.' She pretend swoons.

I don't know if she's being sarcastic, but I don't think so. Stacey is a proper mate. It's just that when it comes to Steve, lots of girls are jealous. For all they say about Steve being a player, I'm not lying: they'd all jump at getting their claws into him, given half a chance.

'Well, yeah, in a roundabout way, everything's worked out for us. It made Steve realise how I felt about him and Dad knew I wasn't going to stay away from him, so, yes, whoop-whoop, happy days, girl.' We clink our water glasses.

'I have to hand it to you,' Stacey says, 'when you want something, you really go after it. I admire you, Andi. It took guts to tear off to London on your own. Fair play to you.'

Our waiter comes back with our cans of Coke.

'I won't keep you beautiful ladies much longer; your order's coming right up.' He winks again, and Stacey winks back. We both giggle as he disappears back into the kitchen.

'Don't be encouraging him,' I say. 'He'll be asking you out next.'

She collapses with laughter. 'Well,' she says, 'it might be the only offer I get.' She flicks back her hair flirtatiously. 'Go on anyway. London. Love was in the air. The ride was fantastic. You took precautions? I don't want to hear it if you didn't.'

Our food arrives and Stacey tucks in, swirling her chip through the little dishes of barbie sauce and then garlic mayo and inhaling the aroma before she takes a bite. 'Crunchy and soft inside. The perfect chip,' she says, wiping her mouth with a napkin. 'Anyway, I'm waiting.'

'Look, Thursday night, I told you, when I met him, I swear I nearly fainted. Just seeing him again, Stace. We went for an Indian and then back to his mother's flat. She's clean since Christmas, getting her life together again. Herself and Ray, her partner, are really nice. We slept in the spare room. Linda didn't have any problem with that.'

'And Steve didn't either.' She clicks her tongue and smiles.

'Obviously. And he didn't know I was coming. And I hadn't seen him since Sunday morning, and in a single bed . . . oh, I wasn't thinking straight, you know how it is.'

'Actually, I don't' – she smiles – 'but I'm taking notes.' Her face becomes serious. 'Did you take the morning-after pill, Andi? I mean, that's the second time – you're playing with fire.' She puts down her fork and counts the days. 'That was Thursday, Friday . . . today's Tuesday, that's five days, Andi! You're pushing your luck. You better get to a pharmacy today.' She looks at her watch. 'You'll make it, but it mightn't even work at this stage. You are one crazy girl.' She takes a bite from her burger and scoops some coleslaw.

'Don't freak me out, Stace, I'll be fine.' I feel like saying, *A lot you'd know.* But I know that's just me being pigheaded and that she's probably right. We eat in silence for a few minutes, listening to Lizzo belt it out on the radio.

'There's no way I'm going in to a pharmacy here in Glengarvan, Stace. Somebody would tell my mother. You know what it's like in this town.'

She nods, her mouth full. 'But you've no choice. Think about it: embarrassment for five minutes, a termination, or pregnant for nine months. Choose A, B, or C.'

'Don't eat with your mouth full,' I say. 'And yes, okay, point taken. I will call in to the pharmacy on my way home. Satisfied?'

I look at the last few St Brendan's boys at the table inside the door as Stacey finishes off my fries. They are all slagging each other off, throwing shapes. One of them – Kieran Kiely, he plays rugby for the Blue Tigers – waves over at me, tries to catch my attention. These college boys, they are only imitation boys, really, hard lads who try to impress each other and impress the girls. They don't impress me. They're not like Steve. Steve has something these pampered lads could never even understand. And if they got you into bed, they probably wouldn't know what to do. All talk. Not like Steve. How could they ever compete? Steve makes me feel like I'm a goddess, perfect just as I am. It's hard to beat that feeling. And Steve is his own man. He knows how to make a girl feel alive. He'll just kiss your mouth and your throat, and, well, it's hard to get your head in gear after that.

The boys get up to leave. Kieran gives me a thumbs-up.

'Andi, you're not listening to me.'

'Sorry, Stace, just wondering if I could fix you up with Kieran Kiely down there.'

She looks behind her and smiles. 'From the Blue Tigers? He's well out of my league. Anyway, I'm going to be late for my grind. Will you pay? I'll Revolut you later.'

I nod. Wave her away. 'Okay, scoot.' I need time to sit and think for a minute. I decide to head back down Main Street towards Mahers Pharmacy. There's a queue. I'm not waiting and risking an audience when the pharmacist starts quizzing me. I cut across Finbarr Street and make for the Pharmacy Express near the shopping centre. I linger outside, rehearsing my story. I checked online, so I know it's not just going to be ask, get, and go. There'll be twenty questions and I'm underage, and what if I'm in trouble or if I get Steve into trouble? Could they tell my parents – I mean, unofficially? If they thought it was in my *best interests*?

I decide to go in, stand tall. Act relaxed, like I'm a Leaving Cert student and it's no big deal. Which it isn't. Or it shouldn't be.

There's an old man buying a box of paracetamol at the counter, and he's enquiring about whether he may need a cough bottle for a dry or a chesty cough. 'Sometimes it's a dry cough.' He clears his throat. 'Did you hear that now? And sometimes, at night especially, it's quite chesty, and my wife said to me . . .' I hover around the shampoos, trying not to listen. When he's done, the coast will be clear. But what happens then, if I'm in the middle of *my* story and someone comes in and hears *my* business?

The man settles on his cough bottle, pays the girl, and shuffles out. God, I hope I never get old.

'Hello, Andrea.' I jump and turn around. It's Ms Trout, our principal. Of all people. *Great timing, you old trout*, I think, but I smile back at her.

'Next, please,' the assistant says, looking at me.

'No, you don't have it,' I say, pointing to the display of shampoos. I slip past Ms Trout and out the door, murmuring a goodbye and a 'See you tomorrow, Miss.' Imagine if she'd come in two minutes later – she'd have heard the lot. Someone was praying for me. Must have been my granny. I whisper a thank-you to her and head back across town, skirting past the river path and onto the Mill Road. I sprint up the hill to Bluebell Grove. I'd say I'll be grand. Stacey, let's face it, is a bit of a stress bunny. Her thing is, if the worst can happen, it probably will.

My dad is in the kitchen. He has his twenty-four-hour blood pressure monitor on, and it's puffing and whirring as he stirs the lamb stew. 'You're like a robot, Dad,' I say, and he pretends to move his arms mechanically like the little guy in Star Wars. He's in better form, even though I know Ger Mac's death really upset him.

'Any more news on Doll?' I ask, but he shakes his head.

'Your mother is on her way. They said there's no need to stay the night; they'll call us if there is any change in her.'

'Just the three of us, so,' I say. 'A nice quiet night in.'

He smiles. 'Just what the doctor ordered,' he says, raising the arm with the monitor, 'a nice quiet night in.'

Sometimes, I think, the simple things in life are the best.

CHAPTER 31

DOLL

Tessa has left a yellow hairband on my bed, and I put it on, smiling as I brush my hair. 'Yellow's your colour,' I say to the mirror.

Mr Cage has already arrived when I go down to the great hall for dinner. He's sitting opposite Lord Carbery at the blazing fire and leans forward to shake my hand. 'Good to see you are safe and well, Doll.' He frowns. 'I heard that poor Tiger was distraught when you went missing.'

Lord Carbery is wearing a pale-grey suit with a pink bow tie. He gestures for me to sit on the stool between them. 'Welcome, Doll, I'll fetch you an iced lemonade.' He hands me a fizzing glass. 'I've filled Alistair in on your, let's say, your misdemeanours. Just to save your blushes.'

I'm mortified, but grateful he spared me the ordeal.

'I'm sorry, Mr Cage,' I say, looking at him from under the safety of my eyelashes. 'We were foolish. We thought if you really were a killer, then we could . . .'

'Be heroes?' Lord Carbery says, curling his lip.

'We might save other children, and we wanted to help, to see if Dr Ashe was right.'

'Leave the child be, Lord Carbery,' Mr Cage looks at me directly. 'I'm sure you thought you were doing the right thing. We'll say no more about it, eh?'

'Thank you, Mr Cage.'

'Hopely Ashe should have had more sense,' Lord Carbery says, shaking his head. 'I mean, telling children about her suspicions . . . very imprudent, I do think, very imprudent altogether.'

'She just wanted us to keep an eye, to see if, well . . . it wasn't her idea for us to search the house or anything. The police didn't seem to believe her, and she was worried, that's all.'

'I remember that study on facial recognition she was referring to,' Mr Cage says, taking a drink from his glass. 'It was debunked afterwards. I thought it might help my case. Still' – he takes off his jacket and settles back in his chair – 'she crossed a line telling you two. Unprofessional, to say the least.'

'Tell her,' Lord Carbery says, taking a sip of red wine and smacking his lips. 'Tell her your story.'

Mr Cage hesitates for a moment, then leans towards me. He looks uncomfortable. 'I never killed anyone, Doll. I was pardoned years ago. My prison record has been erased. I am officially an innocent man.' He closes his eyes, and a cloud of pain crosses his face.

My lemonade tastes of peaches and lemons and fizzes up my nose. 'How did you end up in prison, so?'

He looks at me. 'I was in the wrong place at the wrong time, I'm afraid.' He sighs. 'I witnessed a stabbing on a late-night express MP. The woman was known to me. I was able to disarm her assailant, but it was too late. I couldn't stem the blood.' He shudders. 'I can still remember her perfume, and whenever I smell that same scent now, I have to go outside to be sick.' He takes off his glasses, and his hand is shaking as he cleans them with a handkerchief he takes from his pocket.

'But you were only trying to save her.'

He nods and nods. 'They constructed a case. The truth was irrelevant. The whole trial was a farce. The killer had escaped before the MP stopped, and there were no witnesses.' He joins his hands like a prayer. 'My fingerprints were on the knife. I knew the woman. The prosecution made a ludicrous case, and throughout the trial, the judge was drinking.'

'Drinking what?'

'Alcohol, Doll. Dulling the senses.'

'The killer had very powerful friends,' Lord Carbery says. 'Evidence was tampered with. Alistair was the scapegoat. It was a shocking miscarriage of justice.'

'Eventually, the real culprit was brought before the courts and convicted. I was pardoned. It took time, but on my second appeal, I was free to go. Justice delayed, but all the sweeter.' He kisses his thumb and finger. 'In prison, my music saved me.'

'You didn't give up, my man,' Lord Carbery says. 'You didn't give up, you marched on, the sign of a true soldier indeed. I salute you.'

Mr Cage smiles. 'Enough talk of prison and tribulation,' he says, 'We must dwell on happier things. Like our wonderful win in Vanistra last night.'

'Indeed. Congratulations,' Lord Carbery says. We all raise our glasses and clink them together before taking a long drink. 'A wonderful achievement, Alistair, and well deserved.'

'The choir are stupendous, I agree. And the win is a distraction from the recent tragedies in the Academy.'

'Terrible business.' Lord Carbery plucks a pink handkerchief from his breast pocket and dabs his forehead. 'Very strange events indeed. Who can explain it?'

'Actually, I think the mystery is about to be solved.' Mr Cage is smiling. 'Very positive news on that front, I'm glad to say.'

Lord Carbery looks at me in surprise. 'We are all ears, Alistair. Tell us, please do.'

Tessa comes in, balancing three plates, and we take our seats at the long polished table. The candlelight throws shapes and shadows around the wood-panelled walls, giving the two men's faces a sinister glow. Alexander stirs by the fire, rising up before settling back to sleep.

'This is indeed a feast, Tessa,' Mr Cage says, spearing a piece of shrimp from his salad plate and dipping it in pink sauce.

'Try Doll's scones,' Lord Carbery says with candlelight teeth. He passes the basket to Mr Cage. 'She's a natural-born baker.' He slices his own, adds butter, and crunches on the toasted sesame seeds. 'You were saying, Alistair, the mystery is about to be solved. Please amplify.'

Mr Cage takes a long drink of his wine. 'Well, it's confidential, but' – he taps the side of his nose – 'I know you'll be discreet, and you will hear soon enough at any rate.'

'Don't keep us in suspense. Let it out, sir.'

Mr Cage dabs the corner of his mouth with his napkin. 'It's a virus.'

Lord Carbery looks at him, his fork held midair. 'A virus? You're joking, surely?' He leaves his fork back on his plate and spreads his elbows on the table. 'Two children died. Two are in a serious psychotic state, a girl almost drowns and cannot explain why, and this child here' – he taps my head – 'is thrown to her near death by her friend . . . and you're saying it's all down to a virus?'

'What? Is that true? Tiger pushed you?' Mr Cage's eyes widen. 'She lost you when you were out exploring . . .'

'She pushed me down the hillside into the Long Valley. I'm telling you the truth.'

Mr Cage is shaking his head. 'I am appalled to hear that. Shocked, absolutely shocked.'

'She could've died,' Lord Carbery says. He takes up a shrimp and chews slowly. 'So all this strange behaviour – this dangerous and sinister behaviour, might I say – it's all down to a virus?' He taps his chin with his finger. 'Perhaps it is so, perhaps, perhaps.'

'Have you heard of Professor Laurence Lavelle?' Mr Cage asks.

'*The* Professor Lavelle, founder and director of the Almazova Neuroscience Institute?'

'The very man. The most eminent authority on neural circuitry and brain systems. Scholar, surgeon, academic; he is one of the great innovators of our age, especially in the area of neurology.'

'Yes, yes, a great man.'

'What does he actually do?' I ask.

Lord Carbery smiles. 'Yes, good question, Doll. Well, one of his cases involved enabling a woman who had lost the use of her legs to walk again by altering her brain codes. It was a breakthrough moment in science.'

'And he's done transformative work on neurological disease and ageing. The man is a genius.'

'Go on, Alistair.'

Mr Cage takes another sip of wine and lowers his voice. 'Mother Bodica has summoned him to discover the cause of the dysfunction in the children and to investigate the tragic events.'

'And?' We both lean in to hear every word.

'Apparently he's already met with Thomas and Kristin and their doctors. He's studied their files, and tonight he is arriving at the Academy. He'll meet the druidesses first, and in the morning he will interview Amber.'

'And Tiger, he needs to see her too,' I say.

'Absolutely, Doll. I will talk to Mother Bodica about that.'

'And his theory is?' Lord Carbery asks, stroking his chin.

Mr Cage mops his plate with the last of his bread. 'According to Mother Bodica, his theory is that the children may have contracted a virus that temporarily interfered with their brain circuitry.' He waves his hand in a circle. 'I don't fully understand these things, but that is his prognosis.'

'Surely the medics would have picked that up before now, Alistair?'

'Yes, you would have thought so. But, apparently, some viruses can disappear from the body leaving no obvious trace, so the cause and effect is hard to prove. And some virus particles hide in sanctuary sites in the human body, areas our immune system doesn't monitor as closely as the rest of our bodies.'

'That is fascinating. So he believes the virus theory is a possibility?'

'More than a possibility; he is convinced of it. And Kristin and Thomas are responding well to antiviral medication and are beginning to communicate again – though with some memory loss around the tragic events. Which may be a blessing for them.'

Tessa comes to clear the empty plates and sets down a platter of roast pork along with herbed potatoes and peas. She leaves a dish of applesauce in the middle of the table.

'Fit for a king,' Mr Cage says, helping himself. 'My, my, this is a wonderful evening.'

'So it's all good news, the mystery is solved,' I say. 'It's a virus that made the children think and do things they didn't want to?'

Mr Cage nods, his mouth full. 'That's it, you have it. No foul play.'

'I wasn't aware, Alistair, I must confess, I was *not* aware of the existence of a virus that would affect the cognitive processes in such a fashion.' His Lordship looks at me. 'Could your friend have been outside her mind when she pushed you? It would certainly explain the other events too.'

Mr Cage nods. 'Professor Lavelle has encountered this phenomenon some years back, apparently. The similarities are striking, he says.'

Lord Carbery adds some butter to his potatoes. 'Mother Bodica must be so relieved. The nightmare is over, she can breathe again. We will drink to that.' He raises his glass and takes a dainty sip.

A match strikes in my head. The room blurs along with the delicious food, the peach lemonade, my new friends. Soon – sooner than I thought – I'll be saying goodbye to all this. The Academy, Amber, Tiger, my new self, my happy self – my golden future, snapped off like a twig. And this time I haven't even gotten to be a hero. Instead, I'll be plucked away quietly, no fuss. Sent tumbling through space back to my hospital bed and then to number six Bluebell Grove, bitter and wordless inside the skin of the old Doll. My future no longer belongs to me. I lick the salty tears off my chin. I have to scrape my heart off the floor. The men continue to talk.

'Doll, you haven't eaten much. You must have some raspberries and ice-cream.' Lord Carbery passes me a silver dish. His kindness brings more tears, and I swallow them with the raspberries. And my dreams.

The two men are laughing now. 'I insist, please,' Lord Carbery is saying, and Mr Cage bows and lifts the violin from its case by the fireplace and begins to play. Despite the smallness of my thoughts, the tune takes me whirling towards the castle rafters and sets me down before lifting me off again. I watch Mr Cage as he plays, gliding his bow over the strings, skimming and sliding and plucking and picking as his grey-black curls bob against the collar of his shirt. A happy man.

Lord Carbery jumps to his feet, crying, 'Whoop-whoop,' and begins to dance across the great hall, clapping his hands above his head and swaying from side to side, his jacket tails rising and falling like sails.

Mr Cage stands up too and starts to stomp his feet as the bow dances across his violin like a frenzied bee. Such a thread of joy. Well, I can't help it. I leap from my seat and take Lord Carbery's hand, and he throws his head back and laughs as we swing around in circles, skipping and stomping to the music. I've lost my future, but right now, here, in the aliveness of this moment, I am happy and light as a bird. Even Alexander is up, hissing and swaying from side to side, doing the python twist.

CHAPTER 32

SALLY

'Every brain is different. It's impossible to accurately predict when she will regain consciousness,' Doctor Valera is saying. We are standing by Doll's bed. It's Wednesday morning. The doctor folds his arms. He's talking about PT scans and being able to measure the glucose metabolism of the brain and what that can tell us. Dan is nodding, following the thread.

'I can tell you that impaired consciousness is not the end of the road,' he says. 'You must not think of this as a setback.'

'We'd hoped she'd regain consciousness at this stage,' Dan says. 'It's forty-eight hours since the ventilator was removed, and she is still not responding.'

'It's not unusual. There is some room for optimism. Think of this minimally conscious state as a route to recovery,' the doctor says.

'There is hope, you're saying,' Dan says.

'We have to factor in her condition; that is a complication,' Dr Valera says. 'There are a number of elements at play here, but my best advice is to give it a little time. The brain swelling has almost completely subsided, and that is a plus.'

'Can we actually *do* anything,' I say, 'other than what we have been doing?' Which isn't very much – holding her hand, talking to her. They say people in a coma can hear the voices around them. If that's true, it must be a comfort to hear familiar ones.

'There's a lot of research on sensory stimulation,' he says, 'and how it can impact on patients in a comatose state. So, yes, you could play her favourite music, spray some favourite smells, and, yes, keep talking to her. The human voice is a wonderful healer in many situations.'

We sit there after he's gone. We'd built our hopes up. 'We didn't expect this,' I say. Dan nods, squeezes my hand.

'Poor Doll, hovering in no-man's-land, maybe some glacial wasteland, all alone.'

'Don't think like that, Sally. She's asleep and she's here, and she'll come round.'

But *is* she here? I was reading about it in a science magazine, about the possibility of parallel worlds and the mysteries of time and space. I didn't fully understand it, the notion that anything that *can* happen *does*. And that we're only living in one set of happenings. Living in a three-dimensional world when entire universes are hovering above us in nine and even ten dimensions. Apparently, there's a super-universe we can't access, and it's all around us. We humans are the goldfish in the pond – oblivious to the mega-world above the pond water. A membrane away. And, one day, they think, we might be able to slip through the skin of the membrane and glimpse other worlds. This is science. Not science fiction.

'Sal, hello? You're miles away.' Dan waves his hand in front of my eyes.

I shake myself out of my thoughts. 'Dan, do you believe in the possibility of life in other dimensions?' I ask. 'Do you think she could be living another, wilder life, on another plane?'

Dan looks from Doll to me. 'You mean astral travelling? No, Sally, I do not.'

'Not that. I don't believe in that nonsense either, but science says, according to the rules of quantum mechanics . . .'

'Sounds to me,' Dan says, 'that you need a hot cup of coffee. And so do I. How about we discuss quantum theories over a real-life scone and raspberry jam?'

The hospital canteen is busy, and we find a table at the back behind some oversized potted plants. Dan disappears and comes back with two Americanos and scones. 'Only strawberry jam, I'm afraid,' he says, wrinkling his nose.

'Don't look now,' I say, 'but Emily Murray, that woman we met the night of Doll's accident – well, she's making her way towards us.' He groans as she approaches the table.

'Good morning,' she says brightly. Dan nods coolly as he transfers the mugs and plates from the tray.

I smile politely. 'Hello, Emily.'

'I was hoping to catch you,' she says. 'You're pretty hard to get a hold of.'

I gesture for her to sit down, though Dan is giving me the evil eye.

'I left a number of messages on your phone, Mrs Redmond.'

Her disapproving tone gets my back up. She perches on the chair opposite mine, opens the buttons of her beige jacket.

'I know. I'm sorry. My head's been all over the place.'

Her eyes flicker to Dan. 'And the public health nurse, Ann Brophy, told me she spoke to you last week when she called to your home, and you assured her—'

Dan touches the heel of his palm to his forehead. 'Clean went out of my head,' he says, looking at me. 'I forgot to tell you that, Sal.' He drops a cube of sugar into his coffee, and I know by the way he stirs it that he's irritated. 'I hope, Emily, you're as vigorous in your pursuit of the genuinely feckless parents as you are with us. You deserve a gold medal for persistence!'

Emily does not like the tone. She bites her lip. 'As I said before, Mr Redmond, we are only doing our job. Our priority is the welfare of the child, and we need you' – she sweeps her eyes to include me – 'we need both of you to engage with the services. We all want what's best for Doll, don't we?'

Dan slaps his spoon on the table. 'I'm sorry? Engage with the services? Do you think you are talking to a couple of deadbeat parents who might need some tips on child safety? Perhaps we need to attend a parenting course?' He looks sideways at her. 'I fail to understand, I really do, what is it exactly that you want from us.'

Emily's face colours, and she chews her lip. 'A child, unsupervised, has fallen out a first-floor bedroom window. This is a serious incident and one that warrants investigation.'

'Unsupervised?' Dan's voice is rising. I give his foot a tap under the table. 'For Chrissake, she was in her bed. Asleep. Are you suggesting we should have posted a sentry at her bedside?'

'The window was left open.' Her mouth is a thin straight line.

'It wasn't,' I say. 'We've already told you this. It was not left open. Read your notes, Emily.'

'She was able to reach the catch, evidently. Look' – she turns her palms up – 'I don't want to get into an argument with you. The issue is that the child fell out and was badly injured.'

'We know that,' I say. 'It was an appalling accident.'

'Yes it was, Mrs Redmond. So why the reluctance to engage with us? We are all on the same page, surely?'

'And what page is that?' Dan says, but she ignores him and looks at me, hoping I'll be the good cop versus Dan's bad cop. 'We just want to ensure that it can't happen again. Perhaps some simple steps.'

Dan sighs heavily. 'Oh Jesus, spare us. Of course the window will be secured. Do you think we are complete morons? You people.' He rolls his eyes and takes a sip of lukewarm coffee.

'In any event—' Emily fiddles with the brass buttons on her jacket, rubbing her fingers across the embossed anchors. When she lowers her tone, I know she's applying the classic *Calm the aggressor* tactic: *Slow your pace, lower your tone, and they will unconsciously mirror your behaviour.* 'In any event, we are planning to hold a case conference here at the hospital, and we'd like all parties involved to attend. In fact' – she smiles – 'you have a *right* to be there, and that's why we've been anxious to make contact.'

I can't believe what I'm hearing. 'A case conference? Are you serious? And who are 'all parties,' might I ask?'

'Oh, this is normal procedure; there's no cause for alarm, Mrs Redmond. It's not a reflection on yourselves. Ann Brophy, the public health nurse, will attend, along with a nurse and a representative from Tusla, the child protection agency who—'

'We know who Tusla are, Emily,' Dan says. 'Please don't patronise us.'

She sniffs and ignores him. 'And your good selves, of course, that's if you want to attend; it is your prerogative.' Her voice is cold.

'Oh, is it? It's good to know we won't be handcuffed and frog-marched in against our will.'

Keep it down, I mouth at Dan. The conversation is getting out of control, and I sense that our names could end up in highlighter on some HSE file.

'Emily, my husband has had a serious health scare over the weekend. We are all under stress, as you can imagine. Doll is still unresponsive. It is a difficult time for the family.'

'I do understand. Yes indeed. I'm sorry to hear that.' She adopts a look of concern. 'And there's no suggestion or evidence, might I add, of wilful neglect, so please don't be concerned about that.' She hesitates. 'At the end of the day, though, the child has to be our priority, and sometimes, if that means stepping on parents' toes, well . . .' She shrugs.

I kick Dan under the table. 'Yes, I see. You are just being thorough.'

'That's it, Mrs Redmond, we have to ask the hard questions.'

'I understand.' I hold Dan's eye. 'We both do. And we will have a child lock placed on that window, I can assure you.'

She smiles. 'Just one final question I have for you, a minor concern – I'm just curious.'

'Oh?'

'Those wounds on Doll's face? They look quite sore and concerning, don't they?'

Dan says, 'Jesus wept.'

'Doll self-injures,' I say. 'You already know she has special needs.'

'I see.' She almost seems . . . is it my imagination? She almost looks disappointed.

'What *do* you see, Emily?' Now it's my turn.

'I mean, I understand. She has emotional and behavioural issues.' She nods. 'Difficult. But that's what we are here for. Support for you, help in managing these issues. I can imagine the stress and the upset. It can be overwhelming having a child with special needs. Easy to crack under the strain. We see it all the time.'

What is she trying to say? Is she actually suggesting that child neglect or even abuse might be understandable in the circumstances?

Fury washes over me like a tidal wave.

'And the case conference is an excellent place to discuss these very issues. With professionals who know what they're talking about.'

'You don't,' I say, quietly.

'Sorry?'

'You don't.'

'*I don't?* I'm sorry. How do you mean?' A brittle smile. She's thrown momentarily. She was on a roll there: problem families, problem parents. Emily's speciality.

'You said, *I understand*, but you don't.'

She's cross. 'Yes, well, I don't mean—'

'You haven't a clue.' I say it slowly. Dan is trying to catch my eye, trying to warn me off, but it's too late for logic. The wave is already in motion.

'People like you, Emily—'

She stares at me.

'You haven't a clue. You say you're just doing your job. But you're not very good at your job. For starters, you don't listen – and you should listen, because that's how you can best evaluate a situation. You're patronising, you're judgemental, and you have a supercilious attitude that does your profession no favours. And you get people's backs up.'

She stands up. 'I'm afraid I don't have to—'

I stand too. 'I'm not finished,' I say. She continues to stare at me like I've lost the plot.

'I hope you will never find yourself in our situation. But if you were to, you'd understand the only thing that keeps you going is having an endless supply of patience, resilience, and love. And no professional degree or thesis is going to teach you that.'

Inside, I'm shaking. She backs away, buttoning her jacket. 'I'll be in touch about the case conference,' she says, and she hurries away, getting temporarily entangled in the line of potted plants.

We both suppress a giggle as she almost trips over one of them, and then, flustered, she straightens her skirt and disappears out the canteen door.

'Well, fair play,' Dan says, 'you certainly nailed it. She is some operator. Every word you said was correct.'

'I went too far, Dan. I shouldn't have let fly. I couldn't help it. She is so irritating.'

'I'd say it's parent prison for us,' he says, laughing. 'Can you just imagine the notes she'll be making about the pair of us?' We can't stop laughing. 'The look on your face,' Dan says, 'like thunder.' He makes a face.

'And the look on her face,' I say.

Dan guffaws. 'Especially when you told her she wasn't very good at her job. I thought her jaw would hit her chest.'

We are like two children, creasing over, tears of laughter streaming down our faces. We haven't laughed like this for a long time. It feels good. You have to laugh, really. Life is so absurd, so random, well, you just have to laugh.

CHAPTER 33

DOLL

Next morning, Lord Carbery is waiting for me in the castle courtyard. He's sitting on a bike with two saddles.

'Hop up,' he says, gesturing to the cushioned seat behind him.

'We can't cycle down all those steps,' I say, horrified. 'One fall is enough, thank you very much.'

'I know every twist and turn in those one hundred and twenty steps,' he says, grinning. 'Hold steady, we'll be down in a minute.'

I close my eyes as we zigzag down the winding steps and onto the track that will bring us to the Academy. The bike seems to skim the steps in places, whizzing effortlessly through the air. Lord Carbery starts to whistle a tune, and as we cross the Long Valley, pedalling past fields of poppies and lavender, I hum along behind him. The man just cheers me up every time. I wish he was my granddad.

Mother Bodica greets us when we arrive and invites Lord Carbery for morning tea. 'I'd love you to meet Professor Lavelle,' she says. 'A giant of a man, a genius.'

Lord Carbery beams, bowing his head. 'Honoured, to be sure, ma'am. A pure delight.'

She changes her tune with me though, glowering down at me. 'I'll speak to you later, miss. For now, go to your dorm and await an appointment with Dr Ashe. We want to be sure you are healthy and strong before you resume classes.'

Back in the dorm, Tiger is lying on her bed, hands laced behind her head. She jumps up when she sees me. 'Doll, at last, you're back! I was so worried about you. When you went missing, I was frantic.' She comes towards me. 'I'm so relieved—'

I take a step back. 'I didn't go missing. You pushed me, remember? You pushed me and I could have died.'

She looks horrified. 'Pushed you? I did not! What are you saying, Doll?'

'You sent me tumbling into the Long Valley.'

She backs away, smiling awkwardly. 'Why would you say that? I'm your friend. I would never hurt you.'

'But you did.'

She slumps down on the bed and covers her face with her hands. Her body is trembling. 'You're lying, Doll,' she says.

'Huh. You don't remember?'

She looks up at me, her face stricken. 'Bits of me are going missing,' she says. 'I only remember looking for you in the dark. Shouting your name over and over.'

'Really?'

'How could you even think I would hurt you? I have no memory of it.'

She starts to cry then, and I go and sit next to her. She sobs as she leans into me, and I put my arm around her. 'I believe you,' I say. 'It's like Amber. She was confused too, that night she went into the lake.'

She looks at me. 'I wouldn't hurt you, Doll, not in a million years.'

'I know, Tiger,' I say, giving her a tissue from the bedside table and feeling guilty now for doubting her.

She dabs her eyes. 'The druidesses searched all night for you. I was so relieved when they got word you were safe.' She lowers her voice. 'I didn't tell them what we were doing. Not even Hopely.'

'I told Lord Carbery, Tiger. I had to. Mr Cage is innocent, you know.' I fill her in on his story. 'And after all that, it seems there *was* no killer.'

She nods. 'I know. I heard about Professor Lavelle. The news is all over the Academy. He thinks it's a virus that affects the brain and causes dangerous thoughts and behaviours. Totally weird.'

I nod. 'You know he's already seen Kristin and Thomas, and he's here today to talk to Amber? You'll be called to see him too, Tiger.'

She nods again, her eyes still red and puffy. 'Yes, I'm not myself these last few days. I'm meant to see Dr Ashe this morning anyway.' She sighs. 'It's hard to believe, isn't it? A virus can make you do evil things and you don't even remember them.' She shudders. 'It's crazy and scary, but if the top scientist in Almazova says it's true, well, it must be true. He'd *know*, wouldn't he?'

'Of course. And it means that you're not going mad. No one is. And it's treatable. Everyone is going to be fine.'

'Except the ones who didn't make it.'

'Yes. Poor Matthew and Ava.'

Her face crumples. 'I've been feeling so strange, Doll. Like I'm not me anymore. And my dreams, they frighten me.'

'Doll! You're back!' Amber appears in the doorway and runs to hug me. 'We missed you so much.' She looks at Tiger. 'You're to go over now, Tiger. Professor Lavelle and Hopely are waiting for you.' She skips in a little circle, kicking her heels.

'What's he like?' Tiger asks, lacing up her shoes.

'He was so friendly, Tiger, and I'm so relieved it's down to an infection. He gave me some antivirals.' Amber makes a funny face. 'And there was I, thinking I was cracking up!' We all laugh. Amber is back to her old self.

Tiger jumps off the bed. 'I'd better go. I'll see you later.'

When Tiger's gone, Amber whispers, 'It's going around that Tiger pushed you. Poor you.' She squeezes my hand. 'It's that virus, Doll. Her brain was invaded too.'

'Looks like it's over now,' I say. 'Professor Lavelle has made sure the Academy is safe again. The druidesses must be so delighted.'

She nods. 'Mother Bodica is practically smiling. She would not want all this stuff getting out. The Academy has such a high reputation; this would have destroyed it.'

Sister Fidelma puts her head around the door. 'Welcome back, Doll. You're safe and well, I heard. The Gods were looking after you.' She smiles and looks at Amber. 'For you,' she says, dropping a parcel onto Lia's bed. 'Arrived this morning.' She bustles off.

'I wasn't expecting any treats,' Amber says, tearing open the paper. 'Oh, my books.' She looks at me, and her eyes are filling up. 'The Harold Hansen books I lent to Matthew.' She reads the note inside. 'It's from his parents. Returning the books they found amongst his things.' She shakes her head. 'He loved the Harold Hansen stories. Poor Matthew.' She kisses one of the books. 'I'll treasure these, knowing Matthew read them too.'

She passes them to me, and as I skim through the pages, a pink sheet of folded paper floats to the floor. Amber picks it up and scans it.

'Some sort of report.' She holds her palm up to shush me. Her lips move, and her brow creases in concentration. 'I don't understand,' she says.

'What is it?'

'It's a memo from Hopely Ashe. But that can't be.'

'What can't be?'

'This is a memo from Dr Ashe to Professor Lavelle, dated four weeks ago.'

'So? They probably know each other.'

Amber looks at me. 'That's the thing. They don't.'

'How do you know that?'

'Because I was with Hopely when Mother Bodica brought the professor to meet her this morning.'

'And?'

'And Hopely said she had always admired his work and never expected to meet him and was . . . what did she say? Yes, she was honoured to make his acquaintance.'

'Make his what?'

'Honoured to meet him. And he said something like, "I didn't catch your name," and she repeated it. So it was obvious they didn't know each other.'

'That's odd. And what does the memo say, Amber?'

She scans the page again. 'Oh, no, it couldn't be.'

I look over her shoulder. She points to a column of letters on the left-hand side of the page.

'That's so odd.'

'What's odd?'

'It's about us. What's been happening at the Academy. I think these are initials.' She jabs each pair of letters in the row. 'MM, KB, AH, TL. Oh, wow.'

'They mean nothing to me,' I say.

She looks at me. 'Why would they? This is only your first week. The initials match the children's names – Matthew Morley, Kristin Bell, Ava Harding, Thomas Lee . . .' Her eyes widen. She scans the column on the right.

'What does it say?'

She peers closer. 'Just notes I can't make out, stuff about depressive emotional states, intrusive thoughts, confusion, anxiety, adverse reactions. *Spec re SIs: Risk factors. Direction required.*'

She looks up. 'There are a lot of words and abbreviations I don't recognise.' She sets the paper down beside her. 'There's something funny going on,' she says, tapping her feet on the floor. 'It's dated' – she lowers her voice, glancing towards the door – 'two days before Matthew died.'

'She was obviously contacting him for support with the children's mental health issues. What's so odd about that?'

'But she didn't know him. Or she just pretended not to know him this morning, which is weird, right?'

'Why would Hopely lie, Amber?'

'Exactly. Why would she lie?' She pauses for a minute, chewing her lip. 'There must be something we're missing here.'

'But it was Mother Bodica who brought the professor here, didn't she? It was her idea, right?'

'You two still here?' Tiger is beaming as she comes through the doorway. 'You were right, Amber. He's so friendly. I can't believe I actually met the great professor.'

'What did he say?' I ask.

Tiger grimaces. 'Mostly he explained the virus, how it intercepts the neural pathways, causing disorientation and irrational thoughts. Blow me down, it's scary stuff, but he thinks we should be okay after the meds.' She looks at Amber. 'Same?'

Amber nods.

'Such a relief to know we are not going insane.' Tiger checks her watch. 'C'mon, are we going for our break?'

'Tiger, wait,' I say.

Amber looks at me, shaking her head almost invisibly.

'We have to tell her, Amber.'

Tiger spins around. 'Tell me what?'

I hand her the sheet of paper. 'Amber found this in a book Matthew's parents returned to her.'

She scans the page. 'It's just a report from Dr Ashe to Professor Lavelle. How did Matthew have it? It's marked confidential. We're not supposed to read it, right?'

'Look again at the date, and the initials on the left. The children with problems,' Amber says. 'MM – Matthew Morley, Kristin, Ava, Thomas.'

'You think?' Tiger says.

'What do *you* think, Tiger?' Everyone knows Hopely is her hero.

She sits down heavily on Lia's bed. 'This is what I think: she sent him a confidential memo about the kids at the Academy. She was puzzled and worried. She was looking for advice from a respected neurologist; maybe they worked together at some point. I don't see anything odd about that.'

'She didn't know him,' Amber says. 'I was there this morning when they were introduced. They acted like they'd never met.'

'So?' Tiger says, smiling. 'Maybe she didn't want Bodica to know. Maybe, I don't know, maybe she's just private. I mean, who cares?' She shrugs. 'You two are looking for mystery where there is none. All the weird stuff is down to a virus. It's sorted now.' She points to the sheet of paper. 'I'd get rid of that. She'll get into trouble if the druidesses see it.'

'I still think there's something odd,' Amber says, but Tiger cuts her short.

'C'mon, let's go.' She looks at me when I hesitate. 'Look, Doll, if you feel that strongly about it, why don't you ask her yourself? She said to send you over at twelve bells for your checkup.'

I'm feeling uneasy as we head to the dining hall. My white pearls have turned black again, and I think of Lord Carbery and his ramblings about the birds crying and how snake pearls can warn of danger by changing colour.

When Amber is out of earshot, Tiger whispers, 'Don't get Hopely into trouble, Doll. She's on our side. And look what happened when we went after Mr Cage. Let's forget about the whole thing.' She gives me a nudge and smiles. 'Anyway, we know now what happened. There is no mystery after all.'

'Which means,' I whisper, 'it's goodbye, Almazova, for me. Goodbye, Academy, goodbye, Tiger.' I'm beginning to realise that there's no way I could stay. Where could I run to? I'd be caught in five minutes. It was only a silly dream, really. Thinking I'd stay on. All talk.

'I've been thinking about that,' Tiger says. 'You need to ask Nan-Nan to put in a word for you. It can't hurt to ask.'

'Nell won't allow it. There's no point. It's one of the rules.' We take our seats at the long table. 'I could run away,' I say. 'Just disappear. If they can't find me, then they can't send me back.' The thought is beyond thrilling, but I know in my heart I just don't have the courage.

'You could, but where would you go? And wouldn't you miss your family, Doll? It's very final. If you run and disappear, how would you ever get back home? Better to ask Nan-Nan.'

I take a bite of my pastry. 'Maybe.'

'It's worth asking, Doll.'

She helps herself to some fruit, and the subject is dropped. I'll have to contact Nan-Nan with the news, and then it'll all be over. The food tastes like dust. I leave my pastry and head back to the dorm. I'm going to plead with Nan-Nan to leave me here. It can't hurt. It's a glimmer of hope. It's all I have.

Sitting on my bed, I drag a tissue around my weeping face and reach for the journal-screen. It's been two days, and a lot has happened. I fill in Nan-Nan about Mr Cage's story, Tiger flipping, Lord Carbery, and now the news of the strange virus and Professor Lavelle's theories. I copy her the memo, for what it's worth.

I add at the end, *Nan-Nan, please, could I stay just for another while?* Who knows, she might be able to persuade Nell. Things might be different this time. I keep my fingers crossed as I head towards Dr Ashe's office in the temple.

CHAPTER 34

DAN

The funeral cortege wends its way up the hill. Eileen Mac is wearing a long black dress with gold buttons and a black scarf wound like a noose around her throat. The three children are by her side, the youngest clutching her mother's black-gloved hand. The little girl is carrying a rucksack where a cheery-faced ragdoll peeps out, staring wide-eyed at the crowd. There is a low murmur of voices behind us, but up ahead everyone keeps a respectful silence.

St Mary's Church overlooks the Lainey River, and today it looms above us in sparkling sunshine. The brightness doesn't feel right; it should be raining, a wild and vicious rain bucketing down in solidarity with Ger Mac, deceased. The sun has no right to dazzle us today, of all days. Up on the hill, the light shimmers and bounces off the stained-glass windows. The hearse moves slowly, hundreds of black shoes shuffling along behind it.

A bell tolls; it's the loneliest sound. Sally reaches for my hand, and I'm grateful. A blackbird sings, oblivious to grief. In the midst of untimely death, she insists on bursting forth regardless. All along the hedgerows, new life is clamouring to be seen, lusting to feel the throb of living, saying, *It's our turn now.* But it feels wrong when, just ahead of us, Ger Mac lies cold, in a blue satin frill. Even the buttercups in the verges are an affront. Brazen and arrogantly yellow, they strain to catch the mourners' eyes – *Look at us, look at us* – as we all walk by, heads bent. They should be ashamed of themselves. Summer and all her glossy greenness should show some respect instead of showing off.

The Lord is my shepherd, I shall not want.

The priest is stained in purple and orange as wafers of sunlight light up the pulpit. The words of the psalm are comforting.

In pastures green he leadeth me, the quiet waters by.

I hate funerals, though, all the sadness compressed inside the walls of the church. A choir of schoolchildren sings 'Be Still My Soul', their innocence soaring up through the arches. Reminders of Ger's life are carried to the altar – a Man United jersey, a book on fishing, a family photo, and his intercounty hurling medal, which, we are told, was his pride and joy. They're placed around the pale-wood coffin, the last physical links to a man we all knew and loved. A family man, a hardworking man, a man of the community. There's a cough, a sniffle, and the sound of swallowed tears. You can almost inhale the loneliness and the loss.

Afterwards, we stand around in the windy cemetery, our heels sinking into soft grass while a piper plays 'Mise Éire', the notes floating off like incense into the cloudless sky.

Sally is quiet on the way home. 'What's it all about, Dan? All the suffering and the pain.'

There's no answer to that, is there?

'I don't know, Sally. I don't know how people get through. Life is for living, I suppose. That's the lesson.'

She sighs and takes a compact from her handbag, dabbing puffy eyes, reapplying mascara and lipstick. 'That's better.' She checks her face in the mirror, brushes her hair. 'Would you not go to the hotel for an hour? Eileen would want you to be there.'

'No, Sal. I couldn't face it. Anyway, we were there at the house last night, and I've the GP to see in the afternoon.'

'Drop me off at home,' she says. 'I'll drive straight to the hospital. Dr Valera will be around in the afternoon, and I want to see if there's any update.'

'Have lunch before you go,' I say, swinging into Bluebell Grove.

She shakes her head as she fishes her car keys out of the bag. 'No, I'm not hungry. I'll get a sandwich at the hospital canteen later.'

'Mind you don't bump into Emily,' I say as she reaches over to kiss my cheek and slides out of the car.

Sally's Honda disappears down the Avenue, and just as I twist the key in the front door, I notice two missed calls. From Lavinia. I switch my mobile off silent mode and curse under my breath.

I never got back to her. How could I have forgotten? She was coming to Dublin. I promised her I'd work something out. Has she arrived? For a mad moment, I'm tempted to jump back in the car, zip off to Dublin. Let her know I'm on my way and I'll see her later. It's doable. It's only just one o'clock, and I'd be there shortly after four thirty. But what excuse have I got to go to Dublin? I can forget that plan.

I feel a stab of guilt. Lavinia was intent on making this work, and I wasn't fair or honest. I was holding back. Because of Sally. Because of my family. I ring her, but there's no reply. Serves me right. I let her down. The week was a crazy one, in fairness – the TIA diagnosis, Ger's funeral today, and still no change in Doll, and then all that business with Andi and Steve.

In the kitchen, I pour a can of tomato soup into a saucepan and turn on the heat. The only sound is the ticking clock, and I'm grateful for this quiet time. The silence is as soothing as a hymn. Today I get the results of the BP monitor and presumably a prescription to medicate my blood pressure.

I was lucky. And it's true, life is for living. We need to reach out and grasp every opportunity, because it can disappear like a puff of smoke. Like it did for poor Ger.

The phone makes me jump. It's Lavinia. My heart judders as I answer it.

'Lavinia?'

'Dan, I missed your call. I'm sorry. And you missed mine earlier.' She gives a little laugh.

'I know. I know. I got yours just a few minutes ago. I'm sorry.'

'No, no, there's no problem, Dan. I'm here in Dublin. Are we going to see each other?'

'I'm here in Cork, Lavinia. I am so sorry. I actually meant to be there, but this week, you wouldn't believe . . . actually, I've almost forgotten what day I have.' Oh God, it sounds lame.

'You don't have to explain, Dan. We'll do it again some other time.' Her voice carries no rancour. There's no *You promised* or *Why didn't you* or *You should have*. 'It happens,' she says, 'weeks like that. Don't I know it.' A tinkly laugh. She's a sweetheart.

'It was an exceptional week; there's a lot happening. But, Lavinia?'

'Yes?'

'I'll explain when we next meet.'

'I don't want to put you under pressure, Dan.' Her voice sounds concerned. 'I know you have a family. I understand. It's not easy to get away.'

'Trust me, I want us to meet again, Lavinia. And again. And again. I know I haven't said it to you, but I need you to know this: I want you in my life.'

'Oh,' she says. 'That's lovely to hear, Dan.'

'That's if, of course, if you feel the same?'

'Absolutely,' she says. 'Meeting you was . . .' She laughs softly. 'Well, there's no going back. Not for me, anyway.' To hear her say it almost makes me cry. It must be the funeral earlier, and all those buried emotions they stir up inside you.

'There's no going back for me either.' I mean it too. There *is* no going back. But I knew that already.

There's a comfortable silence for a moment, and we both laugh.

'So,' I say. 'How did the callback go?'

'I'm just heading in there, in an hour. Wish me luck.'

'You'll be great. Are you going back to London tonight?'

'Tomorrow,' she says. 'I'm staying with a girlfriend in Clontarf tonight.'

'Oh, I'm so disappointed I'm missing your visit,' I say.

'So?' she says. And I know she means, *What's next? Your move.*

'I'll come to see you in London, Lavinia. Soon, very soon. I promise. Let me know what works for you.'

Her voice is warm. 'That would be wonderful, Dan. I'm so excited. Leave me know when you can get away, and we'll arrange it. I can meet you at the airport.'

'Leave it with me, darling.' Oh Jesus, there I go again. *Darling!* My hands are clammy. The soup has nearly boiled dry. 'Good luck this afternoon. Let me know how you get on, won't you?'

'I will. See you soon. Look forward to it.' She clicks off.

I dump the pan in the sink and run the cold tap on it. I smile to myself; she gives me joy. She cheers me up.

I sense a movement behind me. I spin around. Sally is standing there, just inside the kitchen door. Her face is ashen, her arms hanging at her sides as if they've broken off her shoulders.

'Christ, you gave me a fright. How long were you . . . ?'

Her face crumples like an old tissue.

'I didn't hear you come in.'

'No, you didn't, Dan. You were on the phone.' Her voice is a whisper.

'I was going to tell you.'

She leans her hip against the kitchen table. 'I heard it all, Dan. The lovely Lavinia, the one you want *to meet again and again and again.*' She mimics my voice. '*I want you in my life.* I heard every word.'

'It's not like it sounds, Sal.'

Tears spill from her lashes. 'How *does* it sound? *There's no going back for me either.* You make me sick to my stomach. Don't even try to deny it.' She wipes tears from her cheeks. 'And you're off to London, Dan? Soon? That will be so lovely for you. While I'm here – your idiot wife – keeping vigil in the hospital and ironing your bloody shirts.'

Her face changes. She looks me directly in the eye, holding her palms out. 'You're a bastard. How could you do this, Dan? You're nothing but a liar and a cheat. *Leave it with me, darling.* I just want to vomit. You disgust me.' She snatches a breakfast plate from the table and hurls it at me. Crusts of toast swoop into the air. The plate misses me and crashes on the floor. 'How dare you! I should have listened to my gut. I knew it.' Another plate sails past me and lands upside down on the draining board.

'Go easy, Sally, calm down. You're jumping to conclusions. I swear, I can explain, if you'll just listen, for once.'

She reaches into the fruit bowl on the table and flings one orange after another in my direction. One of them thumps my head. 'Listen? I *did* listen, that's the trouble. And I've heard enough!' A lemon grazes my ear. 'Get your things and get out of here, right now.' Two avocados sail past my shoulder, one after another.

She sweeps the empty fruit bowl to the floor. 'I mean it. Pack your things. Get out, now. You can't stay in this house.'

'Steady on, Sally.'

I'm sure the neighbours can hear everything. 'Would you just calm down? You're hysterical,' I say, and she stops abruptly.

The kitchen looks like it's been hit by a tornado. Her voice reduces to a whisper. 'I trusted you. After everything we've been through. It meant nothing to you, did it, Dan?'

Andi appears in the doorway, her hands on her hips. 'What the fuck is going on? Mom? Dad? What happened here?'

Silence. We all look at each other. Sally speaks first. Her voice is pretend-calm. 'What are you doing home so early?'

'Our teachers are gone to the funeral, so we have the afternoon free. Can you tell me please, what is going on? The front door is wide open. I could hear you arguing down the Avenue.'

Sally runs her fingers through her hair. Her shoulders slump. 'Your father will explain.' She squeezes past Andi, and I can hear the Honda starting up and screeching off.

'Dad?' Andi hunkers down and picks up the fruit, the shards of plate, the bowl, still intact, rolling under the table. 'Wow, this better be good, Dad. What have you done?'

'It's my fault. I haven't been straight.'

She looks aghast. 'Is it a woman, Dad? Are you having an affair? Because if you are—'

'It's between me and your mother, love. I need to talk to her first. Please leave it, Andi.'

'She's so angry. Poor Mom. I've never seen her like this. You better go after her, Dad. She's in some state.'

I feel I've been hit by a bus. I grab my keys and head for the hospital. Halfway there, I pull in for petrol and try her mobile. It's powered off. In the hospital car park, I switch off the ignition and slump back, listening to the *tick-tick*-ing sound of the engine cooling. Dark clouds are gathering, and it looks like rain. I watch people hurry past the windscreen, chattering. Cars circle round, looking for a parking space, and nearby, a child wails as its being strapped into a car seat.

I could have avoided all this. I could have sat down with Sally months ago. I could have made her understand. She'd have heard me out. I think she would. But I didn't. Because, at heart, I'm a coward, unable to confront the sorry reality: that when I needed to come clean, I just ran away. And boy, do you pay the price in the end.

There's no sign of her in ICU. The nurses haven't seen her. As far as they know, she hasn't come in yet today. Dr Valera is in surgery; he'll talk to us later.

I wait, sit by Doll's bed. Andi rings at four o'clock and again at five. There is no sign of Sally. Her phone is still off.

'She's not here,' I say when Andi rings again at six.

'She hasn't been in work either. I'm worried, Dad. What if she's had an accident?'

'We'd have heard by now, love. I'd say she just wants to be alone for a few hours.'

'You have to fix this, Dad.'

'I know, Andi, and I will. Keep trying her, and let me know when you hear from her.'

At the hospital, I leave a voice message again, but I don't expect a response. When the phone rings, I jump, but it's only the GP enquiring about my missed appointment. I replay the argument in my head, trying to figure out exactly what Sally might have overheard. It must have sounded pretty damning. The sleeping child beside me doesn't move. 'What have I done, Doll? What have I done?' I stroke her arm, thin and pale and lifeless, and I curse myself for the mess I've created.

Footsteps approach the bed. It's Dr Valera. He smiles and nods. 'Mr Redmond, is your wife here?' I stand up, feeling the tingle of pins and needles in my arm. I massage it back to life. 'She's not here at the moment, Dr Valera. Is there anything new to report?'

He rubs the back of his neck. 'Is she due in?'

'Ah, no, not this evening, I don't expect . . .'

He looks at Doll, then turns his head sideways, as if seeing her from a different angle might help. His face is grave.

'You know where we are,' he says. 'There is still a possibility of full recovery, but on the other hand, she may not improve for weeks, months, if at all.'

'And there's no way of telling which way it may go?'

'Yes, it's unpredictable. All we can do for now is monitor the situation.'

As his footsteps echo across the tiles, I look at Doll's ashen face. I hold her little hand in mine. The past is unfixable, the future looks grim, and all I have is this moment and her hand in mine.

CHAPTER 35

DOLL

Dr Ashe drops her glasses onto her chest and smiles.

'Come in, Doll. Come in. You poor, unfortunate child. Take a seat.'

She points to a chair on my right, and she pulls her own chair out so there's no desk between us.

'You look well, considering.' She fingers the cuts on my face, looks into my eyes with a light, checks my temperature. She nods. 'All good.' She takes a wipe and cleans the cut on my leg. 'My, my,' she says, shaking her head, 'that looks nasty. You'll need a tetanus injection.' She clicks her tongue. 'You shouldn't have both wandered off like that. It was very foolish.'

I keep my head down, and she hands me the jar of sweets. I take one.

'At least you are okay.' She tut-tuts as she moves about. 'You've been through the wars. Now, take a deep breath.' She jabs a needle into my arm and rubs the spot with some cotton wool. 'Just in case.' She smiles and takes a sweet herself. 'Tiger is very shaken,' she says, 'but we can put it all behind us now.'

The door opens, and a man in a neat suit walks in. He smiles briefly at me. 'Hello, my dear.'

'This is Professor Lavelle, Doll,' Dr Ashe says.

His smile disappears as he looks at her, pointing to his watch.

'Any minute now,' Dr Ashe says, and I can see she's on edge.

The professor keeps looking at her as he takes a seat, tapping his patent-leather shoe against the tiled floor. A thin hairy leg peeps between his grey sock and the hem of his pants. He turns a handsome, bony face towards me. 'And where do you hail from, Doll?'

I close my eyes, pretending not to hear.

'She's going off,' he says. 'You need to hurry, Hopely. I'm under pressure.' He sighs.

She doesn't answer. When I open my eyes, I can see two professors. Their faces shimmy and blur. I blink. Dr Ashe has also become a twin. Both her mouths are saying, 'Can you hear me, Doll?' But some glue has fused my lips together. She comes closer to me, and I roll my eyes closed.

'This has been a messy business, but now we've another complication?' The professor sounds exasperated. 'You've been careless – reckless, even.'

Dr Ashe says, 'I know how it looks, Lar, I know. But it's early days. There were bound to be some challenges.' Her voice is grim. 'It's under control now. We've learnt a lot.'

'We have,' he says. 'An incredible amount. Valuable data, right enough. But we need to step back now and assess where this is going.'

Their voices fade off into the ceiling. Someone cups the side of my head, and I can feel a stinging sensation behind my ear.

When I come round, I'm in sick bay. Dr Ashe is sitting by my bed, her face anxious. 'You fainted,' she says. 'And you hit the side of your head.' She hands me a glass of water. 'You've been through a lot, Doll. You need plenty of rest.' She smiles. 'I've asked Tiger and Amber to come over and take you out for some fresh air. Professor Lavelle had to leave, but I'm much happier now that we've some answers. It's a comfort to know that all will be well. The problem is solved for all the children.' She sighs in relief.

'Except Matthew and Ava,' I say.

'Yes indeed, poor children. A tragedy. But it could have been much worse – that is what we must remind ourselves: it could have been so much worse. The professor put us on the right track.'

'Yes, we were so lucky you knew him.'

'Oh, I didn't know him, Doll. It was Mother Bodica called him in. She has many friends in high places.' She laughs. 'Would that *I* was so well connected!'

Why is she pretending to not know him? He called her Hopely and she called him Lar – you don't do that with strangers, do you? But Amber and Tiger arrive, and that's the end of our conversation.

Outside, we stretch out on the grass and eat ice-cream. 'Did you ask about the memo?' Amber says.

'I forgot all about it,' I say, taking it out of my pocket and handing it to her. The truth is, I didn't have the courage to say anything. I don't want any more hassle. And now that the reason for all the strange behaviours has been found, is there any point? 'You were right about one thing, Amber,' I say quietly. 'Hopely and the professor do know each other well. You were right about that.'

Later, in bed, I take out my journal-screen to see if there's any news back about staying on at the Academy. I tell Nan-Nan about meeting the professor and Amber's suspicions about Hopely pretending not to know him.

I settle down to sleep, but I can't get the professor out of my head. How he was with Hopely. Cold. Impatient. Not at all friendly.

I drift into unsettling dreams. There are two of me. My hand is glued to the other me, and I can't break free. She's pulling me towards a window, and I have to follow.

I snap awake and sit up, feeling the sweat on my forehead. My heart is thudding, and when I close my eyes again, the other me is back, beckoning me downstairs.

The night is still. I can hear the sugar glider in the distance, and the moonlight is pooling quietly on my bed. I push the covers back and tiptoe out of the dorm and down the silent staircase. The door is locked, but I open a window and squeeze out easily. The night air is cool and clean, and the moon is like a giant egg resting its shell on the lake. How beautiful it looks, lighting up the inky water. I follow the soft sounds of the ripples. The lake is quiet, the stars reflected on the surface, like silver brooches across the lapels of a velvet suit.

And I know, instantly, it is time for me to go. My beautiful thoughts beckon me out, past the ripples to the gentle deep, where nothing can hurt me or sting me or stain me or make me howl. I move through the quiet water, the pebbles rough under my toes. I mean, it's true. The world is a suffering place, isn't it? A place where you can lose your way in the fog – a fog that clings to you, rolling its hopeless tongue around you, taking your breath.

The water curls around my feet, cold as glass. Wouldn't it be a relief – it would, wouldn't it? – to sink like a stone, sheltered and safe. And after that, my body would rise up, swollen and silent as a leaf, floating along, free from the jagged underworld of longing and despair.

I feel the earth breathing in me. The trees are breathing in me – long, low, sighing breaths. The water is breathing in me. It's saying, *Doll, be wild. Be wild, Doll.*

I'm calm. I'm ready to glide off. The water is wrapping silky arms around my shoulders. I can see my face shimmering on the surface, like a surprised ghost. All the greasepaint of my life is washed away. This is the real me. The deeper I go, the more alive I feel, finding at last that peaceful place inside me. The glue that held me to the world is softening, the globules melting. I will be restored now and free. In these silver waters, I will be free. My lonesome heart cries out and is grateful.

CHAPTER 36

ANDI

I check the puppy calendar on my dressing table for the third time, just to be sure. Not that I'm worried. I'm not. Okay, it does look like I'm two days late, but I've looked it up, and your cycle can get out of sync for lots of reasons. Stress, for example. And I'm not lying – the last few weeks have been very stressful, with Doll in hospital and me and Dad at war for a while, and then him collapsing and the worry of all that, and now him and Mom not even speaking. And there was all that hassle before I got back with Steve; Jesus, I was in bits there for a while. At least we're good now, though. More than good.

I count back twenty-eight days and check my diary. I check the previous month and the one before that. I always flag it in my diary, because I always feel so crap that day, my stomach knotted with cramps, my head aching. I can see now – it's clockwork. Two days, though? Think about it; it's nothing, really.

I do my eyes carefully and add some lippy and highlighter. It's only a breakfast date with Steve, but he says he's got a surprise to show me, so I'm making an extra effort. Wear a jacket, he said, something warm. What's that about? I love surprises.

But not, I think, looking at the calendar again, *those kinds of surprises.*

I pull on my black skinnys and my new lime-green sweater from Zara. Good to go. I spray on some Marc Jacobs Daisy; Steve loves it.

I'm not letting anything spoil my morning. Not even my parents' big row yesterday. I'm stuck in the middle, and I don't know who to believe. Dad is saying it's all a misunderstanding, and Mom is saying nothing. She is staying over in her friend Terri's house for the weekend. No, she said when she called over last evening, she wasn't coming home yet. She packed a few things into a bag. Sunday, she said; maybe Sunday she'd face back.

'Talk to him, Mom,' I said. 'Hear him out. Dad is in a right state. What has he done to get you so worked up?'

'I'm sorry, Andi,' she said, hugging me. Her eyes were puffy. 'I hate that you're in the middle of all this. It's between me and your dad, and it's not fair on you. But please, I need a few days, and, well, you and I – we'll talk then, I promise.' She kissed my forehead. 'I'll check in with the hospital,' she said, getting into the car, 'but if there's any news, let me know immediately.'

'Of course, Mom. What'll I tell Dad?'

'Tell him I'm staying with Terri and he's not to call over. I'll be in touch. And please tell him to stop ringing me,' she said.

Maybe tomorrow, when she gets back home, they'll work it out.

'Morning, Dad,' I say now. He is sitting at the kitchen table reading the paper.

He looks up when I come in. 'Any news from your mother?' I actually feel sorry for him; he looks like a lost puppy.

'Nothing this morning, Dad.' I say. 'I told you she said she'll be back tomorrow, so will you two please sort it out then? I mean, right now, Doll needs you both, together. We all do.'

He nods absentmindedly.

'I'm meeting Steve,' I say, getting my leather jacket from the closet in the hall. 'We're having breakfast in town.'

He takes off his reading glasses and massages his lids. 'Will you get my prescription in Mahers, love? Dr O'Brien left it in for me yesterday.'

'No problem, Dad. You look tired. Are you feeling okay?'

He nods and fishes in his pocket for cash. He hands me a fifty. 'Here, that should cover it.'

I fold the note and tuck it into my bag. 'See you later, Dad.'

*****

Steve is already waiting for me outside O'Herlihy's Sales & Repairs on Grattan Street. It's where he's worked as a trainee mechanic for the last two years. Bertie O'Herlihy, his boss, took over the business from his father Ollie when he retired fifteen years ago, and he's built it up into a huge success. Steve gets on great with Bertie, and he loves the buzz of work. Repairing bikes, cars, trucks, you name it – he's a natural. Not that I know anything about cars or bikes, but the way he talks about the work, well, you can tell he loves it. It's more than just a job.

He kisses my cheek. 'Mmm. You smell lovely.' He takes my hand, and we cross the yard to the display area round the back next to a long Portakabin. Rows of bikes form a gleaming line – silver, white, red, and blue metallic. We stop halfway down. 'Isn't she beautiful?' He leans forward, rubbing his hand over the leather seat of a white bike with alloy wheels. 'A Yamaha YZF-R3. Some machine.' He whistles, massaging the metalwork.

'I really like the colour,' I say. He fist-bumps my arm. 'You like the colour? Ah, man! I have to educate you, girl.'

'Oy, Stevie!' A man with a black baseball cap and a grizzly beard steps out of the Portakabin and hurries towards us. 'Well, I can guess what brings you in this morning.' He slaps Steve on the back, like you do with someone you feel comfortable with, someone you like.

'Meet Bertie,' Steve says, as the man pushes back his cap with blackened fingers and grabs a rag from the waistband of his jeans. 'I won't shake your hand, missy.' He peers at me from over the top of his glasses. 'Who have we here, Stevie boy?'

He cleans his hands vigorously. 'Don't tell me; it's the beautiful Andi, am I correct?' He looks from me to Steve. 'I'm right, aren't I?' Steve smiles and nods. 'Nice to meet you, Andi love. He never stops talking about you, you know.' He rolls his eyes. 'To be honest, he's turning into a right bore.' He throws back his head and laughs. He gives Steve a dig. 'I'm only pulling your leg, lad.'

Steve smiles. 'I'm showing her the Yamaha,' he says. 'At least she likes the colour.'

Bertie guffaws again, winking at me. 'Well, sure, that's the decision made. Off you go and get your chequebook.' He gives the wheel a gentle kick with the heel of his scuffed boot. 'Seriously, though, she's in good shape, a humdinger.' He stops. 'I mean the bike, Stevie, not young Andi here.' He thinks this is hilarious, and I'm not sure whether to smile or take offence.

'She'll be snapped up,' Bertie continues. 'She's lightweight, and the cylinders are pure aluminium. She's a smooth ride too, a lot smoother than a regular Ténéré.' He smacks his lips. 'A class act, in fairness.'

He pulls a key out of his jeans pocket and throws it to Steve. Steve catches it in midair, grinning, and looks at me. 'You up for it?'

I nod. 'Try and stop me.'

'Go on,' Bertie says, 'take her away for a spin.' He disappears inside the Portakabin and comes back with two helmets. 'There ye go, and no showing off, Stevie boy. You mind that precious cargo behind you.'

Steve revs up the engine, turns around to wink at me. 'You okay, babe?' I nod and tighten my helmet strap.

We roar out of the yard, then idle in the traffic along Grattan Street. I keep my head down. The last thing I need is my mother seeing me on a motorbike. Last summer, some nosy neighbour told her she'd spotted me, helmetless, on my boyfriend's bike, going, according to the old bitch, a hundred miles an hour up the N71. I never found out who reported me. At the time, I had to promise my mother I wouldn't ever get up on that bike again. This, though, I could point out, is a different bike, and I might just get away with that as a defence.

Soon we're out on the N71 and heading west. I can feel the sun on my shoulder and the throb of the engine beneath me. Best of all, I can feel the firm band of muscle beneath Steve's leather jacket. We cruise along, trees whizzing past us, the tarmac gobbled up as we weave through winding country roads. The wind whips our voices away, and I press my cheek against his jacket and feel the thrill of the outdoors and the emotional speed rush. Clouds puff across the sky and along the coast road, I can see seagulls swooping above the white paws of the waves rolling in from the ocean.

Just before Rosscarbery, we take a left and follow the road to Owenahincha. Steve slows as we approach the beachfront and kills the engine. As we take off our helmets, we can hear the roar of the sea.

'How was it for you?' Steve leans in and pushes my hair off my face. He kisses me on the mouth.

'Exhilarating,' I say. 'Wow, fabulous. I love it.'

'The bike ride or the kiss?'

'Both,' I say, entwining my fingers in his. His hands are warm; mine are so cold.

'Come on, girl, you're freezing. Let's get breakfast. I heard they do amazing pancakes here.' He points to a blue wooden sign over a rickety building farther up the beachfront.

We're soon sipping hot chocolate, waiting for our pancakes and crispy bacon to arrive. From our table by the window, we can see surfers getting their boards ready for the water. 'How do they do it?' I say. 'It's cold out there.'

Steve isn't even listening. 'Andi, I'm going to buy it.' His amber-and-blue eyes are shining. 'I always wanted to own a Yamaha, and she's a real beauty.' He leans in and covers my hands with his. 'Imagine, we could tear off on a Sunday and go wherever we want. Just the two of us.'

'It sounds amazing. I'd love it, Steve. Can you afford it?'

He grins. 'With a little help from the credit union, yes I can. I've worked it out, and Bertie will give me a good deal.'

'He likes you,' I say.

'Yeah, he's like a father to me, is Bertie. The father I never had.' He gives a little laugh. Steve never talks about his dad. I know it's a sore subject, so I don't ask questions anymore.

'It's good to have that relationship with him, Steve. And your gran, she adores you. When is she coming back from Limerick?'

'Monday,' he says, 'I have to throw a party for her. Maybe she'll come out for a spin on the bike with me?' The two of us laugh at the idea of Joanie riding pillion.

Our pancakes and bacon arrive with a little dish of maple syrup on the side.

Steve spears a piece of pancake and dips it in the syrup. 'I was thinking – I mean, not this year, obviously, but maybe next year or even the year after.'

'Steady on, Steve,' I say, laughing.

'I'd love to do a road trip to Morocco. I mean the two of us. Down to Bilbao, overland to Málaga, and then we'd take the ferry to Casablanca.'

'Steve, you haven't bought the bike yet, and don't forget, insurance will cost a fortune.'

The look on his face is priceless. I muss up his hair. 'I'm only teasing,' I say. 'It's a fantastic idea. I love it. OMG, what an adventure.'

'There are your parents to consider, though. They might have other ideas.'

'Listen, I'm eighteen in eighteen months, Steve. I can do whatever I want after that.' I raise my mug. 'Here's to Casablanca and us.'

He smiles, and my heart does a double flip. 'The future belongs to us.'

He clinks my mug, and as the waitress passes, she smiles. 'Lovebirds,' she says, and we both laugh.

An hour later we're back in O'Herlihy's Yard.

'My name's on that bike, Bertie,' Steve says as we drop off the key in the office.

Bertie takes the helmets from us. 'Make sure you have a fistful of dollars in here on Monday morning, so,' he says, winking at me. He gives Steve another playful dig. 'Go on, get out of here before I give you a job to do. We're up the walls here today.'

Steve is meeting Rizla in O'Donoghue's to watch a Man United match for the afternoon, and I remember I need to get my dad's prescription.

'See you at the Carlton at seven, babe.' I kiss him goodbye and head towards Main Street to Mahers Pharmacy.

As I'm waiting for my dad's meds, my eye catches the row of pregnancy testing kits on display. First Response, Clearblue, Suresign, all 99 per-cent accurate. I look around me, like a thief. There's only a young mother trying to calm her screaming toddler and an old woman, coughing and sneezing at the counter, shifting from one foot to the other as the girl inside the counter bags her medicines. 'I'm nearly dead,' she's saying, but the girl isn't listening. On impulse, I pick up a testing kit. The girl says, 'Redmond?'

'That's mine,' I say, 'and I'll take this too.' I thrust the box into her hand and give her the fifty. She doesn't bat an eyelid.

'Will I give you a bag?' She doesn't even wait for me to answer and drops the kit and Dad's meds into a small paper carrier bag. 'Thirty-two fifty and your change.'

On the walk back to Bluebell Grove, I tell myself I only bought it to put my mind at rest. I won't actually use it unless I'm really, really late. Say, Monday or Tuesday – and I'm not expecting that to happen – but say, on Tuesday . . . yes, maybe by Tuesday I might do the test. Just to put my mind at rest, for once and for all.

Walking home, it feels like I'm carrying a secret bomb – I mean, if the neighbours could see through the brown paper bag, they'd be pursing their lips, shaking their heads in disapproval: *What has that young one been up to? Up to no good, I'd say. A pregnancy kit, at her age? A silly, silly girl. She's only a schoolgirl. Does her poor mother know? Tsk-tsk.*

Small-town people with small-town thoughts. I swing the bag as I walk up the Avenue towards home. Casablanca. Morocco. A road trip. Me and Steve. I can see us walking the golden beaches, hanging out in cool bars with palm trees, and on hot nights, our bodies entwined on a huge bed as we listen to the roar of the waves crashing on the shore. And the gleaming white Yamaha, sitting under the balcony, waiting to whisk us off across deserts, maybe, to our next adventure.

In my room, I slip the kit under the bed, hoping that soon I'll feel that headache coming on or those awful cramps and I'll breathe properly again. And I promise myself that I will never, never, never again take a risk. I swear on my granny's grave. Never again.

CHAPTER 37

DOLL

'You don't seem to understand. You're not scientists. I've tried to explain. Back then, I was doing my PhD. I was fascinated by neuroscience and AI, you see, and how parts of the brain could be stimulated to produce particular thought patterns.' The voice belongs to Dr Ashe. 'It was so exciting, you know? The concept that thoughts are the genesis of everything. All plans and dreams, inventions, innovations, movements, start with a thought. It's what quantum physicists believe – that everything we experience is a product of thought energy.'

I'm lying in sick bay, and there's a taste of vomit in my mouth. I don't know why I'm here, and I'm frantically trying to recall a recent memory – the moon sitting on the lake and the peace I found in the lake's watery arms. The voice is drifting in from Hopely Ashe's office across the corridor. She sounds like she's teaching a class, but there's another voice.

'There's nothing novel in what you are saying. We are all well aware of the power of thought.' Mother Bodica's voice is cold.

Hopely carries on, breathing heavily. 'Wait. Let me finish. What's interesting is that thoughts can be constructive and creative or destructive and disabling, right? And we are frequently prisoners of those thoughts – you can agree with that, eh?' She doesn't wait for an answer. 'So my research was about helping subjects to *think* more creatively, amplifying high performance, disabling dysfunction. Lives could be improved dramatically. *As within, so without.* Our thoughts create our reality.'

'So your research was about how the brain can be manipulated for the common good. Very noble, I'm sure. Are you seriously trying to justify your hypothesis and your subsequent actions?' I don't recognise this man's angry voice.

Hopely Ashe sighs loudly. 'I don't think you're listening. My research, my ideas, were revolutionary. We could give subjects access to a quality of thinking they couldn't have dreamt of. This tiny sensor implant has taken me twenty years to develop. The technology is groundbreaking.'

'Heartbreaking,' Mother Bodica cuts in.

'Please, with respect, Mother Bodica, hear me out.'

Silence. Dr Ashe continues. I hold my breath and try to figure out what is going on.

'It's simple. The sensor stimulates the brain – we can do this remotely – helping to redirect thoughts and enhance motivation and focus. Over time, it can effectively rewire the brain. In a positive way.' She pauses. 'Think about it – this is a force for good. We can eliminate crime, addiction, depression, anxiety, all negative brain input. Imagine!' You can hear the excitement in her voice. 'Using the telemetric data we collect, we can refine our coding, make the interface more targeted, and—'

The man's voice says, loudly, 'Dr Ashe, stop! You are remotely programming individuals – unwilling and unknowing children – to perform like monkeys. The risks were monstrous. Yet you continue to justify your actions. As a scientist, have you no code of ethics?'

Hopely Ashe's voice rises in frustration. 'All radical new ideas carry risks. That is what happens when you throw open the door to new frontiers. Have you never heard of autotelic flow?' She snorts. 'Of course not. You are a policeman and obviously too stupid to understand these things.'

A policeman? What is going on?

'Two children have died in horrendous circumstances. Do you say that this is acceptable? Mere collateral damage?' This was the man's voice again.

'Not all subjects respond in the same way. It is impossible to know in advance how each individual will react. Sometimes the brain – we know this now – becomes confused by opposing instructions and can shut down as a protective mechanism.' She sounds pleased when she adds, 'We are learning so very much.'

'And Matthew?' Mother Bodica says.

'Yes. Very unfortunate. I'm afraid his thoughts became self-destructive. Poor boy.'

'That's not entirely true, is it, Dr Ashe?' *It's Nan-Nan!* What is she doing here? I slip out of bed. My legs are wobbly, but I have to move closer to the door, where the voices are clearer.

'Matthew discovered what you were up to, didn't he? He understood how the sensor worked.'

More silence.

Nan-Nan says, 'He discovered how you were able to stimulate the brain remotely. That you were able to programme the children's thoughts and somehow manipulate their emotions and behaviours. You could, it seems, even erase certain memories, though all this, I gather, is a work in progress.'

Hopely Ashe is responsible for the deaths? The kind Dr Ashe, Tiger's hero?

'Yes, yes,' Dr Ashe says. 'And all for the benefit of the citizens of our good planet. Can't you at least acknowledge that?'

When I nudge the door open a little more, I can see Nan-Nan as she paces over and back. There's a bulky man sitting at the edge of Hopely's desk. His arms are folded across his chest, and he's sucking a sweet. Dr Ashe is out of my line of sight.

'The sensors were inserted,' Nan-Nan is saying, 'at the same time as the Academy tattoo was engraved behind the ear. A tiny incision was all that was required. Ingenious, may I say, Doctor.'

How does Nan-Nan know so much? I think back to yesterday and the sharp pain behind my ear before I fainted. Did Hopely Ashe implant a sensor? Is that why my memory is blurred? I mean, why was I down at the lake at night? And how did I get here?

Nan-Nan is still talking. 'Matthew confronted you. When you realised he knew too much, you programmed him to self-destruct. Ava, we suspect, also became suspicious. That made her a threat, so Kristin was programmed to push her off the parapet. How easily you sent them to their deaths. And for what?'

'Matthew drowned,' Hopely says.

'Because you controlled his thoughts,' the policeman says. 'Just as you programmed Kristin's.'

'Nonsense,' Hopely Ashe says, laughing. 'It's preposterous. Try proving that in a court of law, Inspector.'

'Amber was a risk too,' Mother Bodica says. 'Matthew may have confided in her. They were very close. You weren't sure what she knew.'

'She knew nothing.' Hopely screams the last word.

'But you weren't sure. She was another risk. As was Doll,' Nan-Nan says quietly. 'You knew Doll wasn't all she seemed. Maybe you extracted that information from Tiger, but Doll had to go, and you knew how to orchestrate one more death. What's one more?'

It starts to make sense. I would have died, Lord Carbery said. When I survived, Dr Ashe had to make sure I would disappear for good. I remember the lake now, how the voice in my head lured me into the water.

The policeman sounds sympathetic. 'It all got very messy, didn't it, Dr Ashe? The beautiful dream was all starting to fall apart.' He reaches for another one of Hopely's sherbet sweets and unwraps it.

Hopely's voice is barely a whisper. 'These glitches were inevitable, Inspector. I had high hopes. Oh, but we are so close to refining the software.' She pauses. 'Mother Bodica, think of the educational possibilities. Think beyond the now. Be radical. Please. See the bigger picture.'

Mother Bodica's voice is chilly. 'Someone *did* see the bigger picture, didn't they, Dr Ashe? Someone who recognised the value of your work. Someone who understood the advantage of controlling the minds of high-performing children.' The words fall like ice-cubes from her mouth. 'The very people who would become the politicians, the thinkers, the leading figures in medicine, law, finance, and education in Almazova. Now *that*,' she says, 'is indeed a powerful and sinister weapon. A pliable top layer of society. It's a chilling concept, Dr Ashe. Your amorality astounds me.'

'No! You're wrong. We wanted to benefit society. We could now eradicate mental illness, negativity, dysfunction. Quality thinking for all! Think of the advantages.'

Nan-Nan's voice is strong. 'Professor Lavelle saw the bigger picture, didn't he, Dr Ashe? Admit it. He brought his expertise. He brought funding. He enabled and encouraged you. Though he wanted to remain very much under the radar, am I right?' Nan-Nan stops and looks to her side. 'Well?'

'The professor has nothing to do with this. I didn't even know the man.'

The policeman snorts. 'We've run the checks. You were in university together and were close associates on many projects. But let's not waste time on that now. You will have ample time to jog your memory when you meet him in the Central Penitentiary.' He checks his wrist. 'Just about now, the good professor is being escorted to his nearest police station for questioning.'

There's a gasping sound, and Nan-Nan disappears out of sight. Her voice is saying, 'Get a glass of water – quickly. Now, breathe slowly . . . keep your head down . . . that's it . . .'

The meeting is breaking up. I scurry back to my bed as Nan-Nan appears in the doorway. She hurries towards me and kisses my forehead. 'Sweetheart, you're awake.'

'I heard all that,' I say, waving my hand towards the door.

'So you now know what was going on.' She shakes her head. 'The woman is mad.'

'Fill me in, Nan-Nan.'

She sits at the end of the bed and folds her arms. 'Well, the memo told us a lot.' She shudders. 'We started from there. Back here, you almost drowned, Doll. Amber and Tiger saw your empty bed and raised the alarm.'

'So, there *is* no virus. It was her all along, and the professor.'

Nan-Nan purses her lips. 'No, there is no virus.' She sighs. 'The whole experiment was a shocking betrayal of trust. Innocent children used as guinea pigs to further her wild dreams.' She sits down on the bed. 'The thing is – she very nearly got away with it.'

'How did you find out what she was up to, Nan-Nan?'

'When I got your message at lunchtime and saw the copy of the memo, it was clear there was something odd going on.'

'We couldn't work out what some of it meant.'

'Mostly scientific abbreviations and medical terms, but they flagged up some worrisome scenarios. She referred to neuropsychiatric conditions developing, and brain structural changes. We were concerned at the reference to BCIs – brain-computer interfaces – and EEG technology. The memo was a damning piece of evidence.' Her face is grim. 'We were asking ourselves what Dr Ashe was thinking of, divulging confidential information to an external professional and talking about complications from thought-monitoring sensor implants. It warranted urgent investigation. I spoke to Nell. She got the wheels turning. And when we started digging, we found that the good doctor has quite a history of questionable research.'

'Like what?'

'Three years ago she used SIs – sensor implants – to control behaviour in rats. She'd altered some results or made exaggerated claims, and the work was discredited. And there were more examples.' She shakes her head. 'It didn't take long to unravel. The Bureau of Investigation spoke to Mother Bodica. She was adamant Dr Ashe and the professor didn't know each other. She knew of his work in neuroscience, and Hopely Ashe had suggested calling him in – though claiming not to know him. We knew differently. Things began to click.'

'You knew I might be in danger too?'

'We did. Two children had died. Amber came close. Tiger had tried to harm you. We needed to ask the lady some questions. Mother Bodica also had her own suspicions.'

'So you flew over here as soon as you could?'

'We arrived as you were being brought from the lake to sick bay. Dr Ashe was not happy to see you – or us. We searched her office, and we found all we needed. Notes, files, computer reports, analysis.' She jerks her thumb behind her. 'It's all there, being bagged.'

Nan-Nan places a tiny silver wire in my hand. 'There's the infamous sensor. Yours was implanted only yesterday. She had to make sure she could direct you to the lake. We gave you a sedative, and our medical team removed it.'

'It's so tiny,' I say, rolling the wire between my fingers. Nan-Nan nods. 'Tiny but deadly. It can do a lot of damage.' I rub my finger across a sore spot behind my ear. 'And the other girls?'

'Yes, the medical team are with them now. There's a lot of clearing up to do here at the Academy.'

'And me? What happens now?' My voice is barely a whisper.

There's a long silence. Nan-Nan looks away towards the door. 'You already know, Doll.'

'I was thinking maybe, like I said, if you asked, if you say, if you . . .'

Nan-Nan looks at me and looks away again. 'You know the answer. Please, Doll. Don't let's go through this again. You must prepare yourself to return home.'

She sees my face crumple. 'I'm so sorry, Doll.' She gets up from the bed without looking at me. She smooths her skirt and ties the buttons of her Space Agency jacket. 'You'll want to say your goodbyes to the girls.' She looks at her pocket watch. 'It's mid-afternoon. The hovercar will leave at eight bells. Nell will want to see you before you leave.' And with that, she's gone. She doesn't even look back.

I sit in the silence thinking of my mom and dad, almost strangers to me now. Part of an old life, a skin I want to shake off. Guilt smothers me. Anger vomit bubbles up my throat. My future-life at the Academy is already a dust dream, and there's no going forward. Only backwards now into my old cell. It's enough to make me scream, and that's exactly what I do. As quietly as I can.

CHAPTER 38

SALLY

I'm going to be strong for once. I'm going to take control. I look at my eyes in the rearview mirror, but I can see only fear and pain. I'm disappointed in myself. Why do I feel so powerless? Like someone has pulled the rug from under me?

I turn on the ignition and buzz my window down. Terri is waving me off from her doorstep. Thank God her partner Donie was away this weekend. Nothing new, she said; he's married to that Glengarvan Rowing Club. She always rolls her eyes when she mentions his obsession with rowing. This time they were off at some event in Glasgow. But it meant I had a safe crying space for the weekend.

I mouth my thanks, and she gives me a double thumbs-up. Her mouth makes a shape like *You go, girl*, and I force a smile. It dissolves like an aspirin as I drive down Orchard Wood and past the almost deserted Sunday morning footpaths along Forest Road. It's only a seven-minute drive home.

Home. Home doesn't feel like home anymore.

I swing left towards the Mill Road. Where was I? Oh yes, I am going to be strong. *Don't be a victim*, Terri says. She's right. *Don't let him dictate how you feel. Only you can decide that. You need to take back your power. Lean in,* as Sheryl Sandberg says. But it's easier said than done. Isn't it? When you're broken-hearted, do you just pretend you're not? Is that how it works? If you can't stop yourself crying, are you a wimp? I'm always confused, but other women seem to know how to behave and feel. It's instinctive. That talent to hold it together, inside and out – I'd love to be like that.

Terri said anger is better than sadness; I need to hold on to the anger. As fuel, she said. He needs to be told his deception is inexcusable. No lame explanations will do. I must be ruthless. And wear heels, she said. She didn't approve of the cream pants and blue linen shirt I threw on this morning.

'You can't confront him in that,' she said. 'You need to power-dress for the occasion.'

'I'm not confronting him, Terri. We are meeting to talk. I told him he has ten minutes.'

In the end, I agreed to take a little longer over my makeup and to wear her new Faith cream ankle boots.

'You'll be taller, you'll look good, you'll feel good. And no harm to remind him what he's going to be missing.' She sprayed some floral scent in my general direction. 'Just a hint,' she said.

'It's not a date, Terri,' I said crossly. 'Why would I want to tart myself up for a showdown?' But we laughed about it in the end, and she's right, I did feel a little better as I was leaving.

It didn't last long, though. I'm only two minutes away now from Bluebell Grove. So, right, I'll say, *You have ten minutes, Dan. Spare me the lies and the excuses.* I need to preempt what he'll say then. It will either be *Sally, I love this woman, I'm sorry, it's over between us*, or, *I got carried away, I met her, she was available, and I'm sorry, it was a fling, it won't happen again.* Either way, he's gone. Right? And I need to hold tough. I need to say, *Pack your bags and leave.* I'll insist on it. As Terri said – and she's so right – how could you stay with someone who cheated on you? You can't. End of. I must remember that. And I can't help thinking, did the beautiful Shirley Lovett come on to him last year, or was it the other way round? I only have his word for it. It was only a kiss, he said; how do I know it didn't go a lot further than that? But I believed him, more fool me.

I pull into the driveway just after eleven. I take a few quiet deep breaths – he may be looking through the blinds, so I need to start acting the part. Calm, in control. Firm. Focused. I switch off the ignition. My heart is thumping as I walk towards the front door.

He opens it before I even get my key ready.

'Hi, Sally.'

I nod and head through to the living room. He follows me.

'Andi isn't here.' He shrugs. 'Just so you know.' The sleeves of his new blue shirt are rolled up. I can see the dark hairs on the backs of his arms.

I sit on the edge of one of the fireside chairs. 'You've got ten minutes. Dan.'

He takes the chair opposite me and leans forward, his arms resting on his thighs, his fingers interlocked, almost in prayer.

We sit in an awkward silence for a few moments, not looking at each other.

'Get on with it, Dan.'

He looks uncomfortable. 'Thanks for agreeing to hear me out.'

'Dan, get on with it, please.'

'I didn't mean for you—' He stops and starts again. 'For a long, long time I've been meaning to have this conversation. But I'm a coward.'

A long, long time? So this affair is not new. My heart feels like it's exploding. I've been such a prize idiot.

I hear his swallow. 'I knew if I told you, well, you'd react. I couldn't blame you. It would have changed everything between us. I'd have lost you, and I couldn't risk that, you know? You'd have been appalled.'

'How perceptive of you, Dan. How right you are. I *am* appalled.'

He ignores me and looks out the window behind me, like he's trying to recall something from the past, a memory.

'I knew you'd hate me if you knew. You wouldn't trust me again. I knew you'd be unforgiving. Because, admit it' – he looks straight into my eyes – 'you can be a bit like that, Sally. Unforgiving.'

'Oh, hang on. It's *my* fault? Of course. This is really about me not understanding. I'm the unforgiving type, so you had to keep your dirty little secret.' I laugh. 'You really are something.'

He raises his palms. 'I'm sorry. No. That came out wrong.' He runs his fingers through his hair. 'It's just that I knew you'd be furious, and—'

'What did you expect, Dan? You're a pathetic joke. You're having an affair with another woman – for years, for all I know – and you were afraid to tell me in case I'd be mad.' I throw my hands in the air. 'Is that the best you can do? Has that stroke affected your brain?'

'I've already told you . . . I'm not – it's not what it looks like.'

I get up from the chair. I have to pace back and forth to keep myself from shouting. I look at him. 'She's a nun, is she, Dan? Hang on; maybe she's your long-lost sister? Or wait, I know. She's a friend with benefits? Which is it, Dan? And why are you still lying? I heard the conversation, remember?'

'Lavinia is my daughter.'

I stop pacing and sit down again. My legs might give way otherwise. The breath seems to have exited my body without me noticing. Lavinia is his lover's daughter?

'What are you saying? I'm sorry?'

'Lavinia is my daughter.' The words are like a knife across my arm.

'You have an adult daughter?' My head is spinning. I met Dan when I was twenty-one, he was twenty-two. I'm trying to think back to the early years of our marriage. Were there any signs? Did I miss something under my nose? Is he lying?

My mouth is dry. 'How old is she, Dan?' Each word drops out like a stone.

'She's twenty-two since March.'

I'm doing frantic calculations. Twenty-two years ago on the seventh of March, we got married. In Rome. We'd only met the previous August on a Greek island. Looking back, we were half-crazy, and stone in love. It's the way you feel, isn't it, when you think you've found your soulmate and you can't imagine ever feeling anything less than wonderful. You're dipped in gold. That's how it felt for me, anyway.

'Sorry, Dan, you're telling me that when we were going out, getting married even, you had a pregnant girlfriend?'

He doesn't take his eyes off me. '*Ex*-girlfriend. You knew about Juliette. We'd split before I met you.'

He'd mentioned Juliette; of course he had. She was English. I'd seen pictures of her with her long ringlet curls and wide smile. She was graduating from art college, and they'd split in June, just after Dan's finals. Well, that's what he told me, of course. She went back to the UK, and he went off to Germany for his last student summer off. And that August, in a huge outdoor club in Mykonos, we locked eyes.

I remember – enviously, at the time – thinking how Bohemian she looked in those old photos. As those posh, arty girls often do, with their patterned dresses and funky knits and floppy hats. There was something self-assured about her. The way her eyes looked straight at the camera, sexy and confident, the opposite of me. And I remember feeling vaguely jealous of her, though I'd never met her. And I was grateful Dan never really talked about her very much.

'When we met that night in Mykonos, don't deny it, Sally, you knew, I knew, you were the one. That was it. I'd made up my mind before we even got back home.' He sighs. 'Look, you know all this. You felt the same.' He looks at me. 'Don't you remember how it was?'

He's right about that. It was every cliché you could think of. It was more than sex. More than wanting to be with him every minute of the day. I couldn't imagine my life without him in it. Like I say, every cliché under the sun.

I nod.

'Me and Juliette were finished at that stage. She'd gone back to the UK. I was in Hamburg for the summer with the lads. End of story.'

'Well, obviously it wasn't the end of the story.'

'No. It wasn't. In October I got a call from her out of the blue. There was no caller ID. She told me she was five months gone. She'd decided to keep the baby. And she said that I should at least know the child was mine.'

'And you walked away?'

His eyes flash. 'I didn't walk away. She made it very clear she wanted nothing from me. And then she hung up.' A flicker of pain moves across his face.

October . . . October. I'm trying to remember when we moved in together. We both got jobs in Dublin when we came back from Greece, and we moved into a flat in Ranelagh with two other friends in early October. I remember it was my mother's birthday on the third, and she came to see our new flat and we went out for dinner to celebrate.

'You never thought to mention it? We were living together, talking about running off to Rome to get married, and you had a baby on the way. Did it ever cross your mind to tell me?'

His eyes avoid my gaze. 'I was afraid you'd walk away. You *would* have walked away. I know you. You'd have told me to face up to my responsibilities.'

'I wouldn't have. I was in love with you. I'd have been too selfish.'

But would I? I was only twenty-one. I don't think I could have gone ahead and married Dan if I thought another woman was carrying his baby. The truth is, I probably *would* have walked away. As it was, people were telling us to slow down, wait, don't rush into anything, you're too young. This baby news would have definitely been a game changer.

'And your mother? Can you imagine telling her my ex was pregnant? She thought we were too young to get married anyway. With this news, there would have been World War III.'

'When was the child born?'

'A week after we got married. When we came back from Italy in March, there was a letter from Juliette – forwarded by my mother – with a photograph of the baby.' He goes to his briefcase and pulls out a folder. He hands me a faded photograph. It's a baby in a pink fleece babygro. Her eyes are wide and cornflower blue, and on her wispy blond head, a hairband with a pink bow. I turn it over. In Biro it says *Lavinia Evans, March 2nd*.

I am numb. 'All these years and you never said a word. Our kids have a half sister they never met. You never confided in me, and even worse, Dan, you turned your back on your own child. How could you live with that?'

His voice is emotional now. 'I didn't turn my back on her. I wanted to meet her, I wanted to be in her life, but I never heard from Juliette again. And yes, as the years went on, it was harder to tell you.'

'Did you ever try to find her?'

'In the early years I did. But no one knew anything about her. People move on, old friendships fade. But I often thought about her. Lavinia, that is. Of course I did.'

'Did she contact you?'

'No. Last year I met Declan Feeney, an art dealer. A complete random meeting in a pub on Stephen's Green at lunchtime. He used to go out with a friend of Juliette's back in the day. We got chatting, and he told me he'd been at Juliette's wedding in London about ten years back. They'd kept contact on and off. She'd married the painter Louis Templemore. You've heard of him? His brother is the photographer, Robert Templemore?'

I nod. The Templemore brothers are often in the art world news, both very talented and successful. 'So you tracked her down?'

'Yes, it was easy to find their address in Primrose Hill. There aren't many Templemores, and there's only one Louis. A few clicks and I found it. I wrote to Juliette, and she called me.'

'When was this?'

'About four months ago.'

'Your deception is breathtaking. When were you going to tell me?'

He twists the wedding band on his finger. 'I know. It's indefensible. I was planning on telling you, I swear it.'

'What did Juliette say?'

'She told me she'd leave it up to Lavinia herself whether she wanted to make contact or not. She was an adult, it was her own choice, she said.'

'And she did?'

He folds his arms and nods. 'I wasn't sure if she'd want to. Louis has been in her life since she was six or seven, and she took his name long before Juliette and him got married. I mean, I understand he is her father. He raised her.'

Lavinia Templemore. The name has a pretentious ring to it. Like *Juliette*. 'So she contacted you recently?'

'Yes, she said she'd like us to meet. We exchanged emails. Spoke on the phone a few times. Then a few weeks back, she said she was coming over to Dublin for an audition – she's a ballet dancer – and, well, I met her in the Gibson. We had dinner.' He smiles for the first time. 'I can't lie; we just clicked, Sally.'

I feel a spear of jealousy. A new girl in his life. His firstborn, precious daughter. He loves her. He wants her to be part of his life. She gives him joy. I feel like a secondhand jacket, shabby, cast aside. It's ridiculous, but there it is.

'Does she look like you?'

He laughs, his face lighting up again. 'You know, looks-wise, it's hard to tell, but some of her mannerisms – it's extraordinary, they are so like my brothers', or mine. Sort of family quirks.'

'Have you thought about a paternity test? You can't even be sure she's yours.' I so want to puncture his happiness.

He looks at me, his brows furrowing. 'Are you serious? Why would Juliette lie, especially after all these years? The timeline fits. It's definitely my child.' He says it like he's proud of it.

'Is she like her mother? To look at, I mean?'

'Yes. I can see a resemblance. She's slim, small boned – expressive, you could say.'

'Ballet dancers usually are.'

'And she has two half brothers.' He hesitates, looks at me warily. 'I want her in my life, Sally.'

'Of course you do. A child is a precious thing.'

I can see a weight lifting off Dan. An ease I haven't noticed for a while. His voice as he talks about Lavinia is bright, excited, anticipatory. There's a joy hovering about him. I can see it – a lightness. And I feel a corresponding heaviness within me. And I resent it. Like the scales, he's rising up while I land with a thud. She's his new girl, his firstborn. A part of him I'm excluded from. It's not all about me, I tell myself that. I tell myself to be grateful. There is no affair, just an old deception that I need to forgive.

'Can we get past this, Sal?' There's a lilt of hope in his voice. He's sure we can, I'd say.

I look at the man I fell in love with, the man I've raised a family with. My husband. The father of my kids. I see someone unfamiliar. A changeling Dan, replacing the husband I knew.

I shrug. I feel worn down, like an old shoe. 'It's not the girl,' I say. 'It's not Lavinia. I can get past that.' It's not entirely true, but I don't want to think about that now. It makes me feel sick. A shared inheritance I'm not part of.

'So what is it?'

'The deception. You don't get it, do you, Dan?'

'That you're hurt? Shocked? Of course I do.' I can see he's uncomfortable. 'You have no idea how sorry I am.'

'It's fake, Dan. Fake. Fake. Fake. The marriage. Our relationship. It's all fake. That's how it feels for me. For twenty-two years you said nothing. You held on to this secret. You kept me in the dark. And now you're only telling me because you have no choice. You're a fake.'

There's a shift in the room. I can sense it. A distance between us, like galaxies speeding away from each other. Some thread is slipping through my fingers.

The hope in Dan's eyes dies abruptly. There's a long silence.

'I see,' he says. He says it gently, like he actually does see. 'The trust, I mean, it's gone, that's what you're saying.' He massages his temples. 'What did I expect?' In a moment he says, 'If there's anything else I can say or do? If there's anything, Sal, anything at all?'

'Don't. Leave it, Dan. I know. I hear you.'

He rests his elbows on his knees and covers his face with his hands. After a minute, he looks up. 'Is it . . . do you think? Are we, I mean, um, is it rescue-able?' He doesn't take his eyes off me, willing me to answer.

Silence hangs in the air like smoke. It's my move on the chessboard.

When I don't reply, he sighs heavily and says, 'It's your call, Sal.' I stare out the window, unseeing, feeling a withering, the edges of me curling in. I don't feel like fighting back or taking control or leaning in or out. I just want to withdraw, exit the stage.

A few minutes later, I hear his car drive off down the Avenue. I'm grateful for the emptiness in the house. A space where I can hang out my washing line of thoughts, separate out the past from the future. To look at what had meaning and what is now meaningless. Is there even a difference?

I make myself a cup of tea and sit at the kitchen table. I look around at the scattered blue cushions on the chairs, the cream Aga puffing its warmth across the room. And as I sit here on this quiet Sunday afternoon, it feels like all the colours in my life are leaching away. And when I furiously try to recall them, all those bright memories and touch-points of my past, they all start to move out of focus, twirling in circles like a children's carousel.

CHAPTER 39

DOLL

Tiger is sitting cross-legged on her bed. She unwraps a bar of chocolate and breaks off a piece for me. 'We can thank Matthew for holding on to that memo,' she says. 'I wonder how he got his hands on it?'

My rucksack is packed by the door. In just a few hours I'll be back in that hospital bed, waking up again to my old life. The din in my head is the sound of my future cracking and splitting.

Amber is sitting on her bed, peeling a tangerine, trying to do it in one go. The orange skin coils onto her lap, and I can smell the citrus. 'You know what Hopely was like – completely disorganised. Her files were always overflowing. I'd say he found it on her desk when he went looking.' She pops a segment of fruit into her mouth. 'And, Doll, you sending the memo to Nan-Nan was a class idea.' She gives me a thumbs-up.

'She's a scientist,' I say, 'so I knew she'd understand it better than us.'

Tiger winks at me. We haven't told Amber why I've been at the Academy or who I really am. I'd say that even if I did, she wouldn't believe me.

'Imagine,' Amber says, 'the whole virus story was just a ruse to cover up what they were really up to.' She looks at Tiger. 'You loved her, didn't you?'

Tiger nods, looping her hair into a ponytail. 'I think Hopely did really want to do good – she just got carried away. She couldn't see beyond her grand experiment.'

Amber finishes her tangerine and starts to peel another. 'And you're leaving us, Doll. Why won't your guardian let you stay? It's safe now. I don't get it.'

'I don't have a choice, Amber, I have to do as she says.'

'Ask her. Plead with her. Don't give in, Doll.'

'I did. She won't listen.'

'You could run away. Then she might listen.'

'She has to go, Amber. She has no choice.' Tiger breaks off another square of chocolate. 'Sadly.'

'You always have a choice,' Amber says. She rubs sticky hands with a tissue and wipes her mouth. 'I ran away when my parents moved to Holberg, a small town in the south. It didn't have a dance school. I was heartbroken. No dancing? I couldn't bear it, so I ran away.'

'Where did you go?' I look at Amber greenly. Dancing was her life and she wasn't giving up on it. Why am I not surprised?

She tucks her legs under her on the bed and leans against the pillow. She grins. 'I didn't get far. I walked about ten thousand steps and I ending up staying with two old sisters in a farmhouse, but they contacted the police, and the very next morning they came for me.'

'And?'

'And my folks listened to me then and got me in here.' She punches the air. 'I get to dance here every day, and if I qualify – which I intend to – I hope to be accepted into the Almazova Academy of Dance in two years' time.'

'I'd be in big trouble if I ran away, Amber. And anyway, they'd find me and I'd still be leaving, trust me.'

Amber looks at the time and jumps up. She comes and gives me a hug. 'I have to go to dance class, Doll.' She looks sad. 'I'll miss you loads. I won't ever forget you, my dear friend.' She squeezes my hand and then she's gone, skipping off down the corridor, and I know I'll never see that girl again. My heart is flat. You meet a friend, you envy her wildness, you love her daring, she's funny, she's kind, she shows you how you could be, and then . . . then she's gone. And you can only ever meet her again in the pages of your heart – when you remember back to the girl with the bouncy curls and bright smile. The girl who danced on a table and somersaulted over the waiter. A girl, stepping out, fearless.

Tiger comes and puts her arm around my shoulder. 'Doll, don't cry.' She hands me a tissue and brings me to sit on her bed. 'Maybe Amber's right. Maybe you should run away?' she says.

'I'm afraid.' I blow my nose.

'Well, it sounds like there's not a lot for you back home.'

I look at her, annoyed. 'I have my family.'

She sits back and hugs her knees. 'I know that means a lot, Doll. But is it enough? That's what you have to decide.'

'I want to stay more than anything.'

'So, run away.'

What would Amber do? There's something fizzy rising up in my chest, some brew bubbling in a cauldron. *A wicked thought.* Everything starts with a thought. Hopely Ashe was right about that. And some thoughts are like whizzbangs – they zip around inside your head, leaving a trail of glitter, tiny silvery bits of hope. And you can't hoover them all up, even if you wanted to. Dare I run away?

'Where would I go?'

'I don't know, Doll. Get on an MP and see where it takes you. Maybe Amber is right – they would listen then, they might give in. They'd see how important it is for you to stay.'

'If they caught me, they'd never let me back into Almazova.'

'There's no guarantee you'd be back anyway, is there?'

'No.'

She reaches for my hand and squeezes it. I'm crying again.

Amber said, *You always have a choice*, and she's right. It's my choice to make – will I stay or go back?

I feel like I've swallowed a bowlful of butterflies. The thought of actually staying in Almazova is like finding a magic wand. If I go back, I'll just be climbing out of my pit, falling back, climbing out, sliding back, climbing and falling all the days of my life.

'You've just got to go for it,' Tiger whispers. 'You only live once.'

She's right. *You only live once.* Inside my head I can hear the distant sound of dreams roaring. I stand up and rub the water from my eyes. 'Meet me at the lake, Tiger, in five minutes. Bring my rucksack; I better not be seen with it. Don't say a word to anyone.'

Tiger's eyes widen. 'You're going to go for it, Doll? Where will you go?'

'I'll work something out, Tiger.'

It's teatime, so everyone is in the dining hall. It means I can slip to the lake unnoticed. I wait for Tiger there, staying hidden under the trees. The water is still, the ripples barely making a sound against the shingle. The thought has turned into a dream, the dream has turned into a plan. And now I must follow the plan. I cannot fail. *I cannot fail.* I lean against a tree trunk, staring at the lake. I don't hear Tiger approaching.

'What's the plan, Doll?'

I jump. 'Oh, it's you.' I take the rucksack from her.

'I've been thinking,' she says, 'You should go to Mistletoe Castle and ask Lord Carbery to help you.'

'I don't have a plan,' I lie. 'I might just keep walking and see if I can get an MP somewhere.'

'We'll meet again, Doll, won't we?' There's a quiver in her voice as she wraps her arms around me. 'Best friends forever.'

'Best friends forever.'

'Let me know where you are. I'll come to you, I swear. Remember, Doll, you're the Child of Summer. No harm will come to you.'

I feel her hand in mine, and the touch of her strong, sun-bronzed fingers says, *I'll miss you and I love you and I'm sad you're going, and mind yourself.* I can feel her kind heart present in her fingers. It's a blessing, a holy blessing, friend to friend, and it over-wells my heart.

I hear her footsteps retreating on the shingle. I don't turn round. Instead, I start walking into the oak forest. *I cannot fail. I cannot fail. I cannot fail.* The pulse in my blood mirrors the rhythm of the words. Trees waltz past me. They move so fast – have I got wings? It's marble quiet here in the cool green. Even the birds are holding their breaths. I thank them aloud. Their silence is itself a melody. There's a carpet of flowers at my feet, and their scent clings to me and carries me along, lifting me so that my toes are barely skimming the tips of the petals.

My thoughts are weaving a basket of hope. My body feels like a sheet of silk billowing through the trees and out into the fading light of the Long Valley. Soon, Mistletoe Castle appears up on the frowning hill ahead, the turret windows glinting orange. The air is swimming with moths and the scent of lavender, and I trudge along the path that skirts the castle hill. Soon the pink sky starts to fade to a purple glow.

I'm gasping as I climb the steps to the castle. Stopping, hinged over, I try to catch my breath at the entrance. I ring the bell rope, and I hear it jangle inside. I wait. A spider has woven a lace of threads across a door-side shrub. I watch her as she moves across it like an acrobat on a tightrope.

Lord Carbery himself opens the door.

'Well, well, well. Doll is back.' He sweeps his arm to the right. 'Come in, child. You have something to say, you definitely have something to say.'

His eyebrows arch when he sees my rucksack, but he takes it from me without a word and ushers me towards the library. The fire is lighting, and Alexander is coiled on the rug like a hose pipe. I sit in the same chair as before, and Lord Carbery turns down his violin music. He sits opposite me, flicking some imaginary dust from the sleeve of his cream wool jacket.

'Pink lemonade?'

I nod, and he gets up to pour me a glass from the bottle on the table between us.

He sits back, watching me as I drink every drop.

'You were thirsty?'

I nod again, wiping my mouth and setting the glass back on the table.

'Speak to me, child. Something is up, and I'm all ears.' He settles back into his chair and takes a sip from his own glass. 'Ah,' he says, 'a very good year indeed.' He's a strange one.

He waits and waits, and then, after a long silence, I tell him everything. I leave nothing out. I tell him things I never told nobody. About my coffin-couch and my special knees and Nan-Nan and the Grandmothers. I tell him about my mission and Dr Ashe and the professor. And about me nearly drowning. It all spills out, falling all around me like feathers.

He nods his head again and again, cupping his jaw with his palm. He says, 'I see, I see,' so I know he's listening.

I don't even realise I'm crying until he leans over and hands me a tissue.

'So you see, I can't go back. I won't go back.' I blow my nose and wait.

'Yours is an extraordinary tale, Doll.' He rubs his chin.

'Every word is true!'

'I believe you.' He doesn't take his eyes off me.

'You do?'

'Yes. I knew when I met you there was something.' He trails off, takes a sip of wine. 'Then, at dinner the other night, the candle flame inclined towards you. Very strange, I thought. Uncanny. You seemed to have some gravitational pull, some invisible energy force. I could feel it myself.' He refills my glass. 'And the Child of Summer – well, I'm very familiar with the Manuscripts and what they say about her.'

'So, you'll help me?'

He runs his finger around the rim of his wine glass. 'And what, Doll, what can *I* do to help you?'

'I need to . . . I thought maybe I could, you know, stay here just for a while. Till they give up looking for me.'

'You're asking for refuge?' He turns to look out the window. It's twilight, and the hills are black against the purple sky. 'They'll be looking for you now.'

'I know.'

'They'll come here.'

'They will, I know.'

'Now, now, Doll! You want me to lie, to break the laws of the land, to harbour a child, to pervert the course of justice, to betray the Council of Grandmothers, the ruling matriarchs of Almazova?'

He goes to draw the curtains closed and comes back to stand with his back to the fire. 'Do you realise what you are asking me to do?'

I cannot fail. I cannot fail.

'Please, Lord Carbery! It's my life we're talking about. Don't I get any say? Who made up the rules, anyway? I'm not a puppet! *I want to live a life.*'

'The Council of Grandmothers—'

'I don't care about that lot! Or their stupid protocols. Talk is cheap.' I jump to my feet. 'If you won't help me, I have to go.'

'You wouldn't last five minutes out there.' He's quite cross now. 'What about your family? We cannot interfere with your destiny; there are interplanetary rules of engagement.' He runs his hand through his hair.

'Would you want to go back there, Lord Carbery? Would you, if you were me?'

'That's not the point.'

'But would you?'

He chews his lip, then moves his tongue around his mouth. 'No.'

'You see?'

'But—'

'Please. My destiny *can* be here. The future belongs to me. If I can only stay. *My future is in your hands.*'

He sits down again and closes his eyes. Is he gone to sleep? After a long silence, he says, 'You can't stay here.'

I get up to go.

'Sit down,' he says. So I sit again.

'You can't stay here, because the druidesses will find out. They'll report you, have no doubt of that.' He pauses. 'You have to disappear.'

'Disappear? Where to?'

He pauses, tapping his fingers against his chin. Another long silence before he says, 'Kilcoran Island. It's in the southern region. There's an academy for young girls there. A boarding school with an excellent reputation. My friend's daughter, Kat, is principal there.'

My heart is hammering. 'Are you serious?'

'You must leave early in the morning. First light.'

The doorbell jangles, making us both jump. Lord Carbery puts his finger to his lips and frowns. 'Not a sound.' He moves towards the front door.

My heart is like an animal in my chest; my legs are cotton-wool. I hear snatches of conversation. Lord Carbery is saying, 'Yes, dreadful, dreadful,' and 'I see, I see,' and 'Of course, of course.' The door closes. He comes back to the library and taps his cane against the wood floor. 'I've crossed the line,' he says.

'Thank you, Lord Carbery.' My heart nestles back in my chest.

He stands in the doorway and takes a deep breath. 'I couldn't send you back. My conscience would not allow it.' He pauses. 'I may regret it. I hope you don't.'

I jump up. 'You won't regret it. And I certainly won't. I promise.'

'I'm getting you some tea and toast. Leave the rest to me.'

When he's gone, I say a prayer to my family. *Forgive me, I* whisper. I try to explain. *I got a chance, you see, so I've got to go for it.*

The room has brightened, and the violins are playing again. I find myself floating off my chair, my legs dangling as I drift up towards the ceiling, carried by some magic charm. There are flowers in a vase below, and their perfume rises up. I make a plane shape with my arms. Tonight, I'm truly free. I can feel the invisible chains clatter to the floor with an almighty thud, and Alexander looks up, startled.

CHAPTER 40

DAN

The street is a kip. I pull up outside number three Brandon Terrace. Andi steps out, turning to kiss loverboy goodbye. His hand lingers on her elbow, his fingers lightly rubbing the sleeve of her denim jacket. As she slides into the car beside me, he bends and waves his hand in salute. Jesus, will I ever accept this relationship?

'How's his gran?' I say, trying to make an effort. She smells of perfume, something young and fresh and flowery.

She tosses her bag into the back seat. 'She's back home tomorrow but still wheezing a bit, poor thing.' She adds then, 'You'd like her, Dad. She's a great sense of humour.'

You'd have to, living in a place like this, is what I'm thinking, but I don't say it.

'Well, Dad?' She looks at me warily as I turn onto Forest Road.

'We talked. It was civil.'

'And?'

'And nothing. It's not resolved, Andi.'

'You're having an affair? Is it something to do with a woman? I've a right to know, Dad.'

I take the slip road, heading east towards the city. The traffic is light, still a bit early for the Sunday afternoon drivers. 'Your mother will explain. I'm sure you'll see her at the hospital later.'

She folds her arms. 'This is ridiculous Dad. I'm sixteen, not a child. Tell me now. After all, it's your story, isn't it?'

She's right. It *is* my story. 'Well, I suppose you're going to know, one way or another.'

'Exactly. So spill, Dad.'

I take a deep breath. 'You have a half sister.'

I can't read her face. She pauses for a beat, and her hand moves to her chest.

'Older or younger?'

'Older.'

'And she's your daughter, not Mom's?' There's a sharpness in her tone.

'Yes. She's mine. Her name is Lavinia.'

She looks straight ahead, as if the drizzly motorway holds some instant fascination.

'How old, Dad?'

'She's twenty-two.'

'Oh. So you . . .' She's counting on her fingers. 'Will's almost twenty-one. Hang on.' She trails off and looks at me. 'So it was before you and Mom got married?'

'It was around the same time.' I fill her in on the dates and details and about Juliette.

'Jesus, Dad, that's a bombshell. I don't know what to say.' She fixes her hair behind her ears. 'I mean, you never told Mom? She never knew? All these years, you never said a word?'

'I should have told her. Of course I should. But at the time, I thought your mother would call the whole thing off.'

'She would have. Any girl would.'

'Are you upset?' You never know with Andi.

'No. Not upset, but not saying anything, all these years – it's a big secret to keep.'

'It is.'

She takes a chewing gum from the packet on the dash. 'You should've told Mom. She had a right to know.' After a long silence, she says, 'Have you met her? What's she like, Lavinia?'

'You'd like her. She's fair, green eyes, a lovely young woman. Very sweet.' I don't add that she makes my heart sing. That I can't wait to get to know her.

She looks at me. 'So, I'm not your eldest daughter after all, then, am I?'

'This makes no difference to us, Andi. Don't even go there.'

'Will I get to meet her?'

'Yes. I don't know. In time, maybe.'

She takes another chewing gum. 'Mom'll come round, Dad. It's just the shock. Finding out you had a secret love child.'

'Don't be so dramatic, Andi.'

'Actually,' she says, 'I think it's quite exciting – knowing I have a half sister. I always wanted a sister I could talk to. And now' – she touches my arm – 'now I have. Cool.' As we turn in the hospital gates, she says, 'It wasn't your fault, Dad. All this started before you even met. I'll talk Mom round.'

I smile inside. For Andi, it's assimilated and processed; she's seeing some advantages already. And she's cool with it. And I'm grateful for that.

I pull into a parking space and switch off the engine. Liam Clancy is singing 'Shenandoah' on the radio. On impulse I say, 'You know I love you very much, Andi, and nothing will ever change that.'

She nods slowly, twirling a ring on her middle finger. We sit listening to the music.

'We do fight a bit, Dad. You and me. It used to be different. Back along.'

'Come on,' I say, 'you're a teenager; I'm your old man. It's normal. We're not going to see eye to eye on everything.'

She grins. 'Tell me about it.'

'Do you hear that song "Shenandoah", Andi?'

'It's beautiful. What does it mean?'

'It's a Cherokee word meaning *beautiful daughter of the stars*.'

After a minute, she leans closer and lays her head on my shoulder. I put my arm around her, and for a few moments the years peel away and she's five again.

After a while she says, 'I'm lucky I've had you my whole life, Dad; Lavinia is only getting to know you now.'

Some moments really are worth safety-pinning to your heart, and this is one of them.

*****

In the ICU, the nurse smiles as we approach the bed. She's writing something on a chart and adjusting the angle of the bed frame. 'Dr Valera is doing his rounds,' she says. 'I'll tell him you're here. He'll be with you shortly.'

'I'll ring Mom,' Andi says, and disappears out through the double doors.

'It's just you and me, Doll,' I say out loud. Doll starts to smile. I've seen it before. It's not unusual, they told us; patients in a state of unconsciousness can make involuntary movements. I take her hand and can't help thinking, *As I'm gaining a daughter, am I losing a daughter?* Is this my punishment for keeping secrets? Is there a vengeful God up there who doesn't think I deserve both?

There's a flickering movement behind her eyelids. 'Are you coming back to us, Doll?' I lean forward and touch her face. The smile plays around her mouth. Is she dreaming? Is she, as Sally said, inside another life, in another dimension? If that's true, just to know it would change everything.

Andi's back. 'Mom's on her way, Dad.' She sits on the other side of the bed. 'Doll will recover, won't she? Eventually.'

'Yes, I think so, Andi. It may take time.' Even as I say the words, my heart sags. It's not looking good.

It's just after four when Sally arrives. There's an awkward silence, broken by the arrival of Dr Valera. He swishes the curtain around the bed. His eyes look weary behind the black frames.

'It's an anxious time,' he says, nodding at Doll, 'and I'm afraid there is no good news on the horizon.'

He looks at Andi, but Sally says, 'It's okay, Doctor, she's sixteen.'

He nods. 'We expected – we'd hoped – that once we reduced the sedation, Doll would gradually recover consciousness. That she would progress to longer periods of wakefulness. This hasn't happened, I'm afraid.'

'But the brain swelling has reduced?' Sally says.

'Yes, from what we can see.' He steeples his fingers. 'But recovery, as I said, can be unpredictable.'

'What are you saying exactly?'

'I'm saying we need to manage expectations. The longer the patient is in this state . . .' He waves his hand towards the bed.

'You mean the longer this goes on, the worse the outcome?' I ask. Why doesn't he spell it out? These doctors, always beating around the bush.

'Exactly, Mr Redmond. Every injury is different and follows its own timeline, but, no, this is not good. We have to be realistic.' He adds, 'It can be overwhelming for the family, all this uncertainty.'

'But there is some hope of recovery, isn't there?' Sally says.

He hesitates. 'Yes. And she may or may not need rehabilitation if and when that happens. It may be weeks, even months, and there is the possibility she may never recover. That is the stark reality.'

Andi looks pale. She excuses herself and slips out.

Dr Valera folds his arms and rocks gently back and forth. 'That is it, I'm afraid, for now. The stats tell us there is about a fifty per-cent chance of recovery a month after the injury. We're still only two weeks in. And we need to manage any risk of infection – the body is vulnerable in this state.'

Sally sits down, staying perfectly still like an artist's model.

'I'm sorry. I wish I could give you something more.' He turns to leave. 'I'll ask our rehab management consultant to drop in before you go. Professor Carbery will be leading the multidisciplinary team managing your daughter's needs. You won't find better.'

'Thank you, Doctor.' We both say it together, and he half bows and says goodbye.

Sally leans forward in her chair and places her forehead on Doll's bed.

'There's still hope, Sally, you heard him.'

She shakes her head, her shoulders pulsating. I want to put my palm on her back and say some soothing words, but instead I place a tissue in her hand, and she takes it without looking up. She straightens after a minute, patting red eyes. 'Her life was one tough day after another.' She blows her nose and sniffles. 'And this year she was improving, she was starting to engage . . . and now, fucking this.' She shouts the last bit.

She focuses on a point beyond my shoulder. 'She doesn't want to come back.' She waves away my protests. 'No, Dan, she doesn't. Stop. It's true. She wants out. She's sick of it all. Sick, sick, sick of it all.'

'She's not able to make decisions like that, Sal.'

Her voice is flat. 'She is. And who could blame her? I don't.' The tears snake down her face and drip onto the collar of her red jacket. 'I'm so tired of it all.'

'I know you are, Sal.'

'She wants to say goodbye.'

'That's not true. She can't think like that. And you're not to.' I hunker down next to her and take her hand. She doesn't pull away. 'I'm here for you, Sal.'

'I know that.'

'We need each other.'

She nods. There's a long silence. 'It's okay about Lavinia.'

I leave out a long breath. 'I wasn't expecting that.'

'Me neither.' She half smiles. 'It was Andi. On the phone, earlier.'

'What did she say?'

'That you were wonderful. That you kept quiet because you loved me and didn't want to lose me.'

'Go on.'

'That I was to build a bridge and get over it!' She rolls her eyes. 'Oh, yes, and that she was looking forward to meeting her half sister, and I should be too.'

'Good advice, Andi. I need to give that girl some cash.'

Sally smiles at that and squeezes my hand. 'I was jealous. I was angry and jealous. Don't ask me to explain it. It's ridiculous.'

'It was a bombshell. I understand that.'

'You should have told me years ago.'

'I know.'

'I'd like to meet her sometime. When the time is right.'

'She'd love that. I know she would.'

'Mr and Mrs Redmond, good afternoon.' The voice is deep and authoritative, but the smile is dazzling. 'I'm Professor Carbery. Call me Tim.' He comes closer and touches Doll's hand. 'You'll probably be seeing a lot of me over the next while.'

'Yes, Dr Valera said you'd be round.'

'It's very difficult for you, very difficult I am sure.' He grimaces. 'I've no doubt that this is an intolerable journey, an intolerable journey and an unwelcome one.'

'We had high hopes,' Sally says. 'And now, well, we are all at sea.'

He nods, stroking his chin. 'Be assured, both of you, we will be doing all we can for little Doll. And she may well return to us . . .'

'You think she might?'

He holds up a well-manicured finger. 'Anything is possible, Mrs Redmond. Life is cruel, but it is also strange and wonderful. We will wait and see how the weeks unfold.'

'Thank you. We appreciate all the care Doll is getting.'

He nods and smiles. 'It is our privilege.' And then he's gone.

'Where's Andi disappeared to? I hope she's all right,' I say. 'She looked very pale.'

'It's period pains, Dan; she gets them bad. I told her to get some Nurofen when she was on the phone earlier.'

'We were just talking about you,' I say as Andi comes back in. She sits on the edge of the bed. 'You look a bit better.'

She takes Doll's hand and shakes her head. 'I'm fine; the tablets are working.' She takes in the body language. 'You two sorted things out, yeah?' She doesn't wait for an answer but smiles and comes round the bed towards us, her arms outstretched. 'Group hug.' She wraps her arms around us. 'The fight isn't over; we still have hope, don't we?'

'We do,' Sally says. 'Always, there's hope.'

'Shenandoah,' Andi says, moving to kiss Doll's tiny hand. 'Our Shenandoah, beautiful daughter of the stars.' She hums the tune and we all join in, and Doll smiles again. And if ever there was a moment I felt blessed, it is now.

The End

Acknowledgements

Writing a book is like heading off on a journey – you don't know how it's going to go, where exactly you're even going, and how long it's going to take to get there. You don't even know if you will get there. If you'd any sense, you might decide to skip the trip altogether, and stay at home and read a book instead.

So, to keep on track, you need people along the way who believe in you. That's the most important thing. People who you know are rooting for you, and who'll be there to cheer you on, win or lose. A huge thank you to those terrific friends, allies and writing buddies for all their amazing support along the way; Katherina Conneally-Sloane, Rosaleen O'Leary, Angela Crowley, Neasa Browne, Gretta Power, Maria Gillivan, Katherine O'Kelly-Lynch, Zoe Morrison, Maire O'Donoghue, Nicola Garrett-Elovsson, Marguerite Lynch, Anita McKenna, Dr Mary Murphy, Miriam Nash, Mary Buckley, Dr Anne Rath, Terri Murphy, Anne Riordan-Connolly.

A debt of gratitude to my brilliant Listowel gang of writers and my Write Night group of lovely poets and story-weavers – thank you for the encouragement and for all the laughs.

And to my beta readers – Mary McNulty, Colette Doonan, Rosaleen O'Leary, Alannah O'Kelly-Lynch, Neasa Browne and Aileen Quirke – thank you all for your helpful insights and comments.

To the people who bring it all together, many thanks to publisher Orla Kelly, whose expert knowledge and attention to detail were invaluable; to wonderful editor Rachel Keith, a joy to work with; to Louise McSharry, Funkidesign, a real find. And to the Narration team who get the book out there – Rachel, Stephen, Alina and Alona – I couldn't do it without you.

A special thanks to Anne O'Reilly and Teresa Kiely for their insights into the hospital setting and procedures and to Sophia O'Kelly-Lynch for always, always inspiring me, how lucky I am.

And to my readers, I am so grateful, thank you for making my dream come true.

A final word of thanks to my husband for making me laugh every single day as well as being tea-maker, backstage organiser, promoter, marketeer, all round good guy. Thanks, Der.

About the Author

🌐 www.eleanorokellylynch.ie

✉ eleanorokellylynch@gmail.com

📷 eleanoroklynch

𝕏 @eleanoroklynch

𝐟 Eleanor O'Kelly Lynch

Dear Reader,

Thank you for taking the time to read my book. If you enjoyed it, I'd really appreciate if you'd tell others about it. And if you could leave a review in Goodreads – or anywhere online – that'd be the icing on the cake.

I'm always happy to hear from readers and engage with them, so please feel free to contact me on social media, on email or through my website. All details are above. Look forward to hearing from you.

Thank you,

Eleanor O'Kelly-Lynch

Milton Keynes UK
Ingram Content Group UK Ltd.
UKHW030140180324
439604UK00005B/790